BEYOND RUE MORGUE

FURTHER TALES OF EDGAR ALLAN POE's 1st DETECTIVE

BEYOND RUE MORGUE

FURTHER TALES OF EDGAR ALLAN POE's 1st DETECTIVE

EDITED BY PAUL KANE & CHARLES PREPOLEC

TITAN BOOKS

DID YOU ENJOY THIS BOOK?

We love to hear from our readers. Please email us at:
readerfeedback@titanemail.com, or write to us at the above address.
To receive advance information, news, competitions, and exclusive offers
online, please sign up for the Titan newsletter on our website.

WWW.TITANBOOKS.COM

Beyond Rue Morgue: Further Tales of Edgar Allan Poe's 1st Detective
Print edition ISBN: 9781781161753
E-book edition ISBN: 9781781161760

Published by Titan Books
A division of Titan Publishing Group Ltd
144 Southwark Street, London SE1 0UP

First edition: July 2013
10 9 8 7 6 5 4 3 2 1

Acknowledgements
Special thanks to Cath Trechman, Jo Boylett, and all the team at Titan—and, of course, all
the contributors. But especially to Mr. Poe, our inspiration.

CONTENTS

INTRODUCTION
THE FIRST DETECTIVE

Given the popularity and fame of Sherlock Holmes, many might be forgiven for thinking that Sir Arthur Conan Doyle's sleuth was the first fictional detective to make his mark. However, long before Holmes and Watson were tackling Moriarty or chasing a spectral hound across Dartmoor, Edgar Allan Poe's creation C. Auguste Dupin was solving cases on the gritty streets of his native Paris. In fact, Poe wrote his stories before the word "detective" was even coined, laying the foundations for the mystery stories that followed, and single-handedly defining the dominant tropes of the detective genre that are still very much in evidence today.

Poe cleverly established the concept of the eccentric genius who relies on deductive reasoning, the sidekick/narrator who serves as the reader's proxy, and shifted focus from the puzzle to how it is unraveled. Indeed, the impact of Poe's Dupin cannot be underestimated and the influence is readily apparent in almost every amateur sleuth from the Golden Age of Christie (Hercule Poirot), Allingham (Albert Campion), and Sayers (Lord Peter Wimsey), right through to the latest slew of television detectives on shows such as *Castle* and *The Mentalist,* as well as the reinvented Sherlock Holmes in both the BBC's *Sherlock* and CBS's *Elementary*.

Dupin, and his nameless narrator, first appeared in "The Murders in the Rue Morgue" (1841)—published in *Graham's Magazine* and reprinted in this anthology—and then featured in two more stories: "The Mystery of Marie Rogêt" (first published in *Snowden's Ladies' Companion* in three installments between November 1842 and February 1843) and "The Purloined Letter" (which was originally included in the literary annual *The Gift for 1845* in 1844). Sadly, in spite of the impact Dupin would have on the world of the fictional crime-buster, between then and now he has become somewhat overlooked by the general readership.

A series of seven new short stories featuring Dupin were written by Michael Harrison for *Ellery Queen's Mystery Magazine* in the 1960s and collected as *The Exploits of the Chevalier Dupin* (1968), with a further five stories added to the later UK edition. These capture the methodology of Dupin, but lack many of Poe's more outré elements; Poe having been known for his horror and fantasy tales, as well. Dupin also cropped up in publications such as *The Murder of Edgar Allan Poe* (1997), with author George Egon Hatvary calling on him as a narrator, Alan Moore's *The League of Extraordinary Gentlemen* (1999), and bizarrely, *Edgar Allan Poe on Mars* (2007) by Jean-Marc and Randy Lofficier.

His cinematic existence, compared with that of Holmes, also falls a little short. He featured in movies such as *Murders in the Rue Morgue* (1932) and *The Mystery of Marie Roget* (1942)— both Universal productions, starring Leon Ames then Patric Knowles as Dupin (Dr. Paul Dupin in the latter, a character who would again turn up as a professor in 1954's *Phantom of the Rue Morgue*, played by Steve Forrest). And though "...Rue

Morgue" itself was adapted quite a number of times, the results often bore little resemblance to the original story: Gordon Hessler's 1971 film, for example, starring Herbert Lom. Either that, or it distorted the character of Dupin so completely as to be nearly unrecognizable. Closest to the mark might be George C. Scott's portrayal of the detective, alongside Rebecca De Mornay and Ian McShane, in the 1986 TV version.

In putting together an anthology celebrating Dupin we wanted to redress the balance a bit: simultaneously paying homage to Poe's creation and adding to the canon in a way we hope the author might have been proud of. We've gathered together a talented and diverse group of writers for this project, all giving Dupin their personal and unique interpretation. Some have set their tales around the same time as his previous stories, while others have explored later incarnations and descendants. Some are straight crime, while others blend mystery with horror or fantasy. All are fascinating and thoroughly entertaining, we can assure you.

So, without further ado, we encourage you to rekindle your love for Dupin, and are delighted to introduce him to others who may not know him so well. You're in for a treat, either way.

Ladies and gentlemen, we give you the grand original, the master of ratiocination, the first detective: the Chevalier C. Auguste Dupin!

Paul Kane & Charles Prepolec
January 2013

THE MURDERS IN THE RUE MORGUE

By

EDGAR ALLAN POE

*What song the Syrens sang, or what name Achilles assumed
when he hid himself among women, although puzzling
questions are not beyond all conjecture.*

SIR THOMAS BROWNE, *URN-BURIAL*

The mental features discoursed of as the analytical, are, in themselves, but little susceptible of analysis. We appreciate them only in their effects. We know of them, among other things, that they are always to their possessor, when inordinately possessed, a source of the liveliest enjoyment. As the strong man exults in his physical ability, delighting in such exercises as call his muscles into action, so glories the analyst in that moral activity which *disentangles*. He derives pleasure from even the most trivial occupations bringing his talents into play. He is fond of enigmas, of conundrums, of hieroglyphics; exhibiting in his solutions of each a degree of *acumen* which appears to the ordinary apprehension preternatural. His results, brought about by the very soul and essence of method, have, in truth, the whole air of intuition. The faculty of re-solution is possibly much invigorated by mathematical study, and especially by that highest branch of it which, unjustly, and merely on account of its retrograde operations, has been called, as if *par excellence*, analysis. Yet to calculate is not in itself to analyze. A chess-player, for example, does the one without effort at the other. It follows that the game of chess, in its effects upon mental character, is greatly misunderstood. I am not now writing a treatise, but simply prefacing a somewhat peculiar narrative by observations very much at random; I will, therefore, take occasion to assert that the higher powers of the reflective intellect are more decidedly and more usefully tasked by the unostentatious game of draughts than by all the elaborate frivolity of chess. In this latter, where the pieces have different and *bizarre* motions, with various and variable values, what is only complex is mistaken (a not unusual error) for what is profound. The *attention* is here called powerfully into play. If it flag for an instant, an oversight is committed, resulting in injury or defeat. The possible moves being not only manifold but involute, the chances of such oversights are multiplied; and in nine cases out of ten it is the more concentrative rather than the more acute player who conquers. In draughts, on the contrary, where the moves are *unique* and have but little variation, the probabilities of inadvertence are diminished, and the mere attention being left comparatively unemployed, what advantages are obtained by either party are obtained by superior *acumen*. To be less abstract—Let us suppose a game of draughts where the pieces are reduced to four kings, and where, of course, no oversight is to be expected. It is obvious that here the victory can be decided (the players being at all equal) only by some *recherché* movement, the result of some strong exertion of the intellect. Deprived of ordinary resources, the analyst throws himself into the spirit of his opponent, identifies himself therewith, and not unfrequently sees thus, at a glance, the sole methods (sometimes indeed absurdly simple ones) by which he may seduce into error or hurry into miscalculation.

Whist has long been noted for its influence upon what is termed the calculating power; and men of the highest order of intellect have been known to take an apparently unaccountable delight in it, while eschewing chess as frivolous. Beyond doubt there is nothing of a similar nature so greatly tasking the faculty of analysis. The best chess-player in Christendom *may* be little more than the best player of chess; but proficiency in whist implies capacity for success in all these more important undertakings where mind struggles with mind. When I say proficiency, I mean that perfection in the game which includes a comprehension of *all* the sources whence legitimate advantage may be derived. These are not only manifold, but multiform, and lie frequently among recesses of thought altogether inaccessible to the ordinary understanding. To observe attentively is to remember distinctly; and, so far, the concentrative chess-player will do very well at whist; while the rules of Hoyle (themselves based upon the mere mechanism of the game) are sufficiently and generally comprehensible. Thus to have a retentive memory, and to proceed by "the book," are points commonly regarded as the sum total of good playing. But it is in matters beyond the limits of mere rule that the skill of the analyst is evinced. He makes, in silence, a host of observations and inferences. So, perhaps, do his companions; and the difference in the extent of the information obtained, lies not so much in the validity of the inference as in the quality of the observation. The necessary knowledge is that of *what* to observe. Our player confines himself not at all; nor, because the game is the object, does he reject deductions from things external to the game. He examines the countenance of his partner, comparing it carefully with that of each of his opponents. He considers the mode of assorting the cards in each hand; often counting trump by trump, and honor by honor, through the glances bestowed by their holders upon each. He notes every variation of face as the play progresses, gathering a fund of thought from the differences in the expression of certainty, of surprise, of triumph, or chagrin. From the manner of gathering up a trick he judges whether the person taking it can make another in the suit. He recognizes what is played through feint, by the air with which it is thrown upon the table. A casual or inadvertent word; the accidental dropping or turning of a card, with the accompanying anxiety or carelessness in regard to its concealment; the counting of the tricks, with the order of their arrangement; embarrassment, hesitation, eagerness or trepidation—all afford, to his apparently intuitive perception, indications of the true state of affairs. The first two or three rounds having been played, he is in full possession of the contents of each hand, and thenceforward puts down his cards with as absolute a precision of purpose as if the rest of the party had turned outward the faces of their own.

The analytical power should not be confounded with simple ingenuity; for while the analyst is necessarily ingenious, the ingenious man is often remarkably incapable of analysis. The constructive or combining power, by which ingenuity is usually manifested, and which the phrenologists (I believe erroneously) have assigned a separate organ, supposing it a primitive faculty, has been so frequently seen in those whose intellect bordered otherwise upon idiocy, as to have attracted general observation among writers on morals. Between ingenuity and the analytic ability there exists a difference far greater, indeed, than that between the fancy and the imagination, but of a character very strictly analogous. It will be found, in fact, that the ingenious are always fanciful, and the *truly* imaginative never otherwise than analytic.

The narrative which follows will appear to the reader somewhat in the light of a commentary upon the propositions just advanced.

Residing in Paris during the spring and part of the summer of 18—, I there became acquainted with a Monsieur C. Auguste Dupin. This young gentleman was of an excellent—indeed of an illustrious family, but, by a variety of untoward events, had been reduced to such poverty that the energy of his character succumbed beneath it, and he ceased to bestir himself in the world, or to care for the retrieval of his fortunes. By courtesy of his creditors, there still remained in his possession a small remnant of his patrimony; and, upon the income arising from this, he managed, by means of a rigorous economy, to procure the necessaries of life, without troubling himself about its superfluities. Books, indeed, were his sole luxuries, and in Paris these are easily obtained.

Our first meeting was at an obscure library in the Rue Montmartre, where the accident of our both being in search of the same very rare and very remarkable volume, brought us into closer communion. We saw each other again and again. I was deeply interested in the little family history which he detailed to me with all that candor which a Frenchman indulges whenever mere self is the theme. I was astonished, too, at the vast extent of his reading; and, above all, I felt my soul enkindled within me by the wild fervor, and the vivid freshness of his imagination. Seeking in Paris the objects I then sought, I felt that the society of such a man would be to me a treasure beyond price; and this feeling I frankly confided to him. It was at length arranged that we should live together during my stay in the city; and as my worldly circumstances were somewhat less embarrassed than his own, I was permitted to be at the expense of renting, and furnishing in a style which suited the rather fantastic gloom of our common temper, a time-eaten and grotesque mansion, long deserted through superstitions into which we did not inquire, and tottering to its fall in a retired and desolate portion of the Faubourg St. Germain.

Had the routine of our life at this place been known to the world, we should have been regarded as madmen—although, perhaps, as madmen of a harmless nature. Our seclusion was perfect. We admitted no visitors. Indeed the locality of our retirement had been carefully kept a secret from my own former associates; and it had been many years since Dupin had ceased to know or be known in Paris. We existed within ourselves alone.

It was a freak of fancy in my friend (for what else shall I call it?) to be enamored of the night for her own sake; and into this *bizarrerie*, as into all his others, I quietly fell; giving myself up to his wild whims with a perfect *abandon*. The sable divinity would not herself dwell with us always; but we could counterfeit her presence. At the first dawn of the morning we closed all the massy shutters of our old building; lighted a couple of tapers which, strongly perfumed, threw out only the ghastliest and feeblest of rays. By the aid of these we then busied our souls in dreams—reading, writing, or conversing, until warned by the clock of the advent of the true Darkness. Then we sallied forth into the streets, arm and arm, continuing the topics of the day, or roaming far and wide until a late hour, seeking, amid the wild lights and shadows of the populous city, that infinity of mental excitement which quiet observation can afford.

At such times I could not help remarking and admiring (although from his rich ideality I had been prepared to expect it) a peculiar analytic ability in Dupin. He seemed, too, to take an eager delight in its exercise—if not exactly in its display—and did not hesitate to confess the pleasure thus derived. He boasted to me, with a low chuckling laugh, that most men, in respect to himself, wore windows in their bosoms, and was wont to follow up such assertions by direct and very startling proofs of his intimate knowledge of my own. His manner at these moments was frigid and abstract; his eyes were vacant in expression; while his voice, usually a rich tenor, rose into a treble which would have sounded petulantly but for the deliberateness and entire distinctness of the enunciation. Observing him in these moods, I often dwelt meditatively upon the old philosophy of the Bi-Part Soul, and amused myself with the fancy of a double Dupin—the creative and the resolvent.

Let it not be supposed, from what I have just said, that I am detailing any mystery, or penning any romance. What I have described in the Frenchman, was merely the result of an excited, or perhaps of a diseased intelligence. But of the character of his remarks at the periods in question an example will best convey the idea.

We were strolling one night down a long dirty street, in the vicinity of the Palais Royal. Being both, apparently, occupied with thought, neither of us had spoken a syllable for fifteen minutes at least. All at once Dupin broke forth with these words:—

"He is a very little fellow, that's true, and would do better for the *Théâtre des Variétés*."

"There can be no doubt of that," I replied unwittingly, and not at first observing (so much had I been absorbed in reflection) the extraordinary manner in which the speaker had chimed in with my meditations. In an instant afterward I recollected myself, and my astonishment was profound.

"Dupin," said I, gravely, "this is beyond my comprehension. I do not hesitate to say that I am amazed, and can scarcely credit my senses. How was it possible you should know I was thinking of—?" Here I paused, to ascertain beyond a doubt whether he really knew of whom I thought.

—"of Chantilly," said he, "why do you pause? You were remarking to yourself that his diminutive figure unfitted him for tragedy."

This was precisely what had formed the subject of my reflections. Chantilly was a *quondam* cobbler of the Rue St. Denis, who, becoming stage-mad, had attempted the *rôle* of Xerxes, in Crébillon's tragedy so called, and been notoriously pasquinaded for his pains.

"Tell me, for Heaven's sake," I exclaimed, "the method—if method there is—by which you have been enabled to fathom my soul in this matter." In fact I was even more startled than I would have been willing to express.

"It was the fruiterer," replied my friend, "who brought you to the conclusion that the mender of soles was not of sufficient height for Xerxes *et id genus omne*."

"The fruiterer!—you astonish me—I know no fruiterer whomsoever."

"The man who ran up against you as we entered the street—it may have been fifteen minutes ago."

I now remembered that, in fact, a fruiterer, carrying upon his head a large basket of apples, had nearly thrown me down, by accident, as we passed from the Rue C— into the thoroughfare where we stood; but what this had to do with Chantilly I could not possibly understand.

There was not a particle of *charlatanerie* about Dupin. "I will explain," he said, "and that you may comprehend all clearly, we will first retrace the course of your meditations, from the moment in which I spoke to you until that of the *rencontre* with the fruiterer in question. The larger links of the chain run thus—Chantilly, Orion, Dr. Nichols, Epicurus, Stereotomy, the street stones, the fruiterer."

There are few persons who have not, at some period of their lives, amused themselves in retracing the steps by which particular conclusions of their own minds have been attained. The occupation is often full of interest; and he who attempts it for the first time is astonished by the apparently illimitable distance and incoherence between the starting-point and the goal. What, then, must have been my amazement when I heard the Frenchman speak what he had just spoken, and when I could not help acknowledging that he had spoken the truth. He continued:

"We had been talking of horses, if I remember aright, just before leaving the Rue C—. This was the last subject we discussed. As we crossed into this street, a fruiterer, with a large basket upon his head, brushing quickly past us, thrust you upon a pile of paving-stones collected at a spot where the causeway is undergoing repair. You stepped upon one of the loose fragments, slipped, slightly strained your ankle, appeared vexed or sulky, muttered a few words, turned to look at the pile, and then proceeded in silence. I was not particularly attentive to what you did; but observation has become with me, of late, a species of necessity.

"You kept your eyes upon the ground—glancing, with a petulant expression, at the holes and ruts in the pavement, (so that I saw you were still thinking of the stones), until we reached the little alley called Lamartine, which has been paved, by way of experiment, with the overlapping and riveted blocks. Here your countenance brightened up, and, perceiving your lips move, I could not doubt that you murmured the word 'stereotomy,' a term very affectedly applied to this species of pavement. I knew that you could not say to yourself 'stereotomy' without being brought to think of atomics, and thus of the theories of Epicurus; and since, when we discussed this subject not very long ago, I mentioned to you how singularly, yet with how little notice, the vague guesses of that noble Greek had met with confirmation in the late nebular cosmogony, I felt that you could not avoid casting your eyes upward to the great *nebula* in Orion, and I certainly expected that you would do so. You did look up; and I was now assured that I had correctly followed your steps. But in that bitter tirade upon Chantilly, which appeared in yesterday's *Musée*, the satirist, making some disgraceful allusions to the cobbler's change of name upon assuming the buskin, quoted a Latin line about which we have often conversed. I mean the line

Perdidit antiquum litera prima sonum.

I had told you that this was in reference to Orion, formerly written Urion; and, from certain pungencies connected with this explanation, I was aware that you could not have forgotten it. It was clear, therefore, that you would not fail to combine the ideas of Orion and Chantilly. That you did combine them I saw by the character of the smile which passed over your lips. You thought of the poor cobbler's immolation. So far, you had been stooping in your gait; but now I saw you draw yourself up to your full height. I was then sure that you reflected upon the diminutive figure of Chantilly. At this point I interrupted your meditations to remark that as, in fact, he *was* a very little fellow, that Chantilly, he would do better at the *Théâtre des Variétés*."

Not long after this, we were looking over an evening edition of the *Gazette des Tribunaux* when the following paragraphs arrested our attention.

"EXTRAORDINARY MURDERS—This morning, about three o'clock, the inhabitants of the Quartier St. Roch were aroused from sleep by a succession of terrific shrieks, issuing, apparently, from the fourth story of a house in the Rue Morgue, known to be in the sole occupancy of one Madame L'Espanaye, and her daughter, Mademoiselle Camille L'Espanaye. After some delay, occasioned by a fruitless attempt to procure admission in the usual manner, the gateway was broken in with a crowbar, and eight or ten of the neighbors entered, accompanied by two *gendarmes*. By this time the cries had ceased; but, as the party rushed up the first flight of stairs, two or more rough voices, in angry contention, were distinguished, and seemed to proceed from the upper part of the house. As the second landing was reached, these sounds, also, had ceased, and everything remained perfectly quiet. The party spread themselves, and hurried from room to room. Upon arriving at a large back chamber in the fourth story, (the door of which, being found locked, with the key inside, was forced open), a spectacle presented itself which struck every one present not less with horror than with astonishment.

"The apartment was in the wildest disorder—the furniture broken and thrown about in all directions. There was only one bedstead; and from this the bed had been removed, and thrown into the middle of the floor. On a chair lay a razor, besmeared with blood. On the hearth were two or three long and thick tresses of grey human hair, also dabbled in blood, and seeming to have been pulled out by the roots. Upon the floor were found four Napoleons, an ear-ring of topaz, three large silver spoons, three smaller of *métal d'Alger*, and two bags, containing nearly four thousand francs in gold. The drawers of a *bureau*, which stood in one corner, were open, and had been, apparently, rifled, although many articles still remained in them. A small iron safe was discovered under the *bed* (not under the bedstead). It was open, with the key still in the door. It had no contents beyond a few old letters, and other papers of little consequence.

"Of Madame L'Espanaye no traces were here seen; but an unusual quantity of soot being observed in the fire-place, a search was made in the chimney, and (horrible to relate!) the corpse of the daughter, head downward, was dragged therefrom; it having been thus forced up the narrow aperture for a considerable distance. The body was quite warm. Upon examining it, many excoriations were perceived, no doubt occasioned by the violence with which it had been thrust up and disengaged. Upon the face were many severe scratches, and, upon the throat, dark bruises, and deep indentations of finger nails, as if the deceased had been throttled to death.

"After a thorough investigation of every portion of the house, without farther discovery, the party made its way into a small paved yard in the rear of the building, where lay the corpse of the old lady, with her throat so entirely cut that, upon an attempt to raise her, the head fell off. The body, as well as the head, was fearfully mutilated—the former so much so as scarcely to retain any semblance of humanity.

"To this horrible mystery there is not as yet, we believe, the slightest clew."

The next day's paper had these additional particulars:

"THE TRAGEDY OF THE RUE MORGUE—Many

individuals have been examined in relation to this most extraordinary and frightful affair" [the word "*affaire*" has not yet, in France, that levity of import which it conveys with us], "but nothing whatever has transpired to throw light upon it. We give below all the material testimony elicited.

"*Pauline Dubourg*, laundress, deposes that she has known both the deceased for three years, having washed for them during that period. The old lady and her daughter seemed on good terms—very affectionate toward each other. They were excellent pay. Could not speak in regard to their mode or means of living. Believed that Madame L. told fortunes for a living. Was reputed to have money put by. Never met any persons in the house when she called for the clothes or took them home. Was sure that they had no servant in employ. There appeared to be no furniture in any part of the building, except in the fourth story.

"*Pierre Moreau*, tobacconist, deposes that he has been in the habit of selling small quantities of tobacco and snuff to Madame L'Espanaye for nearly four years. Was born in the neighborhood, and has always resided there. The deceased and her daughter had occupied the house in which the corpses were found, for more than six years. It was formerly occupied by a jeweler, who under-let the upper rooms to various persons. The house was the property of Madame L. She became dissatisfied with the abuse of the premises by her tenant, and moved into them herself, refusing to let any portion. The old lady was childish. Witness had seen the daughter some five or six times during the six years. The two lived an exceedingly retired life—were reputed to have money. Had heard it said among the neighbors that Madame L. told fortunes—did not believe it. Had never seen any person enter the door except the old lady and her daughter, a porter once or twice, and a physician some eight or ten times.

"Many other persons, neighbors, gave evidence to the same effect. No one was spoken of as frequenting the house. It was not known whether there were any living connections of Madame L. and her daughter. The shutters of the front windows were seldom opened. Those in the rear were always closed, with the exception of the large back room, fourth story. The house was a good house—not very old.

"*Isidore Musèt, gendarme*, deposes that he was called to the house about three o'clock in the morning, and found some twenty or thirty persons at the gateway, endeavoring to gain admittance. Forced it open, at length, with a bayonet—not with a crowbar. Had but little difficulty in getting it open, on account of its being a double or folding gate, and bolted neither at bottom nor top. The shrieks were continued until the gate was forced—and then suddenly ceased. They seemed to be screams of some person (or persons) in great agony—were loud and drawn out, not short and quick. Witness led the way up stairs. Upon reaching the first landing, heard two voices in loud and angry contention—the one a gruff voice, the other much shriller—a very strange voice. Could distinguish some words of the former, which was that of a Frenchman. Was positive that it was not a woman's voice. Could distinguish the words '*sacré*' and '*diable*.' The shrill voice was that of a foreigner. Could not be sure whether it was the voice of a man or of a woman. Could not make out what was said, but believed the language to be Spanish. The state of the room and of the bodies was described by this witness as we described them yesterday.

"*Henri Duval*, a neighbor, and by trade a silversmith, deposes that he was one of the party who first entered the house. Corroborates the testimony of Musèt in general. As soon as they forced an entrance, they reclosed the door, to keep out the crowd, which collected very fast, notwithstanding the lateness of the hour. The shrill voice, the witness thinks, was that of an Italian. Was certain it was not French. Could not be sure that it was a man's voice. It might have been a woman's. Was not acquainted with the Italian language. Could not distinguish the words, but was convinced by the intonation that the speaker was an Italian. Knew Madame L. and her daughter. Had conversed with both frequently. Was sure that the shrill voice was not that of either of the deceased.

"—*Odenheimer*, restaurateur. This witness volunteered his testimony. Not speaking French, was examined through an interpreter. Is a native of Amsterdam. Was passing the house at the time of the shrieks. They lasted for several minutes—probably ten. They were long and loud—very awful and distressing. Was one of those who entered the building. Corroborated the previous evidence in every respect but one. Was sure that the shrill voice was that of a man—of a Frenchman. Could not distinguish the words uttered. They were loud and quick—unequal—spoken apparently in fear as well as in anger. The voice was harsh—not so much shrill as harsh. Could not call it a shrill voice. The gruff voice said repeatedly '*sacré*,' '*diable*' and once '*mon Dieu*.'

"*Jules Mignaud*, banker, of the firm of Mignaud et Fils, Rue Deloraine. Is the elder Mignaud. Madame L'Espanaye had some property. Had opened an account with his banking house in the spring of the year—(eight years previously). Made frequent deposits in small sums. Had checked for nothing until the third day before her death, when she took out in person the sum of 4000 francs. This sum was paid in gold, and a clerk sent home with the money.

"*Adolphe Le Bon*, clerk to Mignaud et Fils, deposes that on the day in question, about noon, he accompanied Madame L'Espanaye to her residence with the 4000 francs, put up in two bags. Upon the door being opened, Mademoiselle L. appeared and took from his hands one of the bags, while the old lady relieved him of the other. He then bowed and departed. Did not see any person in the street at the time. It is a bye-street—very lonely.

"*William Bird*, tailor, deposes that he was one of the party who entered the house. Is an Englishman. Has lived in Paris two years. Was one of the first to ascend the stairs. Heard the voices in contention. The gruff voice was that of a Frenchman. Could make out several words, but cannot now remember all. Heard distinctly '*sacré*' and '*mon Dieu.*' There was a sound at the moment as if of several persons struggling—a scraping and scuffling sound. The shrill voice was very loud—louder than the gruff one. Is sure that it was not the voice of an Englishman. Appeared to be that of a German. Might have been a woman's voice. Does not understand German.

"Four of the above-named witnesses, being recalled, deposed that the door of the chamber in which was found the body of Mademoiselle L. was locked on the inside when the party reached it. Every thing was perfectly silent—no groans or noises of any kind. Upon forcing the door no person was seen. The windows, both of the back and front room, were down and firmly fastened from within. A door between the two rooms was closed, but not locked. The door leading from the front room into the passage was locked, with the key on the inside. A small room in the front of the house, on the fourth story, at the head of the passage, was open, the door being ajar. This room was crowded with old beds, boxes, and so forth. These were carefully removed and searched. There was not an inch of any portion of the house which was not carefully searched. Sweeps were sent up and down the chimneys. The house was a four story one, with garrets (*mansardes*). A trapdoor on the roof was nailed down very securely—did not appear to have been opened for years. The time elapsing between the hearing of the voices in contention and the breaking open of the room door, was variously stated by the witnesses. Some made it as short as three minutes—some as long as five. The door was opened with difficulty.

"*Alfonzo Garcio*, undertaker, deposes that he resides in the Rue Morgue. Is a native of Spain. Was one of the party who entered the house. Did not proceed upstairs. Is nervous, and was apprehensive of the consequences of agitation. Heard the voices in contention. The gruff voice was that of a Frenchman. Could not distinguish what was said. The shrill voice was that of an Englishman—is sure of this. Does not understand the English language, but judges by the intonation.

"*Alberto Montani*, confectioner, deposes that he was among the first to ascend the stairs. Heard the voices in question. The gruff voice was that of a Frenchman. Distinguished several words. The speaker appeared to be expostulating. Could not make out the words of the shrill voice. Spoke quick and unevenly. Thinks it the voice of a Russian. Corroborates the general testimony. Is an Italian. Never conversed with a native of Russia.

"Several witnesses, recalled, here testified that the chimneys of all the rooms on the fourth story were too narrow to admit the passage of a human being. By 'sweeps' were meant cylindrical sweeping-brushes, such as are employed by those who clean chimneys. These brushes were passed up and down every flue in the house. There is no back passage by which any one could have descended while the party proceeded upstairs. The body of Mademoiselle L'Espanaye was so firmly wedged in the chimney that it could not be got down until four or five of the party united their strength.

"*Paul Dumas*, physician, deposes that he was called to view the bodies about daybreak. They were both then lying on the sacking of the bedstead in the chamber where Mademoiselle L. was found. The corpse of the young lady was much bruised and excoriated. The fact that it had been thrust up the chimney would sufficiently account for these appearances. The throat was greatly chafed. There were several deep scratches just below the chin, together with a series of livid spots which were evidently the impression of fingers. The face was fearfully discolored, and the eye-balls protruded. The tongue had been partially bitten through. A large bruise was discovered upon the pit of the stomach, produced, apparently, by the pressure of a knee. In the opinion of M. Dumas, Mademoiselle L'Espanaye had been throttled to death by some person or persons unknown. The corpse of the mother was horribly mutilated. All the bones of the right leg and arm were more or less shattered. The left *tibia* much splintered, as well as all the ribs of the left side. Whole body dreadfully bruised and discolored. It was not possible to say how the injuries had been inflicted. A heavy club of wood, or a broad bar of iron—a chair—any large, heavy, and obtuse weapon would have produced such results, if wielded by the hands of a very powerful man. No woman could have inflicted the blows with any weapon. The head of the deceased, when seen by witness, was entirely separated from the body, and was also greatly shattered. The throat had evidently been cut with some very sharp instrument—probably with a razor.

"*Alexandre Etienne*, surgeon, was called with M. Dumas to view the bodies. Corroborated the testimony, and the opinions of M. Dumas.

"Nothing farther of importance was elicited, although several other persons were examined. A murder so mysterious, and so perplexing in all its particulars, was never before committed in Paris—if indeed a murder has been committed at all. The police are entirely at fault—an unusual occurrence in affairs of this nature. There is not, however, the shadow of a clew apparent."

The evening edition of the paper stated that the greatest excitement continued in the Quartier St. Roch—that the premises in question had been carefully re-searched, and fresh examinations of witnesses instituted, but all to no purpose. A postscript, however, mentioned that Adolphe Le Bon had been arrested and imprisoned—although nothing appeared to criminate him, beyond the facts already detailed.

Dupin seemed singularly interested in the progress of this affair—at least so I judged from his manner, for he made no comments. It was only after the announcement that Le Bon had been imprisoned, that he asked me my opinion respecting the murders.

I could merely agree with all Paris in considering them an insoluble mystery. I saw no means by which it would be possible to trace the murderer.

"We must not judge of the means," said Dupin, "by this shell of an examination. The Parisian police, so much extolled for *acumen*, are cunning, but no more. There is no method in their proceedings, beyond the method of the moment. They make a vast parade of measures; but, not unfrequently, these are so ill adapted to the objects proposed, as to put us in mind of Monsieur Jourdain's calling for his *robe-de-chambre—pour mieux entendre la musique*. The results attained by them are not unfrequently surprising, but, for the most part, are brought about by simple diligence and activity. When these qualities are unavailing, their schemes fail. Vidocq, for example, was a good guesser, and a persevering man. But, without educated thought, he erred continually by the very intensity of his investigations. He impaired his vision by holding the object too close. He might see, perhaps, one or two points with unusual clearness, but in so doing he, necessarily, lost sight of the matter as a whole. Thus there is such a thing as being too profound. Truth is not always in a well. In fact, as regards the more important knowledge, I do believe that she is invariably superficial. The depth lies in the valleys where we seek her, and not upon the mountain-tops where she is found. The modes and sources of this kind of error are well typified in the contemplation of the heavenly bodies. To look at a star by glances—to view it in a side-long way, by turning toward it the exterior portions of the *retina* (more susceptible of feeble impressions of light than the interior), is to behold the star distinctly—is to have the best appreciation of its luster—a luster which grows dim just in proportion as we turn our vision *fully* upon it. A greater number of rays actually fall upon the eye in the latter case, but, in the former, there is the more refined capacity for comprehension. By undue profundity we perplex and enfeeble thought; and it is possible to make even Venus herself vanish from the firmament by a scrutiny too sustained, too concentrated, or too direct.

"As for these murders, let us enter into some examinations for ourselves, before we make up an opinion respecting them. An inquiry will afford us amusement" [I thought this an odd term, so applied, but said nothing] "and, besides, Le Bon once rendered me a service for which I am not ungrateful. We will go and see the premises with our own eyes. I know G—, the Prefect of Police, and shall have no difficulty in obtaining the necessary permission."

The permission was obtained, and we proceeded at once to the Rue Morgue. This is one of those miserable thoroughfares which intervene between the Rue Richelieu and the Rue St.

Roch. It was late in the afternoon when we reached it; as this quarter is at a great distance from that in which we resided. The house was readily found; for there were still many persons gazing up at the closed shutters, with an objectless curiosity, from the opposite side of the way. It was an ordinary Parisian house, with a gateway, on one side of which was a glazed watch-box, with a sliding panel in the window, indicating a *loge de concierge*. Before going in we walked up the street, turned down an alley, and then, again turning, passed in the rear of the building— Dupin, meanwhile, examining the whole neighborhood, as well as the house, with a minuteness of attention for which I could see no possible object.

Retracing our steps, we came again to the front of the dwelling, rang, and, having shown our credentials, were admitted by the agents in charge. We went upstairs—into the chamber where the body of Mademoiselle L'Espanaye had been found, and where both the deceased still lay. The disorders of the room had, as usual, been suffered to exist. I saw nothing beyond what had been stated in the *Gazette des Tribunaux*. Dupin scrutinized everything—not excepting the bodies of the victims. We then went into the other rooms, and into the yard; a *gendarme* accompanying us throughout. The examination occupied us until dark, when we took our departure. On our way home my companion stopped in for a moment at the office of one of the daily papers.

I have said that the whims of my friend were manifold, and that *Fe les ménageais*—for this phrase there is no English equivalent. It was his humor, now, to decline all conversation on the subject of the murders, until about noon the next day. He then asked me, suddenly, if I had observed anything *peculiar* at the scene of the atrocity.

There was something in his manner of emphasizing the word "peculiar," which caused me to shudder, without knowing why.

"No, nothing *peculiar*," I said; "nothing more, at least, than we both saw stated in the paper."

"The *Gazette*," he replied, "has not entered, I fear, into the unusual horror of the thing. But dismiss the idle opinions of this print. It appears to me that this mystery is considered insoluble, for the very reason which should cause it to be regarded as easy of solution—I mean for the *outré* character of its features. The police are confounded by the seeming absence of motive—not for the murder itself—but for the atrocity of the murder. They are puzzled, too, by the seeming impossibility of reconciling the voices heard in contention, with the facts that no one was discovered upstairs but the assassinated Mademoiselle L'Espanaye, and that there were no means of egress without the notice of the party ascending. The wild disorder of the room; the corpse thrust, with the head downward, up the chimney; the frightful mutilation of the body of the old lady; these considerations with those just mentioned, and others which I need not mention, have sufficed to paralyze the powers, by putting completely at fault the boasted *acumen* of the government agents. They have fallen into the gross but common error of confounding the unusual with the abstruse. But it is by these deviations from the plane of the ordinary, that reason feels its way, if at all, in its search for the true. In investigations such as we are now pursuing, it should not be so much asked 'what has occurred?' as 'what has occurred that has never occurred before?' In fact, the facility with which I shall arrive, or have arrived, at the solution of this mystery, is in the direct ratio of its apparent insolubility in the eyes of the police."

I stared at the speaker in mute astonishment.

"I am now awaiting," continued he, looking toward the door of our apartment—"I am now awaiting a person who, although perhaps not the perpetrator of these butcheries, must have been in some measure implicated in their perpetration. Of the worst portion of the crimes committed, it is probable that he is innocent. I hope that I am right in this supposition; for upon it I build my expectation of reading the entire riddle. I look for the man here—in this room—every moment. It is true that he may not arrive; but the probability is that he will. Should he come, it will be necessary to detain him. Here are pistols; and we both know how to use them when occasion demands their use."

I took the pistols, scarcely knowing what I did, or believing what I heard, while Dupin went on, very much as if in a soliloquy. I have already spoken of his abstract manner at such times. His discourse was addressed to myself; but his voice, although by no means loud, had that intonation which is commonly employed in speaking to some one at a great distance. His eyes, vacant in expression, regarded only the wall.

"That the voices heard in contention," he said, "by the party upon the stairs, were not the voices of the women themselves, was fully proved by the evidence. This relieves us of all doubt upon the question whether the old lady could have first destroyed the daughter, and afterward have committed suicide. I speak of this point chiefly for the sake of method; for the strength of Madame L'Espanaye would have been utterly unequal to the task of thrusting her daughter's corpse up the chimney as it was found; and the nature of the wounds upon her own person entirely preclude the idea of self-destruction. Murder, then, has been committed by some third party; and the voices of this third party were those heard in contention. Let me now advert—not to the whole testimony respecting these voices—but to what was *peculiar* in that testimony. Did you observe anything peculiar about it?"

I remarked that, while all the witnesses agreed in supposing the gruff voice to be that of a Frenchman, there was much disagreement in regard to the shrill, or, as one individual termed it, the harsh voice.

"That was the evidence itself," said Dupin, "but it was not the peculiarity of the evidence. You have observed nothing distinctive. Yet there *was* something to be observed. The witnesses, as you remark, agreed about the gruff voice; they were here unanimous. But in regard to the shrill voice, the peculiarity is—not that they disagreed—but that, while an Italian, an Englishman, a Spaniard, a Hollander, and a Frenchman attempted to describe it, each one spoke of it as that *of a foreigner*. Each is sure that it was not the voice of one of his own countrymen. Each likens it—not to the voice of an individual of any nation with whose language he is conversant— but the converse. The Frenchman supposes it the voice of a Spaniard, and 'might have distinguished some words *had he been acquainted with the Spanish*.' The Dutchman maintains it to have been that of a Frenchman; but we find it stated that '*not understanding French this witness was examined through an interpreter*.' The Englishman thinks it the voice of a German, and '*does not understand German*.' The Spaniard 'is sure' that it was that of an Englishman, but 'judges by the intonation' altogether, '*as he has no knowledge of the English*.' The Italian believes it the voice of a Russian, but '*has never conversed with a native of Russia*.' A second Frenchman differs, moreover, with the first, and is positive that the voice was that of an Italian; but, *not being cognizant of that tongue*, is, like the Spaniard, 'convinced by the intonation.' Now, how strangely unusual must that voice have really been, about which such testimony as this *could* have been elicited!—in whose *tones*, even, denizens of the five great divisions of Europe could recognize nothing familiar! You will say that it might have been the voice of an Asiatic— of an African. Neither Asiatics nor Africans abound in Paris; but, without denying the inference, I will now merely call your attention to three points. The voice is termed by one witness 'harsh rather than shrill.' It is represented by two others to have been 'quick and *unequal*.' No words—no sounds resembling words—were by any witness mentioned as distinguishable.

"I know not," continued Dupin, "what impression I may have made, so far, upon your own understanding; but I do not hesitate to say that legitimate deductions even from this portion of the testimony—the portion respecting the gruff and shrill voices—are in themselves sufficient to engender a suspicion which should give direction to all farther progress in the investigation of the mystery. I said 'legitimate deductions'; but my meaning is not thus fully expressed. I designed to imply that the deductions are the *sole* proper ones, and that the suspicion arises *inevitably* from them as the single result. What the suspicion is, however, I will not say just yet. I merely wish you to bear in mind that, with myself, it was sufficiently forcible to give a definite form—a certain tendency—to my inquiries in the chamber.

"Let us now transport ourselves, in fancy, to this chamber. What shall we first seek here? The means of egress employed by the murderers. It is not too much to say that neither of us believe in preternatural events. Madame and Mademoiselle L'Espanaye were not destroyed by spirits. The doers of the deed were material, and escaped materially. Then how? Fortunately, there is but one mode of reasoning upon the point, and that mode *must* lead us to a definite decision. Let us examine, each by each, the possible means of egress. It is clear that the assassins were in the room where Mademoiselle L'Espanaye was found, or at least in the room adjoining, when the party ascended the stairs. It is then only from these two apartments that we have to seek issues. The police have laid bare the floors, the ceilings, and the masonry of the walls, in every direction. No *secret* issues could have escaped their vigilance. But, not trusting to *their* eyes, I examined with my own. There were, then, *no* secret issues. Both doors leading from the rooms into the passage were securely locked, with the keys inside. Let us turn to the chimneys. These, although of ordinary width for some eight or ten feet above the hearths, will not admit, throughout their extent, the body of a large cat. The impossibility of egress, by means already stated, being thus absolute, we are reduced to the windows. Through those of the front room no one could have escaped without notice from the crowd in the street. The murderers *must* have passed, then, through those of the back room. Now, brought to this conclusion in so unequivocal a manner as we are, it is not our part, as reasoners, to reject it on account of apparent impossibilities. It is only left for us to prove that these apparent 'impossibilities' are, in reality, not such.

"There are two windows in the chamber. One of them is unobstructed by furniture, and is wholly visible. The lower portion of the other is hidden from view by the head of the unwieldy bedstead which is thrust close up against it. The former was found securely fastened from within. It resisted the utmost force of those who endeavored to raise it. A large gimlet hole had been pierced in its frame to the left, and a very stout nail was found fitted therein, nearly to the head. Upon examining the other window, a similar nail was seen similarly fitted in it; and a vigorous attempt to raise this sash, failed also. The police were now entirely satisfied that egress had not been in these directions. And, *therefore*, it was thought a matter of supererogation to withdraw the nails and open the windows.

"My own examination was somewhat more particular, and was so for the reason I have just given—because here it was, I knew, that all apparent impossibilities *must* be proved to be not such in reality.

"I proceeded to think thus—*à posteriori*. The murderers *did* escape from one of these windows. This being so, they could not have re-fastened the sashes from the inside, as they were found fastened—the consideration which put a stop, through its obviousness, to the scrutiny of the police in this quarter. Yet the sashes *were* fastened. They *must*, then, have the power of fastening themselves. There was no escape from this conclusion. I stepped to the unobstructed casement, withdrew the nail with some difficulty, and attempted to raise the sash. It resisted all my efforts, as I had anticipated. A concealed spring must, I now knew, exist; and this corroboration of my idea convinced me that my premises, at least, were correct, however mysterious still appeared the circumstances attending the nails. A careful search soon brought to light the hidden spring. I pressed it, and, satisfied with the discovery, forbore to upraise the sash.

"I now replaced the nail and regarded it attentively. A person passing out through this window might have reclosed it, and the spring would have caught—but the nail could not have been replaced. The conclusion was plain, and again narrowed in the field of my investigations. The assassins *must* have escaped through the other window. Supposing, then, the springs upon each sash to be the same, as was probable, there *must* be found a difference between the nails, or at least between the modes of their fixture. Getting upon the sacking of the bedstead, I looked over the headboard minutely at the second casement. Passing my hand down behind the board, I readily discovered and pressed the spring, which was, as I had supposed, identical in character with its neighbor. I now looked at the nail. It was as stout as the other, and apparently fitted in the same manner—driven in nearly up to the head.

"You will say that I was puzzled; but, if you think so, you must have misunderstood the nature of the inductions. To use a sporting phrase, I had not been once 'at fault.' The scent had never for an instant been lost. There was no flaw in any link of the chain. I had traced the secret to its ultimate result—and that result was *the nail*. It had, I say, in every respect, the appearance of its fellow in the other window; but this fact was an absolute nullity (conclusive as it might seem to be) when compared with the consideration that here, at this point, terminated the clew. 'There *must* be something wrong,' I said, 'about the nail.' I touched it; and the head, with about a quarter of an inch of the shank, came off in my fingers. The rest of the shank was in the gimlet hole, where it had been broken off. The fracture was an old one (for its edges were incrusted with rust), and had apparently been accomplished by the blow of a hammer, which had partially imbedded, in the top of the bottom sash, the head portion of the nail. I now carefully replaced this head portion in the indentation whence I had taken it, and the resemblance to a perfect nail was complete—the fissure was invisible. Pressing the spring, I gently raised the sash for a few inches; the head went up with it, remaining firm in its bed. I closed the window, and the semblance of the whole nail was again perfect.

"The riddle, so far, was now unriddled. The assassin had escaped through the window which looked upon the bed. Dropping of its own accord upon his exit (or perhaps purposely closed), it had become fastened by the spring; and it was the retention of this spring which had been mistaken by the police for that of the nail—farther inquiry being thus considered unnecessary.

"The next question is that of the mode of descent. Upon this point I had been satisfied in my walk with you around the building. About five feet and a half from the casement in question there runs a lightning-rod. From this rod it would have been impossible for any one to reach the window itself, to say nothing of entering it. I observed, however, that shutters of the fourth story were of the peculiar kind called by Parisian carpenters *ferrades*—a kind rarely employed at the present day, but frequently seen upon very old mansions at Lyons and Bordeaux. They are in the form of an ordinary door (a single, not a folding door), except that the lower half is latticed or worked in open trellis—thus affording an excellent hold for the hands. In the present instance these shutters are fully three feet and a half broad. When we saw them from the rear of the house, they were both about half open—that is to say, they stood off at right angles from the wall. It is probable that the police, as well as myself, examined the back of the tenement; but, if so, in looking at these *ferrades* in the line of their breadth (as they must have done), they did not perceive this great breadth itself, or, at all events, failed to take it into due consideration. In fact, having once satisfied themselves that no egress could have been made in this quarter, they would naturally bestow here a very cursory examination. It was clear to me, however, that the shutter belonging to the window at the head of the bed, would, if swung fully back to the wall, reach to within two feet of the lightning-rod. It was also evident that, by exertion of a very unusual degree of activity and courage, an entrance into the window, from the rod, might have been thus effected. By reaching to the distance of two feet and a half (we now suppose the shutter open to its whole extent) a robber might have taken a firm grasp upon the trellis-work. Letting go, then, his hold upon the rod, placing his feet securely against the wall, and springing boldly from it, he might have swung the shutter so as to close it, and, if we imagine the window open at the time, might have swung himself into the room.

"I wish you to bear especially in mind that I have spoken of a *very* unusual degree of activity as requisite to success in so hazardous and so difficult a feat. It is my design to show you, first, that the thing might possibly have been accomplished: but, secondly and *chiefly*, I wish to impress upon your understanding the *very extraordinary*—the almost preternatural character of that agility which could have accomplished it.

"You will say, no doubt, using the language of the law, that 'to make out my case,' I should rather undervalue, than insist upon a full estimation of the activity required in this matter. This may be the practice in law, but it is not the usage of reason. My ultimate object is only the truth. My immediate purpose is to lead you to place in juxtaposition that *very unusual* activity of which I have just spoken, with that *very peculiar* shrill (or harsh) and *unequal* voice, about whose nationality no two persons could be found to agree, and in whose utterance no syllabification could be detected."

At these words a vague and half-formed conception of the meaning of Dupin flitted over my mind. I seemed to be upon the verge of comprehension, without power to comprehend—as men, at times, find themselves upon the brink of remembrance, without being able, in the end, to remember. My friend went on with his discourse.

"You will see," he said, "that I have shifted the question from the mode of egress to that of ingress. It was my design to suggest that both were effected in the same manner, at the same point. Let us now revert to the interior of the room. Let us survey the appearances here. The drawers of the bureau, it is said, had been rifled, although many articles of apparel still remained within them. The conclusion here is absurd. It is a mere guess—a very silly one—and no more. How are we to know that the articles found in the drawers were not all these drawers had originally contained? Madame L'Espanaye and her daughter lived an exceedingly retired life—saw no company— seldom went out—had little use for numerous changes of habiliment. Those found were at least of as good quality as any likely to be possessed by these ladies. If a thief had taken any, why did he not take the best—why did he not take all? In a word, why did he abandon four thousand francs in gold to encumber himself with a bundle of linen? The gold *was* abandoned. Nearly the whole sum mentioned by Monsieur Mignaud, the banker, was discovered, in bags, upon the floor. I wish you, therefore, to discard from your thoughts the blundering idea of *motive*, engendered in the brains of the police by that portion of the evidence which speaks of money delivered at the door of the house. Coincidences ten times as remarkable as this (the delivery of the money, and murder committed within three days upon the party receiving it), happen to all of us every hour of our lives, without attracting even momentary notice. Coincidences, in general, are great stumbling-blocks in the way of that class of thinkers who have been educated to know nothing of the theory of probabilities—that theory to which the most glorious objects of human research are indebted for the most glorious of illustration. In the present instance, had the gold been gone, the fact of its delivery three days before would have formed something more than a coincidence. It would have been corroborative of this idea of motive. But, under the real circumstances of the case, if we are to suppose gold the motive of this outrage, we must also imagine the perpetrator so vacillating an idiot as to have abandoned his gold and his motive together.

"Keeping now steadily in mind the points to which I have drawn your attention—that peculiar voice, that unusual agility, and that startling absence of motive in a murder so singularly atrocious as this—let us glance at the butchery itself. Here is a woman strangled to death by manual strength, and thrust up a chimney, head downward. Ordinary assassins employ no such modes of murder as this. Least of all, do they thus dispose of the murdered. In the manner of thrusting the corpse up the chimney, you will admit that there was something excessively *outré*—something altogether irreconcilable with our common notions of human action, even when we suppose the actors the most depraved of men. Think, too, how great must have been that strength which could have thrust the body *up* such an aperture so forcibly that the united vigor of several persons was found barely sufficient to drag it *down*!

"Turn, now, to other indications of the employment of a vigor most marvelous. On the hearth were thick tresses—very thick tresses—of gray human hair. These had been torn out by the roots. You are aware of the great force necessary in tearing thus from the head even twenty or thirty hairs together. You saw the locks in question as well as myself. Their roots (a hideous sight!) were clotted with fragments of the flesh of the scalp—sure token of the prodigious power which had been exerted in uprooting perhaps half a million of hairs at a time. The throat of the old lady was not merely cut, but the head absolutely severed from the body: the instrument was a mere razor. I wish you also to look at the *brutal* ferocity of these deeds. Of the bruises upon the body of Madame L'Espanaye I do not speak. Monsieur Dumas, and his worthy coadjutor Monsieur Etienne, have pronounced that they were inflicted by some obtuse instrument; and so far these gentlemen are very correct. The obtuse instrument was clearly the stone pavement in the yard, upon which the victim had fallen from the window which looked in upon the bed. This idea, however simple it may now seem, escaped the police for the same reason that the breadth of the shutters escaped them—because, by the affair of the nails, their perceptions had been hermetically sealed against the possibility of the windows having ever been opened at all.

"If now, in addition to all these things, you have properly reflected upon the odd disorder of the chamber, we have gone so far as to combine the ideas of an agility astounding, a strength superhuman, a ferocity brutal, a butchery without motive, a *grotesquerie* in horror absolutely alien from humanity, and a voice foreign in tone to the ears of men of many nations, and devoid of all distinct or intelligible syllabification. What result, then, has ensued? What impression have I made upon your fancy?"

I felt a creeping of the flesh as Dupin asked me the question. "A madman," I said, "has done this deed—some raving maniac, escaped from a neighboring *Maison de Santé.*"

"In some respects," he replied, "your idea is not irrelevant. But the voices of madmen, even in their wildest paroxysms, are never found to tally with that peculiar voice heard upon the stairs. Madmen are of some nation, and their language, however incoherent in its words, has always the coherence of syllabification. Besides, the hair of a madman is not such as I now hold in my hand. I disentangled this little tuft from the rigidly clutched fingers of Madame L'Espanaye. Tell me what you can make of it."

"Dupin!" I said, completely unnerved; "this hair is most unusual—this is no *human* hair."

"I have not asserted that it is," said he; "but, before we decide this point, I wish you to glance at the little sketch I have here traced upon this paper. It is a *fac-simile* drawing of what has been described in one portion of the testimony as 'dark bruises, and deep indentations of finger nails,' upon the throat of Mademoiselle L'Espanaye, and in another (by Messrs. Dumas and Etienne), as a 'series of livid spots, evidently the impression of fingers.'

"You will perceive," continued my friend, spreading out the paper upon the table before us, "that this drawing gives the idea of a firm and fixed hold. There is no *slipping* apparent. Each finger has retained—possibly until the death of the victim—the fearful grasp by which it originally imbedded itself. Attempt, now, to place all your fingers, at the same time, in the respective impressions as you see them."

I made the attempt in vain.

"We are possibly not giving this matter a fair trial," he said. "The paper is spread out upon a plane surface; but the human throat is cylindrical. Here is a billet of wood, the circumference of which is about that of the throat. Wrap the drawing around it, and try the experiment again."

I did so; but the difficulty was even more obvious than before. "This," I said, "is the mark of no human hand."

"Read now," replied Dupin, "this passage from Cuvier."

It was a minute anatomical and generally descriptive account of the large fulvous Ourang-Outang of the East Indian Islands.

The gigantic stature, the prodigious strength and activity, the wild ferocity, and the imitative propensities of these mammalia are sufficiently well known to all. I understood the full horrors of the murder at once.

"The description of the digits," said I, as I made an end of reading, "is in exact accordance with this drawing. I see that no animal but an Ourang-Outang, of the species here mentioned, could have impressed the indentations as you have traced them. This tuft of tawny hair, too, is identical in character with that of the beast of Cuvier. But I cannot possibly comprehend the particulars of this frightful mystery. Besides, there were two voices heard in contention, and one of them was unquestionably the voice of a Frenchman."

"True; and you will remember an expression attributed almost unanimously, by the evidence, to this voice, the expression, '*Mon Dieu!*' This, under the circumstances, has been justly characterized by one of the witnesses (Montani, the confectioner), as an expression of remonstrance or expostulation. Upon these two words, therefore, I have mainly built my hopes of a full solution of the riddle. A Frenchman was cognizant of the murder. It is possible—indeed it is far more than probable—that he was innocent of all participation in the bloody transactions which took place. The Ourang-Outang may have escaped from him. He may have traced it to the chamber; but, under the agitating circumstances which ensued, he could never have re-captured it. It is still at large. I will not pursue these guesses—for I have no right to call them more—since the shades of reflection upon which they are based are scarcely of sufficient depth to be appreciable by my own intellect, and since I could not pretend to make them intelligible to the understanding of another. We will call them guesses then, and speak of them as such. If the Frenchman in question is indeed, as I suppose, innocent of this atrocity, this advertisement, which I left last night, upon our return home, at the office of *Le Monde* (a paper devoted to the shipping interest, and much sought by sailors), will bring him to our residence."

He handed me a paper, and I read thus:

CAUGHT—*In the Bois de Boulogne, early in the morning of the —inst.*, [the morning of the murder,] *a very large, tawny Ourang-Outang of the Bornese species. The owner, (who is ascertained to be a sailor, belonging to a Maltese vessel,) may have the animal again, upon identifying it satisfactorily, and paying a few charges arising from its capture and keeping. Call at No. —, Rue —, Faubourg St. Germain—au troisième.*

"How was it possible," I asked, "that you should know the man to be a sailor, and belonging to a Maltese vessel?"

"I do *not* know it," said Dupin. "I am not *sure* of it. Here, however, is a small piece of ribbon, which from its form, and from its greasy appearance, has evidently been used in tying the hair in one of those long *queues* of which sailors are so fond. Moreover, this knot is one which few besides sailors can tie, and is peculiar to the Maltese. I picked the ribbon up at the foot of the lightning-rod. It could not have belonged to either of the deceased. Now if, after all, I am wrong in my induction from this ribbon, that the Frenchman was a sailor belonging to a Maltese vessel, still I can have done no harm in saying what I did in the advertisement. If I am in error, he will merely suppose that I have been misled by some circumstance into which he will not take the trouble to inquire. But if I am right, a great point is gained. Cognizant although innocent of the murder, the Frenchman will naturally hesitate about replying to the advertisement—about demanding the Ourang-Outang. He will reason thus: 'I am innocent; I am poor; my Ourang-Outang is of great value to one in my circumstances, a fortune of itself—why should I lose it through idle apprehensions of danger? Here it is, within my grasp. It was found in the Bois de Boulogne—at a vast distance from the scene of that butchery. How can it ever be suspected that a brute beast should have done the deed? The police are at fault—they have failed to procure the slightest clew. Should they even trace the animal, it would be impossible to prove me cognizant of the murder, or to implicate me in guilt on account of that cognizance. Above all, *I am known*. The advertiser designates me as the possessor of the beast. I am not sure to what limit his knowledge may extend. Should I avoid claiming a property of so great value, which it is known that I possess, I will render the animal at least liable to suspicion. It is not my policy to attract attention either to myself or to the beast. I will answer the advertisement, get the Ourang-Outang, and keep it close until this matter has blown over.'"

At this moment we heard a step upon the stairs.

"Be ready," said Dupin, "with your pistols, but neither use them nor show them until at a signal from myself."

The front door of the house had been left open, and the visitor had entered, without ringing, and advanced several steps upon the staircase. Now, however, he seemed to hesitate. Presently we heard him descending. Dupin was moving quickly to the door, when we again heard him coming up. He did not turn back a second time, but stepped up with decision and rapped at the door of our chamber.

"Come in," said Dupin, in a cheerful and hearty tone.

A man entered. He was a sailor, evidently—a tall, stout, and muscular-looking person, with a certain dare-devil expression of countenance, not altogether unprepossessing. His face, greatly sunburnt, was more than half hidden by whisker and *mustachio*. He had with him a huge oaken cudgel, but appeared to be otherwise unarmed. He bowed awkwardly, and bade us "good-evening," in French accents, which, although somewhat Neufchatelish, were still sufficiently indicative of a Parisian origin.

"Sit down, my friend," said Dupin. "I suppose you have called about the Ourang-Outang. Upon my word, I almost envy you the possession of him; a remarkably fine, and no doubt a very valuable animal. How old do you suppose him to be?"

The sailor drew a long breath, with the air of a man relieved of some intolerable burden, and then replied, in an assured tone—

"I have no way of telling—but he can't be more than four or five years old. Have you got him here?"

"Oh no; we had no conveniences for keeping him here. He is at a livery stable in the Rue Dubourg, just by. You can get him in the morning. Of course you are prepared to identify the property?"

"To be sure I am, sir."

"I shall be sorry to part with him," said Dupin.

"I don't mean that you should be at all this trouble for nothing, sir," said the man. "Couldn't expect it. Am very willing to pay a reward for the finding of the animal—that is to say, anything in reason."

"Well," replied my friend, "that is all very fair, to be sure. Let me think!—what should I have? Oh! I will tell you. My reward shall be this. You shall give me all the information in your power about these murders in the Rue Morgue."

Dupin said the last words in a very low tone, and very quietly. Just as quietly, too, he walked toward the door, locked it, and put the key in his pocket. He then drew a pistol from his bosom and placed it, without the least flurry, upon the table.

The sailor's face flushed up as if he were struggling with suffocation. He started to his feet and grasped his cudgel; but the next moment he fell back into his seat, trembling violently, and with the countenance of death itself. He spoke not a word. I pitied him from the bottom of my heart.

"My friend," said Dupin, in a kind tone, "you are alarming yourself unnecessarily—you are indeed. We mean you no harm whatever. I pledge you the honor of a gentleman, and of a Frenchman, that we intend you no injury. I perfectly well know that you are innocent of the atrocities in the Rue Morgue. It will not do, however, to deny that you are in some measure implicated in them. From what I have already said, you must know that I have had means of information about this matter— means of which you could never have dreamed. Now the thing stands thus. You have done nothing which you could have avoided—nothing, certainly, which renders you culpable. You were not even guilty of robbery, when you might have robbed with impunity. You have nothing to conceal. You have no reason for concealment. On the other hand, you are bound by every principle of honor to confess all you know. An innocent man is now imprisoned, charged with that crime of which you can point out the perpetrator."

The sailor had recovered his presence of mind, in a great measure, while Dupin uttered these words; but his original boldness of bearing was all gone.

"So help me God," said he, after a brief pause, "I *will* tell you all I know about this affair; but I do not expect you to believe one half I say—I would be a fool indeed if I did. Still, I *am* innocent, and I will make a clean breast if I die for it."

What he stated was, in substance, this. He had lately made a voyage to the Indian Archipelago. A party, of which he formed one, landed at Borneo, and passed into the interior on an excursion of pleasure. Himself and a companion had captured the Ourang-Outang. This companion dying, the animal fell into his own exclusive possession. After great trouble, occasioned by the intractable ferocity of his captive during the home voyage, he at length succeeded in lodging it safely at his own residence in Paris, where, not to attract toward himself the unpleasant curiosity of his neighbors, he kept it carefully secluded, until such time as it should recover from a wound in the foot, received from a splinter on board ship. His ultimate design was to sell it.

Returning home from some sailors' frolic on the night, or rather in the morning of the murder, he found the beast occupying his own bedroom, into which it had broken from a closet adjoining, where it had been, as was thought, securely confined. Razor in hand, and fully lathered, it was sitting before a looking-glass, attempting the operation of shaving, in which it had no doubt previously watched its master through the key-hole of the closet. Terrified at the sight of so dangerous a weapon in the possession of an animal so ferocious, and so well able to use it, the man, for some moments, was at a loss what to do. He had been accustomed, however, to quiet the creature, even in its fiercest moods, by the use of a whip, and to this he now resorted. Upon sight of it, the Ourang-Outang sprang at once through the door of the chamber, down the stairs, and thence, through a window, unfortunately open, into the street.

The Frenchman followed in despair; the ape, razor still in hand, occasionally stopping to look back and gesticulate at its pursuer, until the latter had nearly come up with it. It then again made off. In this manner the chase continued for a long time. The streets were profoundly quiet, as it was nearly three o'clock in the morning. In passing down an alley in the rear of the Rue Morgue, the fugitive's attention was arrested by a light gleaming from the open window of Madame L'Espanaye's chamber, in the fourth story of her house. Rushing to the building, it perceived the lightning-rod, clambered up with inconceivable agility, grasped the shutter, which was thrown fully back against the wall, and, by its means, swung itself directly upon the headboard of the bed. The whole feat did not occupy a minute. The shutter was kicked open again by the Ourang-Outang as it entered the room.

The sailor, in the meantime, was both rejoiced and perplexed. He had strong hopes of now recapturing the brute, as it could scarcely escape from the trap into which it had ventured, except by the rod, where it might be intercepted as it came down. On the other hand, there was much cause for anxiety as to what it might do in the house. This latter reflection urged the man still to follow the fugitive. A lightning-rod is ascended without difficulty, especially by a sailor; but, when he had arrived as high as the window, which lay far to his left, his career was stopped; the most that he could accomplish was to reach over so as to obtain a glimpse of the interior of the room. At this glimpse he nearly fell from his hold through excess of horror. Now it was that those hideous shrieks arose upon the night, which had startled from slumber the inmates of the Rue Morgue. Madame L'Espanaye and her daughter, habited in their night clothes, had apparently been arranging some papers in the iron chest already mentioned, which had been wheeled into the middle of the room. It was open, and its contents lay beside it on the floor. The victims must have been sitting with their backs toward the window; and, from the time elapsing between the ingress of the beast and the screams, it seems probable that it was not immediately perceived. The flapping-to of the shutter would naturally have been attributed to the wind.

As the sailor looked in, the gigantic animal had seized Madame L'Espanaye by the hair (which was loose, as she had been combing it), and was flourishing the razor about her face, in imitation of the motions of a barber. The daughter lay prostrate and motionless; she had swooned. The screams and struggles of the old lady (during which the hair was torn from her head) had the effect of changing the probably pacific purposes of the Ourang-Outang into those of wrath. With one determined sweep of its muscular arm it nearly severed her head from her body. The sight of blood inflamed its anger into frenzy. Gnashing its teeth, and flashing fire from its eyes, it flew upon the body of the girl, and imbedded its fearful talons in her throat, retaining its grasp until she expired. Its wandering and wild glances fell at this moment upon the head of the bed, over which the face of its master, rigid with horror, was just discernible. The fury of the beast, who no doubt bore still in mind the dreaded whip, was instantly converted into fear. Conscious of having deserved punishment, it seemed desirous of concealing its bloody deeds, and skipped about the chamber in an agony of nervous agitation; throwing down and breaking the furniture as it moved, and dragging the bed from the bedstead. In conclusion, it seized first the corpse of the daughter, and thrust it up the chimney, as it was found; then that of the old lady, which it immediately hurled through the window headlong.

As the ape approached the casement with its mutilated burden, the sailor shrank aghast to the rod, and, rather gliding than clambering down it, hurried at once home—dreading the consequences of the butchery, and gladly abandoning, in his terror, all solicitude about the fate of the Ourang-Outang.

The words heard by the party upon the staircase were the Frenchman's exclamations of horror and affright, commingled with the fiendish jabberings of the brute.

I have scarcely anything to add. The Ourang-Outang must have escaped from the chamber, by the rod, just before the breaking of the door. It must have closed the window as it passed through it. It was subsequently caught by the owner himself, who obtained for it a very large sum at the *Jardin des Plantes*. Le Bon was instantly released upon our narration of the circumstances (with some comments from Dupin) at the *bureau* of the Prefect of Police. This functionary, however well disposed to my friend, could not altogether conceal his chagrin at the turn which affairs had taken, and was fain to indulge in a sarcasm or two, about the propriety of every person minding his own business.

"Let them talk," said Dupin, who had not thought it necessary to reply. "Let him discourse; it will ease his conscience. I am satisfied with having defeated him in his own castle. Nevertheless, that he failed in the solution of this mystery, is by no means that matter for wonder which he supposes it; for, in truth, our friend the Prefect is somewhat too cunning to be profound. In his wisdom is no *stamen*. It is all head and no body, like the pictures of the Goddess Laverna—or, at best, all head and shoulders, like a codfish. But he is a good creature after all. I like him especially for one master stroke of cant, by which he has attained his reputation for ingenuity. I mean the way he has '*de nier ce qui est, et d'expliquer ce qui n'est pas.*'" *

---

* Rousseau, *Nouvelle Héloïse.*

THE SONS OF TAMMANY

By

MIKE CAREY

My name is Thomas Nast. I'm sixty-two years old, and to be honest I don't expect to be able to hold up my hand after another year's seasonal turnings and returnings to say I'm sixty-three. I'm dying, at long last. And death dissolves all the bonds of obligation except the ones I owe to God. That being the case, I feel like I'm free at last to talk about the events of August 1870, which formerly I had held back from doing on account of they implicate a whole lot of people in a whole lot of queasy doings, and I couldn't really back up what I was saying with anything you might count as actual proof.

But when a man's staring straight down the barrel of his *nunc dimittis*, and the writing's not just on the wall but on the face that stares back at him out of the mirror, he stops fretting about the legal niceties and starts to think about setting the record straight. Which is what I aim to do.

In 1870, I was residing in New York City and working as an artist and cartoonist on that excellent periodical, the *Harper's Weekly*, under the editorship of George Curtis. I counted Curtis as a friend as well as an employer. But when he called me into his office on the morning of August 13th of that year, he was wearing the boss hat rather than the friend one.

Curtis gave me a civil nod and gestured me into one of the two visitor chairs. Already ensconced in the other chair was a man of a somewhat striking appearance. Although, having said that, I'm going to show myself a weak sister by admitting that I can't really say what it was about this gentleman that was so singular.

He was a good deal older than I was, and he'd seen enough summers to get a slightly weather-beaten look around his cheeks and jowls. He was kind of short and dumpy in his build, which was neither here nor there, but he had one of those half-hearted little mustaches that looks like it's about to give up and crawl back inside, and to be honest that was sort of a point against him in my book. If a man's going to go for a mustache, he should go all-in for one, say I, and Devil take the hairiest. He was toying with a cane that had a carved ivory handle in the shape of a lion's head—an effete sort of a gewgaw for a man to be playing with. And he had a suit with a waistcoat, and the waistcoat had a pattern to it. In my experience, that doesn't speak to a man's moral seriousness.

I guess, thinking about it, it was the eyes that were the selling point. They were a dark enough brown to count for black, and they had a sort of an augur-bit quality to them. It was the most startling thing. Like when this gentleman looked at you, looking wasn't really the half of it, and maybe you needed a whole other verb.

"Tommy, this here's Mr. Dupin," Curtis said. "Visiting from Paris. Not the Texas one, t'other one, over in France."

"Well, it's good to meet you, Mr. Dupin," I said, taking the collateral of the eyes against the rest of the stuff that was on offer. Curtis pronounced the name "du*pan*," which I estimate is French for "out of the pan," as in the thing you bail out from before you end up in the fire. Which wasn't a bad name at all for this particular customer, as things transpired.

"Only he ain't a mister," Curtis added, scrupulous as you'd expect a good editor to be. "He's a *Chevalier*."

"What does that mean?" I asked.

"Means he's got a horse stashed somewhere, as I understand it."

"Good job," I said. "With that waistcoat, he may need to access it in a hurry."

"Monsieur," the little man said in a waspish voice, "I speak excellent English, and I thank you for the compliment. I can, if you wish, give you the address of my tailor."

"Oh, that won't be necessary," I told him. "I think one of those things in the world at any one time answers the purpose pretty well."

The Frenchman surprised me by laughing at that—and it was a big, loud horse-laugh, too, not the little snigger you'd expect would come from underneath that lamentable mustache. "Perhaps you are right," he said. "One at a time. Yes."

And then Curtis got to the point, which was that Mr. Du-Frying-Pan wanted to see something of New York while he was here. What's more, he carried letters of introduction from a job lot of people who were (as you might say) the human equivalent of big guns on big limbers, and could blast Curtis and me and Mr. Harper and the subs' desk and Uncle Tom Cobley and all into the Hudson if we didn't show their friend Dupin a good time.

"So I thought perhaps he could come with you today when you go to sketch the bridge," Curtis wound up.

I knew that was where he was aiming at, so I took it in my

stride. "I think that's a swell idea," I said. "Sure. Mr. Dupin, come and see my city. She's something to see. George, you want to come along?"

"Oh no," Curtis said hurriedly. "I'm tied up every which way here, and I won't see daylight this side of Tuesday. You guys go and have a good time. Lunch is on Mr. Harper, so long as you don't get into a second bottle... And you can take a cab to get down there." He waited a decent length of time—maybe a slow count of five—before adding, "Trolley car will bring you back."

"And what is it you do, way over there in Paris, Mr. Dupin?" I asked, as we toiled down the stairs. The Equitable Life Building, which they'd just finished building over on Broadway, had its very own hydraulic elevator, but every time I mentioned that to Curtis he walked the other way.

"What do I do?" Dupin repeated doubtfully.

"Yeah. What's your motive and your métier? What's the singular thing that you pursue?"

"Ah." The little man's face lit up with understanding, but then it closed down again as he took that question over the threshold of his ruminations and worried it some. "The truth," he said at last. "The truth is what I pursue."

"Really? There any profit to be had in that?"

He gave out with that belly laugh again. "No. Not usually."

We waited for a cab on the corner of 41st Street right next to Peason's cigar store. Mr. Du-Griddle-Tray kept taking sideways glances at the cigar store Indian as though he might be looking to pick a fight. "That there is Tamanend, of the Lenape nation," I told him. "He's widely known in these parts, despite having turned up his toes back in sixteen-ought-eight."

The Frenchman's answer surprised me. "Yes," he said. "Of course. Because of the Society of St. Tammany, to which many members of New York's current civic administration belong."

I gave him a nod, and probably my face showed him that I was impressed. "One up to you, Dupin. That's the connection, all right. The Great Wigwam, they call it—the Tammany Hall, down on 14th Street. And it's got its share of famous patrons, like you say. Our illustrious mayor, Oakey Hall. Judge George Barnard, who doles out wisdom to the city benches. Hank Smith, who's the president of the Police Commission. Oh, there's a whole ring of them."

I didn't mention the Grand Sachem, William "Boss" Tweed, in the same way that you don't speak of the Devil—in case you turn around and find him breathing over your shoulder.

"Political corruption," Dupin mused. "It is a scourge."

And yes, it is. But this was my city we were lambasting, and I don't care to see my city, good-time girl though she may be, roughly handled by a stranger. So I changed the subject and talked about the bridge instead. And not long after that, we managed to hail a cab.

In deference to Du-Sausage-Cutter's hind parts I picked out a Duncan Sherman, which had a sprung undercarriage and a horse with something of an imperturbable nature. Truth to tell, we could have made better time walking—but you've got to push the boat out when you've got a guest to entertain, and besides it was setting in to rain a little. On a rainy day, Fifth Avenue is a lot more fun to ride down than to walk down.

As we rode, I carried on waxing lyrical about the bridge. "Over yonder," I said, pointing, "to the east of us, those buildings you see are not a part of the fair city of New York. They belong to our neighbor polity, Brooklyn, which like New York is a thriving metropolis, home to close on half a million people. It's got just as many warehouses and factories and refineries as we do, and we'd like nothing better than to increase the ties of mutual amity and profit between the two cities. Only trouble is, there's sixteen hundred feet of water laying between them. It would need a bridge longer than any in the world to cross that gap."

"That would seem to be an insuperable problem," said Dupin, who knew what was required of a straight man.

"Well, sir, you'd think so. But Mr. John Augustus Roebling, of Ohio, drew up a plan for a suspension bridge whose spans would be supported by steel wires redoubled inside flexible housings. He died before he could start in to build the thing, but his son, Washington Roebling, took over. Then Washington got sick from the Caisson disease, and deputed his wife, Emily, to see the project to completion. Now the Brooklyn tower's mostly up and they're laying the foundations for the New York side. Hell of a thing to see, I'll tell you. When it's done, it will bestride the East River like a colossus."

"Remarkable," Dupin observed, dryly.

"Yes, sir, it is."

"And yet, dogged by ill fortune and tragedy."

I shrugged that off. I was a younger man, then, and more easily impressed by big dreams and big ideas. The misfortunes of the Roebling family didn't seem like such a big almighty deal to me. "Well, the salient fact is that this will be the biggest suspension bridge in the whole damn world. Biggest one right now is in Kentucky, and Roeblings built that, too. America is a place where anything's possible, Mr. Dupin."

The Frenchman nodded solemnly. "Yes," he agreed. "I believe that is so. That is one reason why I wished to see it."

I was opening my mouth, about to parrot some more facts and figures about steel wires and three-way overlapping joists, when I realized that I'd lost my audience. Mr. Dupin was staring ahead down the street toward the Centre Street Pier, or rather just before it, which was where they'd erected the scaffolding for the tower on the New York side of the river.

"It seems," Mr. Dupin said, "that we have chosen a busy day."

And in truth there was a crowd milling in the street beside the pier, the like of which I hadn't seen since the draft riots. They didn't seem to be up to any mischief, but there was a lot of shouting and shoving of the kind that normally signals something unusual has happened, and—undeterred by that past tense—people are jostling to line up in its wake. A few city police were trying to keep some kind of order, along with a crew or two from the new paid fire service which had replaced the volunteer brigades a few years back. They were having a lively time of it.

I paid off the cab and we pushed our way through the crowd, my press badge making little difference to the citizens, but winning me a little headway with the cops and the firemen. Finally we got through the police line and into the building yard. In front of us was the massive, complicated apparatus known as a *caisson*—the chief aid and comfort of bridge builders everywhere, and (sadly) the scourge and terror of their workers. It only showed six or seven feet above the ground, but it extended a great long way beneath us.

Normally, this building site was such a humming pit of industry that you had to duck and weave as you walked along, leading with your elbows like a forward in the Princeton University Football game. Today, though there were a lot of workers around, nobody was actually working. Most of the men were sitting around looking unhappy or sullen. The rain was coming down steadily now, turning the earth to mud, but it seemed like nobody cared about the cold or the wet. Some had their heads in their hands. The winch that lowered food and coffee to the men down in the caisson was standing idle, and the old Italian man who ran it was slumped against the scaffolding, his arms draped over it, like a prize fighter who's only just made it to his corner. He looked to have been crying.

I collared a foreman who was bustling past, red-faced and urgent, and compelled him to stop. "See here, brother," I told him, "we're from the *Harper's Weekly* and we'd like to know what's going on here."

The yegg tried to pass us off with some mumble about asking the shift manager, but Dupin spoke up then, and either his gimlet eyes or his weird accent took the wind out of the foreman's sails. "What is your name?" he demanded.

"O'Reilly," the man mumbled, truculently.

"Your given name, as well as your family name," Dupin snapped, for all the world as though he had some kind of right to ask. "Come, come."

"John. John O'Reilly."

"*C'est ça.* Tell us what has happened, John. Be brief and precise, if you please."

The foreman didn't seem to know what to make of this strange little guy in the fancy clothes. But on the principle that most people he met were going to turn out to be more important than he was, he coughed it up. "We got twenty men dead. The whole night shift. I went away to sign in the morning crew, and when I got back they was all…" He faltered into silence and pointed down into the caisson, as if the period of his sentence might be found down there.

"Twenty men?" Dupin echoed, and O'Reilly nodded. "Twenty men is a full complement, then? A full workforce?"

"It depends what's going on," O'Reilly said. "There's less men on at night, on account of we just light the lanterns up in one half of the caisson. There's a fire hazard, see?"

"No," Dupin said forcefully.

"What?"

"No, I do not see. Show me."

"Listen here, I got to…"

"Show me."

If the situation hadn't been so tragic, I might have laughed at the spectacle of this queer little foreigner taking charge so decisively. Dupin followed the foreman and I followed Dupin, my materials case clutched in my hand like a doctor's Gladstone bag—only there wasn't going to be any good I could do down there, I thought, as we skirted round the wheezing steam pump. Not unless you count bearing witness.

The caisson was eighty feet long, sixty wide and forty deep. The last ten feet or so were under the bedrock of the East River, so the air had a hellish dampness to it. We went down through several successive chambers, each sealed off by greased tarpaulins laid out in overlapping sheets. You had to lift a corner of the tarpaulin each time, like turning the page of a massive book, to expose the trapdoor and carry on down to the next level. Below us, candle flames flickered fitfully like someone was keeping vigil down there. The bellows of the steam pump kept up a consumptive breathing from up over our heads, and from below us that sound was compounded by the muttered conversations you mostly get around the bedsides of dying men.

The floor of the caisson was one half packed earth and one half new-laid stone. There weren't any dying men there, only hale ones and dead ones. The dead ones were laid out in rows, like men sleeping in a dormitory. The living ones stood over them, candles in their hands, looking impotent and terrified as behooves men who are in the presence of such a disaster.

The shift manager—a clerkish-looking man of middle age, named Sittingbourne—introduced himself to us, and we returned the favor. I was vague about exactly who Dupin was, but emphasized our association with the *Harper's Weekly*. That put a woeful look on Sittingbourne's face, as well it might. This was the sort of thing he would probably have wanted to keep out of the papers until he'd talked to his bosses about what shape his future might likely take.

"See here," he said, "don't you go talking to none of my people without me being in on the conversation. Is that understood?"

"You got any people left for me to talk to?" I countered—and he deflated like a punctured soufflé.

"It was an accident," he said. "A terrible accident. I don't see how anyone could have foreseen this, or done anything to guard against it."

"Perhaps not," Dupin said acerbically. "But perhaps—yes. That is what we must ascertain. I wish to see the bodies."

This came as a surprise to all of us, but principally to Mr. Sittingbourne, who thought he was dealing with newspapermen and now wondered if he was maybe dealing with something even scarier than that. A state commissioner, maybe.

"The... the bodies?" he temporized.

Dupin brushed past him, taking his candle out of the man's hand in an *en passant* move that made me wonder if he'd ever done any fencing. He squatted down beside the nearest body and brought the candle up close to its face.

I winced, but I didn't look away. I'm a sketch artist, and looking away isn't in my religion. The dead man's face was lividly pale, his lips blue rather than a healthy red. His face was twisted in a desperate travail, the eyes bulging half out of his head. All in all, it looked like death when it finally came for him might have been something of a relief.

"Poor bastard," I muttered.

"*Oui, le pauvre gosse*," Dupin said. He moved the candle from face to face. "They all seem to have died in the same way. Or at least, they all display the same symptoms."

"It's known that working in the caissons is dangerous," Sittingbourne said. He was hovering at my elbow, nervously wringing his hands. "There's a condition…"

"Caisson sickness," I said.

"Caisson sickness, to be sure. And we've had our fair share of it. But nothing like this. Nothing on this scale. I honestly… I don't know what to say. I really don't."

He was talking to Dupin's back. Dupin was still examining the bodies, his mouth puckered into a grimace. "The light is inadequate," he commented.

Sittingbourne looked around, startled. "Get your candles over here!" he called out to the other men. They clustered round us looking like they were about to burst into a Christmas carol.

Dupin stood. "Who turned out the lanterns?"

"I don't know," Sittingbourne confessed.

"Then find out."

The Frenchman swept past us and headed back for the ladder, but he couldn't climb up because there was a whole posse coming down. It was hard to tell in the sepulchral light of the candles, but they looked to be in uniform. Once they touched down, I was able to identify them as New York City cops—the Eastside variety called spudpickers elsewhere in the City because they're bog Irish and Tammany men to a fault.

The two in the vanguard were Sergeant Driscoll and his

lackey, Flood. Driscoll looked as saintly as a christening cloth, and Flood looked like a nasty stain that somehow got smeared onto it, but I knew for a fact they were as bad as each other and a good deal worse than most.

"What are we having here?" Driscoll asked mildly. "Mr. Nast, is it? You must have sneaked past us all quiet like, when we were quelling the angry mob."

"I'm sorry, sergeant," I lied emolliently. "I didn't realize you were restricting access. But I'm here as a representative of the press."

"A guy who draws funny pictures!" Flood sneered.

"My associate makes a cogent argument," Driscoll said. "You can't be painting pictures in the dark, Mr. Nast, so I'll thank you to bugger off out of this." To the room at large, he added, "These workings are hazardous, and they're not being properly maintained. I'm closing them down, herewith. You can apply at City Hall for a new license, subsequent to a complete overhaul of the safety procedures and a thorough inspection at the contractor's expense."

"But…" Sittingbourne protested. "Please, sergeant. If I can consult Mrs. Roebling, I'm… I'm sure we can…"

"I'm sure you can't," Driscoll told him, deadpan. "Not unless you want to go around Boss Tweed."

That shut Sittingbourne up, *instanter*. You could go around William Tweed, of course. Topographically speaking, I mean. He was a mighty obstacle, but you could do it. The trouble was, you'd need to be properly provisioned for a journey like that, and your troubles would set in as soon as you were out of sight of the high road, as it were. I knew men who'd tried it. I even knew where some of them were buried.

"Might I inquire as to why this is being done?" The voice was

Dupin's, the tone was sharp, and nobody was more surprised to hear it than I was. Well, maybe I was runner-up. Driscoll's face was a picture. He made a show of peering around on his own eye level for a little while before he looked down and found Dupin a foot or so below.

"Who the hell are you?" he demanded.

"*Le Chevalier* Auguste Dupin, at your service. I repeat, why is this being done?"

Driscoll didn't seem inclined to dignify that question with an answer, so Flood obliged us instead. "He already told you, you moron. These workings ain't safe. Twenty men died here."

"Twenty men died here," Dupin agreed, "but not because of the presence or absence of adequate building standards."

"And you'd know?"

"Yes. I would know. They were murdered."

Flood's face went through a series of discrete states, like a slide show. Astonishment, then a sort of ghastly dismay, then anger. "You fuck!" he spluttered. He balled his hand into a fist and drew it back.

Driscoll caught it in mid-air and held onto it. He moved as quick as a snake, and he didn't seem to be exerting any particular effort to hold the constable immobile. "I think you should get your friend home, Mr. Nast," he said mildly. "Otherwise, I'll have to arrest him for breach of the peace."

"Breach of the peace?" The Frenchman glanced at me with an interrogatory expression.

"Means you're stirring up a riot," I translated. "Come on, Mr. Dupin, we're leaving."

"Yeah, you better," Flood spat. The sergeant gave him his hand back and he glared at us, rubbing his wrist, as I hauled Dupin over to the ladder.

"I have further questions for the gentleman in charge," Dupin protested.

"They'll have to keep," I muttered. "Trust me, these two will break your head as soon as look at you."

"They are agents and representatives of the law."

"Nope, of the city. Not the same thing at all."

I steered him ahead of me halfway up the ladder, but then he stopped—which meant I had to stop, too, since the only way up was through him. "Monsieur!" he called down to Sittingbourne. "Hola, monsieur! Who put out the lanterns?"

Sergeant Driscoll slipped his nightstick out of his belt and tapped it meaningfully against his palm.

Sittingbourne made a helpless gesture. Dupin tutted, and carried on up. But he'd got the bit fairly between his teeth now, and he certainly didn't seem interested in leaving. He went over to the steam pump and started to walk around and around it, inspecting it from all angles. It looked a little beaten up here and there—especially around the protuberant valve assemblies to which the hoses were attached. A pump such as this was like a heart in a human body, working mightily without cease. It was an amazing thing in its own right, that allowed even more amazing things to be done.

"You know how a caisson works?" I asked Dupin.

"Yes," he said. "I believe so. It is a hyperbaric environment, no?"

"It's a what?"

"It utilizes air at higher than atmospheric pressure to create a dry working space below sea level. Or, in this case, river level. Air is pumped in by artificial means to maintain the pressure, which may be two or three times greater than that in the ambient air outside the caisson."

"Well, yeah," I said. "That's more or less how it's done."

Actually, Dupin seemed to understand the process better than I did. He was starting to fiddle with the controls on the steam pump now, and the foreman came running over hell for leather.

"Say hey, now," he yelped. "You don't want to be messing with this. This is delicate equipment. And that outlet connection there is loose!"

Dupin gave him a withering glare. "Nonsense!" he snapped. "This is a Jacquard-Sevigny pump, made from a single molding. You could take a hammer to it—and indeed, it looks as though someone has—but still it would not break."

O'Reilly faltered a little, but only for a moment. "It's private property," he said. "You keep your hands off it, or I'll sic the police on you, see?"

I felt like we'd had more than enough of that already, so I took Dupin by the arm with a view to getting him moving again, but he slipped out of my grip and went after O'Reilly like a terrier after a rat. "You found the bodies?" he demanded.

O'Reilly backed away. "Yeah, I did," he said. "So?"

"So. How did you find them? Tell me."

"I just... well, I went away, and I come back, and they was dead. I don't know how. I don't know anything about it."

"When was this?"

"It was eight o'clock. On the turn of the shift."

"Did you disturb the bodies?" The foreman was still moving backward and Dupin was still following, almost stepping on his toes.

"No! I never touched them!"

"And yet they were arranged in rows. Was that how they died?"

"No. Yes. I moved them, obviously. But that was afterward."

"And the lanterns?"

The foreman was looking a little bit desperate now. "The what?"

"The lanterns. Did you extinguish them?"

"No. They was already out."

Dupin stopped dead, and turned to me. "*Bien*," he said. "We are finished here."

That was news to me, since I was the one who was meant to be showing him the sights. But I guess we'd gone off that agenda a while before. "Okay," I said. "You want to go see the Equitable Life building? It's got a hydraulic elevator, made by Elisha Otis, and you can ride all the way up to the…"

"I want to see the lady you mentioned, Monsieur Nast," Dupin interrupted forcefully. I was a little mystified at this, and I must have looked it. "Madame Roebling, I think the name was? The lady who builds this bridge."

I tried to explain to him that we couldn't just walk in on the Roeblings, but Dupin wasn't having any of that. There's a thing called a New York minute, and inside of one of those we were pulling up at the door of the Roebling house in midtown in another cab that Curtis was going to get all sore about paying for. And Dupin was explaining to some sour old curmudgeon in a spiffy black and silver livery that he was the godson of Colonel Maximilian Roebling-Lefevre of the *Légion d'Honneur*, and on that basis would be delighted to pay his respects to the lady of the house.

The curmudgeon went away and came back with a different face on. Mrs. Roebling would be delighted to see us in the morning room.

She didn't look all that delighted, though. It was like walking in on a funeral, which I guess in one sense we were. Mrs.

Roebling looked as pale as death, and though she rallied enough to greet us, she couldn't find a whole lot to say.

"You'll have to forgive me, gentlemen," she said. "I–I've just had some very bad news. Twenty workers on one of our construction projects have died in the most tragic of circumstances. It appears that our working practices may be to blame. The caisson sickness has incapacitated a number of our masons and navigators, and laid my husband low. And now— now it seems it's taken a score of men at a single stroke!"

She started in to crying at this, which was a distressing thing to see. I made the usual *there, there* noises, but Dupin surprised me—surprised both of us—by laughing. Not the belly laugh, this time, but a little snort like a steam kettle saying it's ready. Mrs. Roebling gave him a startled look.

"Pray, sir," she said, affronted, "what can you find in these awful facts to amuse you?"

Dupin made a dismissive gesture. "The facts, Madame," he said, "the facts are not amusing at all. What is amusing is the refusal of all parties concerned to acknowledge them. You feel responsible for the deaths of these men?"

Mrs. Roebling blanched at the blunt question. "Why yes," she said, "to some extent, I do."

"Then calm yourself. You are not responsible at all, and I will prove it. But tell me, how was the news brought to you?"

"By a runner," Mrs. Roebling said. "Sent by the foreman, Mr. O'Reilly, shortly after eight o'clock."

"And then?"

"And then, hard on his heels, an attorney came from the mayor's office to tell me that my building permits had been revoked. We now owe the city a great deal of money. We must pay for a full inspection, which will be expensive and onerous.

There will be a fine, besides, for so serious a breach of safety regulations. And of course, compensation for the families of the dead men must also be found. I fear this may sink our project completely."

Dupin glanced at me. "The mayor's office?" he queried. Evidently I'd been appointed his personal perambulatory encyclopedia.

"253 Broadway," I said. "Don't tell me you want to go see the mayor, Dupin. It's a long haul back the way we came, and a long haul west, and I let the cab go."

Dupin didn't seem to be listening. He'd turned his attention back to Mrs. Roebling again. "At what time, precisely, did these runners arrive?"

Mrs. Roebling couldn't say—not precisely—but the butler (the gent in all the black and silver) was called and he knew the times to a nicety. See, that's what I mean about clothes and moral seriousness. The runner from the works had arrived at 8.27, and the clerk from City Hall at 8.33.

Dupin absorbed this news in solemn silence, then turned to me again. There was a kind of a gleam in his eye. "I do not, Monsieur Nast, wish to see the mayor. But I think perhaps I would like to see the commissioner of police."

Mrs. Roebling gasped. "Do you honestly believe, sir, that a crime has been committed?" she demanded, her face clouded with bewilderment.

"I believe, in fact," Dupin said, "that several crimes have been committed. But I will not speak of things I cannot prove. Of this morning's events, however, I can speak with absolute certainty. Those men were murdered, and the culprit is already known to you." He turned to the lady again. "Madame," he said, "I request you to remain here, and to ignore for the moment any communications from the mayor's office or from city officials of whatever provenance. I will tell what I know, and we will see what we will see. But I assure you, you will pay for no inspections nor levies. The compensation, yes, since the men are dead and you would not wish to leave their families destitute. But that will be the limit of your exposure."

We left the lady in a pretty confused state—and to be honest, I was more than a little consternated myself. Otherwise, I think I would have put up more resistance. But Dupin had the hang of summoning cabs now, and that was a terrible power to put in a Frenchman's hands. He waved his cane like an orchestra conductor, and a two-horse rig rolled to a halt right in front of us. He was jumping up onto the running board even while I was explaining that this was a fool's errand. I had no choice but to jump up after him.

"You can't just walk into the police commissioner's office and make wild assertions, Dupin," I told him, in something of a panic. "Especially not in this city. It just won't wash."

"*Pourquoi ça*, Monsieur Nast?" Dupin snorted. "Why will it not wash?" He wasn't even looking at me. He'd taken out a fancy silver pocket watch and was consulting it with a look of deep deliberation.

Where to begin? "Well, for starters, you're not even armed."

"But yes. I am armed with the truth."

"Oh, jumping Jehoshaphat!"

I carried on remonstrating with him, because I kind of felt like it was incumbent on me to be the voice of reason. But there wasn't any way of shifting him. I just got sucked along in his wake, and before I knew it we were walking up the steps of the police headquarters building.

Two officers standing up on the top step, like bouncers at

the door of a bar room, looked us up and down and asked our business. Dupin was looking at his watch again, so I handled the introductions myself—with something of a sinking feeling in my stomach. I said we were from the *Harper's Weekly* and we'd love to talk to Commissioner Smith and maybe sketch his portrait for the papers.

One of the cops led us inside, leaving the other one to take care of the business of looking tough and surly by himself for a while. We got some curious glances from the flatfoots sitting in the bullpen, and the officers in their little working cupboards. Dupin looked neither left nor right, but when we finally approached the commissioner's door, he put on a turn of speed and got there first.

"See here," our tutelary spirit said, "I got to announce you, is what."

"I am the Chevalier Auguste Dupin," the Frenchman declaimed, with fine contempt, "and I will announce myself."

The door was already ajar. Dupin threw it wide with a thrust of his cane and walked inside. I followed him, into a fug of smoke chopped into lines of solid white and solid black by the sunlight filtering through the window blinds. It looked like the men in that room had put the sun in jail, almost. Had thrown it behind bars. A fanciful notion, obviously, but they were the men to do it, if such a thing could be done.

There were six of them, but I only saw four out of the gate. Police Commissioner Hank Smith, whose office this was, his doughy face overshadowed by a massive brow like the ledge over a cave. James Kelso, his superintendent, who looked like a cardinal of the Church of Rome, thinning hair swept back and thin lips pursed. Mayor Oakey Hall, with his pendulous, bifurcated mustache like the mandibles of a huge spider.

They were sitting around a big table, off to one side of Smith's desk. At the head of the table sat not Smith, but Smith's boss and the boss of everyone else here.

William Magear Tweed rose slowly from his chair as we entered the room. He towered above us. The man was architectural in his build—well over six feet in height, three hundred pounds or more in avoirdupois. But he looked a whole lot bigger and a whole lot heavier than that. His tiny round eyes might have looked weak on another man, in his face, the eyes being the windows of the soul, they looked like pinholes pricked into a black inferno.

"Well, now," he said. His voice was a deep basso rumble like a trolley car going by. "It's Mr. Nast, and his friend with the dapper clothes and the funny accent. You going to introduce us?"

"Actually, Mr. Tweed," I said, "we just come here to sketch the commissioner's portrait. But since he's busy, we'll come back another time."

"Wouldn't hear of it," Tweed said. "Pull up a chair for Mr. Nast, and... I don't know, what do you say to a high stool for the little guy?"

He was talking to the two remaining men, who stepped out of the smoke and shadow then. Sergeant Driscoll closed the door. Constable Flood kicked two chairs in our general direction, his face suffused with a nasty grin as with a bruise.

That sinking feeling I was talking about sunk about another twelve storys, quicker than any hydraulic elevator yet invented.

"Sit down, you yeggs," Flood sneered. I slumped down in one of the chairs, but Dupin didn't even acknowledge the loaded courtesy.

"You are Boss Tweed?" he demanded. "I have heard of you."

"Most people have," Tweed allowed. "As a humble servant

of the City of New York, I hope. So you gents came here to paint a pretty picture?"

I opened my mouth to answer, but Dupin was in there a sight too fast for me. "No."

"No?"

"Not at all. We are here to report an act of mass murder."

Something like a soundless shockwave went through the room. The two cops and the three seated officials braced themselves against it, and seemed to tremble slightly as it passed. Not Tweed. He just raised his eyebrows up a little and let it go by him.

"Mass murder," he ruminated. "I thought you ran a tighter ship than that, Hank. Any mass murderers you know of that you didn't put on payroll yet?"

The police commissioner gave a sickly grin. "Very droll, Bill," he muttered. "Very droll. You better watch what you say, Mr. Nast. Perjury's still a crime in this state."

"Although it's also somewhat of an industry," Tweed added. Everyone except Smith laughed at that, even the two cops.

Now I hadn't said a thing to the purpose, let alone under oath, so the perjury shot went wide. But then it wasn't a writ I was afraid of here. I took Dupin by the shoulder, hoping we could still steer a way out of these choppy waters, but he didn't budge an inch. And it probably wouldn't have mattered if he had, because Driscoll and Flood had taken up station at the door. Driscoll had his hand resting on the holster at his belt and Flood had his nightstick out, casually resting it athwart his shoulder. There wasn't any way out except forward.

"The murders I speak of," Dupin said, "were committed at eight o'clock this morning at the site of the bridge that is being constructed close to the Centre Street Pier. The principal agent and perpetrator is most likely the foreman at that site, a gentleman named O'Reilly, but I believe he had confederates whose names he might be made to divulge under questioning."

"Oh, you believe that?" Tweed asked politely.

"Yes."

"Those weren't murders," Jimmy Kelso said, all windy self-importance. "We already looked into that. Those men was killed by the caisson disease."

"That," said Dupin, "is an absurd conclusion. Every single observation that can be made says otherwise."

"And what observations are those?" Tweed asked. He was looking highly amused, which I didn't like at all.

Dupin seemed pretty happy too, and I realized he'd been building up to this. He struck a stance. "To begin with," he said, "caisson sickness is a malady with a slow onset and a slow progression. The idea that it might afflict a score of people all at the same time, and kill them at a stroke, is absurd."

"Horse pucky!" Kelso said with force. "Nobody even knows how the caisson disease even works, so nobody can say what it can and can't do."

Dupin's lips turned at the corner as he stared at the superintendent. "There is already a body of literature relating to hyperbaric environments," he said.

Kelso blinked. "There's a what?"

"There are essays, monsieur, and monographs, and longer studies, about the conditions in which these unfortunate men worked. The caisson sickness seems to be a side effect of those conditions—conditions which, though they may be imperfectly understood, are extremely well documented. I have myself visited *le professeur* Fontaine's hyperbaric chamber at the Sorbonne and studied its operation. Air from the outside world is excluded by welded seals and tight-fitting doors. Breathable air, under higher than atmospheric pressure, is injected into the caisson by means of a Jacquard-Sevigny steam-driven pumping apparatus. The same machine draws away exhaled air and expels it outside the caisson, so that the level of oxygen—that indispensable gas identified by Monsieur Lavoisier, another of my countrymen—remains constant."

"You talk beautifully," Boss Tweed said, every bit as easy as before. "But not to the purpose. Who cares how the pump works?"

"I do, monsieur," Dupin said. "I care very much. When I examined the bodies in the caisson, I found that they all had livid skin and blue lips."

"So?"

"*Alors*. If they had died from caisson sickness, their skin would be bright red. An urticarial rash, as from the touch of nettles, would have been visible on their faces and necks. This in itself was enough to arouse my suspicions. What confirmed them was the fact that the lamps in the caisson, essential to the continuing work there, had all been extinguished.

"And that, monsieur, could mean only one thing. A wind or breeze, in that space where air was so carefully rationed, was impossible. The only thing that could have put out those flames was the absence of the oxygen on which they fed. The lights died for the same reason that the men died. They had no oxygen to consume, and without it, had not the wherewithal to continue in existence."

Something like a frown passed across Tweed's big, heavy-featured face, but he rallied pretty quickly and managed a pained smile. "You're saying someone stole the air?"

"*Bien sûr que non*. Not the air. Only the oxygen from the air."

"And how does a man go about stealing that, exactly?"

"A man," Dupin said with grim emphasis, "attaches the outlet hose on the steam pump back into the inlet valve, creating in effect a closed system. A *boucle*. A loop. The men's exhaled air, depleted of the vital oxygen, is fed back to them, again and again, until they suffocate. Which does not take long at all."

There was a deathly silence in the room. The men at the table looked to Tweed, as if they weren't willing to venture an opinion on this subject until the Boss had spoken. I kept quiet too, but for a different reason. I was thinking of those men's last moments, and my mind was reeling. I couldn't imagine a worse way to die—and I couldn't imagine the mind that could have cooked up something like that. At the same time, I was starting to put things together the way Dupin had, running along after his thought processes the way a dog runs after a fire tender.

"The marks on the pump," I said. "That outlet valve did look all beaten up. As though…"

"As though someone had levered it off, with a wrench or a crowbar," Dupin finished. "And then replaced it again, after it had served its purpose. Yes, I believe that to be the case."

"But whatever you believe," Boss Tweed said with the calm of complete indifference, "you can't prove who did it."

"Ah, but I think that I can," said Dupin, sealing our fate. "The runner, who came from City Hall to announce that the workings were unsafe and had to close, arrived at thirty-three minutes past the hour. Let us assume that a message was sent from the worksite as soon as the deaths were discovered, and that the mayor—" He gave Oakey Hall a perfunctory bow. "—delivered his decision immediately. The two journeys, cross-town and then north to Mrs. Roebling's house, require a minimum of fifty minutes to complete. It can therefore be established by a very simple calculation that the messenger sent from City Hall must have been dispatched before any notification could have arrived from the site."

Hall blanched as Boss Tweed shot him a cold, disapproving glance. "That true?" he demanded.

"I thought we wanted to shut them down fast," the mayor protested, with something of a whine in his voice. "I didn't think anyone was going to be standing on the street with a damn stopwatch."

"No," Tweed agreed, "you didn't think. You never do, Oakey. Maybe it's time I replaced you with someone who does." He gave a hitch of his shoulders, which was evidently a sign to Driscoll and Flood. Driscoll put his gun in my back, and Flood grabbed a hold of Dupin.

"But... but why?" I demanded. Given the extremity of the situation, talking back to the Boss didn't feel like quite as fearful a prospect as it would normally have been. "Why would you do something like this?"

Tweed seemed surprised to be asked. He shrugged his massive shoulders. "The usual reason," he said. "Come on, Nast. You're a newsman, not a babe in arms. The New York to Brooklyn Bridge is the biggest building project this city has ever seen. All we wanted was a decent kickback. The old man was dragging his feet, so we arranged a little accident for him. We started leaning on the son, and he was just about to roll when he got sick. That left us with the lady, who's the toughest nut of the lot. Or maybe just the stupidest. She didn't seem to understand that when we said we could help her with her licenses and her on-site security, we were asking for a bribe. She just said thank you and goodnight. So we thought we'd move things along a little."

"By killing twenty men?" I asked, my throat dry.

Those tiny black eyes blinked slowly, the way a cat's eyes do. "Well, you know what they say about omelets. If you're serious about making them, you can't afford to get sentimental about eggs."

"You murdering bastard," I said. "Some of those eggs had wives and kids."

"They'll break, too," the Boss replied laconically. "Sooner or later, makes no difference. It's not like eggs are built to last." He gave Driscoll a meaningful look. "Get rid of them," he said. "Somewhere real quiet. Say a few words over the bodies, then take the evening off."

That was the end of the interview. Driscoll and Flood hauled us out of there, and took us via the back door of the building to a paddy wagon. They pushed us inside and locked the door. We could hear Flood hitching up the horses, with a lot of cursing, while Driscoll berated him for his clumsiness.

It was a long, uncomfortable ride, all the way uptown to the northern tip of Manhattan Island. The swampy ground around the Palisades was slowly being reclaimed, and the city was obviously going to head out that way in its own good time, but back then it was a wilderness. The few tracks there were petered out quickly, leaving you adrift in an endless expanse of couch grass and stunted trees.

"I'm real sorry, Mr. Dupin," I muttered.

"About what?" Dupin demanded.

"All this. Dying in a ditch is a poor sort of a way for your day of sightseeing to end. And I'm the native guide here. I should have headed this off before you got too far into it. Mind you," I added, "I didn't know you were going to be accusing Boss Tweed himself of multiple counts of homicide."

"*Je vous en prie,*" Dupin demurred, and since I had no clue what that meant, the conversation ended there.

The paddy wagon slowed to a halt. We heard Driscoll and Flood jump down from the driver's seat, and a second later the doors were hauled open. Driscoll had a pistol leveled at us, and Flood had some kind of a sap—shorter than his nightstick, but just as lethal-looking.

"Last stop, my buckos," the constable said cheerfully.

We climbed down out of the wagon into a desolate landscape. We were only a few miles outside the city limits, but there wasn't a building in sight. The sun was touching the horizon, and there was a sharp wind getting up, making the leafless trees lean over like they were hunching down against the cold.

Sergeant Driscoll chucked me on the chin with the barrel of the pistol, as though to coax a smile out of me. "Any last words, Mr. Nast?" he asked mildly. "A prayer, perhaps? Or a confession? We're not in any hurry."

It was a thoughtful offer in the circumstances, but I couldn't think of anything either reverential or splenetic that was worth detaining him with. I'd sort of resigned myself to death, now, and I just wanted to get the unpleasant business over with. I shook my head.

Dupin seemed even more detached. He wandered over to a flowering bush and prodded it with his cane. Flood stood over him, sap in hand, guarding him until it was his turn to be dispatched.

"Right then," Driscoll said. "May the good Lord have mercy. I can speak for my shooting, so your only worry's what happens afterward."

He took aim at my forehead, and I braced myself for the world to come.

At that point, Constable Flood gave a sudden, constricted

gasp and sank to his knees. Driscoll turned, astonished.

"What's the matter with you, you idiot?" he demanded.

Flood opened his mouth, but nothing came out of it except a thin trickle of blood. He pitched forward onto his face.

Dupin swished the sword that had appeared from nowhere in his hand. "Direct your thoughts, monsieur," he suggested, "to what happens afterward."

Driscoll was as fast as a snake, a trait I believe I've remarked on earlier in this narrative. He swung the pistol round in the blink of an eye, but Dupin's arm dipped and rose and intersected the other man's at some significant point in its arc. The gun went flying away through the air and Driscoll started back with a cry, nursing his hand.

The sword flashed again and the sergeant's legs buckled under him. A spurt of crimson from his severed throat splashed my sleeve as he fell. I stared at it stupidly, only decoding its meaning when Dupin slid the slender blade back into its housing in his cane. "*Voilà*," he said.

"Y–You had…" I stammered. "You were…"

"Armed," Dupin agreed. "The truth is all very well, but sometimes one needs a little more. Come, Monsieur Nast. We have a carriage and horses, but not much daylight left. It would be a good idea, I think, to get back to the city before night is fully upon us."

In fact, he left me at the edge of town. He purposed to hire a boat or a berth at the tiny harbor on Spuyten Duyvil Creek, rather than risk buying a ticket home anywhere in New York City itself. He had a shrewd suspicion that Boss Tweed might be looking for him, once he realized that his two spudpicker assassins had misfired. The haulage men at Spuyten Duyvil would take him on up the coast to Bridgeport or Westhaven, and he could continue on his travels from there.

"My survival, Monsieur Nast," the Frenchman assured me, "will be the earnest and guarantor of yours. Tweed and his associates will want you dead, but they will not dare to move against you so long as I am free and able to speak of what I know. I cannot, of course, prove that he was involved in these murders, but I can embarrass and clog the machine of which he is a part. And I will do so, if he defies me."

We shook hands and parted company. Dupin rode away northwards and I hiked down to Morningside. There, I was able to prevail on a fisherman to give me a lift on the back of his cart when he took his day's catch down to Peck Slip, and I was home only an hour or so after sunset.

Dupin, I learned later, had put pen to paper before he embarked from Spuyten Duyvil. Whatever it was he wrote to Tweed, the Tammany machine rescinded its writs and remands against the Roebling family and their great construction project and withdrew any and all accusations of unsafe working practices. A warrant was issued for the arrest of the foreman, O'Reilly, on twenty counts of murder, but his room in a seedy boarding house at Red Hook was found to have been emptied of all moveable items. Verbal descriptions were issued, along with a promise of reward, but O'Reilly never turned up again, and I doubt he will now—not until the last trump brings the dead up out of their graves.

Dupin wrote to me, too, enclosing a letter for Mrs. Emily Roebling, but also a few lines for my own edification. *Your Mr. Tweed*, he wrote, *trades very strongly on the appearance of invulnerability. If you wish to harm him, you must first encourage the perception that he is susceptible to harm. I mention this, my dear friend, because your own trade of cartooning seems* to me to be very admirably suited to this purpose. You asked me a question when we first met: what is your motive and your métier? What is the singular thing that you pursue? I ask you now to consider this very question yourself. I believe that your answer will be the same as mine—that you are a servant of truth. And you will know to what I am referring when I say she arms her servants well.

Well, I chewed that over a while, and I saw clear enough that he was right. So I took up my sword (it was shaped somewhat like a Woodson & Penwick number 1 black sable paintbrush) and I went to war.

ADDENDUM: From 1870 to 1873, Thomas Nast's editorial cartoons mercilessly lampooned the corrupt activities of the Tammany Ring, and its formidable front man, William "Boss" Tweed. Harper's Weekly rallied behind him, and one by one the other New York newspapers joined the crusade. In 1873, Tweed was arrested on multiple charges of fraud and racketeering. He died in prison five years later, having been convicted on all counts.

THE UNFATHOMED DARKNESS

By

SIMON CLARK

...the Lucifugus demons are eminently malicious and
mischievous, for these, said he, not merely impair men's intellect,
by phantasms and illusions, but destroy them with the same
alacrity as we would destroy the most savage wild beast.

MICHAEL PSELLUS'S DIALOGUE ON THE
OPERATION OF DEMONS, 1050 AD

Books! Books! Books! I always considered them to be the sole reason to continue to live upon our dreary Earth. Books, however, were on this November night, very nearly the death of me, and my friend, Monsieur C. Auguste Dupin.

I am writing this account just hours after the extraordinary events that nearly led to our destruction. I confess that as well as smoking pipe after pipe of strong tobacco I have drunk several invigorating glasses of absinthe. My friend, Dupin, slumbers in his bedchamber, but I am in such a state of profound excitement that I am far from the shores of sleep—so, by the light of candles, and with the heat of that powerful spirit of wormwood putting fire in my belly, I am attempting to exorcise the ghost of what I experienced tonight by writing down all that I saw, heard, and felt.

And it all began with our addiction to books that drove us out into the snowy night, where we heard the terrible sound of a woman's scream.

Dupin had received a letter informing him that a sailor would sell him a cache of tomes acquired on his travels of the Eastern Mediterranean. One of these is a sublime rarity, entitled *Dialogue on the Operation of Demons*, penned by that Byzantine philosopher and educator of princes, Michael Psellus. Dupin has little in the way of money, yet the purse put aside for food was hastily retrieved from beneath the boards of his study; thereafter, we lit a lantern apiece and hurried out into the Parisian night. Snow had fallen steadily all evening, veiling the ground with a pristine shroud. The footprints and cart tracks left by the sparse midnight traffic soon vanished entirely as we headed out amongst the open fields beyond Montmartre.

"Books, books, books!" panted Dupin. "The word hurtles through your head like a musket ball through its barrel."

"I know your tricks by now," I replied. "You saw me mouthing the word to myself."

"No, absolutely not. You are *obsessed* with books. I hear you at night chanting the word over and over in your sleep. You covet books, you crave books, monsieur. You sit at a table and curl your arms over a book, like a hawk protecting its freshly killed prey, so no other creature can steal it."

"Is that so? Then I am morbidly diseased by my love of the printed page. My soul must be liquefying into printer's ink."

"Ha!" His teeth flashed in the light of our lanterns as he smiled. "I am gripped by the same *contagion bibliotheque*. The reading germ nests snugly in both our brains."

We continued to chatter thus as our feet crunched on freshly fallen snow. A distant church clock struck the half hour after midnight, and although the bitterly cold air wormed its way through our cloaks to shiver our skin we were so eager to hold that eight hundred-year-old book of Psellus' in our hands that we almost ran along the deserted lane, our lamps throwing out splashes of light.

It was as the lane cut through broad, flat meadows that we heard the scream.

"A woman is being murdered!" I cried.

"Not being murdered," Dupin corrected. "That's the sound of grief, despair, and a heart-breaking realization of loss—the woman has found the lifeless body of someone she loves." He stood absolutely still; the lamp was held high, as he carefully and precisely stored the sound away in that remarkable brain of his. Chevalier Dupin is a man who methodically preserves memories of the sights, sounds, and odors produced by the horrors of this world, as I would methodically place books on my library shelves. He is the consummate archivist of the accouterments of tragedy.

The woman screamed again, this time the sound being much fainter, suggestive of increased distance, rather than her becoming weaker, or overcome in some way. Dupin and I hurried through dense bushes that lined the track. Within moments, we found ourselves in a broad meadow that possessed a smooth covering of snow. Our lanterns shone across that pristine shroud of white. Nothing had disturbed the snow—neither birds, animals, nor people. We scrunched onwards, searching for the distressed female. From the dark sky above, a lazy snowflake or two descended. We heard no sound. The woman had fallen silent.

"Perhaps there was no woman?" I suggested as the search revealed nothing but a winter's meadow. "Might the cry have been made by a fox?"

"That was no fox, monsieur. You know as well as I." Dupin raised the lamp higher, endeavoring to push back the darkness. "That was a lady in distress. Ha!" He pointed. "Now do you see what caused said distress?"

The light revealed a figure lying face down in the midst of the snowy landscape. I immediately began to hurry closer. However, Dupin stopped me by gripping my arm. "No, do not move. Not a single step. Something is wrong here... profoundly wrong."

"Of course there is—a man lies dead. I can see his corpse with my own eyes."

"Yes, you see the body... What is it that you *don't* see?"

"He's not wearing a coat or hat. See, he's dressed in a cotton shirt and breeches."

"What else don't you see?" demanded Dupin. His manner wasn't terse or annoyed; on the contrary, his eyes glittered with excitement. My friend detested the mundane routines of everyday life—this was anything but mundane.

I attempted to put myself inside Dupin's remarkable mind, and apply his unique talent for observation, which he'd used to explain so many mysterious crimes. "Fifty paces from us, there is the body of a young man, wearing indoor garments," I said, "but we must be four hundred meters from the nearest farmhouse. It's a bitterly cold night, so he wouldn't have been out walking when he was attacked."

"Yes."

"He must have been killed elsewhere and carried or dragged here."

"No."

"Then, Monsieur Dupin, what is it that I am *not* seeing?"

"Imagine the marks in the snow are our beloved hieroglyphics —decipher them, interpret them, extract information from every dot, swirl, and line."

Not for the first time did I wonder if madness had taken root in my companion's brain. "There are no marks in the snow," I pointed out.

"Exactly." Dupin extended his free hand to indicate the unblemished whiteness. "The body lies face down, his arms outstretched like a fallen bird. There are no marks in the snow. Not one within forty paces. He has only been here a short while, because he lies *on top* of freshly fallen snow, there is none on the cadaver. There are no footprints near the body to suggest that attackers approached him and struck him down there on that spot."

I stared in astonishment. "What is even more inexplicable is how the man arrived in this meadow. He hasn't left any footprints."

"Carried by angels?" Dupin's eyes gleamed with impish delight—a veritable witch-fire blazed there. The mystery enthralled him. "Or was the gentleman thrust from beneath the ground by the Devil? So, monsieur. From above? From below? What is it to be?"

I stood there in the forbidding snowfield that might have been conjured here from some Arctic wasteland. The cold air put its icy claws on my throat. The darkness grew even thicker... denser... the darkness of a tomb that imprisoned children's ghosts. *Listen to them cry*, I thought, *listen to their sorrow*. The despairing sobs of tiny children, who had been cast lifeless and forgotten into the grave-pit, came a-creeping through my flesh to chill my blood, until shiver upon shiver poured through me, and I longed to run from that evil place that no longer seemed part of the natural world.

Dupin spoke in a low, hollow voice, as if his words, too, came ghosting from some melancholy realm of the dead: "To your right. Forty paces from us. See those indentations in the snow?"

He moved in the direction of which he spoke. Presently, I saw footprints, which I counted quickly. There were twelve of them; however, they were scuffed and elongated, suggesting that the person had moved with strange haste. The footsteps had simply appeared in the midst of that whiteness then stopped again. Yet where the footsteps ended there were a series of broken lines in the snowfall that created a series of dashes like so: - - - - - - These ran for perhaps fifty paces in all before they, too, simply vanished.

"I do not understand," I confessed. "A corpse lies in a field. There is an impossibility about the manner of its arriving. No footprints led to the corpse, none led away. Then there is a smattering of footprints—impossible footprints!—as they suddenly appear from nowhere in the middle of a meadow before vanishing again... In addition, there is a line of marks in the snow that abruptly end. This is the mystery of all mysteries, Dupin. A mystery that must surely contain the supernatural at the center of its dark heart. There is no other explanation that I can see, other than witchcraft."

"The mystery *does not* embody magic in any form whatsoever. This enigma can be traced back to the French name of Montgolfier." He put his hand on my shoulder and looked me in the eye. "I would prefer to savor the mystery. To peel back its exquisite layers one by one, and reveal its solution to you in a languid manner over many glasses of amontillado. But there is no time, my friend. Lives are at stake." With a sudden impetuousness he rushed toward the corpse. "The snow is fifteen centimeters deep. This young gentleman has been thrust down through it with great force. His bones are broken. Death arrived in a single second. He had no time to writhe or struggle." He swung the lantern round, casting its glow over the winter shroud. "No footprints, so he did not walk here to the place of his death, nor was he carried."

"You spoke the name Montgolfier. Are you suggesting this individual fell from a balloon?"

"Fell, pushed, cast out, jettisoned!"

"But who would ascend in a balloon in this dreadful weather?"

The excited man spoke faster—ever faster. "Since Montgolfier rose over French soil—*this* French soil—undertaking the first manned balloon flight over half a century ago, there have been hundreds of astonishing ventures into the sky. In 1841, Charles Green ascended to a height of eight kilometers above the Earth. The temperature on that summer's day dropped to twenty-seven degrees below freezing. Ice formed on the balloon's rigging, and the sky turned from blue to black. Soon, another English gentleman by the name of Monck Mason intends to travel through the atmosphere all the way to America. It is recorded historical fact that many extraordinary voyages have taken place, successfully reaching halfway to heaven, using an envelope of silk containing hydrogen or coal gas. Men fly, monsieur. The ground cannot hold them."

"The woman who screamed, where is she?"

He beckoned me to the footprints. "Female feet made these.

They move fast, then the feet are dragged. I believe she climbed from a grapple hook that had descended from the basket of the balloon, made those messy, hither-thither prints before climbing onto the grapple hook once more. The iron hook made those dash marks in the snow as the balloon rose and fell while it moved southwards. The marks end because the craft gained altitude. See the yellow particles on the snow? The captain of the flying ship discharged a ballast of sand in order to rise into the sky."

"I thought I was beset by witchcraft," I said in a breathless daze. "For a moment I believed I heard the ghosts of weeping children."

"You heard children weeping, indeed." Dupin looked upward. "But the children you heard crying in sorrow are very much alive and are high above our heads."

"By the saints! Who would subject infants to such an horrific ordeal?"

The man gravely studied the dark, cloud-burdened skies before all of a sudden shouting a warning. "Look out!"

He pushed me aside. At that moment, I heard a thin, whistling note, which rapidly swelled into an alarming rush of noise. A black object sped from the sky to strike the ground where I'd been standing before Dupin pushed me away. There, embedded in the field, was a black pole that was as long as my arm and tipped with a sharp, iron point.

"That is most definitely not Cupid's arrow of love." Dupin began to run. "We are under attack, monsieur. Hurry!"

"Shouldn't we run for the road, if we are to escape?"

"We're not escaping. We will do our utmost to capture the balloon and bring a murderer to justice."

We ran, carrying our lanterns. Barely had we covered forty meters when I beheld a remarkable vision. A lady clad in pure white stood on a branch, high in a tree. She shouted some words I could not identify. Yet without a shadow of doubt I realized that this was the same woman who had made the dreadful scream that had sent us running into the field in the first place.

"Behold!" Dupin sang out. "The female aeronaut!"

"Mademoiselle," I shouted, fearing that she would fall, "hold tight to the branch. We will rescue you."

The young woman called down in a language I didn't understand. Then she asked a question in passable French: "Is this Belgium, monsieur?"

"This is France, mademoiselle," Dupin replied. "You have alighted near Paris."

"I see you are respectable gentlemen," she shouted. "I wish you to guide me to a magistrate. I have to make a charge of murder."

"Where is the balloon now?" asked Dupin.

"Do you not see it? There, above your heads, gentlemen. I have captured the balloon *and* the murderer."

I gazed up into the dark sky. In the combined light of both our lamps, I made out a vast, rounded form. This was the envelope filled with gas that was so much lighter than air. Beneath the titanic balloon hung a basket, one of considerable dimensions that had been fashioned like the superstructure of a galleon, so it had a deck and what appeared to be an arrangement of cabins at either end. A rope of twenty meters descended to a grapple hook that had been jammed into the branches of the tree, no doubt by the woman in white.

"Did you throw the dart at us?" I asked.

"The lady did not," Dupin answered on her behalf. "The hurler of the weapon will be that slayer of the unfortunate man lying in the field."

"Where is the killer?" I asked.

This question required no verbal answer. A burly figure in black appeared on the deck of the craft above our heads, and a second dart whistled out of the gloom to embed itself in the frozen soil.

Dupin beckoned to the woman. "Hurry down. You'll be slain, too, if you remain there."

The lady moved as nimbly as a cat. White skirts fluttering, she rapidly descended. A third dart pierced the darkness, its point grazing the toe of my leather boot.

"His aim is improving," I warned.

"Here I come!" With that the woman leapt from a branch.

Dupin managed to hand the lantern to me before catching her in his arms. Without setting her down, he ran with her. I followed as he led the way through a line of bushes to where I glimpsed a building not thirty paces from the tree and its captive balloon.

The building, it transpired, was a barn. Therein, were bales of straw arranged around a large plow sitting in the middle of the floor. Dupin put the woman down, and bade me to enter; he then closed the stout timber door before shooting home a pair of formidable bolts.

"Safe, I trust," I pointed upward, "from that devil's javelins."

The woman appeared remarkably self-assured and free from hysteria, considering her ordeal.

"We cannot remain here," she insisted. "We must report the murder—your soldiers must capture the balloon before the Pastor can free it."

"What happened?" Dupin asked gently.

"Did you not hear? I must find a magistrate and demand that an arrest warrant be issued."

"We cannot leave yet. We will be struck down by the darts

before we have covered twenty paces."

"But the man killed my fiancé. I will not rest until he faces the guillotine."

"We are confined to this barn for a time, mademoiselle. Please tell us what befell you."

The woman was pretty, with pale blue eyes, and blonde ringlets. Yet she was no swooning damsel. A storm of anger boiled behind that blue-eyed gaze. "I will kill him with my own hands, if need be."

"Kill whom?"

"Pastor Larsson." She took a deep breath as she realized she could put her trust in us. And there in the golden lamplight within the barn, she told her story. "My name is Annette Lamberg. My fiancé and I worshiped at the same chapel in Denmark. The pastor is a man of great oratory power and conviction. Pastor Larsson could, I'm sure, persuade birds to swim and fish to fly. He convinced his congregation that the Earth suffered from contagion. That a plague germ had infected the soil, and everyone who walked upon it would soon be struck down by a foul pestilence and die. Pastor Larsson told us that an angel had appeared and told him that the only way to escape the plague was to build an 'Ark of the Air.' The angel explained how to build an enormous balloon that would safely carry the God-fearing high above the ground until the plague had passed. Once it had, he and his congregation would inherit an Earth free from both sin and plague." She looked upward as if she could see the balloon suspended there above the red tiles of the barn. "You see, winds blow from the north during the winter. The Pastor calculated that prevailing winds would carry us south over Europe and over the Mediterranean to Africa. Accordingly, thirty-six hours ago, we boarded the *Seraphiel*—that is the name of our craft—

and ascended into the skies above Denmark. As the pastor had predicted, the breeze carried us south at great speed. On board the *Seraphiel*, there are thirty-five men, women, and children. We have provisions for a month, and a system for collecting rainwater to drink. Therefore, we have the means of sailing the skies above the African wilderness, far from tainted humanity, until the angel returned to Pastor Larsson and told him that he may land his craft."

"And your fiancé?"

"He suffered from a head fever. I'm sure it was nothing more. Pastor Larsson heard him sneezing and immediately the man flew into a rage. Before we could react the pastor had seized Johann and flung him from our craft. Even as I watched my beloved falling through the air to the ground, the pastor screamed at us that Johann had become infected, claiming that his depravities had allowed the evil germ into his body." She wiped a tear from her eye. "Pastor Larsson ordered his flock to their knees; he demanded that they pray harder than they had ever prayed before. They did as he ordered, yet the children were so frightened by what the pastor had done to poor Johann, they sobbed in such a heart-rending way. While the adults were at prayer, I flung the grapple hook over the side. I climbed down in the hope I could reach Johann. I prayed to God, too... however, I prayed that Johann hadn't been killed." She shivered. "My prayers weren't answered. I saw that he was dead even before I reached the ground."

"And you screamed."

"Yes, the shock of seeing Johann's broken body was more than I could bear."

"You did alight briefly?"

"Yes, I jumped from the cable to the ground, intending to report the murder; however, I was too angry to grieve yet, and

I promised myself I would stop the pastor from escaping. There and then, I resolved to capture the balloon. So I leapt back onto the hook after taking just a few mere steps in the snow. By sheer good fortune I succeeded in lodging the grapple in a tree; after that, I tied the rope to a branch, now the balloon is tethered. I have trapped the murderer."

"Alas, it is we three who are trapped." Dupin gazed up at the barn's roof.

"Moreover," I said, "the pastor and his balloon will not be trapped for long. He could simply cut the cable."

"Indeed," she said with a sigh. "My head was so muddled with anger that I had not considered that."

The moment she finished speaking there was a tremendous crash. Shards of red tile fell inward with a shower of snow that must have accumulated on the roof. We rushed backward to the relative safety of the walls. Immediately we saw that a grapple iron had landed in our midst. The barbs of its four-pronged hook embedded themselves in the woodwork of the farmer's plow.

Dupin ran toward the hook and tried to wrench it free. He knew devilry was afoot—and that devilry required the use of the grapple. Yet he was driven back to the wall as an entire salvo of lethally sharp darts punched through the roof tiles to embed themselves in the bales of straw. Seizing a lantern, I directed its glow up through the roof beams. The iron-tipped darts had left holes through which snowflakes fell. The rope tied to the grapple hook pulled taut. A moment later it began to quiver.

"The Indian fakir's rope trick in reverse, I fear." Dupin pulled a dart from the floor so he'd at least have a weapon. I retrieved one from a bale of hay.

A loud crash made me look up. Straight away, I saw tiles

shattering beneath an almighty impact. Very shortly after that I saw the head of an ax cleaving the roof in order to form a large hole. In the light of the lamp, I beheld men's faces as they stared down at us. The men were armed with more of those spears. A young man also carried a cutlass, while a large, bearded clergyman—with blazing eyes—carried an ax, which he used to smash yet more of the tiles. Above our captors floated that vast, rounded shape of the balloon. As Dupin had said, *the Indian fakir's rope trick in reverse.* The men had climbed down the grapple hawser and onto the roof before hacking at that aperture.

Dupin pointed the dart upward, lest the men should jump down. In response, the bearded clergyman produced a pistol, which he aimed at my friend.

Annette Lamberg cried, "Pastor Larsson! These are Frenchmen. They have done you no harm, so do not harm them."

The bearded Pastor gazed down. "Is that so?" he asked in French. "Which part of France is this?"

"You are just an hour's walk from Paris," Dupin told him.

"An hour's walk? I will not take a single step on this world's poisoned soil until the plague has passed."

"What plague?"

"The soil beneath your feet, monsieur, teems with active microbes—germs that feed on all manner of putrefaction; they mate and spawn and multiply. With a powerful microscope I have seen them with my own eyes."

"Yes, such germs exist, but in the main they are harmless."

"On the contrary, they are lethal to Mankind. What is more, they are increasing in number, just as a hostile army will mass on a nation's border prior to invasion."

Dupin endeavored to persuade the man with logic. "Such

microbes teem in our bodies, too, without causing illness. Even in the smallest drop of saliva one will find a million amoeba. These tiny creatures have been created by God for His divine purpose, just as He populated the Earth with plants and animals in a myriad of diverse forms."

"Nonsense!" thundered the Pastor. "There is no word of microbes in the Bible—not a single mention of those profoundly tiny germs that swarm and multiply and kill the God-fearing. Bacterial creatures are the work of demons. An angel, by our Lord's good grace, visited me, and explained that I should take my flock to the skies until the plague has run its course."

"An angel?"

"Do you doubt me, Frenchman?"

"I believe in angels," replied Dupin. "I don't believe, however, they advise on the construction of flying machines."

"Insolent devil." The hand that gripped the pistol began to shake. "You are alleging that I am a liar?"

"There are maladies, pastor, that produce visions of things which are not there in reality."

"A liar and a madman—that is what you believe me to be." The man's eyes bulged with fury. "I will send you to Hell right now!" He aimed the pistol squarely at my friend's heart.

Annette Lamberg stepped in front of Dupin, shielding him from the gun. "Pastor! You hurled my fiancé to his death, because he suffered from the most trivial of fevers."

"Johann was infected. His sins allowed the bacillus to enter his body."

"Pastor, he did but sneeze."

"No, Annette, you must believe what I tell you. Johann was riddled with vile germs. They would have infected every single one of us aboard our craft. I had no choice but to cast him out."

"You are wrong."

"I am *never* wrong. The angel will endorse my words."

"You are afflicted with madness. Do you not see?"

"Stand aside." His eyes were red and bloodshot in the light of the lanterns. "Stand aside, so I can despatch the Frenchman to Hades!"

"No, uncle. Fire the ball through me if you must, but I will not stand aside."

The word "uncle" made the lunatic flinch. The other men on the roof had been ready to cast those darts down upon us; however, now they paused and looked to the pastor for guidance.

"Annette, my child, I promised your father—my late, lamented brother—that I would see no harm come to you. I sincerely hoped that you would pray for forgiveness then re-join our vessel."

"That I will never do, uncle."

"I see."

"Nor will I permit you to kill these men."

"The angel told me... He whispers in my ear even now." The pastor gazed upward. "Do none of you hear? Or see his wings of gold? Or that he has the body of an eagle and sings so sweetly. There, beside our vessel, he gazes down upon us, and there is such a shining about him."

The men on the roof appeared uneasy now. They cast uncertain glances at one another.

Dupin seized the moment. "Pastor, speak to us about the angel. Describe his features."

The man threw a belligerent stare at Dupin. "I have listened enough to your snake-ish words. You have a demon's shadow, monsieur, not a mortal one. Even if the angel descended to Earth to stand face-to-face with you, you would not see it with your ungodly eyes."

"Uncle," Annette spoke softly, "I do not believe you are a well man. You have become infected with illusions."

"*Pah!* You are the one who has been infected, for you have walked upon the germ-drenched soil. You must remain here, Annette. I will pray for your soul, because the plague will undoubtedly claim you."

"*Uncle*—"

Ignoring the woman's cry, Pastor Larsson issued orders to his companions: they quickly climbed upward to the basket that hung beneath the balloon. I now saw the reason for such apparent agility—wooden pegs had been inserted into the weave of the rope to form something akin to a rope ladder.

The pastor carefully released the gun's cocking mechanism so it would not fire, then he thrust the weapon into his belt beneath that billowing coat of his.

"May Christ's blessing be on you all," he said from his lofty position. "I wish I could have opened your eyes to the terrible fate that creeps toward you. But your innate depravity has blinded you to what so obviously squirms and breeds in the dirt beneath your feet. Salut!" With that he began to climb the rope, too. Above him, the balloon swayed in the breeze. That aerial leviathan strained at its leash, seemingly eager to dash to the south, and the hot, clear skies of Africa.

The other men had already reached the vessel. Pastor Larsson was perhaps some ten meters above the barn's roof, and halfway to the basket-weave cabins, which housed the *Seraphiel*'s passengers.

Dupin gave a sigh of regret. "I am very sorry that we have not been able to apprehend the slayer of your fiancé, mademoiselle. But the pastor has the advantage of both manpower and weaponry."

The woman screamed—this sounded altogether different from the cry of dismay we'd heard earlier when she beheld the body of her husband-to-be. Instead, this raw shriek was shot through with rage and a fierce longing for vengeance. Even at that moment, I noticed that Dupin took care to preserve the sound in his memory. I confess my eyes were on him, so the woman had no difficulty in seizing the lantern from me.

In an instant she dashed the light against the blades of the plow. Flames immediately gushed upward as the glass vessel that contained the lamp oil burst open and its contents were ignited by the burning wick. And at that point a spectacle unfolded that was as horrific as it was extraordinary.

The grapple rope caught alight. Just as a burning fuse rushes toward a keg of gunpowder, so the flame raced up the rope—one no doubt soaked in tar to preserve it from the corrupting effects of rain. Meanwhile, Pastor Larsson had scaled upward to within five meters of his craft. The passengers watched in shock as the ball of fire ran up the rope toward the basketwork of the craft. That structure would catch alight quickly, but Dupin had recognized an altogether greater hazard—one of calamitous enormity.

"The balloon is inflated with hydrogen," he breathed. "Hydrogen is the most explosive gas known to Man—just one lick of flame; just one spark. The explosion will destroy the balloon and its passengers—and the fireball will incinerate us, too."

The fire that ascended the rope had reached the pastor. Like a burning fuse, the flame raced past him as he clung to the line. The fire seared his face and hands, yet he did not release his grip. All of a sudden, we heard the man's shouts of *"MIN GUD!"* He'd reverted to his Danish tongue to implore the Almighty: *Min Gud*—my God!

And still he climbed. The small halo of fire, however, that

encircled the cable would reach his craft first. Then there would be an explosion of such force that nobody would survive aboard the balloon... or beneath it.

The passengers on that craft, floating almost thirty meters above the ground, realized that destruction was merely seconds away, and their families would be wiped out by the searing heat of igniting hydrogen. The man with the cutlass did not pause and hacked clean through the rope. As soon as the tether parted, the balloon soared into the darkness. The burning rope fell harmlessly back to the ground. Pastor Larsson fell with it.

He plunged through the roof with such force the building shuddered. Then silence reigned supreme. We approached the clergyman, who lay face up in the center of the floor, and across the plow. His neck was broken.

His mad eyes remained open wide as they stared up toward the glory of Heaven.

The man's niece, and executioner, at last began to weep for her dead fiancé as the snow once more began to fall. Flakes of the purest white gently descended through the gash in the roof tiles. Perhaps, if we could but return to the innocence of childhood, we would imagine those flakes as tiny, feathery angels. And, moreover, that those shining angels had come to safely chaperone the souls of the dead to an infinitely better realm than the one in which you and I, my friend, do currently dwell.

THE WEIGHT OF A DEAD MAN

By

WESTON OCHSE AND YVONNE NAVARRO

MEXICAN–AMERICAN BORDER. ARIZONA TERRITORY. 1895

He stands with his back to the painting, protecting it with his life as the men array themselves before him, their faces masks of red death, their every bone and muscle tightened in outrage over what he'd just done. But nothing matters except the painting— St. John tries to flee, Jesus forgives Judas, two soldiers dressed in fifteenth-century Spanish armor move to arrest Jesus, and Caravaggio himself, part of the painting he so idealized with light and brushstrokes, shines a lantern on all of them like a divine voyeur. In the Garden of Gethsemane, it is the betrayal by one so beloved that is represented by the humility and tiredness on the face of Jesus.

Today, if he is to survive, he needs something *not* portrayed in this timeless, famous painting to happen soon.

The men move one step closer.

Escape, perhaps.

Not soon.

Now.

DOUGLAS, ARIZONA. THREE DAYS EARLIER.

The word was *ratiocination* and his grandfather had been an alleged expert at its implementation. But as Nate Dupes stood and stared at the rheumy-eyed gunslinger at the end of the bar, he couldn't help wonder if it wasn't a load of Old World crap his father had bestowed upon him, forever trying to impress a young man with tales of a famous relative who'd solved what Edgar Allan Poe had fictionalized as *The Murders in the Rue Morgue*. The idea of *ratiocination* was to so firmly place yourself inside the mind of a criminal that you would know as much about the crime as the criminal, in this case the thief of the missing painting known as *The Taking of Christ* by the fifteenth century Baroque master Michelangelo Merisi da Caravaggio; the very same painting which had been commissioned for recovery by the British Royal Art Society through the Pinkerton Detective Agency.

"You staring at me like you want to have my child," the gunslinger said, his words like sawdust.

Nate sighed, still baffled that such a thing as *ratiocination* really existed. The further idea that he could even remotely have the other man's child sickened him to the point where Nate had to cover his mouth with the back of his left hand. "If you'll pardon me," Nate said, careful to speak in small-syllable words, "I'm looking for a man known as Burt Johnson. I thought you might be him."

The man, who just a moment before seemed about to pass out from too much rye, suddenly straightened and adjusted his cowboy hat. He levered his tired frame from the stool. Dressed like every other cattle puncher in southern Arizona, the thing that set him apart was the way he let his gun ride low and easy on one hip, as if they were old friends and had gone places together. "What if I might be this man you looking for? You got some kind of beef?"

Nate shook his head, acutely aware of his own appearance. Where the other man was large and filled out with bulky muscle, Nate was small-boned and more finely muscled. Instead of dusty canvas and stained cotton attire, Nate wore wool pants and a vest over a clean white shirt beneath a gold and brown brocade coach jacket. He had a pistol as well, but his was a German Mauser 9mm Zig-Zag kept tucked under his left arm, rather than the Peacemaker the other wore like a third limb. There was, of course, the additional fact that Nate's green-tinted sunglasses were a little off-putting. He hadn't seen anyone else wearing sunglasses since he'd left Saint Louis three weeks earlier. He had never liked wearing a hat, preferring to let his blond hair bleach beneath the hard desert sun and his face take on the hue of well-tanned leather.

"No beef, Mr. Johnson. I'm on a search and rescue mission, as it were."

"Rescue? Who is it you're going to rescue?"

"Not who, Mr. Johnson—as I do believe you are the man I'm looking for." When the other gave an almost imperceptible nod, Dupes continued. "Rather, a *thing*. A painting, to be exact. Mr. Oliver in Saint Louis said you'd appropriated it for a Mr. J.C. Magillicutty, formerly from Chicago, Illinois, but now residing here in Douglas. Do I have my facts about right?"

"I didn't '*propitiate* nuthin.'" The big man spat tobacco on the floor as if to accentuate his innocence.

"*Appropriate*. It means you received and took it to the man who hired you."

"Then why didn't you say that yourself?"

"I have no idea," Nate replied, trying very hard not to roll his eyes. "So then you are that man."

"So what if I am?"

"Then I'd like to give you twenty dollars."

Greed won over guile. "Yeah, I'm him."

Nate reached into his vest pocket and brought out a gold piece with two fingers. "Just one thing before I give this to you."

Johnson's watery eyes fixed on the gold eagle coin. "What?"

"Please describe the painting you delivered to Mr. Magillicutty."

"The painting? I don't know art. It was just a painting."

Nate pulled out another gold piece and tucked it neatly into the same two fingers that still held the first coin. "I was hoping you knew art just a little bit, Mr. Johnson."

It was all the big man could do to keep from drooling. "It was a picture of Jesus with soldiers and stuff."

"Was it a small picture?"

Johnson shifted his eyes from the coins to Nate's face. "Who you kidding? It was a huge painting. The size of a man, only rolled up and pushed into a wooden tube."

"And you delivered this to your boss?"

Johnson nodded.

Nate handed over the coins.

"Is that all you want to know? You don't want to see it?" Johnson asked. He rolled the coins in one hand, obviously hoping for more.

"That's enough for now." Nate touched a finger to his forehead in a small salute, then turned and left the bar, mindful that Johnson didn't follow. It would be better, he decided, to get back to his hotel than continue his search tonight; perhaps he could get the owner to once again scrounge up some ice. This town was beyond hot. Even the night gave almost no respite. But before he could get relief, he had one more chore, a telegram to send and one which should have gone out the moment he'd arrived.

This evening a cold water bath was the best the owner could provide, so Nate sat in the beaten copper tub with his legs hanging over one edge and his head resting on another while he read the latest issue of the *Douglas Dispatch*. A newspaper told a lot about a town if one paid attention. His grandfather Le Chevalier C. Auguste Dupin believed that even a bad newspaper could provide a good detective with the necessary links one would need to determine the major players.

Douglas, it seemed, was fighting to become an incorporated township. The odds looked good because of the railhead and the silver mines, but certain landowners, such as the infamous J.C. Magillicutty, were against it because of its possible disruption of the free-range cattle business.

There had also been several recent fires. Two occurred at warehouses, but a third destroyed the home of a ranch hand who'd been accused of raping a Mexican girl, but released for lack of evidence. The cattle worker himself was nowhere to be found.

Sears, Roebuck and Co. had just established a catalogue store.

Buffalo Soldiers, a Negro cavalry unit out of nearby Camp Huachuca, were assisting elements of the 10th Cavalry in the relocation of several Apache Indian tribes.

Twin girls, Eloise and Marie Duvall, had been missing for several days with no clues as to their whereabouts.

A gunfight on Main Street had resulted in the death of one Mr. Frank Dorsett, a known card shark and cheat.

Agnes Moffit brought in another pail of cold water from the

well. A one-time girl of Madame Menadue's, she was now house woman of the inn where Dupes was staying, and she was no stranger to the sight of a naked male body. However, what had stunned her when she'd first helped him out of his clothes were the tattoos covering his back and arms. Many of them were done in black and white ink, but several more were in color; all sported a Far East Asian motif and were indelible memories of the five years Nate Dupes had spent in China.

"I see you're reading the newspaper of our fine city," she said. He could tell she was trying to sound as civilized as possible in front of him.

"I am, dear Agnes. Just pour that water in and—" His words broke off as the cold water hit his stomach and groin. He let out a surprised gasp, then inhaled and smiled. When he had his air back, he asked the question he'd been wanting to for at least half an hour. By then Agnes had settled on a rocker with her back to him; ready to assist if needed, she was passing the time by crocheting a doily. "So, what's interesting that *isn't* in the newspaper?"

"I'm sure I don't know what you mean," she said without looking up from her work.

"Well, take this man whose house burned down. What's the real story behind that?"

"If you mean that no good rapist Billy Picket, then he got exactly what he deserved."

"Says here there was a lack of evidence."

"Ain't no evidence found around here that can stand up in an American court when it's a Mexican against an American."

"So he was guilty?"

He watched her back as she paused in her crocheting. "I'm not knowing if he was guilty or not, but if he did rape that woman, it wasn't the first Mexican girl he'd forced himself on."

Ah. So the fire was payback.

"Looks like people are going to be able to order anything they want now that Sears and Roebuck has a catalogue store."

"Oh, yes," she said as she went back to her doily and rocked backward. "Mr. Magillicutty brought one all the way from Chicago. Says we need to be as civilized as the rest of America."

Nate raised one eyebrow behind the woman's back. He had seen how civilized America really was and thought the remark more than exaggerated. Born in Paris, Nate's father had immigrated to America, allowing the administrators on Ellis Island to change the family name from Dupin to Dupes. That single deed had ruined America for his father, a man who had continually basked in the shadow of his own sire. All his life the elder Dupin had been unable to do anything but promote the brilliance of the fictionalized accounts of Nate's grandfather, the very real Le Chevalier C. Auguste Dupin. Nate, however, didn't care a bit. While he appreciated the fame of his grandfather, he was determined to make a name for himself. His only nod to his ancestor was to take a similar job, which was why Nate had not only been a detective in the employ of Lloyd's of London, but most recently worked for the famous American Pinkerton Detective Agency.

"It's a shame about these twin girls," he said. "Any hope of finding them?"

She ceased crocheting and sat, not moving or speaking. He'd struck a nerve.

"Their mother must be crazed with concern," he added, hoping for something... anything. He waited a few moments, then decided to let it go.

Then she surprised him by speaking in a low, slow voice.

"Girls have been disappearing around here for a long time. Three years, maybe. No one knows who's taking them, or even how they do it."

"The article doesn't mention anything about it."

"And it won't. Because up to now it was only Mexican girls."

"What happens to them?"

She turned, her eyes shining with tears. "I don't know. I just heard they sometimes find a body in the desert, buried and curled into a ball just like when they came out of their mother's womb."

The next morning Dupes had two messages waiting for him. One was from none other than Mr. J.C. Magillicutty requesting his presence. Nate's forty dollars in gold pieces was as useful as the thirty pieces of silver Judas Iscariot had been given to betray a certain other J.C. The other message was from the sheriff, so Dupes decided to attend to that one first. He was late in presenting his *Bona Fides* to the local constabulary anyway. So after a meal of toast and eggs, Nate made his way to the sheriff's office, and it took only a few moments of pretending that the sheriff was in charge and showing his Pinkerton credentials before he was allowed to leave. He held back his warrant for the missing painting, signed by the Secretary of the Interior; he'd use that when needed, but there was no hurry to reveal its existence now. With such an endorsement, not even the territorial governor had the power to countermand the warrant.

Magillicutty's property was an hour away by horseback, due east along the border. Nate got there, but watched the place for an hour before he descended a small hill and rode down the front road. Surrounded by pastures, the main house was an impressive three-story Tudor mansion that seemed as out of place in the American southwest as a Caravaggio painting. An old silver mine rose out of the hillside behind it, the tailings scattering down the side of the mountain like a black and red veil.

A couple of men lolled around the front door, but they stood straight as he strode toward them. Both kept their hands near their pistols, but at least they didn't have the bad grace to draw. He gave one the reins to his horse and bade the other announce him, providing a card with his name and title. The man looked at Dupes like the visitor had made his stomach go sour, but complied.

A few minutes later a big man with ruddy skin and a lion's mane of red hair burst through the door. "Nathanial Dupes," he said as he reached out a hand to shake, "no one told me you were a Pinkerton Detective. My man Johnson left that part out."

"I might have forgotten to tell him," Nate said, observing the quality of tailoring on Magillicutty's Savile Row wool suit.

"Well, come on in. We're still unpacking," Magillicutty said. "Please forgive the mess."

Nate followed him inside, realizing immediately that the other's statement was nothing but platitudinous. Everything was in its place and seemed perfectly arranged. He'd always felt he had an eye for decorating, and he could find no fault in the decidedly European interior. "How long have you been here?"

"Five years, but it took some time to build the house and have my things shipped." They'd made it to a library and the homeowner shoved his hands in his pockets. "I had three homes and consolidated everything into this one."

Nate nodded, noting several statues and two paintings whose provenance, once established, would make each of them worth more money than he was likely to ever see in his life. The man was definitely a collector.

They exchanged some polite talk for a few minutes after Dupes accepted a seat in a comfortable leather chair, then he and Magillicutty got down to brass tacks.

"So why are you interested in my painting?" his host asked. As it had turned out, the J.C. was short for John Christopher and he'd asked to be called John.

"Because it's not your painting," Dupes told him bluntly. "It was stolen sixty years ago and it's taken this long to track it down."

John sat very still for a few moments behind his massive desk. Finally, he sighed. "I'm sorry. You seem like a nice enough and responsible fellow, but you can't have it."

Nate had been waiting for this. He leaned forward and drew out the piece of paper he'd kept close at hand for these past four months. "I'm afraid you don't understand, I have a warrant for its return, signed by the Secretary of the Interior."

John smiled slightly. "No, I'm afraid you're the one who doesn't understand. It's true that I had the painting at one time, but I don't have it any longer."

Nate's smile fell. "You lost it? Sold it?"

"I don't have it," John repeated. "If you like, feel free to check every room."

"I will," Nate said stiffly. "What happened to it?"

John leaned back and shrugged mightily. "Who knows?"

For the first time in weeks Nate found himself flustered. The man had had the painting, but now it was gone. He'd even offered to let Nate check his house—and Nate definitely would—but the best he could offer was only that he didn't have it anymore?

"I doubt very much it grew legs and walked away by itself,"

Nate said. "Either you gave it away or it was stolen. So who has it now?"

John shrugged again, making a gesture meant to impart his lack of knowledge. Dupes didn't believe it for an instant. Then Magillicutty leaned forward. "Not what you expected, was it?" He grinned the same way he'd probably done to the last dozen business competitors he'd bested and ruined, making Nate wish he could do nothing more than punch out a few of the bigger man's teeth.

The ride back to town was long and depressing. Dupes had little doubt that the local constabulary was in league with the landowners, so trying to get them to open even a cursory investigation would be impossible. Adding to his frustration was the fact that he'd already telegraphed back to Pinkerton Headquarters and told them he'd found the missing painting, so there as a certain expectation that he would actually produce it.

Back in Douglas, he dropped off his horse and went to Calumet House. It was smaller than where he'd met Johnson, but promised to be a little more civilized.

Dupes was on his third glass of claret when a proud-looking young Mexican, wearing a broad-rimmed hat, approached him. He wore a bandolier across his wool suit and his trousers were tucked into shined—but worn—brown boots. At his side was a .40 caliber pistol, the trigger guard released.

"My name is José Doroteo Arango Arámbula," he told Nate as he stopped in front of the table. "But I'm known around here as Arango. Can I join you?"

Nate waved at the empty chair, watching as Arango settled onto it. "I followed you from Magillicutty's," he admitted. "I must tell you that I am curious about your relationship with that man."

Nate weighed his words, then carefully explained that he'd been looking for something he'd been sure Magillicutty had, following with the landowner's denial and that Dupes had no way of figuring out where the object now was.

Arango nodded, not bothering to ask for details. "I have the same problems with this man. He has no respect for Mexican men, women, or children. He'd rather feed a coolie than a Mexican. He's said this."

Admitting that he'd rather feed a Chinese rail worker than a descendant of Spanish ancestors spoke to a larger issue, one which if correctly divined might give Nate the necessary insight to move the proverbial mountain.

Arango was an interesting sort, as well. The Mexican sat with his back ramrod straight, as if he were of royal blood, but Nate could tell by the man's handsome yet broad features that any remnant of the blood from Hernán Cortés de Monroy y Pizarro or his Conquistadors had been so watered down it was nothing but an echo of old Spain. Still, the young man was proud and elegant in a battered fighter sort of way.

Calumet House wasn't the sort that cow punchers frequented, but there was still some rough trade at the bar. Occasionally someone would glance in Arango's direction with conspiracy in their eyes. The Mexican never turned or acknowledged the looks, but Nate could tell he knew everything that was happening.

"Do not worry about me, Nathanial," he said, making the *th* into a hard *t*. "Men like these do not concern me. They look for the now and forget the future. In that, us Mexicans are like Magillicutty's coolies. The Chinese play the long game, as do we. There will be change. There will be revolution. And that which has been taken will be returned to us."

Nate watched the man as he sipped another claret. Arango had a purity of purpose that he couldn't help but admire. That Nate was one of the people Arango would ultimately align himself against didn't bother him at all. As Arango had said, that was then—the future—and this was now.

"The disappearance of the girls must be weighing hard on you," he said. By Arango's reaction, Nate might as well have shot the man.

"It is an unholy thing that Magillicutty is doing," he said in a low voice.

Nate held up a hand. "I'm not making light of it. I'm serious when I say this." After glancing around, Nate asked quietly, "Do you have proof of his guilt?"

Arango shook his head. "No. We watch him. He's careful. But we know."

"There's a place for supposition if you can back it up. Do you have any evidence at all?"

But Arango didn't—it seemed no one did. That meant Magillicutty was innocent, or he was guilty but just too crafty for anyone to figure it out. The latter was the most probable, and Nate decided it was time for a little subterfuge.

Nate returned to his room and changed his appearance. Not being a big man, he'd perfected several different disguises. Although many were designed for a more civilized environment, the presence of the rail hub meant his Oriental persona could just be the key he needed to open certain doors.

A few hours later he was dressed like a Chinese businessman, his skin tinted yellow with a tincture he'd designed from lychee and turmeric. He settled himself at a table in the Silver Stop, a few blocks down from Calumet House and a few hundred levels beneath anyplace J.C. Magillicutty would frequent. Among the many hard-faced men in the dark, single-story bar were several Chinese, who by their pale skin and broken nails had traded the rail hammer for the mine pick. These were the men he targeted, and believing Nate's claim of being the result of a Dutch and Chinese union, they allowed for his passable Chinese and found it easy to speak with him, especially since he kept their mouths loose with drink.

Because he was deep in conversation with the Chinese, Nate wasn't in his room when the men came to get him, nor did they give him a second look when he passed them later on the street.

After all, he wasn't the man they were looking for. He was just some uppity, over-dressed Chinese coolie.

Nate found Arango in Calumet House around noon the next day. At first the Mexican failed to recognize him as he sat down, then it became clear that beneath the makeup was none other than the Pinkerton detective he'd met the previous evening.

"I need my kit," Nate said, meaning his bags. "But there are men up in my room, waiting for me."

Arango smiled slyly. "Why don't you let them take you?"

"I'd rather have more control than that over my immediate future. Besides, I learned something last night that might be of interest to both of us." When he saw he had the other's attention, Nate asked, "Have you ever heard of the Hermetic Order of the Golden Dawn?"

Arango shook his head. "Is this a church?"

"Of sorts. It has a Christian basis for certain, but it propounds the idea that God made the universe by combining four elements and has on hand seven divine spirit guides. It claims that through ritual, one can use these guides to help elevate one's spirit."

That calculating look slipped back into Arango's expression. "Agave will elevate your spirit much easier."

Nate almost laughed. "I agree, although I could do without the hangover."

"You can't have one without the other." Arango's grin showed bright white teeth.

"The Golden Dawn thinks you can. They believe you can ascend to a higher level with no penalty."

Arango studied him. "You asked me about evidence before. Now I ask you: how do you know this?"

"By certain symbols and signs." Nate went on to explain, drawing invisible versions of each symbol on the tabletop as he described them. "Magillicutty brought in a bunch of miners to clear several chambers of the old mine behind his home. There was a symbol of a square and compass etched into one wall, which is a Masonic designation. There were many other symbols the Chinese didn't understand, and my guess is that's because they were Qabalah. But the most telling symbol which was described to me was of an ornate golden cross with six-pointed stars etched into it. These are Stars of David, and their presence on a Christian cross would be deemed sacrilegious… unless that cross was a ritual device of the Golden Dawn."

"How do you know all of this?"

"I'm an art expert. Iconology goes hand in hand with knowing art."

"And these Golden Dawn types are dangerous?"

"*Anyone* who believes in magic is dangerous. More importantly, there is a version I have heard of that says human sacrifices are needed for certain rituals."

Arango's eyes widened. "And this is in Magillicutty's mine?"

"That is what I believe."

"And you have a plan?"

"I do, but it involves you and many men. Are you in?"

Arango grinned again, but there was no joy in his features this time, rather an echo of an unnamed violence that had yet to happen.

Now that things had been arranged, Nate cleansed his skin of the tincture in a trough and then returned to his room. The men waiting were kind enough to let him change before they escorted him out; they took along all of his things, paid his bill, and let him ride his own horse. Nate wasn't fooled by their courtesy; if he suddenly disappeared, there'd be nothing remaining to show he left of anything other than his own free will.

They didn't bother taking him to the big house. Instead, they went straight into the mine, where they tied his horse inside the entrance. Just beyond, the walls were covered with sconces, and chandeliers hung from the ceilings; so many candles were lit it was almost as though the mine had sunlit windows.

Burt Johnson himself escorted Nate into the first chamber, which had benches surrounding a circular raised stage; through the second chamber, which held an altar and had an array of painted diagrams on the floor; and finally into the third and smallest chamber. This was a library with a table holding an alchemist's kit; off to the side were several cages. Inside one stood a goat, bleating pathetically. The middle cage was empty, but the third cage held the prize: twin girls, both alive, but drugged.

Nate had found Eloise and Marie Duvall.

He'd taken a huge risk, and this was the part of his plan he hadn't been able to predict. Would Magillicutty kill him outright—he certainly hoped not—or would Nate be allowed to see them make a different offering? Goats were the classical sacrifice if you couldn't get your hands on a virgin, but here were *twin* virgins, young and innocent, and this promised some kind of special upcoming ritual. Although this made Nate believe that he might not be killed right away, as he stared at the angelic faces of the two lethargic girls, he did not feel better for it.

Locked securely in the middle cage, Nate's captors made him wait until it had to be well past nightfall, with the hours passing as slowly as the sun over a dying man in the desert.

Finally, the sound of men in the other rooms grew louder, and eventually Magillicutty swept into the room, wearing a maroon ceremonial robe and a hat shaped like a pyramid with an all-seeing eye brocaded into the yellow silk. As Magillicutty approached the cage, Nate said casually, "I feel underdressed for the ceremony, Magister."

Magillicutty froze in his tracks and his eyes narrowed. "I'm a Magus!" He examined Nate as if his eyesight could tell him more than what they saw. "And you are?"

"I am Practicus. First Order."

"Who brought you in?"

"Aleister Crowley. We met in Switzerland."

"Who was the second?"

"Algernon Blackwood. I met him at Wellington College."

Magillicutty went to a bookshelf and brought down a tome. He opened it on the table and began to search through it. "When was this?"

"1891."

After a few moments, Magillicutty looked up. His expression

was hard, but there was still uncertainty in his eyes. "I found Blackwood and we know of Crowley, but of you there is no report."

Nate kept his eyes steady. "I see on your shelf you have *De Occulta Philosophia* written by Cornelius Agrippa. I also see you have Baron Rosenroth's translation of the *Zohar*, titled *Kabbala Denudata,* or *Kabbalah Unveiled*. I found it much easier to read than Agrippa's work, especially as it detailed the *sephiroth*."

His words had the desired result. Magillicutty's mouth dropped open and his aura of self-importance wavered.

"If there's to be a ceremony," Nate continued, "I'd like to participate. I've been in the backwater for so long that it's a rare occasion to find someone, much less a *Magus*, with an active order."

Magillicutty glanced back the way he'd come, then at the twins, before he made his decision. "You seem to be a brother. A *Practicus*, you say?"

"I traveled to the Far East and was out of touch for several years. As it is, I am rusty when it comes to ceremony."

The man walked over to Nate's cage and opened it with a key he had tied to his waist. "You may participate, Mr. Dupes, but at the smallest hint of deception, I'll have Johnson shoot you through the heart." He brought his face close enough for Nate to smell onions on his breath. "Even if you are a *Practicus*."

Everything Nate had said was true. He had been inducted into the Golden Dawn, but it wasn't because he believed in all the *ooga booga*. Instead, he'd been desperate for the affection of Maud Gonne, an aspiring Irish actress he'd met in London. He'd followed after her like a sad puppy for the better part of a year, dining where she dined, drinking where she drank, being friends with her friends. Ultimately she'd run off with a

Frenchman, igniting the fuel that had sent Nate to China. Half a world away would put her as far out of sight as possible, and make him incapable of following through on his ill-thought plan of trailing after her to France.

Out of the cage and potentially a free man, Nate followed the Magus into the center chamber, which was now filled with three dozen men. Each wore a colored robe associated with their rank and position on the Golden Dawn Tree of Life.

The First Order was comprised of five ranks, with the Practicus the third. The Second Order was for Adepts and had three levels. The Third Order, those who were given access to the magical texts, also had three levels, Magister Templi, Magus and Ipsissimus. It was a rare occurrence to run into a Magus, and Nate had been told there were only five Ipsissimi in the world.

Nate was handed a light blue robe with three stripes on the arms to designate his rank. He slipped into it and found a place with the others of his color, who made up the outer ring of a half circle, which itself formed around the altar.

He hadn't had the opportunity to fully appreciate the room on his entrance. The walls had been smoothed by chisel work. Here and there he could see the marks made by the coolies, but for the most part, every surface was completely even. Five chandeliers hung from the ceiling, the light from hundreds of candles illuminating the interior. Several large paintings and designs hung on the walls, and with a start he suddenly recognized his Caravaggio. It held a place of reverence above a marble table on which rested a golden ciborium and paten, both of which would have been more at home in a Catholic church than a hermetic temple. Next to these was a dagger formed from a caduceus, two intertwined snakes, each of their bodies coming to stiletto points to form twin blades. The altar was raised between the center of the room and the painting, so that when watching the Magus, one could see the placid face of Jesus forgiving guilt-wracked Judas.

In the end, his grandfather's *ratiocination* had told him how to proceed. Once he'd discovered the linkage to the Golden Dawn, it had been easy to get into the mind of the man who'd accepted the stolen artwork. If there was one thing Nate had learned while chasing the skirt of his actress, it was that above all else, the Golden Dawn members loved ceremony. Even more than Masons, who were all choppy arms and angled feet, the Golden Dawn had a structure to their activities that bordered on the obsessive.

So it was with the cold and objective eye of a detective that Nate watched the Magus stand next to the empty altar and begin his Qabalistic incantations. While Magillicutty droned on, Nate surreptitiously glanced right and left to observe the other members of the First Order. Every single member's eyes were closed; every single pair of hands was folded piously before them. These were believers. These were men who'd stood passively aside as Mexican children were sacrificed, probably on this very altar, trading the innocence of young lives for better crops, or healthy stock—or wealth.

Magillicutty's words ceased. It was finally time for introductions.

"We have a surprise member with us tonight, all the way from England," Magillicutty said in an imperious voice. "Come forward, brother, so that we may recognize you by the sign of a Practicus."

The inner circle of Adepts parted to let Nate pass. Magillicutty made the sign of welcome and Nate made the sign of a Practicus... or at least he hoped he did. Standing with feet angled, knees flexed and fingers intertwined was not something one did every day. It must have been sufficient, however, because he was allowed to live. Even so, as he looked upon the members of the order he spied Burt Johnson; the unrobed cowhand was leaning against a wall and holding a Henry rifle in the crux of one arm.

"Tell us about the order across the pond, Mr. Dupes," Magillicutty commanded. "Explain to these poor men of the continent how well the order fares in England and Europe."

Nate looked into Magillicutty's eyes and knew what the Magus wanted. Behind the beatific smile was a stern and steely gaze. Nate was reminded about what Agnes Moffit had said regarding the man bringing civilization to Douglas with the installation of a Sears, Roebuck and Co. catalogue store. Magillicutty had also brought with him a level of mysticism unbeknownst to the region. Nate doubted if any of the locals had even heard of the Hermetic Order of the Golden Dawn before the big man's arrival. Magillicutty had admitted to arriving in the territory five years ago, and the Mexican children had begun to go missing a couple of years later. It had probably taken Magillicutty two years to firmly establish the order, pulling from local businessmen and ranchers with his promises of good, better, and best everything.

"I asked if you would tell us about the order across the pond, Mr. Dupes." Magillicutty's eyes glittered in the rampant candlelight. "Cat got your tongue?"

A few of the Adepts chuckled.

"The order is strong in London and Paris, Magus. We have thousands of members, each one reaching the pinnacle of their careers."

At his words, need flared in the eyes of the members of Magillicutty's order. They needed to know that they were not alone. They needed to be told that everyone did what *they* did. He saw a few gazes stray to the entrance of the chamber where the girls were being held; the movement spoke volumes to the bill of spiritual goods Magillicutty had sold them.

"And do they perform sacrifice?" one asked in an almost timid tone of voice. The men next to the speaker looked at the ground, but Nate couldn't tell whether they were embarrassed at the question or afraid of the forthcoming answer.

"Members of the order do whatever is needed to promote the order," Nate said, repeating one of the initiation tenets. "If sacrifice is needed, then sacrifice is performed." Although the words were spoken and written in ritual, Nate was fairly certain they referred to personal sacrifice rather than physical. Still, his words would serve to make the members feel as if they'd killed for a higher purpose. Even as a ruse, Nate hated himself for making them feel that way, for excusing their most terrible crimes even for an instant.

"Well done," Magillicutty said under his breath. Then he raised his voice: "Speaking of sacrifice, we have a special occasion this evening. It is the celebration of the birth of Poemander, the bringer of the knowledge of Ra." He spread his arms as if to encompass all the others. "What say you we celebrate this great moment and become one with the universe?"

The men of the order shouted, "Aye!" together, and the sound carried through the chambers. The candle flames above them flickered as though the words had created their own breeze.

Nate moved to go back to his place in the circle, but Magillicutty's hand landed suddenly on his arm, heavy and cold. "Stay," he said. "I would have you participate in the ritual."

Nate's stomach did a sad, sick lurch, then knotted back up when the twins were pushed through the doorway and into the circle. Their mouths were covered by cloth, their hands bound in front of them, and they'd been dressed in small white robes. Crimson bows pulled their blonde hair back from their pale, terrified faces.

Two Adepts placed them on the altar side by side. They were so tiny it only took one man to hold their feet, and another to push down their shoulders.

The Magus spoke again. "Adepts, who art thou?"

"We are followers of Poemander," the Adepts said in unison. "We are the mind of the Great Lord, the most Mighty and absolute Emperor. We know that thou wouldst have us, for we are always present with thee."

The Magus spoke yet again. "First Order, who art thou?"

"We are also followers of Poemander," the members of the First Order said in unison. "We are the mind of the Great Lord, the most Mighty and absolute Emperor. We know that thou wouldst have us, for we are always present with thee."

"And how do I know you?"

Everyone said, "By the third eye, the golden heart, and the rose cross."

"And how shall you be known to each other?"

"By secret sign and by our deeds."

"And what are your deeds?"

"To seek higher spiritual order and to become resident in the Tree of Life."

"So mote it be."

Everyone bowed their heads. "So mote it be."

Nate started to lift his own head then felt a weight pressed into his hand. He looked down and saw the dagger made from the caduceus. Named and formed after the staff of Hermes, the messenger god, Nate supposed that the dagger would hasten the spirit to the afterlife. Glancing over at Magillicutty, he couldn't help but fix on the soft space at the base of the man's throat. But then he followed the man's gaze to where Burt Johnson now held his Henry rifle at eye level, sighting down the barrel and ready to send a bullet through Nate's heart, just as the Magus had promised.

"For Poemander and Thoth and Hermes, we take these lives," Magillicutty intoned. "Repeat after me."

Magillicutty began the Rosicrucian Prayer and everyone followed his words, their eyes on the dagger as they waited for him to finish. Nate knew what was expected of him. Two swift jabs, one through each girl's heart.

What should he do? He could make their deaths swift, remove the fear from their eyes, take them from a world that would allow them to be stolen away to fulfill the maniacal whims of a cult leader who promised others a better harvest if only these two innocents' lives were given in return.

Nate thought of Caravaggio's painting and how the artist had put himself in as witness to the taking of Jesus. How ironic it was that Saint John seemed to flee while the stranger, Caravaggio, stayed. John had been one of Jesus' followers, yet in the betrayal of his master by Judas, he'd tried to run. Had it been curiosity that made Caravaggio seem to stay? Or had it been necessity?

Suddenly the truth came to Nate. Not curiosity, never that. He simply hadn't wanted Jesus to be alone in his last, worst hours.

Nate stared down at the girls with the same feeling. These were truly their last, worst hours.

When the prayer ended, all eyes turned on him. The silence in the room was incredible, almost suffocating… except for the sound of the Henry rifle being cocked.

Nate had no choice. He did what he had to.

He ducked down and stabbed Magillicutty right in the jimmy. When the man shrieked and bent over, grasping his groin, Nate jabbed upward and shoved the dagger home deep into the man's left eye. By then all hell had broken loose, and the row of Adepts surged forward.

Nate stood and hooked an arm around each girl's neck, dragging them off the table until his back was to the Caravaggio painting. As he pressed against the canvas, to his great relief, he felt a breeze at the base of his neck.

The men clambered toward Nate, their faces bright red, as a sea of hands reached forward, ready to rip him apart. He let the girls sag at his feet and urged them under the marble altar. As they crawled underneath it, he spied Burt Johnson trying to aim at him with his rifle, but there were too many heads in the way for a clean shot.

One of the Adepts leaped toward him.

Nate kicked down with the inside of his right foot, catching the man just above the knee and shattering it. He fell aside, screaming, but another one jumped to take his place. Nate caught this one across the throat with the edge of his right hand, dropping the man's bellow into a thin gurgle.

A gunshot made him jerk his head toward Burt Johnson, but instead of the expected bullet through his own head, Nate saw the cowhand fall forward.

Then a Mexican with a wide-brimmed hat and crossed bandoliers stormed into the room, brandishing a pair of pistols—

Arango!

Stunned, the members of the Golden Dawn scattered as more and more Mexicans poured into the chamber. Too late, they flailed at their robes and tried to pull out their own guns, but a full half were shot before they could even tug their weapons free. Others succeeded, and suddenly the noise became unbearable, explosion after explosion as the sounds combined with smoke and the smell of gunpowder to create a ten-second dose of hell just below the surface of the earth.

When it was done, the only ones left standing were seven Mexicans—Arango and six of his men—and Nate Dupes.

Arango picked his way over the bodies to where Nate stood, then helped him pull the girls from their hiding place beneath the altar. Untied and freed of their gags, they clutched at Nate and began to cry.

"This is a delicious revenge," Arango said. He pointed at the room full of dead men. "These are the ones who have been murdering our children."

Nate nodded, suddenly fighting with his emotions. He'd been holding everything so close inside that he felt like spinning with happiness. Instead of making a fool of himself, he grinned and said, "It took you long enough."

"You know us Mexicans, amigo. We love our drama."

"Did you think this was all shit, Nate Dupes?"

Nate and Arango spun at the same time, and Nate gasped at the sight of Magillicutty, standing tall and firm just behind them. The caduceus dagger jutted grotesquely from his eye above a wet stream of blood and clear fluid. Magillicutty raised one hand toward the ceiling and pointed at Nate with the other; his voice was hollow and oddly echoing. *"Did you believe there was nothing to what we do?"*

Nate felt a tingling along his spine and he backstepped, stumbling against Arango.

"I curse you, Nate Dupes. You shall never be happy. You shall never find peace." The words reverberated off the stone walls.

"How is he alive?" Arango demanded. "How can this be?"

Nate tried to answer, but found he couldn't speak. Magillicutty swayed and switched to Greek, his words tumbling out. The ground began to tremble. Pieces of debris fell from the ceiling.

Arango pushed Nate aside and shouted to his men. *"Corre!"*

They scrambled out just before a piece of the wall collapsed and blocked the exit. Without hesitating, Arango drew both of his pistols and shot Magillicutty with every bullet he had, until he was clicking only on empty chambers. The Magus jerked with every gunshot, then stood for a long moment. When he finally fell, the ceiling—first in parts, then the rest—fell with him.

There was no more time to waste.

Nate ripped the painting free, revealing a tunnel bored into the rock wall. Arango went in first, pulling the twins behind him. Nate dove into the hole in the rock just before everything in the room collapsed with a roar. Pulling himself to his feet in total darkness, he felt his way along the tunnel, using his hands as eyes and following the faint sounds farther down. According to the Chinese coolie who'd told him about this escape route, it would twist and turn until it came out the back of the mountain. It seemed like forever until Nate finally smelled the clean and dust-free air of an Arizona night and came out on a ledge about seven feet above the ground. The girls were waiting for him with their backs to the hillside.

Arango had already made his way down. Four horses were staked and waiting for them below. The Mexican leaped atop one and reached out a hand. "Here, let me help."

With the painting dragging from his left hand, Nate reached for the nearest girl.

"The painting first," Arango called.

Nate stopped. "Why?"

"Let's get it out of the way."

Of course—right now it was a hindrance, dragging on the ground and getting in the way. Nate hastily rolled it, then leaned over the edge and handed it down to Arango.

The Mexican grinned broadly. "You have shown me what one has to do, amigo. I thank you for that. My people thank you as well. You are always welcome with us. I shall make it known." He yanked on the horse's reins and spun to the side.

"Wait," Nate cried. "Where are you going?"

"Soon there will be a revolution!" Arango pulled up hard and his horse reared and pawed the air. "We will take back what was taken from us." He hefted the painting above his head in a sign of victory. "And this will help to finance it!"

"You're leaving us," Nate said incredulously.

"You have horses," Arango pointed out. "You have your life. Be thankful."

"But you could help us!"

"*Solo el que carga el cajon sabe loque pesa el muerto*," Arango told him. "It means 'Only he who carries the coffin knows how much the dead man weighs.' Know this, Nate Dupes, and live it. You cannot know what someone else carries in his soul, nor feel the suffering he bears."

Nate's mouth twisted. "Trust no one, you mean."

"It's more than that," Arango said with an almost sad smile. "Much more. Adiós, amigo—and know that you gave birth to the Revolution!"

And Arango was gone, leaving Nate on the side of a hill in the middle of nowhere with twin girls, feeling like he was standing in the Garden of Gethsemane.

* * *

Fifteen years later, after a decade and a half of experiences, but never a day of true happiness, Nate Dupes sits at a café table in New York City and recognizes a picture in the newspaper. The black and white image shows him a Mexican revolutionary bandit whom he knows was born José Doroteo Arango Arámbula.

But now, in this newspaper and forever after, this Mexican is known as Pancho Villa.

THE VANISHING ASSASSIN

By

JONATHAN MABERRY

It should, I suppose, be entirely appropriate that I sat with my friend C. Auguste Dupin in the gloomy autumn shadows inside the cavernous and—some would insist *haunted*—walls of the decrepit mansion we shared at No. 33 Rue Dunot, Faubourg St. Germain. We had been to see a rather melancholy play about phantoms and murder and it had brought us into a discussion of many things gruesome and bloody. Over excellent wine and a tray of small cakes, we whiled away the hours speculating on the nature of the supernatural. I have a tendency toward belief in it, or at least in some parts of it; however, Dupin will have none of it.

"Specters are the product of a lack of information," he said as he lit his pipe, "as well as a failure of perception."

"How so?" I asked, intrigued.

He took several long puffs of the strong Belgian tobacco he had been favoring lately, blowing ghostly clouds of smoke into the air between our chairs. Small vagaries of wind made the smoke dance and twitch before whipping the hazy tendrils from sight.

"There is an example," he said. "Had you, a credulous man, peered in through a frosted window and beheld the dancing smoke that has so recently departed us, and had you not perceived the meerschaum in my hand, might you not have thought that inside this house, haunted as it is, at least in reputation, you beheld a specter? And, had you been even more credulous—as say our charwoman has demonstrated herself to be on so many occasions—wondered if the two gaunt men who sat with heads bowed together were not, in fact, sorcerers who conjured the dead from the dust of this place?"

"Perhaps," I said cautiously, for I know that to agree or disagree too quickly with Dupin is the surest way to put a foot into a bear trap of logic.

"Then consider the nature of a ghostly sighting," he continued, warming to his thesis. "Most of them occur at night, and of those many in remote places, darkened houses, dimly lit country lanes, and church yards—places where proper lighting is seldom provided. Such places lend themselves to morbid thoughts, do they not? Now additionally consider the nature of the sighting itself. So often there is a sense of unnerving coldness, a perception that something unseen is moving so close that its frigid reach brushes against the perceptions of the witness. Add to this the fact that most specters are only seen as partially materialized figures or amorphous blobs of light and shadow. Reflect further on the time of day, and let us remember that at night we are often sleepy and closer to a dreaming state than we are at the height of noon." He sat back and puffed out a blue stream. "The evidence we collect are elements of circumstance and a predisposition of mind that not only lacks clarity and is likely fatigued, but which is also shaped into a vessel of belief because of the macabre atmosphere."

"So it is your opinion that all ghosts are merely the creations of overly credulous minds who witness—what? Mist or fog or smoke on a darkened night? How then do you explain the movement of these specters? How do you dismiss the moans they make?"

"I do not dismiss any sounds or movement," said Dupin, "but I challenge the authenticity of the eyewitness account. Let me hear an account of a ghost who appears on the Avenue des Champs-Élysées at two o'clock on a May afternoon, and present me with at least three unbiased witnesses who have had no time to confabulate, and then perhaps you will ignite a flicker of credulity even in a stoic such as me."

Outside, the wind blew against the house and found some crack in the slate tiles on the roof so that its passage was an eloquent wail, like a despairing spirit.

Dupin nodded as if pleased with the confirmation of his argument.

We sat there, smoking our pipes and listened to the sounds of the old house, some caused by the relentless wind, others by the settling of its ancient bones into the cold earth. Despite the cogency of his argument, we both huddled deeper into our coats and cast curious looks into the shadows that seemed to draw closer and closer to us.

Then there was a sharp *rap-tap-tap* that was so unexpected and so jarring that we both jumped a foot in the air and cried out like children.

However, when the door opened, in came Monsieur G—, the Prefect of the Parisian police, and his presence broke the spell. Dupin and I glanced at each other, aware that we had both been as surely spooked as if we had seen a specter in truth. We burst out laughing.

"Well, well," said G., looking rather startled and confounded by our sharp cries and ensuing gales of laughter, "now behold another mystery. Have I come in upon some great jest or have you two fine gentlemen taken sure and final leave of your faculties?"

"A bit of both, I dare say," said I, and that sent Dupin into another fit of laughter.

G. smiled thinly, but it was clear that he was forcing a cordial face. Dupin saw this, of course, and quickly sobered. He waved G. to a chair.

"Let me pour you some of this excellent wine," I suggested. "It is a Prunier Cognac, 1835. Quite scandalous for a blustery autumn night in a drafty pile such as this, but appropriate for whiling the hours away with dark tales of shades and hobgoblins."

However, G. remained standing, hat in hands, nervous fingers fidgeting with the brim.

"Gentlemen," said he, "I wish I could join you, but I am afraid that those things of which you jest are perhaps out in truth on this wretched night."

Dupin lifted one eyebrow. "Do you say so? And what spectral vapors could possibly conspire to draw the Prefect himself away from a quiet evening at the Jockey Club de Paris?"

"It is a matter of…" began G., but his voice trailed away and stopped. "Wait, how could you possibly know I was at that club this evening?"

Dupin waved the stem of his meerschaum as if dismissing the matter as being of no importance. "A blind man could see it."

"Then I am blind," said I. "Please light a candle to this darkness."

The briefest ghost of a smile flickered across Dupin's mouth and I knew from long experience that although my friend can appear both cold and inhuman at times, particularly in his pursuit of the pure logic of observation and analysis, he has a splinter of perversity that enjoys both the confounding of whatever audience is at hand, and the later satisfaction of their curiosity.

Affecting a face of boredom, Dupin said, "The scandalous matter of race fixing which was resolved so satisfactorily last month was entirely the doing of our good Prefect of the Parisian police. One of the more notable applications by modern law enforcement of the value of evidence collection and the science of observing details to discern their nature rather than forcing assumptions upon them."

G. colored slightly. "I make no pretence to brilliance," he murmured. "And I openly admit to having applied methods I have observed in recent cases with which you were involved."

"Just so," said Dupin without false modesty.

"But how does that place Monsieur G. at the club this evening?" I demanded.

"It is customary of such clubs to grant special memberships to distinguished gentlemen who have been of service to their organization. It would be entirely out of character for the Jockey Club de Paris to have eschewed that policy after G. saved them from scandal and ruin."

"Agreed," I said slowly, taking the point.

"It is also in keeping with the policies of such clubs to hold a gathering to celebrate the induction of a new member. In virtually any other circumstance such a dinner would be held on a Saturday, with much fanfare and mention in the press."

"But there was no mention," I said, having read every paper from front to back.

"Of course not," said Dupin. "Scandal cannot be advertised. No, such a gathering would be on a night when the club would be the least well-visited, and that is a Thursday night because of the big races in England on Friday. Many of the members would be crossing the channel. That would leave only the most senior members and the governors of the board in Paris, and it would be they who would want to offer their private thanks. They lavished food and drink upon you, my dear G., and before you ask how I know, I suggest you look to your cuffs, coat sleeve and waistcoat for evidence. Crème sauce, sherry, aspic and... if I am not mistaken... *pâte à choux*."

G. looked down at his garments and began brushing at the crumbs and stains.

"A gentleman who has had time to go home and brush up would never have ventured out in such a condition. No, you came from that robust dinner to the scene of some crime."

"But it could have been any club that serves a fine dinner," said I.

"True, true," admitted Dupin, "however, I believe I can put a nail in the coffin with the unsmoked cigar I perceive standing at attention in your breast pocket. It is wrapped by a colorful paper band, which is the invention of Cuban cigar makers Ramon and Antonio Allones, and although other cigar makers have begun to similarly band their cigars, the Allones brothers were the first and theirs is quite easy to identify. These excellent cigars are not yet being exported to Europe, but they are often given as gifts by American horse racing moguls to colleagues in Great Britain and France. It is unlikely anyone but a senior official of the Jockey Club would have such a fine cigar; however, it is *very* likely that such a prize would be presented to the man who solved the French horse racing incident."

"By God, Dupin," said G. in a fierce whisper. "Your mind is more machine than flesh and blood."

"Ah," said Dupin, "how I wish that were so. Machines do not fatigue. They are pure in function." He sighed. "There are other bits of evidence as well, both hard clues and inspirations for informed speculation, but I have no desire to show off."

I kept my face entirely composed.

"Nor do I wish to waste any more of our dear friend's time. Tell me, G., what *has* brought you away from food and festivities and compelled you even further to visit us?"

"Murder," said G. "Murder most foul and violent."

"Ah," said Dupin, his mouth curling with clear appetite.

"But come now," I said, "you earlier spoke of something unnatural."

G.'s eyes darkened. "I did, and indeed there is nothing at all *natural* about this case. A man was killed without weapons by a killer who seems to have vanished into thin air."

Dupin's eyes burned like coals through a blue haze of pipe smoke.

"We shall come at once," he said.

And so we did.

We piled into the cab G. had left waiting, and soon we were clattering along the cobblestoned streets of Paris. And within a quarter hour we found ourselves standing outside a building which was divided into offices for various businesses engaged in international trade.

Gendarmes filled the street, keeping back a growing knot of onlookers and preventing anyone but official persons from going into the building. As I alighted I spied an ancient-looking woman swathed in a great muffler of green and purple leaning heavily on a walking stick. She raised a folded fan to signal our cabbie. I paused to help her inside. In a thickly accented voice she asked the driver to take her to the train station.

Dupin, who waited for me while I assisted the lady, glanced at his watch. "She'll have a long, cold wait. The next train isn't for three quarters of an hour."

"Poor thing," I said. "She was as thin as a rail and already shivering with the cold."

But our concern for the old lady was swept away by the Prefect, who loudly cleared his throat.

"Gentlemen," he said with some urgency, "if you please."

Dupin gave a philosophical shrug and we turned to address the building and the knot of police who stood in a tight cordon around the place. They gave G. a crisp salute and stood aside to let him pass. However, they eyed us with some curiosity. The Prefect did not pause to introduce us, as was well within his right.

We climbed three flights of stairs to a suite of offices that occupied half of the top floor. There was a cluster of official-looking persons on hand, including several gendarmes in uniform, two detectives from the Prefect's office, a lugubrious medical examiner waiting his turn, and an ancient cleaning woman who sat shivering with fear on a bench, her face still blanched white from what she had witnessed.

"It was she who alerted the police?" asked Dupin.

"Yes," agreed G. "She heard bloodcurdling screams of fear and agony coming from this floor and, knowing that M. Thibodaux was the sole occupant working this late, she hurried to see if he had done himself an injury. However, she found his door locked. But here is the cause of her greatest consternation— she saw a line of bloody footprints leading away from M. Thibodaux's office, but they vanished mid-stride and were not seen again. The thought that a phantom had come to do cruel harm to M. Thibodaux sent her screaming into the street as if the hounds of hell were on her heels. There she sits now, shaken and frightened half to death. Do you want to interview her?"

Dupin stood for a moment in front of the woman. His dark eyes took in her posture, her mean clothing, the nervous knot of her fingers in her lap, and the florid and puffy countenance of her face.

"No," said Dupin, "she knows nothing."

The Prefect opened his mouth to demand how my friend could be so certain, but then thought better of it and shut his jaws. We both know that Dupin would rather say nothing at all than make a declaration which could in any way be impeached. He had observed this woman and summed up everything there was to know about her—at least from the point of calculating observation—and had reached a conclusion that he could defend.

He turned away from her and glanced down the hall to where the office of M. Thibodaux awaited us.

"The door was locked, you say?" he mused.

The Prefect nodded. "The superintendent had gone home for the evening, which necessitated that the guards break the door down."

"Interesting," said Dupin. He walked over to where the medical examiner sat. "Have you inspected the body?"

"I have," said the doctor, who was as old as Methuselah and as thin as a stick. "He is the victim of—"

But Dupin raised a finger to stop the flow of words. "Thank you, doctor, but I prefer to make my own assessments. I was merely inquiring as to whether it is safe for us to examine the victim."

The doctor looked both skeptical and annoyed. "Yes, there is nothing more of official merit to be learned."

Dupin smiled thinly. "Please remain on the premises, doctor. I may have a question or two for you after I have examined the scene."

"Very well," said the doctor in as cold a tone of voice as I am ever likely to hear.

Dupin moved down the hallway to where a beefy gendarme stood guard before glass-fronted double-doors. When the officer stepped aside I could read the name of the firm written in gold script.

Oriental Artifacts and Treasures
Antoine Thibodaux, Proprietor

However, we all stopped ten paces from the door and cast our eyes upon the floor. As Mrs. Dubois had sworn, there was indeed a line of bloody footprints that trailed from the doors of the murder room and along the runner carpet. Twelve steps in all, the intensity of blood diminishing with each successive footfall.

"A child!" I cried, pointing to the diminutive size of the prints.

Dupin did not immediately comment.

"Surely," I said, "the blood merely wore off by this point and that is why there are no further marks."

Dupin got down on his hands and knees and peered at the last stains. "No," he said. "The blood on these prints was fading, surely, but there was more than enough to leave a trace for several more paces. No, consider this print." He gestured to the last one. "It is somewhat denser in color than the one before it, with an emphasis on the ball of the foot. Then there is an overlay of the edge of the foot as if it was lifted slightly and placed down again with most of the weight on the blade."

He stood up, shaking his head.

"My dear Prefect, may all ghosts be laid as easily as this one and the world will be free of spirits forever more."

"I don't follow," said G.

"The person who left that room stopped here to remove the bloody shoes. When first bending to remove the left shoe, the killer placed weight on the ball of the right foot. The overlay of the edge was likely an attempt to catch their balance while untying the laces. Once the left was off, a bare or stockinged foot was placed here—see the slight indentation in the nap of the carpet? Standing on that foot, the killer removed the other shoe."

G. grunted, seeing it now.

"Come look at the scene of the crime," he suggested, "and perhaps you can dispel the rest of the mystery as easily as this."

Dupin did not answer. Instead he shoved his hands into his pockets as he followed G. inside. I too followed, but stopped nearly at once.

"Good God!" I cried.

"Indeed," drawled Dupin.

The room was a charnel house.

Unless a person is a professional soldier, a slaughterhouse jack, or a member of the police department, it is unlikely that he will chance to encounter a scene of such carnage. I admit that I froze, unable to set foot into that place of slaughter. My heart instantly began to hammer inside my chest and I felt as though my whole body was bathed in frigid dew. I put a hand to my mouth, as much to stay my rising bile as to staunch a flow of unguarded curses.

Even Dupin, with all of his practiced detachment from ordinary emotions, seemed to hesitate before crossing the threshold. Only the Prefect, jaded and hardened by so many years and so many crime scenes, seemed predominantly unmoved. However, his wooden features might well be a tactic to keep his more human emotions to himself.

Despite my misgivings, I shifted around so that I could look over Dupin's shoulder into the room. Except for a solitary figure, the room was entirely unoccupied and thoroughly cluttered. Paintings crowded the walls and filled every inch of space so that not even a sliver of the wallpaper was visible; and each of these works were in a distinctive Asian style. I am no Orientalist, but I could pick out the differences between Chinese and Japanese artwork, and both were represented here, with—perhaps—a bias toward the Japanese. Grim-faced Samurai, demure courtesans, absurd fish, and fierce demons looked down from the walls and regarded the scene with serene dispassion. The furniture was of the kind called "japanned," in which the body of each piece is lacquered in a glossy black, then either over-painted or inlaid with designs of unsurpassed intricacy. There were racks of scrolls, urns filled with hand-painted fans, chests made of polished teak from which spilled tendrils of the rarest silk. Every table, every cabinet, every shelf and surface was crammed with carved combs, silk kimonos with elaborate patterns, knives and swords, ink boxes, trinkets, statues, and many other items whose nature or category was beyond my knowledge.

And all of it was splattered with blood.

Streaks and dots of it were splashed upon the walls, scattered across the tops of tables, and ran in lines down the sides of desks.

And there, slumped in a posture that contained no trace of vitality, was a corpse.

"Dear God," I gasped.

It was the body of a man, but that was all I could tell for sure about him. I turned away, ostensibly to study the walls, but everywhere I looked I saw evidence of the carnage that had been wrought upon this unfortunate individual.

Without turning away from the corpse, Dupin asked, "What has been touched?"

G. cleared his throat. "The gendarmes who responded to the alert broke into this room. They hurried to the man you perceive there in the chair and felt for heartbeat and listened for breath and found neither."

"I daresay," murmured Dupin.

"The officers then made a cursory search of the room, touching as little as possible, but enough to determine that the windows were closed and locked."

Dupin turned to him. "And—? I believe you are omitting some facts, my friend. Out with it. In the absence of information I can be of no value at all."

"It's a queer thing," admitted G. "When the officers entered the building, they held the door for a person who was leaving."

"God in heaven," I cried. "Are you saying that they held the door so the murderer could exit? Did they tip their hats as well and wish our killer their best wishes? Really, G., this is outrageous."

But the Prefect was shaking his head. "No, it was not like that at all. Though in the absence of all other leads I..."

His voice trailed off and he looked uneasy and uncertain.

Dupin said, "Come on, dear friend, out with it. If the bird has flown, then at least tell me your officers had the good sense to record a basic physical description."

G. snapped his fingers to summon a pair of gendarmes. One was as green a recruit as ever I have seen wear the uniform of a Paris police officer. The other, however, was well known to both Dupin and myself. It was none other than Jacques Legrand, a hulking brute of a sergeant whose physique was at odds with the shrewd intelligence sparkling in his blue eyes. On more than one occasion Dupin remarked that Legrand had a real chance in his profession and we should not be surprised if one day this monster of a man wore the Prefect's badge.

The sight of Legrand looking so embarrassed and wretched caused Dupin to throw up his hands and click his tongue in the most disapproving manner.

"Come now, Legrand," said my friend, "surely you will not break my heart by confessing that you let a red-handed criminal walk past you while you held the door."

Legrand drew in a big breath that made his muscular shoulders rise half a foot into the gloom, then exhaled a sigh that would have deflated an observation balloon.

"I fear I have done exactly that," he confessed, "and I'm more the fool for even now being unaware of how my actions might have played out in a different manner."

"Tell me everything," declared Dupin. "Unburden your soul with every fact you can recall and we shall see how low you have sunk."

Legrand drew in another breath and then took the plunge. "It was like this, gentlemen," he said to us, "my partner, Roux, and I were on foot patrol and on such a foggy, cold night many a mugger and footpad is abroad, content that the dense fog and their own mufflers will conceal their identities. Roux and I had made two circuits of this district and we were considering stopping at a café to take our evening break."

"What time was this?" interrupted Dupin.

"A quarter to eight," said Legrand, who checked his notebook, then his watch. "Forty-one minutes ago."

"Forty-two," corrected Dupin absently. "Your watch is off by nearly thirty seconds."

Legrand colored, but he cleared his throat and plowed ahead. "We were within half a block of the café when we heard a bloodcurdling scream. Naturally we came running and intercepted the charwoman, Mrs. Dubois, who was screaming as if she was being chased by half the devils in hell."

"What did she say?"

"It took quite a bit to get her to make sense, but her story was a simple one. She had finished the top floor and was bringing her mops and buckets down to this floor, the third, when she heard a cry of pain coming from the office of Monsieur Thibodaux. She dropped her mops and came hustling down the stairs, only to find the door locked and a trail of bloody footprints. She tried to open the door, but it was solidly locked and it is a stout door, as you've no doubt observed. However, Mrs. Dubois heard Monsieur Thibodaux continue to moan and cry out in great agony. Then... she heard him die, you might say."

"Heard?" I asked.

"Monsieur Thibodaux called out a name, then she heard a solid thump. She pressed her ear to the crack and swears that she heard his last breath and death rattle. It was this grisly sound that broke her and she ran screaming into the streets."

Dupin's eyes glittered. "Monsieur Thibodaux called out a name, eh?"

"Yes, sir. Anna Gata. Or something very like it. A woman's name, I believe, though it is not a name I have ever heard before, and it is not included on the register of occupants of this building, nor in the ledger of visitors."

"You checked?" asked Dupin.

"I did, sir. All occupants' names are engraved on a plaque in the foyer along with accompanying office numbers and floors. The visitors' ledger is on the desk downstairs. I checked it very carefully while waiting for reinforcements to arrive."

"That, at least, was good police work." Dupin pursed his lips. "Gata is an unusual surname. If it is a real name, then we should have little trouble locating the possessor of it, for it cannot be common even in Paris. If it is a nickname, then we have some leads. It is the Catalan word for 'cat' and Fijian name for 'snake'. Perhaps there are clues there, for each is suggestive. However, such speculations are far in advance of the information we yet need to collect." He shook his head to clear his thoughts of such distractions.

"Wait," I said, "we seem to have skipped over a vital clue. The person who exited the building."

"Not skipped over," said Dupin, "but left it to its place of importance." To Legrand he said, "Now tell me of the person who exited the building as you entered, and explain why you thought it was beyond sense or prudence to detain this individual. Every detail now, spare nothing."

"There is little *to* spare," said Legrand. "As Roux and I approached the building we saw the door open and a lady stepped out."

"A lady," I said. "Anna Gata, perhaps?"

Dupin ignored me.

"I do not think so," replied Legrand. "This was no sweetheart for a man the age of poor Monsieur Thibodaux, for this was a crone, a withered old woman, and a foreigner to boot."

"Was she wearing a gray cloth coat with a green and purple muffler?" asked Dupin.

"Why… yes!" gasped Legrand. "However did you guess that?"

"It's not a guess," said Dupin. He cut a withering look at me. "My companion here helped her into a cab."

Legrand did not look at me.

"You said she was a foreigner," said Dupin. "From where?"

"Well, she was all bundled up, as you apparently saw, but I spotted her eyes. I reckon that she was a Chinese or somesuch. Small, slender, and so wrinkled that I believe she must have been a hundred years old. Frail, she was, and she needed to lean heavily on a carved walking stick."

Dupin stood considering this for many long and silent seconds. He cut a look at me. "You were closer to her than I. Did you see her eyes and can you confirm that she was Chinese?"

"I did see her eyes, though briefly," I admitted, "but I cannot tell from those if she was Chinese, Japanese, Korean, or any of countless Orientals. They are all of a piece to me."

Irritation flickered across Dupin's face. "That may be a dead end in terms of apprehending the killer, but surely, Legrand, you had to make some connection between an Oriental woman and the nature of Monsieur Thibodaux's business."

Legrand swallowed. "To tell the honest truth, sir, I thought she was another charwoman. She was dressed in rags except for that scarf, and walked hunched over. In any other circumstance I would have offered her my arm and escorted her to a public house or fetched her a cab."

"Too late for that now." Dupin looked even more disgusted. "Let us leave that for the moment. Is there anything more you can tell me?"

The big sergeant shook his head, and Dupin dismissed him with bad grace. When he was gone, Dupin snarled, "Had that been an old man leaving the building, even a dotard or a cripple, I have no doubt Legrand would have detained him without thought. But he, being a big and powerful man, can barely imagine anyone but a similarly large person committing an act of such shocking violence. It is a blind spot that may hurt his career and may have prevented us from easily solving this case. Bah! It is my curse that I am so often disappointed by believing in the potential of a person only to find them as flawed and shallow as the rest of the herd."

"Surely not," I began, working up some heat in protest to my friend's words, but he dismissed me with an irritable wave of his hand. I bit down on the rest of my words and they left a bitter taste on my tongue.

Dupin stalked back toward the murder room, leaving G. and I to exchange helpless looks. With raised eyebrows, we followed. Dupin walked past the elderly doctor without comment. He once more examined the bloody footprints and then, nodding to himself, entered the room. He was careful not to step on any of the spilled blood, but that care limited him, for the blood was everywhere. He moved slowly through the chamber, speaking in a low murmur as he assessed each item therein and offered commentary to construct a scenario.

"That Monsieur Thibodaux was an Orientalist is evident," said he. "Except for ordinary items of daily convenience— pens, ink bottles and suchlike—there is nothing here of local or common manufacture. It is likewise evident that Monsieur Thibodaux was an antiquarian of some note. These premises are not inexpensive, and his stationery and calling cards are of the very best quality. Likewise his clothes, what we can see of them. He was a man of expensive tastes and deep pockets." He did a complete circuit of the room, peering up and down, sometimes bending quite low to examine one of the countless artifacts on display. "It appears that the late Monsieur Thibodaux was more than a mere Orientalist, but rather a specialist within that field, for virtually everything here, with the exception of a few paintings, is of Japanese origin. This statue of sacred cranes is well known and is surely the work of H—, a noted sculptor from the city of Osaka. There are a number of *Tansu* chests of great value. And see these *Satsuma* vases, *Ko Imari* and *Kutani* covered bowls, *Oribe* tea bowls, *Usuki* stone Buddhas, as well as stone mirrors, jade combs, and many swords."

"But what of it?" demanded G. "Please, my friend, I did not bring you here to inventory the possessions of a murdered man, but to offer advice in the discovery of a murderer."

"The fact that some of these items are even here is surely at the heart of this gruesome matter," said Dupin. "See here, this tea-leaf jar with a design of wisteria? This is a treasure from the seventeenth century and it belongs in a museum. I would venture the same holds true of this fine *Akikusamon* bottle. This is authentic Heian Period, later twelfth century. I know for a fact that this is considered a national treasure of Japan. How then is it in the collection of a Parisian dealer of antiquities? The fact that the man who came to be in possession of these items could not under any circumstances legally own them is undoubtedly tied to the cause of his death."

"Then Thibodaux was naught but a common thief?" exclaimed G.

"Oh, I daresay he was much more than a common thief. More likely a trafficker in stolen items. A most elite fence, for these items are unparalleled in quality, and more to the point, they are treasures of historical and cultural significance. Wars have been waged over the possession of items such as these. Even now Japan is slowly being torn apart by cultural changes, with one faction wanting to move toward a more modern culture— with fractured and fuming Europe as its model; while the other desperately tries to hold onto the ancient values of the Samurai traditions. Look at these items, gentlemen, and you will see their delicacy and exotic beauty, but to the Japanese on both sides of the cultural rift these are emblematic of the spirit of the people."

"How came they here?" asked the Prefect.

Dupin picked up an ornate knife and studied the fine weaving of black silk thread around its handle. "Certainly it is not the traditional faction who would let such items leave Japan. No, gentlemen, this is part of an insidious plan by the modernists, the groups who want to see the old remnants of the Tokugawa Shogunate torn down and replaced by a more corporate and capitalist structure. To that end they have engaged many of the world's greatest thieves, as well as traitors from within the oldest families. Bribery and promises of power are the grease that allows the machinery of theft and exportation to work."

"But why? Bowls and urns and hair combs? Why steal trinkets and baubles?" I asked. "What possible political value could they possess?"

Dupin cocked an eyebrow. "Imagine, if you can, that a similar schism were taking place in, say, Great Britain. What if dissidents were spiriting away the Crown Jewels? And, closer to home, imagine that thieves were walking off with the splendors of Versailles, and doing so in a deliberate attempt to inflict a wound upon the heart of all that we hold dear as Frenchmen. That is the scope of this. That is what is at stake for the Japanese. The treasures of that nation are being looted and men like our dearly departed Monsieur Thibodaux are the parasites and Shylocks who both assist in these crimes and profit handsomely from them."

We looked around the room, seeing it afresh. I could very well now understand the vehemence of the attack. The degree of harm, and the apparently protracted length of the assault, spoke to a passion fed by love of country and horror at the rape of an ancient culture. I found now that I could look upon the corpse with less revulsion and more with a particular repugnance—and a total lack of sympathy.

"We are still no closer to solving the mystery of who committed this murder," said G. "I cannot ignore it because I may sympathize with the murderer's cause. That is for courts, domestic and likely foreign, to decide. And furthermore I am still at a loss for *how* the murder was committed. I daresay the killer took his weapon with him, but I cannot deduce what that weapon may have been."

"*Weapons*," corrected Dupin, making the word clearly plural, "for I perceive that a great many of them were used in the work that was done here."

"But which ones? I see swords aplenty, and even spears, but these are not the cuts and slashes of those weapons."

"No." Dupin's tight mouth wore a strange half-smile. "There is a certain poetry to this carnage."

"In God's name, how?" I demanded.

"Gentlemen," he said, holding wide his arms, "we are surrounded by the murder weapons. Can you not see them? They have been left behind for us to find—for anyone who had the eyes to see."

G. and I looked around, and though we saw blood glisten and drip from virtually every object and surface, there did not appear to be any particular weapon on display except those fashioned for that purpose, but they had inexplicably been eschewed by the killer.

"I cannot see it," confessed the Prefect. "I am all at sea."

"Then let logic bring you safely to shore," said Dupin. He pointed to a particularly deep gouge on Monsieur Thibodaux's scalp. "To identify an object used in a murder as creative as this we need to broaden our minds from thoughts of those things created to be weapons to those which were not, but can nevertheless be used to accomplish harm." He turned and picked up a fragile vase with one hand and then the painted wooden stand with the other. For all of the delicacy of the vase, the stand was a sturdy piece of work. Dupin held it up for our inspection and with our wondering and horrified eyes we could see a smear of blood in which floated a few fine hairs that were a match to the deceased's, and the corner of one leg was an equally perfect match to an indented scalp wound.

"He used a… vase stand?" gasped the Prefect.

"Oh yes. A vase stand is but a piece of wood after all, and wooden weapons have such a rich history, wouldn't you say?" While we continued to gape, Dupin pointed out several other objects, matching each to a specific wound or series of wounds. Decorative chopsticks made from bone had been used to create dreadful rough punctures, the steel ribs of a lady's court fan had been used to create dozens of shallow slashes, an ink-block had clearly been the cause of a broken nose and crushed brow. On and on it went, until Dupin had proved that we, indeed, stood within an arsenal of deadly weapons, though each appeared to be utterly fragile and lovely.

"If we suspected that the murderer was one of the modernist Japanese, then I would have expected to find bullet wounds or the marks of military knives. But no, the fact that commonplace objects—or rather those things never intended for such grim purposes—had been used, reinforces my supposition that the murderer is indeed devoted to the ancient Samurai houses of Japan. But not, I am certain, a Samurai himself."

"Please explain," said G., "so that I may begin composing a rough description for my men."

"The Samurai and their retainers are highly skilled in many fighting arts, not least the sword. But some of these sciences are more obscure, their nature and use coveted by the great families. One such art is called *hadaka-korosu*, and it translates roughly to 'the art of the naked kill.' The name refers not to a person being unclothed in combat, but a fighting art used when the Samurai has no sword. The Japanese, particularly the Samurai, are less mystical than the Chinese in that they endeavor to see things plainly for what they are. And so to them a piece of wood is a potential weapon, whether it has been fashioned into a club or made to support a delicate vase."

"Astounding," said I.

"Subtle," said he. "Look around and you can see how many of these things are surrogates for blades, for truncheons, for garroting wires, for weapons of combat, or—as clearly in this case—for weapons of torture, punishment, and execution." He looked down in disdain at the body. "Think about the care, the patience, and the risks taken by the killer, gentlemen. Even a retainer of a Samurai family would be skilled with every kind of knife. He could have made this quick and silent. Instead, he chose to use the stolen artifacts as the weapons of this man's destruction. This was a performance of murder, a symphony of slaughter, make no mistake. And... think of how poetic that is."

"*Poetic?*" I asked, aghast.

"Oh yes," said Dupin, "and in its poetry the killer is revealed. Remember the words the dying man cried aloud."

"You mean the name," said the Prefect, "Anna Gata."

"No, my dear friend, I do not, for I would doubt that Monsieur Thibodaux ever knew the name of the assassin sent to kill him. My guess is that he arranged a late meeting with what he thought would be a client, someone bringing a new and illegal piece to him that he could never receive during regular hours. The caller was almost certainly a woman."

G. snapped his fingers. "The old Oriental woman Legrand encountered. Surely it can't be she? These wounds are the work of a powerful hand."

Dupin nodded. "And yet Thibodeaux would never feel quite safe meeting a Japanese man after hours, not with the likelihood of a Samurai spy hunting for a broker such as he. No, Thibodeaux expected to meet with a woman, but her name was never 'Anna Gata.'"

"Then what?" I demanded.

"Thibodaux did not, with his last breath, name the killer, but cried out in surprise as he discovered the killer's secret. In the extremis of the situation, Thibodaux realized that it was, after all his precautions, a man who assailed him... but a man dressed as a woman. And therein is the answer to his outcry. Not 'Anna Gata,' gentlemen, but *onnagata*. A Japanese word from the world of Kabuki theater—which we have all seen upon the stage even here in Paris. Like Shakespeare of old, Kabuki does not allow women to perform, and instead young men are chosen to play the female roles, and the word for such a role is *onnagata*. Our killer revealed that he was a man, and quite a lethal one, during the act of murder, but by then Thibodaux was doomed."

The Prefect gaped at Dupin for a long moment, but he did not dare question my friend's veracity or try to poke holes in the chain of his logic. Dupin seldom speaks unless he is sure, even when other men witness the same evidence and are far less certain.

Then G. bellowed for Legrand and his other gendarmes and bade them hurry to the train station to arrest anyone they met there. An old woman, an old man, or even someone dressed like a Buddhist monk, for a Kabuki actor could adopt any of a thousand roles and play them with surpassing conviction.

Dupin hooked his arm in mine and we went down the stairs and out into the cold, foggy night.

"Your knowledge is in itself remarkable," I told him, "but it is in the way that you allow disparate facts from such vastly different closets of your mind to find their way together that continues to astound me."

"It is the result of a practice of logical thought," he said. "It is not a comfortable discipline, for it is very demanding and it can sour one to many aspects of ordinary social behavior. But... but... it has its advantages."

I removed my pocket watch and looked at the time. "Oh dear," I cried, "I doubt that the gendarmes will have time to intercept our suspect before she—or, I should say, *he*—boards the continental express."

Dupin merely shrugged.

I shot him a look. "Surely this distresses you? A criminal— one who you alone have found out—is likely to slip away."

He turned and looked at me with eyes that were as deep as wells and equally dark. "Are you, my friend, so inflexible in your views of justice that you view this man, this deadly actor, as nothing but a common criminal, one to be hunted, tried, jailed, and hanged?"

Before I could answer, he added, "Certainly the actor is an assassin, and surely he is operating on French soil without permission and in ways that contravene so many laws... but tell me and speak true from your heart—if you were he, would you consider yourself a criminal or an agent of justice? Has not the true criminal of this drama already been found, tried, and executed?"

I formed a dozen arguments against so radical a notion, but before I could barrage Dupin with any of them, he turned and began walking along the avenue. Within seconds the darkness and the fog had turned him into a specter and then he was gone entirely. I, on my part, was left standing there with his words ringing in my ears and no clear opinion painted on the walls of my heart.

THE GRUESOME AFFAIR OF THE ELECTRIC BLUE LIGHTNING

From the files of C. Auguste Dupin

By

JOE R. LANSDALE
(translated loosely from the French)

This story can only be described as fantastic in nature, and with no exaggeration, it deals with nothing less than the destruction of the world, but before I continue, I should make an immediate confession. Some of this is untrue. I do not mean the events themselves, for they are accurate, but I have disguised the names of several individuals, and certain locations have been re-imagined— for lack of a better word—to suit my own conscience. The end of the cosmos and our world as we know it is of considerable concern, of course, but no reason to abandon manners.

These decisions were primarily due to the possibility of certain actors in this drama being unnecessarily scandalized or embarrassed, even though they are only mentioned in passing and have little to nothing to do with the events themselves. I do not think historians, warehouse owners, and the like should have to bear the burden of my story, especially as it will undoubtedly be disbelieved.

There are, however, specific players in my article, story if you prefer, that have their own names to contend with, old as those names may be, and I have not made any effort whatsoever to alter these. This is owed to the fact that these particular personages are well enough recognized by name, and any attempt to disguise them would be a ridiculous and wasted effort.

This begins where many of my true stories begin. I was in the apartment I share with Auguste Dupin, perhaps the wisest and most rational man I have ever known, if a bit of a curmudgeon and a self-centered ass. A touch of background, should you be interested: we share an apartment, having met while looking for the same obscure book in a library, which brought about a discussion of the tome in question, which in turn we decided to share in the reading, along with the price of an apartment, as neither of us could afford the rental of one alone. Dupin is a Chevalier, and had some financial means in the past, but his wealth had somehow been lost—how this occurred, we have by unspoken agreement never discussed, and this suits me, for I would rather not go into great detail about my own circumstances.

In spite of his haughty nature, Dupin is quite obviously of gentlemanly countenance and bearing, if, like myself, he is a threadbare gentleman; I should also add, one who in manners is frequently not a gentleman at all. He is also a sometime investigator. This began merely as a hobby, something he did for his own amusement, until I assured him that regular employment might aid in his problems with the rent, and that I could assist him, for a small fee, of course. He agreed.

What I call "The Affair of the Electric Blue Lightning" began quite casually, and certainly by accident. I was telling Dupin how I had read that the intense lightning storm of the night before had been so radical, producing such powerful bolts, it had started fires all along the Rue —. In fact, the very newspaper that had recorded the article lay before him, and it wasn't until I had finished telling him about the irregular events that I saw it lying there and admonished him for not revealing to me he had read the article and knew my comments even before disclosing them for his consideration.

"Yes," Dupin said, leaning back in his chair and clasping his fingers together. "But I appreciate your telling of it. It was far more dramatic and interesting than the newspaper article itself. I was especially interested in, and impressed with, your descriptions of the lightning, for yours was a practical explanation, but not an actual recollection, and therefore perhaps faulty."

"Excuse me," I said.

His eyes brightened and his lean face seemed to stretch even longer as he said, "You described to me lightning that you did not see, and in so doing, you described it as it should appear, not as the newspaper depicted it. Or to be more precise, you only said that the fires had been started by a lightning strike. The newspaper said it was a blue-white fulmination that appeared to climb up to the sky from the rooftops of a portion of the warehouse district, rather than come down from the heavens. To be more precise, the newspaper was supposedly quoting a man named F—, who said he saw the peculiar lightning and the beginnings of the warehouse fire with his own eyes. He swore it rose upward, instead of the other way around. Out of the ordinary, don't you think?"

"A mistake on his part," I said. "I had forgotten all about his saying that. I didn't remember it that way."

"Perhaps," said Dupin, filling his meerschaum pipe and studying the rain outside the apartment window, "because it didn't make sense to you. It goes against common sense. So, you dismissed it."

"I suppose so," I said. "Isn't that what you do in your investigations? Dismiss items that are nonsensical? Use only what you know to be true? You are always admonishing me for filling in what is not there, what could not be, that which faults ratiocination."

Dupin nodded. "That's correct. But isn't that what you're doing now? You are filling in what is not there. Or deciding quite by your own contemplations that which should not be there."

"You confuse me, Dupin."

"No doubt," he said. "Unlike you, I do not dismiss something as false until I have considered it fully and examined all the evidence. There is also the part of the article where F—'s statement was validated by a child named P—."

"But, the word of a child?" I said.

"Sometimes they have the clearest eyes," Dupin said. "They have not had time to think what they *should* see, as you have, but only what they *have* seen. They can be mistaken. Eye witnesses often are, of course. But it's odd that the child validated the sighting of the other witness, and if what the article says is true, the man and child did not know one another. They were on very distant sides of the event. Due to this—and of course I would question their not knowing one another until I have made a full examination—perhaps more can be made of the child's recollections. I certainly believe we can rule out coincidence of such an observation. The child and the man either colluded on their story, which I find unlikely, because to what purpose would they say such an unbelievable thing? Or the other possibility is they did in fact see the same event, and their description is accurate, at least as far as they conceive it."

"That lightning rose up from the ground?" I said. "You say that makes more sense than it coming down from the heavens? I would think suggesting Jove threw a bolt of lightning would be just as irrational as to suggest the lightning rose up from the earth!"

"From a warehouse rooftop, not the earth," he said. "And it was blue-white in color?"

"Ridiculous," I said.

"It is peculiar, I admit, but my suggestion is we do not make a judgment on the matter until we know more facts."

"I didn't realize we cared to make a judgment."

"I am considering it."

"This interests you that much? Why would we bother? It's not a true investigation, just the soothing of a curiosity, which I might add, pays absolutely nothing."

"What interests me are the deaths from the warehouse fire," Dupin said. "Though, since, as you noted, we haven't been hired to examine the facts, that pays the same absence of price."

"Horrid business," I said. "But I believe you are making much of nothing. I know that area, and those buildings are rats' nests just waiting for a spark to ignite them. They are also the squatting grounds for vagrants. Lightning struck the building. It caught ablaze rapidly, and sleeping vagrants were burned to death in the fire. It is as simple as that."

"Perhaps," Dupin said. He leaned back and puffed on his pipe, blowing blue clouds of smoke from between his teeth and from the bowl. "But how do you explain that our own acquaintance the Police Prefect, G—, was quoted as saying that they found a singed, but still identifiable arm, and that it appeared to have been sawed off at the elbow, rather than burned?"

I had no answer for that.

"Of course, G— is often wrong, so in his case I might suspect an error before suspecting one from the witnessing child. G— solves most of his crimes by accident, confession, or by beating his suspect until he will admit to having started the French Revolution over the theft of a ham hock. However, when he has solved his cases, if indeed one can actually consider them solved, it is seldom by any true form of detection. I should also note that there has been a rash of grave robbings of late, all of them involving freshly buried bodies."

Now, as he often did, Dupin had piqued my curiosity. I arose, poured the both of us a bit of wine, sat back down and watched Dupin smoke his pipe, the stench of which was cheap and foul as if burning the twilled ticking of an old sweat-stained mattress.

"For me to have an opinion on this matter, I would suggest we make a trip of it tomorrow, to see where this all occurred. Interview those that were spoken to by the newspaper. I know you have contacts, so I would like you to use them to determine the exact location of these witnesses who observed the lightning and the resulting fire. Does this suit you?"

I nodded. "Very well, then."

That was the end of our discussion about these unique, but to my mind insignificant events, for the time being. We instead turned our attention to the smoking of pipes and the drinking of wine. Dupin read while he smoked and drank, and I sat there contemplating that which we had discussed, finding the whole matter more and more mysterious with the thinking. Later, I decided I would like to take a stroll before retiring, so that I might clear my head of the drinking and heavy smoke.

I also had in mind the ideas that Dupin had suggested, and wanted to digest them. I have always found a walk to be satisfying not only to the legs and heart, but to the mind as well; many a problem such as this one I had considered while walking, and though, after talking to Dupin, I still turned out to be mistaken in my thinking, I had at least eliminated a large number of my fallacies of thought before speaking to him.

Outside the apartment, I found the rain had ceased; the wind had picked up, however, and was quite cool, almost chilly. I pulled my collar up against the breeze and, swinging my cane before me, headed in the direction of the lightning fire in the warehouse district along the Rue —. I didn't realize I was going there until my legs began to take me. I knew the location well, and no research was required to locate the site of the events, so I thought that for once, having seen the ruins, I might actually have a leg up on Dupin, and what he called his investigative methods of ratiocination.

I will not name the exact place, due to this area having recently been renovated, and keep in mind these events took place some years back, so there is no need to besmirch the name of the new owners. But for then, it was an area not considered a wisely traveled pathway by night. It was well known for unsavory characters and poor lighting. That being the case, I was fully aware it was not the best of ideas to be about my business in this vicinity, but what Dupin had said to me was gnawing at my thoughts like a terrier at a rug. I felt reasonably confident that my cane would defend me, as I am—if I say so myself—like Dupin, quite skilled in the art of the cane, and if I should be set upon by more than one ruffian, it contained a fine sword that could help trim my attacker's numbers.

I came to where the warehouse section lay, and found the burned buildings instantly, not far from a large allotment of land where other warehouses were still maintained. I stood for a moment in front of the burned section, going over it with eyes and mind. What remained were blackened shells and teetering lumber; the rain had stirred the charred shambles and the stench of it filled and itched my nostrils.

I walked along the pathway in front of it, and tried to imagine where the fire had started, determining that the areas where the structures of the buildings were most ruined might be the source. I could imagine that the fire jumped from those ruined remains to the other buildings, which though burned beyond use, were still more structurally sound, suggesting that the fire had raged hottest before it reached them.

I was contemplating all of this, when from the ruins I heard a noise, and saw a shape rise up from the earth clothed in hat and overcoat. It was some distance away from me, and even as it rose, it paused for a moment, looking down in the manner of a man who has dropped pocket change.

I can't explain exactly why I thought I should engage, but I immediately set off in that direction, and called out to it. As I neared, the shape looked up, seeing me. I took note of the fact that it carried something, clutched tightly to it, and that this undefined individual was in a kind of panic; it began to run. I wondered then if it might be a thief, looking for some surviving relic that could be swapped or sold, and part of its loot had been dropped when it came up from wherever it had been lurking, and before it could be found, I had startled the prowler.

I took it upon myself to call out again, and when I did, the shape ceased to run, turned, and looked at me. I was overcome with fear and awe, for I was certain, even though the being stood back in the shadows, wore an overcoat, and had the brim of a hat pulled down tight over its face, that staring back at me was some kind of hairy upright ape clutching a bagged burden to its breast.

Unconsciously, I lifted the shaft of my walking stick and revealed an inch of the hidden sword. The beast—for I can think of it no other way—turned, and once more proceeded to run, its hat blowing off as it went. In a flash, it disappeared behind one of the standing warehouses. I remained where I was for a moment, rooted to the spot, and then, overcome with curiosity, I pursued it, running through the burnt lumber, on out into the clearing that led to the street where I had seen the beast standing. As I turned the corner, I found it waiting for me. It had dropped the bag at its feet, and was lifting up a large garbage container that was dripping refuse. I was granted a glimpse of its teeth and fiery eyes just before it threw the receptacle at me. I was able to duck, just in time, and as the container clattered along the cobblestones behind me, the thing grabbed up its bag, broke and ran toward a warehouse wall. I knew then I had it trapped, but considering that what it had thrown at me was heavier than anything I could lift, perhaps it would be I who was trapped. These thoughts were there, but my forward motion and determination succeeded in trampling my common sense.

As I came near it again, my previous astonishment was nothing compared to what I witnessed now. The creature divested itself of the overcoat, slung the bag over its shoulder, and with one hand grasped a drain-pipe and using its feet to assist, began to climb effortlessly upward until it reached the summit of the warehouse. I watched in bewilderment as it moved across the rain-misted night-line, then raced out of sight down the opposite side of the warehouse wall, or so I suspected when it was no longer visible.

I darted down an alley, splashing in puddles as I went, and came to the edge of the warehouse where I was certain the ape-man had descended. Before me was a narrow, wet street, the R—, but the ape-man was not in sight.

I leaned against the wall of the warehouse, for at this point in time I needed support, the reality of what I had just witnessed finally sinking into my bones. I momentarily tried to convince myself that I had been suffering the effects of the wine Dupin and I had drunk, but knew this was wishful thinking. I drew the sword from the cane, and strolled down the R— in search of the ape, but saw nothing, and frankly, was glad of it, having finally had time to consider how close I may have come to disaster.

Replacing the sword in its housing, I walked back to the ruins of the warehouse. Using my cane to move burnt lumber about, throwing up a light cloud of damp ash, I examined the spot where I had seen the thing pulling something from the rubble; that's when I found the arm, severed at the elbow, lying on top of the ash. It had no doubt been dropped there after the fire, for it appeared un-charred, not even smoke-damaged. I knelt down and struck a Lucifer against the tip of the cane, then held it close. It was a small arm with a delicate hand. I looked about and saw that nearby were a series of steps that dipped beneath ground level. It seemed obvious this was where the creature had originated when it appeared to rise out of the very earth. It also seemed obvious this opening had been covered by the collapse of the warehouse, and that the creature had uncovered it and retrieved something from below and tucked it away in the large bag it was carrying. The obvious thing appeared to be body parts, for if he had dropped one, then perhaps others existed and were tucked away in its bag. I lit another Lucifer, went down the narrow steps into the basement, waved my flickering light so that it threw small shadows about. The area below was larger than I would have expected. It was filled with tables and crates, and what I determined to be laboratory equipment—test tubes, beakers, burners, and the like. I had to light several matches to complete my examination—though complete is a loose word, considering I could only see by the small fluttering of a meager flame.

I came upon an open metal container, about the size of a coffin, and was startled as I dipped the match into its shadowy interior. I found two human heads contained within, as well as an assortment of amputated legs, arms, feet, and hands, all of them submerged in water.

I jerked back with such revulsion that the match went out. I scrambled about for another, only to discover I had used my entire store. Using what little moonlight was tumbling down the basement stairs as my guide, and almost in a panic, I ran up them and practically leapt into the open. There was more moonlight now than before. The rain had passed and the clouds had sailed; it was a mild relief.

Fearing the ape, or whatever it was, might return, and considering what I had found below, I hurried away from there.

I should have gone straight to the police, but having had dealings with the Police Prefect, G—, I was less than enthusiastic about the matter. Neither Dupin nor myself were well liked in the halls of the law for the simple reason that Dupin had solved a number of cases the police had been unable to, thereby making them look foolish. It was they who came to us in time of need, not us to them. I hastened my steps back to the apartment, only to be confronted by yet another oddity. The moon was turning to blood. Or so it appeared, for a strange crimson cloud, the likes of which I had never before seen, or even heard of, was enveloping the moon, as if it were a vanilla biscuit tucked away in a bloody-red sack. The sight of it caused me deep discomfort.

It was late when I arrived at our lodgings. Dupin was sitting by candlelight, still reading. He had a stack of books next to him on the table, and when I came in he lifted his eyes as I lit the gas lamp by the doorway to further illuminate the apartment. I was nearly breathless, and when I turned to expound on my adventures, Dupin said, "I see you have been to the site of the warehouses, an obvious deduction by the fact that your pants and boots are dusted heavily in ash and soot and are damp from the rain. I see too that you have discovered body parts in the wreckage. I will also conjecture we can ignore having a discussion with the lightning witnesses, for you have made some progress on your own."

My mouth fell open. "How could you know that I discovered body parts?"

"Logic. The newspaper account spoke of such a thing, and you come rushing in the door, obviously excited, even a little frightened. So if a severed arm was found there the other day, it stands to reason that you too discovered something of that nature. That is a bit of speculation, I admit, but it seems a fair analysis."

I sat down in a chair. "It is accurate, but I have seen one thing that you can not begin to decipher, and it is more fantastic than even severed body parts."

"An ape that ran upright?"

"*Impossible!*" I exclaimed. "You could not possibly know."

"But I did." Dupin paused a moment, lit his pipe. He seemed only mildly curious. "Continue."

It took me a moment to collect myself, but finally I began to reveal my adventures.

"It was carrying a package of some kind. I believe it contained body parts because I found an arm lying in the burned wreckage, as you surmised. Something I believe the ape dropped."

"Male or female?" Dupin said.

"What?"

"The arm, male or female?"

I thought for a moment.

"I suppose it was female. I didn't give it considerable evaluation, dark as it was, surprised as I was. But I would venture to guess—and a guess is all I am attempting—that it was female."

"That is interesting," Dupin said. "And the ape?"

"You mean was the ape male or female?"

"Exactly," Dupin said.

"What difference does it make?"

"Perhaps none. Was it clothed?"

"A hat and overcoat. Both of which it abandoned."

"In that case, could you determine its sex?" Dupin asked.

"I suppose since no external male equipment was visible, it was most probably female."

"And it saw you?"

"Yes. It ran from me. I pursued. It climbed to the top of a warehouse with its bag, did so effortlessly, and disappeared on the other side of the building. Prior to that, it tried to hit me with a trash receptacle. A large and heavy one it lifted as easily as you lift your pipe."

"Obviously it failed in this endeavor," Dupin commented.

"How long did it take you to get to the other side of the ware-house, as I am presuming you made careful examination there as well?"

"Hasty would be a better word. By then I had become concerned for my own safety. I suppose it took the creature less than five minutes to go over the roof."

"Did you arrive there quickly? The opposite side of the building, I mean?"

"Yes. You could say that."

"And the ape was no longer visible?"

"Correct."

"That is quite rapid, even for an animal, don't you think?"

"Indeed," I said, having caught the intent of Dupin's question. "Which implies it did not necessarily run away, or even descend to the other side. I merely presumed."

"Now, you see the error of your thinking."

"But you've made presumptions tonight," I said.

"Perhaps, but more reasonable presumptions than yours, I am certain. It is my impression that your simian is still in the vicinity, and did not scale the warehouse merely to climb down the other side and run down the street, when it could just as easily have taken the alley you used. And if the creature did climb down the other side, I believe it concealed itself. You might have walked right by it."

That gave me a shiver. "I admit that is logical, but I also admit that I didn't walk all that far for fear that it might be lurking about."

"That seems fair enough," Dupin said.

"There is something else," I said, and I told him about the basement and the body parts floating in water. I mentioned the red cloud that lay thick against the moon.

When I finished, he nodded, as if my presentation was the most normal event in the world. Thunder crashed then, lightning ripped across the sky, and rain began to hammer the street; a rain far more vigorous than earlier in the evening. For all his calm, when Dupin spoke, I thought I detected the faintest hint of concern.

"You say the moon was red?"

"A red cloud was over it. I have never seen such a thing before. At first I thought it a trick of the eye."

"It is not," Dupin said. "I should tell you about something I have researched while you were out chasing ape-women and observing the odd redness of the night's full moon—an event that suggests things are far more desperate than I first suspected."

I had seated myself by this time, had taken up my own pipe, and with nervous hand, found matches to light it.

Dupin broke open one of the books near the candle. "I thought I had read of that kind of electric blue lightning before, and the severed limbs also struck a cord of remembrance, as did the ape—which is why I was able to determine what you had seen—and that gives even further credence to my suspicions. Johann Conrad Dippel."

"Who?"

"Dippel. He was born in Germany in the late sixteen hundreds. He was a philosopher and something of a theologian. He was also considered a heretic, as his views on religion were certainly outside the lines of normal society."

"The same might be said of us," I remarked.

Dupin nodded. "True. But Dippel was thought to be an alchemist and a dabbler in the dark arts. He was in actuality a man of science. He was also an expert on all manner of ancient documents. He is known today for the creation of Dippel's Oil, which is used in producing a dye we know as Prussian blue, but he also claimed to have invented an elixir of life. He lived for a time in Germany at a place known as Castle Frankenstein. This is where many of his experiments were performed, including one that led to such a tremendous explosion it destroyed a tower of the castle, and led to a breaking of his lease. It was said by those who witnessed the explosion that a kind of lightning, a blue-white lightning, lifted up from the stones to the sky, followed by a burst of flame and an explosion that tore the turret apart and rained stones down on the countryside."

"So that is why you were so interested in the lightning, the story about it rising up from the warehouse instead of falling out of the sky?"

Dupin nodded, relit his pipe and continued. "It was rumored that he was attempting to transfer the souls of the living into freshly exhumed corpses. Exhumed clandestinely, by the way. He was said to use a funnel by which the souls of the living could be channeled into the bodies of the dead."

"Ridiculous," I said.

"Perhaps," Dupin replied. "It was also said his experiments caused the emergence of a blue-white lightning that he claimed to have pulled from a kind of borderland, and that he was able to open a path to this netherworld by means of certain mathematical formulas gleaned from what he called a renowned, rare, and accursed book. For this he was branded a devil worshiper, an interloper with demonic forces."

"Dupin," I said. "You have always ridiculed the supernatural."

"I did not say it was supernatural. I said he was a scientist that was branded as a demonologist. What intrigues me is his treatise titled *Maladies and Remedies of the Life of the Flesh*, as well as the mention of even rarer books and documents within it.

One that was of special interest was called the *Necronomicon*, a book that was thought by many to be mythical."

"You have seen such a book?"

"I discovered it in the Paris library some years ago. It was pointed out to me by the historian M—. No one at the library was aware of its significance, not even M—. He knew only of its name and that it held some historical importance. He thought it may have something to do with witchcraft, which it does not. I was surprised to find it there. I considered it to be more than a little intriguing. It led me to further investigations into Dippel as not only the owner of such a book, but as a vivisectionist and a resurrectionist. He claimed to have discovered a formula that would allow him to live for 135 years, and later amended this to eternal life."

"Drivel," I said. "I am surprised you would concern yourself with such."

"It was his scientific method and deep understanding of mathematics that interested me. My dear friend, much of what has become acceptable science was first ridiculed as heresy. I need not point out to you the long list of scientists opposed by the Catholic Church and labeled heretics. The points of interest concerning Dippel have to do with what I have already told you about the similarity of the blue-white lightning, and the interesting connection with the found body parts, the ape, and the curious event of the blood-stained moon, which I will come back to shortly. Firstly, however, was Dippel's mention of the rare book. The *Necronomicon*, written by Abdul Alhazred in 950 AD, partially in math equations and partly in verse. He was sometimes referred to as 'The Mad Arab' by his detractors, though he was also given the moniker of 'Arab Poet of Yemen' by those less vicious. Of course, knowing my penchant for poetry, you might readily surmise that this is what first drew my attention to him. The other aspect of his personality, as mathematician and conjuror, was merely, at that time, of side interest, although I must say that later in life he certainly did go mad. He claimed to have discovered mathematical equations that could be used to open our world into another where powerful forces and beings existed. Not gods or demons, mind you, but different and true life forms that he called 'The Old Ones.' It was in this book that Dippel believed he found the key to eternal life."

"What became of Dippel?"

"He died," Dupin said, and smiled.

"So much for eternal life."

"Perhaps."

"Perhaps? You clearly said he died."

"His body died, but his assistant, who was imprisoned for a time, said his soul was passed on to another form. According to what little documentation there is on the matter, Dippel's experiments were concerned with removing a person's soul from a living form and transferring it to a corpse. It was successful, if his assistant, Hans Grimm, can be believed. Grimm was a relative of Jacob Grimm, the future creator of *Grimm's Fairy Tales*. But of more immediate interest to us is something he reported, that a young lady Dippel was charmed by, and who he thought would be his companion, took a fall from a horse and was paralyzed. Grimm claimed they successfully transferred her soul from her ruined body into the corpse of a recently dead young lady, which had been procured by what one might call midnight gardening. She was 'animated with life,' as Grimm described her, 'but was always of some strangeness.' That is a direct quote."

"Dupin, surely you don't take this nonsense seriously."

He didn't seem to hear me. "She was disgusted with her new form and was quoted by Grimm as saying 'she felt as if she was inside a house with empty rooms.' She leaped to her death from Castle Frankenstein. Lost to him, Dippel decided to concentrate on a greater love—himself. Being short of human volunteers who wanted to evacuate their soul and allow a visitor to inhabit their living form, he turned to animals for experimentation. The most important experiment was the night he died, or so says Grimm."

"The ancestor of the creator of *Grimm's Fairy Tales* seems an unlikely person to trust on matters of this sort."

"That could be. But during this time Dippel was having exotic animals shipped to him in Germany, and among these was a creature called a Chimpanzee. Knowing himself sickly, and soon to die, he put his experiments to the ultimate test. He had his assistant, Grimm, by use of the formula and his funnel, transfer his soul from his disintegrating shell into the animal, which in turn eliminated the soul of the creature; the ape's body became the house of his soul. I should add that I have some doubts about the existence of a soul, so perhaps essence would be a more appropriate word. That said, soul has a nice sound to it, I think. The experiment, according to Grimm, resulted in an abundance of blue-white lightning that caused the explosion and left Grimm injured. In fact, later Grimm disappeared from the hospital where he was being held under observation and arrest for alchemy. He was in a room with padded walls and a barred window. The bars were ripped out. It was determined the bars were pulled loose from the outside. Another curious matter was that the room in which he was contained was three floors up, a considerable drop. How did he get down without being injured? No rope or ladder was found. It was as if he had been carried away by something unknown."

"Come, Dupin, you cannot be serious? Are you suggesting this ape pulled out the bars and carried him down the side of the wall?"

"There are certainly more than a few points of similarity between the story of Dippel and the events of tonight, don't you think? Consider your description of how effortlessly the ape climbed the warehouse wall."

"But, if this is Dippel, and he is in Paris, my question is how? And his ape body would be old. Very old."

"If he managed eternal life by soul transference, then perhaps the ape body does not age as quickly as would be normal."

"If this were true, and I'm not saying I believe it, how would he go about his life? An ape certainly could not ride the train or stroll the street without being noticed."

"I am of the opinion that Grimm is still with him."

"But he would be very old as well."

"Considerably," Dupin agreed. "I believe that the body parts you saw are for Grimm. It is my theory that Grimm received a wound that put him near death when Castle Frankenstein blew up. Dippel saved him by transferring his soul to a corpse. Unlike Dippel's lady love, he managed to accept the transfer and survived."

"So why did Dippel go after the body parts himself? Wouldn't he have Grimm procure such things? It would be easier for the one with a human body to move about without drawing so much attention."

"It would. My take is that the human soul when transferred to the soul of a corpse has one considerable drawback. The body rots. The ape body was a living body. It does not; it may age, but not in the way it would otherwise, due to this transformation. Grimm's body, on the other hand, has to be repaired from time to time with fresh parts. It may be that he was further damaged by the more recent explosion. Which indicates to me that they have not acquired the healthy ability to learn from their mistakes."

"After all this time, wouldn't Dippel have transferred Grimm's essence, or his own, into a living human being? Why would he maintain the body of an ape? And a female ape at that?"

"My thought on the matter is that Dippel may find the powerful body of an ape to his advantage. And to keep Grimm bent to his will, to maintain him as a servant, he only repairs him when he wears out a part, so to speak. Be it male or female parts, it is a matter of availability. If Grimm's soul were transferred into a living creature, and he could live for eternity, as male or female, then he might be willing to abandon Dippel. This way, with the ape's strength, and Dippel's knowledge of how to repair a corpse, and perhaps the constant promise of eventually giving Grimm a living human body, he keeps him at his side. Grimm knows full well if he leaves Dippel he will eventually rot. I think this is the Sword of Damocles that he holds over Grimm's head."

"That is outrageous," I said. "And wicked."

"Absolutely, but that does not make it untrue."

I felt cold. My pipe had died, as I had forgotten to smoke it. I relit it. "It's just too extraordinary," I said.

"Yet the *Necronomicon* suggests it is possible." With that, Dupin dug into the pile of books and produced a large volume, thrusting it into my hands. Looking at it, I saw that it was covered in leather, and that in the dead center was an eye-slit. I knew immediately what I was looking at was the tanned skin of a human face. Worse, holding the book I felt nauseous. It was as if its very substance was made of bile. I managed to open the book. There was writing in Arabic, as well as a number of mathematical formulas; the words and numbers appeared to crawl. I slammed the book shut again. "Take it back," I said, and practically tossed it at him.

"I see you are bewildered, old friend," Dupin said, "but do keep in mind, as amazing as this sounds, it's science we are talking about, not the supernatural."

"It's a revolting book," I said.

"When I first found it in the library, I could only look at it for short periods of time. I had to become accustomed to it, like becoming acclimated to sailing at sea, and no longer suffering sea sickness. I am ashamed to admit, that after a short time I stole the book. I felt somehow justified in doing this, it being rarely touched by anyone—for good reason, as you have experienced— and in one way I thought I might be doing the world a justice, hiding it away from the wrong eyes and hands. That was several years ago. I have studied Arabic, read the volume repeatedly, and already being reasonably versed in mathematics, rapidly began to understand the intent of it. Though, until reading the newspaper account, I had been skeptical. And then there is Dippel's history, the words of his companion, Grimm. I believe there is logic behind these calculations and ruminations, even if at first they seem to defy human comprehension. The reason for this is simple; it is not the logic of humans, but that of powerful beings who exist in the borderland. I have come to uncomfortably understand some of that logic, as much as is humanly possible to grasp. To carry this even farther, I say that

Dippel is no longer himself, in not only body, but in thought. His constant tampering with the powers of the borderland have given the beings on the other side an entry into his mind, and they are learning to control him, to assist him in his desires, until their own plans come to fruition. It has taken time, but soon, he will not only be able to replace body parts, he will be capable of opening the gate to this borderland. We are fortunate he has not managed it already. These monsters are powerful, as powerful as any god man can create, and malicious without measure. When the situation is right, when Dippel's mind completely succumbs to theirs, and he is willing to use the formulas and spells to clear the path for their entry, they will cross over and claim this world. That will be the end of humankind, my friend. And let me tell you the thing I have been holding back. The redness of the moon is an indication that there is a rip in the fabric of that which protects us from these horrid things lying in wait. Having wasted their world to nothing, they lust after ours, and Dippel is opening the gate so they might enter."

"But how would Dippel profit from that? Allowing such things into our world?"

"Perhaps he has been made promises of power, whispers in his head that make him outrageous offers. Perhaps he is little more than a tool by now. All that matters, good friend, is that we can not allow him to continue his work."

"If the red cloud over the moon is a sign, how much time do we have?"

"Let me put it this way: We will not wait until morning, and we will not need to question either the boy or the man who saw the lightning. By that time, I believe it will be too late."

* * *

There was a part of me that wondered if Dupin's studies had affected his mind. It wasn't an idea that held, however. I had seen what I had seen, and what Dupin had told me seemed to validate it. We immediately set out on our escapade, Dupin carrying a small bag slung over one shoulder by a strap.

The rain had blown itself out and the streets were washed clean. The air smelled as fresh as the first breath of life. We went along the streets briskly, swinging our canes, pausing only to look up at the moon. The red cloud was no longer visible, but there was still a scarlet tint to the moon that seemed unnatural. Sight of that gave even more spring to my step. When we arrived at our destination, there was no one about, and the ashes had been settled by the rain.

"Keep yourself alert," Dupin said, "in case our simian friend has returned and is in the basement collecting body parts."

We crossed the wet soot, stood at the mouth of the basement, and after a glance around to verify no one was in sight, we descended.

Red-tinged moonlight slipped down the stairs and brightened the basement. Everything was as it had been. Dupin looked about, used his cane to tap gently at a few of the empty beakers and tubes. He then made his way to the container where I had seen the amputated limbs and decapitated heads. They were still inside, more than a bit of rainwater having flooded in, and there was a ripe stench of decaying flesh.

"These would no longer be of use to Dippel," Dupin said. "So we need not worry about him coming back for them."

I showed him where I had last seen the ape, then we walked to the other side. Dupin looked up and down the wall of the warehouse. We walked along its length. Nothing was found.

"Perhaps we should find a way to climb to the top," I said.

Dupin was staring at a puff of steam rising from the street. "No, I don't think so," he said.

He hastened to where the steam was thickest. It was rising up from a grate. He used his cane to pry at it, and I used mine to assist him. We lifted it and looked down at the dark, mist-coated water of the sewer rushing below. The stench was, to put it mildly, outstanding.

"This would make sense," Dupin said. "You were correct, he did indeed climb down on this side, but he disappeared quickly because he had an underground path."

"We're going down there?" I asked.

"You do wish to save the world and our cosmos, do you not?"

"When you put it that way, I suppose we must," I said. I was trying to add a joking atmosphere to the events, but it came out as serious as a diagnosis of leprosy.

We descended into the dark, resting our feet upon the brick ledge of the sewer. There was light from above to assist us, but if we were to move forward, we would be walking along the slick brick runway into utter darkness. Or so I thought.

It was then that Dupin produced twists of paper, heavily oiled and waxed, from the pack he was carrying. As he removed them, I saw the *Necronomicon* was in the bag as well. It lay next to two dueling pistols. I had been frightened before, but somehow, seeing that dreadful book and those weapons, I was almost overwhelmed with terror, a sensation I would experience more than once that night. It was all I could do to take one of the twists and wait for Dupin to light it, for my mind was telling me to climb out of that dank hole and run. But if Dippel succeeded in letting the beings from the borderland through, run to where?

"Here," Dupin said, holding the flaming twist close to the

damp brick wall. "It went this way."

I looked. A few coarse hairs were caught in the bricks.

With that as our guide, we proceeded. Even with the lit twists of wax and oil, the light was dim and there was a steam, or mist, rising from the sewer. We had to proceed slowly and carefully. The sewer rumbled along near us, heightened to near flood level by the tremendous rain. It was ever to our right, threatening to wash up over the walk. There were drips from the brick walls and the overhead streets. Each time a cold drop fell down my collar I started as if icy fingertips had touched my neck.

We had gone a good distance when Dupin said, "Look. Ahead."

There was a pumpkin-colored glow from around a bend in the sewer, and we immediately tossed our twists into the water. Dupin produced the pistols from his bag and passed me one.

"I presume they are powder charged and loaded," I said.

"Of course," Dupin replied. "Did you think I might want to beat an ape to death with the grips?"

Thus armed, we continued onward toward the light.

There was a widening of the sewer, and there was in fact a great space made of brick that I presumed might be for workmen, or might even have been a forgotten portion of the sewer that had once been part of the upper streets of Paris. There were several lamps placed here and there, some hung on nails driven into the brick, others placed on the flooring, some on rickety tables and chairs. It was a makeshift laboratory, and had most likely been thrown together from the ruins of the warehouse explosion.

On a tilted board a nude woman... or man, or a little of both, was strapped. Its head was male, but the rest of its body was female, except for the feet, which were absurdly masculine. This body breathed in a labored manner, its head was thrown back, and a funnel was stuck down its throat. A hose rose out of the funnel and stretched to another makeshift platform nearby. There was a thin insect-like antenna attached to the middle of the hose, and it wiggled erratically at the air.

The other platform held a cadaverously thin and nude human with a head that looked shriveled, the hair appearing as if it were a handful of strings fastened there with paste. The arms and legs showed heavy scarring, and it was obvious that much sewing had been done to secure the limbs, much like the hurried repair of an old rag doll. The lifeless head was tilted back, and the opposite end of the hose was shoved into another wooden funnel that was jammed into the corpse's mouth. One arm of the cadaver was short, the other long, while the legs varied in thickness. The lower half of the face was totally incongruous with the upper half. The features were sharp-boned and stood up beneath the flesh like rough furniture under a sheet. They were masculine, while the forehead and hairline, ragged as it was, had obviously been that of a woman, one recently dead and elderly was my conjecture.

The center of the corpse was blocked by the body of the ape, which was sewing hastily with a large needle and dark thread, fastening on an ankle and foot in the way you might lace up a shoe. It was so absurd, so grotesque, it was almost comic, like a grisly play at *Le Théâtre du Grand-Guignol*. One thing was clear, the corpse being sewn together was soon to house the life force of the other living but obviously ill body. It had been cobbled together in the past in much the same way that the other was now being prepared.

Dupin pushed me gently into a darkened corner protected by a partial brick wall. We spoke in whispers.

"What are we waiting for?" I said.

"The borderland to be opened."

Of course I knew to what he referred, but it seemed to me that waiting for it to be opened, if indeed that was to happen, was the height of folly. But it was Dupin, and now, arriving here, seeing what I was seeing, it all fit securely with the theory he had expounded; I decided to continue believing he knew of what he spoke. Dupin withdrew the *Necronomicon* from the bag and propped it against the wall.

"When I tell you," he said, "light up a twist and hold it so that I might read."

"From that loathsome book?" I gasped.

"It has the power to do evil, but also to restrain it."

I nodded, took one of the twists from the bag and a few matches, and tucked them into my coat pocket. It was then I heard the chanting, and peeked carefully around the barrier.

The ape, or Dippel I suppose, held a copy of a book that looked to be a twin of the one Dupin held. It was open and propped on a makeshift pedestal of two stacked chairs. Dippel was reading from it by dim lamplight. It was disconcerting to hear those chants coming from the mouth of an ape, sounding human-like, yet touched with the vocalizations of an animal. Though it spoke the words quickly and carefully, it was clear to me that Dippel was more than casually familiar with them.

That was when the air above the quivering antenna opened in a swirl of light and dark floundering shapes. I can think of no other way to describe it. The opening widened. Tentacles whipped in and out of the gap. Blue-white lightning flashed from it and nearly struck the ape, but still he read. The corpse on the platform began to writhe and wiggle and the blue-white lightning leaped from the swirling mass and struck the corpse repeatedly and vibrated the antenna. The dead body glowed and heaved and tugged at its bonds, and then I saw its eyes flash wide. Across the way, the formerly living body had grown limp and gray as ash.

I looked at Dupin, who had come to my shoulder to observe what was happening.

"He is not bringing him back, as in the past," Dupin said. "He is offering Grimm's soul for sacrifice. After all this time, their partnership has ended. It is the beginning; the door has been opened a crack."

My body felt chilled. The hair on my head, as on Dupin's, stood up due to the electrical charge in the air. There was an obnoxious smell, reminiscent of the stink of decaying fish, rotting garbage, and foul disease.

"Yes, we have chosen the right moment," Dupin said, looking at the growing gap that had appeared in mid-air. "Take both pistols, and light the twist."

He handed me his weapon. I stuck both pistols in the waistband of my trousers, and lit the twist. Dupin took it from me, and stuck it in a gap in the bricks. He opened the *Necronomicon* to where he had marked it with a torn piece of paper, and began to read from it. The words poured from his mouth like living beings, taking on the form of dark shadows and lightning-bright color. His voice was loud and sonorous, as we were no longer attempting to conceal ourselves. I stepped out of the shadows and into the open. Dippel, alerted by Dupin's reading, turned and glared at me with its dark, simian eyes.

It was hard for me to concentrate on anything. Hearing the words from the *Necronomicon* made my skin feel as if it were crawling up from my heels, across my legs and back, and slithering underneath my scalp. The swirling gap of blue-white lightning revealed lashing tentacles, a massive squid-like eye, then a beak. It was all I could do not to fall to my knees in dread, or bolt and run like an asylum escapee.

That said, I was given courage when I realized that whatever Dupin was doing was having some effect, for the gash in the air began to shimmer and wrinkle and blink like an eye. The ape howled at this development, for it had glanced back at the rip in the air, then turned again to look at me, twisting its face into what could almost pass as a dark knot. It dropped the book on the chair, and rushed for me. First it was upright, like a human, then it was on all fours, its knuckles pounding against the bricks. I drew my sword from the cane, held the cane itself in my left hand, the blade in my right, and awaited Dippel's dynamic charge.

It bounded toward me. I thrust at it with my sword. The strike was good, hitting no bone, and went directly through the ape's chest, but the beast's momentum drove me backward. I lost the cane itself, and used both hands to hold the sword in place. I glanced at Dupin for help. None was forthcoming. He was reading from the book and utterly ignoring my plight.

Blue, white, red, and green fire danced around Dippel's head and poured from its mouth. I was able to hold the monster back with the sword, for it was a good thrust, and had brought about a horrible wound, yet its long arms thrashed out and hit my jaw, nearly knocking me senseless. I struggled to maintain consciousness, pushed back the sword with both hands, coiled my legs, and kicked out at the ape. I managed to knock it off me, but only for a moment.

I sat up and drew both pistols. It was loping toward me, pounding its fists against the bricks as it barreled along on all fours, letting forth an indescribable and ear-shattering sound that was neither human nor animal. I let loose an involuntary yell, and fired both pistols. The shots rang out as one. The ape threw up its hands, wheeled about and staggered back toward the stacked chairs, the book. It grabbed at the book for support, pulled that and the chairs down on top of it. Its chest heaved as though pumped with a bellows.

And then the freshly animated thing on the platform spat out the funnel as if it were light as air. Spat it out and yelled. It was a sound that came all the way from the primeval; a savage cry of creation. The body on the platform squirmed and writhed and snapped its bonds. It slid from the board, staggered forward, looked in my direction. Both pistols had been fired; the sword was still in Dippel. I grabbed up the hollow cane that had housed the sword, to use as a weapon.

This thing, this patchwork creation I assumed was Grimm, its private parts wrapped in a kind of swaddling, took one step in my direction, the blue-white fire crackling in its eyes. Then the patchwork creature turned to see the blinking eye staring out of the open door to the borderlands.

Grimm yanked the chairs off Dippel, lifted the ape-body up as easily as if it had been a feather pillow. It spread its legs wide for position, cocked its arms, and flung the ape upward. The whirlpool from beyond sucked at Dippel, turning the old man in the old ape's body into a streak of dark fur, dragging it upward. In that moment, Dippel was taken by those from beyond the borderland, pulled into their world like a hungry mouth taking in a tasty treat. Grimm, stumbling about on unfamiliar legs, grabbed the *Necronomicon* and tossed it at the wound in the air.

All this activity had not distracted Dupin from his reading. Still he chanted. There was a weak glow from behind the brick wall. I stumbled over there, putting a hand against the wall to hold myself up. When Dupin read the last passage with an oratory flourish, the air was sucked out of the room and out of my lungs. I gasped for breath, fell to the floor, momentarily unconscious. Within a heartbeat the air came back, and with it, that horrid rotting smell, then as instantly as it arrived, it was gone. The air smelled only of foul sewer, which, considering the stench of what had gone before, was in that moment as pleasant and welcome as a young Parisian lady's perfume.

There was a flare of a match as Dupin rose from the floor where he, like me, had fallen. He lit a twist from the bag and held it up. There was little that we could see. Pulling the sword from his cane, he trudged forward with the light, and I followed. In its illumination we saw Grimm. Or what was left of him. The creatures of the borderlands had not only taken Dippel and his *Necronomicon*, they had ripped Grimm into a dozen pieces and plastered him across the ceiling and along the wall like an exploded dumpling.

"Dippel failed," Dupin said. "And Grimm finished him off. And The Old Ones took him before they were forced to retreat."

"At least one of those terrible books has been destroyed," I said.

"I think we should make it two."

We broke up the chairs and used the greasy twists of paper we still had, along with the bag itself, and started a fire. The chair wood was old and rotten and caught fast, crackling and snapping as it burned. On top of this Dupin placed the remaining copy of the *Necronomicon*. The book was slow to catch, but when it did the cover blew open and the pages flared.

The eye hole in the cover filled with a gold pupil, a long black slit for an iris. It blinked once, then the fire claimed it. The pages flapped like a bird, lifted upward with a howling noise, before collapsing into a burst of black ash.

Standing there, we watched as the ash dissolved into the bricks like black snow on a warm window pane.

I took a deep breath. "No regrets about the book?"

"Not after glimpsing what lay beyond," Dupin said. "I understand Dippel's curiosity, but though mine is considerable, it is not that strong."

"I don't even know what I saw," I said, "but whatever it was, whatever world The Old Ones live in, I could sense in that void every kind of evil I have ever known or suspected, and then some. I know you don't believe in fate, Dupin, but it's as if we were placed here to stop Dippel, to be present when Grimm had had enough of Dippel's plans."

"Nonsense," Dupin said. "Coincidence. As I said before. More common than you think. And had I not been acquainted with that horrid book, and Dippel's writings, we would have gone to bed to awake to a world we could not understand, and one in which we would not long survive. I should add that this is one adventure of ours that you might want to call fiction, and confine it to a magazine of melodrama; if you should write of it at all."

We went along the brick pathway then, with one last lit paper twist we had saved for light. It burned out before we made it back, but we were able to find our way by keeping in touch with the wall, finally arriving where moonlight spilled through the grating we had replaced upon entering the sewer. When we were on the street, the world looked strange, as if bathed in a bloody light, and that gave me pause. Looking up, we saw that a scarlet cloud was flowing in front of the sinking moon. The cloud was thick, and for a moment it covered the face of the moon completely. Then the cloud passed and faded and the sky was clear and tinted silver with the common light of stars and moon.

I looked at Dupin.

"It's quite all right," he said. "A last remnant of the borderland. Its calling card has been taken away."

"You're sure?"

"As sure as I can be," he said.

With that, we strolled homeward, the moon and the stars falling down behind the city of Paris. As we went, the sun rose, bloomed red, but a different kind of red to the cloud that had covered the moon; warm and inspiring, a bright badge of normalcy, that from here on out I knew was a lie.

FROM DARKNESS, EMERGED, RETURNED

By

ELIZABETH MASSIE

Peter is dead.

Dear, young Peter Garrett, the handsome fellow who delivered milk with his horse and wagon to all the flats along Riggs Road, dead. Murdered. Killed and dragged into an alley, as his horse Sue stood alone out on the street, pawing the ground, sniffing, and nickering.

My heart is broken, my mind spinning. For I loved Peter. I loved his voice, his face, and the way his large but elegant hands held the reins, patted Sue's broad shoulder, tossed biscuit crumbs to dogs on the street, and ladled milk from the tanks into the jugs left on doorsteps. That someone would hate him enough to steal his life is beyond any sort of reason. That he is dead is beyond comprehension. It was the one bright spot of my life, watching him from my third-floor window, imagining that he might someday come up and carry me off to be his bride. No, we never spoke. We never met. But I knew that, somehow, he would find me and love me.

But such hopes and dreams shall delight me never more.

For Peter is dead. I can barely breathe with the horror of it.

I pull away from the window and fall into my little chair. I pick up my knitting, a partial scarf for my mother, then put it down again. I get up, pace the room barefoot. I have shoes in the bottom of the pie safe, but I don't wear them except in the winter when it is cold, for I never go outside. My feet slap softly against the irregular wooden floor.

This room serves as my bedroom, parlor, and kitchen, collectively. It is eight feet by fourteen feet. We've one other room to our flat; it is eight by six and my mother's bed is in there. She never closes the door, though, because she doesn't like to sleep alone, and when the door is open it's as if we are in the same room.

Back and forth I pace across an anemic puddle of summer sunlight, past the kitchen table, stove, and pie safe, my chair and cot, my mother's chair and the little stand on which she keeps her Bible and the matches that light the gas-lamps at night. The front door is locked but the transom is open, and I can hear people out in the hallway and on the stairway talking, coughing. I can smell the pork and cabbage that Mrs. Anderson across the hall has put on for lunch. Flies, confused and excited by the thick scent, buzz in and out through the transom, seeking the source. I bat at several, but miss.

I return to the window, dabbing sweat from between my breasts with a loose fold of my blouse. Men down on the street are still discussing Peter's murder. It happened only last night, during the thunderstorm, and the news is fresh. Fresh as fish caught off Coney Island and hauled on ice to Mr. Denny's Meat Market. I bite the inside of my cheek so as not to cry. I put one hand to my temple to press away the pain, but it remains.

There is a police officer amongst the men, standing tall in his big hat and shiny badge. I push the window up a bit farther and stick out my head. It's hard to hear over the other sounds down there—children running and squealing, the creaking of the rag man's cart, a mongrel barking at his shadow in a puddle. But I catch bits of the conversation.

"So he was stabbed, was he?" This is Mr. McCary, who owns the hardware store.

"Clear through, you say?" This is Mr. Denny, the butcher. "Then dragged off behind some garbage?"

I cringe.

"Horrid, horrid." This is Mr. Bruce, a hateful old gentleman as round as a beer barrel and red-faced as a tomato. He has no job, but enjoys the business of everyone else. I've spent many hours listening to this man from the vantage point of my window. My mother calls him a busybody, and indeed, he is. Mr. Bruce mutters, "horrid," again, and smiles as if such a dreadful crime is enticing, thrilling. It looks as though he's licking his lips.

The officer says something and the three men shiver and shake their heads. Mr. Denny mumbles and the officer replies, "We think it was done with a pistol. Bit of dark residue at the hole. Shot clean through, and we didn't find the bullet."

Mr. Bruce nods, and purses his lips. "We can't have no criminal like that on the loose."

"Not to worry," says the officer. "We arrested the culprit we think done it. Ugly fellow, head like a crushed can. Had a gun on him, newly fired from the smell of it. Don't speak no English, and he fought like a mad dog. Got him in the jail now. He didn't confess, but we'll get it out of him, don't you worry."

The murderer had already been arrested? That surprises me. The cops on the beat in our neighborhood are hardly careful and often drunk. From tales my mother tells me when she returns home from her work at the clothing factory, the officers are happy to have the jail cells full, regardless of guilt. That keeps the alderman and police chief happy, thinking crime is being properly addressed. I find it highly improbable that Peter's murderer has already been apprehended, due to the incompetence of the force and the interference of the rainstorm that ended just four hours ago.

I wish I could do something. My shoulders and arms sting with the wanting! I wish I could solve the murder, for I don't believe the jailed immigrant did the deed. How terrible to be imprisoned wrongly and facing certain execution. And how terrible for a criminal to still be at large somewhere nearby and planning his next kill.

Yet I cannot leave our flat. Mother won't allow it and the idea frightens me to the core.

I watch as the men fall away from one another, heading off in their own particular directions. I slump down at the window and try to think past the pain. Think.

Think.

Thinking is pretty much all I do, you see. Thinking, pondering, evaluating, considering. I may have a small world, but my mind is large. I read the mysteries of Sherlock Holmes, the brilliant consulting detective, and try to guess the perpetrator before the great man does. I enjoy the large and complex wooden jigsaw puzzles my mother buys for me whenever she finds a spare nickel. I savor poring over my mother's accounting books and planning what she can spend each week for meals and fuel. I love creating new patterns of my own design that I knit into scarves and sweaters and leggings and stockings. Sometimes I count handfuls of rice grains from the lidded tin, or try to guess the number I spill from the tin onto the table top, because I like the order of numbers. I find fascinating the intricate water patterns on the ceiling, which, when I lay on my cot at night, I imagine into fanciful stories of fairies and dragons and knights and ladies.

My desire to untangle matters should not be a surprise, however. My last name, Dupin, means little to those here in Brooklyn, New York. But for those in France, the name would certainly bring awe. My great-grandfather was Monsieur C. Auguste Dupin, a Parisian, a brilliant mind, a deep thinker who solved many mysteries. I like to imagine I take after him.

However, I, Molly Dupin, am wholly American, brought to this country from France in April 1893 when I was but two years old by my mother, Martha Dupin, a gentle, quiet, yet slow-witted woman who now works a sewing machine at the Louder Shirtwaist Factory to keep us fed and clothed. I am eighteen now, a grown woman, and yet, as I've mentioned, I've not stepped foot outside the apartment since I was a little girl. Peculiar to some, but it suits me. The world outside is dangerous, as exemplified by Peter's murder last night. Miscreants, villains, thieves, molesters, killers. My mother rightly encourages me to stay inside. Every morning she kisses my cheek and says, "Be good, my Molly. Stay here and do your chores and I will be back soon." Soon is twelve hours. They work the women to pieces at the factory. I would work there, too, if the world weren't so treacherous.

And so I stay here, doing puzzles, knitting, thumbing through the account book or Holmes books or old magazines Mother finds scattered in the street and brings home to me or making up stories while gazing at the water stains overhead.

I sit in my chair again, pick up the knitting, then put it aside. I close my eyes and imagine all sorts of horrors surrounding Peter's death, and in each one I am a heroine, saving him in the last moment.

In one moment I see Mr. Denny, distraught because Peter's wagon ran over Mr. Denny's beloved dog, Charlie, last week, crushing Charlie's spine and causing Mr. Denny to break the dog's neck to save it from suffering. I saw the crushing of the dog beneath the wheels, or rather I heard about it from the shrieks of some of the women in the street. So vivid in my mind, it is as if I were actually there, and so sad, about the dog and how Mr. Denny cried so pitifully. Peter, shocked and sorry, offered him a dollar to get another dog, but Mr. Denny refused. And so I imagine what transpired late last night. Most of the city is sleeping and Peter is driving his horse home through the rain. Mr. Denny waves at him to stop. Peter ties off the horse and enters the warm, dry meat market. Mr. Denny offers Peter a drink, which Peter accepts, but then Mr. Denny snatches up a meat skewer and makes to stab my young love clear through. But I rush into the shop and shove Peter out of the way just in time. Peter thanks me, then proposes marriage.

My heart pounds with joy.

In another moment I see Mr. McCary, waving Peter down through the rain well after midnight, to tell him he's noticed a wheel wobbling on the wagon and to say he has just the thing to fix it. Peter hasn't noticed the wobble, but is tired and so perhaps Mr. McCary is right. Mr. McCary invites Peter into the hardware store where he grabs a long metal spike from his shelf of wares and plunges it toward Peter's chest for bringing him soured milk that morning, milk that made him vomit for hours on end. Yet I come in again at the right moment, and push Mr. McCary away. The spike clatters on the floor and Peter catches me in his embrace. He tells me he loves me and we plan our wedding date.

The next moment I see a police officer patrolling the street in the pouring rain, bored and a bit drunk, tapping his stick against his thigh, hoping for trouble so he can smack someone on the ear with it. Peter steers his wagon home, exhausted from the long day, hunched down in the rain. The copper waves at him to stop. Peter draws his horse up, waits. The policeman says, "I said get down here now!" Peter frowns, but does as the officer asks. Then the copper punches Peter for no reason, and hits him with his stick. Peter punches him back and the stick goes flying away. The copper laughs, draws a pistol, and aims it at Peter's chest. I am out on the street, and rush over to throw myself in front of Peter. "Don't shoot!" I cry, and the officer scowls and staggers away, pistol hanging limply from his trigger finger. Peter hugs me, kisses me, caresses me so tenderly and completely. He says I will be his forever.

But Peter is dead. I didn't save him.

I weep. I bury my face in my hands and pour out my anguish. If only I were brave enough to go down and outside, I would use my wits, the skills passed down to me by Auguste Dupin, and find the real killer. I would avenge Peter!

Lunchtime comes. I fix a cold biscuit with cold ham. I note that there is a glowing coal down in the stove, which is odd as we haven't cooked or heated our rooms in several weeks. Maybe Mother has taken up smoking after I've gone to sleep, and hides her cigarettes in her purse. I spit on the coal until it winks out. Then I return to the window. I look down and watch as Mr. McCary stands just outside his shop door and shows a handful of nails to a potential customer. Mr. Denny's meat market door is open. He's inside sweeping, and I can see clots of wet dirt and small bits of fat and pinkish meat fly out onto the street with each *whisk*. Mrs. Anderson's daughter, Katherine—likely the prettiest woman in our neighborhood, which irritates me for reasons I can't quite fathom—tries to maneuver her way across the steaming street without stepping in a rain puddle. She fails, topples, and stomps down hard in the middle of one particularly muddy pool. Water splashes her skirt and she curses. The she marches angrily on, over to the butcher shop where she disappears. She loves mutton and pork. I don't know how her family can afford so much meat as her father is a cripple from fighting in Cuba and he begs on the corner. Her brother, James, ran off last year to join the Navy against the wishes of his parents. From what I've heard through the transom, he's never sent home one thin dime.

I sit in my chair in this blasted mid-July heat, my hair damp and clinging to my neck and forehead, and re-read "A Scandal in Bohemia" in an old issue of *The Strand Magazine*. My great-grandfather Auguste was so like brilliant Sherlock, and I often think Sir Arthur Conan Doyle fashioned his character after Auguste. Had my great-grandfather still been alive, and had he been here, I would task him to help me solve Peter's murder. I sorely wish I had the courage to go down, go out and investigate. If I were a man I would go by myself. I would be brave.

I get up and go to Mother's room where I find her little looking glass. I study myself and imagine my appearance adorned in a cap and pipe. Perhaps I could dress as a man and go out in disguise. Maybe that would give me the courage to interview my suspects, to question them in oh, such subtle ways as to coerce the perpetrator into confessing.

But we've no men's clothing.

I think I'll ask Mother if she might steal some from a clothesline behind our building.

No, she is an honest and good woman. And if by chance she acquiesced, she would certainly be caught and arrested. She isn't clever and cautious. And she is so simple, so innocent of mind and heart that she would die in jail. She wishes she were smart, I know that. She told me once that soon after I was born she had surgery on her brain to make her smart, but it didn't work. It was then we left Paris and came to the States, with the assistance of one of her friends who had also decided to emigrate. Her friend found us this flat, helped Mother secure a job, then took a train to Chicago. Mother has a scar on her skull from the surgery where the hair doesn't grow right.

I sit in my chair, pick up my knitting, put it down again. I can't think of anything but Peter's murder. I dump rice onto the table and try to guess how many grains there are, and then I count them. I'm off by twenty-four. Usually I'm a lot closer than that.

I curl up on my cot and fall asleep.

He comes to me in a dream, or perhaps it is a vision. I can't know. But it is my great-grandfather, Auguste Dupin. He is so young, and trim, with night-pale cheeks, and dark eyes that have a strangely vacant yet intense, haunting look. He does not even glance at me, but instead stares out the window, one fist tapping inside the open palm of the other. His brows furrow, twitch. He says, "Take all things into consideration, that you might comprehend most clearly that which has taken place. Consider the facts, great-granddaughter. Motive. Opportunity. Location. Think on these things without emotion, for emotion destroys concentration. You will find your answer."

I stare at him and I want to ask him for help. My jaws do not work, however, and the only sound that issues from my lips is a pathetic and soft grunt.

I awaken to the sound of that grunting. I am sweating, and my great-grandfather, of course, is not there.

The puddle of sunlight has traveled across the well-worn rug, heading for the wall. It's late afternoon. I go into Mother's room and pull her steamer trunk from under her bed. She keeps two blankets in there as well as her winter clothing—woolen stockings, sweaters, several of the scarves I've knitted for her (the others she's given away to people on the street, so that at least no one in our neighborhood has a cold neck come January), a few heavy skirts, and a ratty blouse or two. The trunk is locked to keep mice away. They love to find soft material on which to sleep and piss. Mother hides the key in various places around the flat; I pretend not to see as she moves it from one hiding spot to another. I let her have her fantasy that her simple deviousness will prevent rodents from finding the key, unlocking the trunk, and having themselves a party in her old skirts, or prevents me from finding it and then giving it to the rodents so we can all have a nap and a piss together on Mother's clothes.

Today I find the key in the potato basket on the shelf over the stove and I unlatch the lock. I find the scarves, sweaters, winter cap, stockings with massive runs in them (I take them out; I'll find time to mend them), Mother's winter cloak, and gloves. Two skirts—which are too long for me as I don't have my mother's height—and a lacy scarf from her days in Paris. I take out one of the skirts and hold it up. I could snip and re-sew this into a shawl with a wide hood that would hide my face if I tipped my head down as I walked. I will still look like a woman, but a mysterious woman no one knows.

Back in my chair, the skirt in my lap, I rub my hands over the rough material. It smells old, yet there is also a faint sweetness to it. I wonder if that's what Paris smelled like. I think I hear my great-grandfather whisper, "Think it through. Consider only the facts. Make your plan." I whisper back, "I will."

In my hooded shawl, I shall start with Mr. McCary. I will tell him that my sister sent me to ask him for her handkerchief back. He'll not know what I'm talking about, of course, for it's a lie, but a lie for a better purpose. I'll then say he had best remember, for they had a romantic rendezvous last night here in his very shop after Mrs. McCary had gone upstairs to bed. Mr. McCary might then say, "No! I was not in my shop last evening. I had business elsewhere." Ah-ha, I will think, but will not say. I will then demand to know why he is treating my sister so, pretending their night together never happened. I will scan the floor as I speak, looking for a trace of blood that was not cleaned up well enough before Peter's dear body was dragged away to the alley.

My daydream is broken when I hear Mr. Bruce outside, shouting. I put the skirt down and hurry to the window. He is yelling at another man for bumping into him. The other man says, "Were you not so much of a hog, sir, I should not have knocked you with my shoulder." Mr. Bruce is sensitive about his weight, and I've seen his face go from flour white to tomato red in a heartbeat. His anger and nosiness know no bounds.

Perhaps he killed Peter? Perhaps Peter offended him in some way, and Mr. Bruce knocked him down and stabbed him with the sharp tip of the walking cane he carries with him. Stabbed him clean through to the street.

I sit back down and pick up the skirt. My heart squeezes. Dear Peter. Is he in Heaven? I would think any just god would put him there, for any sin such a beautiful man might have committed on this Earth would surely be minor and forgivable.

I put the skirt down and pace the floor, back and forth in my bare feet. Mother will be home at seven and then we shall dine. After supper, she will read her Bible to me then retire to her room. When she is sound asleep, I shall tear apart the skirt then snip and stitch it into a shawl. Done soon after midnight, I shall venture out. I shall be my great-grandfather's rightful descendant. Bright and sharp and determined.

And outside alone.

Alone for the first time in my life.

I dump rice out on the table and guess the number. I'm off by thirty-seven this time. Where is my focus? My nerves have me careless. I can't be careless. My great-grandfather warned me against emotion.

Back in my chair, I pick up my knitting, rub the soft cream-colored yarn then put it down again. I draw up Mother's skirt to my chin and close my eyes. Behind my lids I see Peter and me, standing in a church overlooking the sea. The preacher declares us husband and wife. I run my hands up and down the fabric.

Then stop.

There is a key deep in the skirt pocket. I take it out and frown. What, now, has Mother locked up? Something I don't know about, clearly. She won't be home for another hour or more, so I return to her room.

Nothing is hidden under her mattress or pillow. There are no loose panels in the walls. I search the drawers of her small bedside dresser, and in the bottom I find her wooden jewelry box. I've seen this box many times, have seen Mother take out the cheap earrings and necklace and hold them to herself in memory of the old days in France. But that is all there is in the box. I know she locks it, but have thought it only habit. She knows I would never take those things from her.

I put the box on Mother's bed and sit beside it. The key does indeed open the box, and inside are the necklace and earrings. Nothing else, save the old newspapers that line the sides and bottom to hold down the splinters. I put the necklace to my own throat and wonder if I will ever have a chance to dress up in something such as this.

Something printed on the newspaper catches my eye, and I carefully pull it up out of the box, unfolding the yellowed, brittle page.

It is a Parisian newspaper, dated June 14th, 1890. I am fluent in French, and so read the story with initial curiosity then a growing, gnawing ill-ease. It is a report of a brutal murder. A man who left a brothel in the late night-hours was bludgeoned and stabbed to death. His shoulders were smashed and his skull crushed, then his heart stabbed clear through. The weapon, which was found in a thatch of weeds, was the leg of a chair, sharpened into a spike at the end and tempered by fire to brutal strength. It was the fourth such murder, and the authorities believed they were close to capturing the killer.

The killer, they were quite certain, was a woman.

I unfold the other papers. The three other, earlier murders are described, all with similar results, with beatings and fatal stabbings. They suspect the weapon is a sharpened, tempered stake. They suspect a small man or a woman in a fit of uncontrollable rage.

All took place in the neighborhood of Route de Pierre Froide. My mother's neighborhood.

My hands shake as I fold the paper back and tuck it down in the box. I replace the jewelry, lock the box, and put it in my mother's bedside table. I hurry out to my chair, fold my hands, and try to think.

But I don't like the dark thoughts that well up.

What I think is impossible.

I hear my great-grandfather whisper, "Consider the facts."

She is on the stairs, coming up a full twenty minutes early, huffing and thumping and muttering to herself as she often does. Quickly I ball up the skirt and shove it beneath my chair behind my sewing box. Mrs. Anderson's door scrapes open and Mother says, "Good evening." Mrs. Anderson returns the greeting, then I hear our neighbor take the stairs down. A key rattles our lock. Our door swings open.

"Molly," says Mother with her slightly lopsided smile. "Have you had a fine day?" She is tall and thin, and limps a bit. Her hands are chewed from laboring in the factory.

I open my mouth. Then snap it shut. Then open it again to say, "Peter Garrett is dead."

"Oh, yes. I know. Poor Peter. I heard the talk. Sad. So sad." She takes off her summer cap and puts it on the ear of her chair. She unfastens the top button of her dress, fans her chest, and pours a cup of water from the pitcher on the kitchen table. She drinks it noisily. "Have you not made us a supper, Molly? I'm so tired."

"It's too hot to cook, Mother," I say. "It's summer, remember. Let's have some cheese and bread."

Mother nods.

"Much too hot to heat the stove," I continue. "I wonder why anyone would do that when the air is so stifling?"

Mother shrugs vaguely, sits down in her chair, which has all four legs, and rubs her arms. "So much work today," she says. Her voice is so light, so childish. So innocent. "Delia got mad at me for looking at her for too long. She said I stared. I didn't think I stared, but maybe so. Sometimes I just forget that I'm looking. My mind wanders. I don't want to cause trouble. I don't like trouble, Molly."

"I know that." I think I know that.

We sit at the table and have our meal of cheese and bread. As much as I try to remain composed, Mother senses something. "Molly, are you ill?"

I don't know how to answer. I just eat and clear the dishes and wash them in the bin and put them away. Mother sits in her chair and opens her Bible then waits for me to sit to hear her read. She doesn't read well, or fast, but this is our nightly ritual.

"What should I read, Molly?" Mother looks at me with her simple eyes, her simple smile.

I hesitate then whisper, "What does the Bible say of murder?"

Mother looks startled. "Why it is a sin, Molly. Whoever kills sins against God Himself."

"I thought so."

Mother struggles with my question and the cool attitude I've pulled on. I look for something in her eyes that I've not looked for before. A keenness? A dangerous spark? If it is there, she hides it well. I have never feared my mother… until now.

I get up, look out of the window. Peter will never again drive Sue up and down the road, never again deliver milk.

Then I speak before I can stop myself. "I found a key in your skirt pocket." Turning, I see her still in her chair, holding her Bible, head tilted in confusion.

"Skirt?"

"The key that opens your jewelry box."

"My necklace and earrings," she says. "Did you want to wear them?"

"Now where would I wear them?"

"Consider the facts," whispers Auguste in the depths of my ear.

"I don't know, Molly, but I wouldn't mind if you did."

Mother, did you find some piece of wood yesterday, bring it home in your skirt, and then... I press my hand to my forehead against a pain that is building up like a foul blister. "Mother, why did we come to America?"

"I don't know. Let me think." She squints at the wall then says, "Oh, yes. It was better to come here. Better than Paris."

"Why? What was wrong with Paris?"

Mother looks at the floor, her face scrunched up as if she is really trying to remember. It looks so sincere. "It's a bad place. Bad things happened."

Oh, God. "What bad things?"

"I..." She rubs her eyes with her fists then stares at me. I see little more than a child there, yet there must be more.

"Tell me what you remember."

"I was in trouble." Mother begins to cry. Silently, though, as if watching one of Edison's films. "I didn't want any more bad, Molly."

"What bad?"

"You'll hate me."

"What bad?"

"You'll hate me!" Mother screams. I'd never heard her scream before.

I take a breath and wipe my forehead, which is clammy and wet. I try to speak kindly, as knotted as my stomach and throat are in this very moment. "Mother, what bad?"

Mother gets up, wringing her hands, goes into her bedroom, comes back out, paces to the window then sits in her chair. Her brow is furrowed and her mouth screwed up. "I don't want you to hate me, Molly!"

"I don't hate you. Did you... did you kill anyone?"

Mother's head drops and she nods. *Merciful Christ!*

"Did you kill four people?"

She nods. "I believe I did, Molly."

For several full minutes I can't speak. My cool and calculating brain is suddenly sluggish and fogged. Mother cries. I sit and stare at her.

Then: "*Why* did you kill them?"

"I got mad. They made me mad!"

"Did you kill Peter?"

"What?" She looks up.

"Did you kill Peter Garrett?"

Mother blinks as if someone has shone a bright light in her face. She frowns and bites her lip, before looking toward the window. "Dr. Burckholdt was a nice man. He made me better, Molly. He fixed my brain."

"What? No, no. You said he tried to make you smarter, but it wasn't successful."

"I didn't tell you the truth, Molly. It was the only time I lied to you. I wanted him to make me... to make me simple. And he did."

I stomp my foot. "You make no sense! Now answer me, Mother. Did you kill Peter Garrett?"

Mother links her fingers. It's as if she hasn't heard my question. "I was like my mother. She was like my grandmother. We were oh, so fancy, don't you see? Fancy women. Perfume. Necklaces. Wine and music. The men liked us."

"What do you mean?"

"I... we let men have us. Have their way with us. For money. Please don't hate me, Molly!"

My teeth are on edge now, but I push ahead. "You were a prostitute?"

"A what? Oh, yes. A whore. I never told you. Don't hate me, Molly."

"Go on."

"My mother got mad easy. She hit me when she got mad. She hit other people, too. She didn't care if she hurt someone then. Or if she killed someone. She killed a man once, and a woman who made her mad. She never got caught. But she was a sinner. God hated her, I know!"

"Yes."

"Her mother was the same way. Marie Dupin. That was my grandmother's name. She was a whore, like all of us. She had a temper. She could be nice. Then in a second would hurt someone. Or kill them. I saw her kill a man once with a knife. The other whores threw him in the river so nobody found out. She didn't remember killing him, but she did. I saw it. Oh! I had nightmares after that, Molly. I might not remember a lot of things. But I remember that."

I clench my fists, one inside the other. I don't want to hear this. But I have to. I am smart. I am not like my mother. I like to put information together, to figure things out. It makes me special.

"Mother…"

"Marie got a baby in her… got my mother in her… from Auguste Dupin. He didn't visit us often at the brothel. But when he did, he liked my grandmother best."

I feel anger stirring in my gut. It is hot like the worst of a summer's day. "You told me my great-grandmother and Dupin were married. But now you say Dupin was only my great-grandmother's customer?"

Mother hangs her head again. She starts to pick at a loose thread on a bodice buttonhole. "I wish they had been lovers, or married. She took his last name, anyway. Who would care what a whore called herself?"

"Mother." I speak slowly through clenched jaws. "Did you kill Peter Garrett?"

Mother shakes her head violently. "No! No! I got my brain fixed, I told you! I *was* smart like my grandfather one time. Smart like *you*! But I was also like my mother and grandmother. I got mad like them. And when I did I didn't always know what I was doing. I killed men who made me angry."

Consider the facts…

"With a chair leg that had been sharpened and tempered in fire."

Mother grimaces. "When you were born I loved you. You were the only person I ever loved. Molly, don't hate me, please!" She picks more furiously at her buttonhole, and I know it will need mending along with the torn stockings. I don't know that I'll do the mending, though. I think I hate my mother now.

"Mother, did Peter make you angry? Were you upset that I loved him? Did you think I'd leave you?"

Mother looks at me. "I didn't know you loved him."

My breathing grows rapid. So do my heartbeats.

Mother shakes her head. "I didn't want to kill any more, Molly. If the Paris coppers caught me they would kill me. Chop my head clean off! What would happen to you, you were such a little thing? I found out about Dr. Burckholdt. A man who operated on brains of people to make them better. To get rid of the bad. The sin. Some of them died, but I wasn't scared. I didn't care if I died. Better die than kill! Dr. Burckholdt visited Paris. I went to see him. I didn't have a lot of money, but

I let him have me. A trade. He said all right. He liked me. Thought I was pretty. When it was over my memory wasn't so good. I wasn't so good with numbers anymore. I got lost a lot. The women at the brothel didn't like me anymore. They made sport of me. But I never killed anybody again. I promise I didn't."

I get up and lean on the window.

"I never ever killed again," Mother repeats.

I look down at the street. Light is fading fast and heavy clouds are gathering. I hear Mother, still whimpering, go into her bedroom. This time she closes the door.

Mr. Denny stands outside his shop, smoking a cigar. Mr. Bruce is beside him, talking about something I can't quite make out. Probably about Peter Garrett's murder and the man they arrested for the crime. A cat laps at a muddy puddle in the middle of the road. It looks like it might rain again tonight.

I hear Mrs. Anderson in her flat across the hall, fussing at Katherine for staying out so late. Katherine, the prettiest woman in our neighborhood, who flounces and tosses her head oh, so haughtily. I saw her kissing Peter a couple of days ago. He laughed and kissed her back before he drove on in his milk wagon.

A dreadful heat that has nothing to do with summer stings the back of my mind.

I go to the pie safe and look down at my shoes. They are coated in mud.

I sit in my chair, pick up my knitting, and make a row with the large wooden needles. The first few stitches of the cream colored yarn are spotted with a gray, ashy residue and dried flecks; something crusty, reddish.

Consider the facts, great-granddaughter.

How terrible for the immigrant to be imprisoned wrongly and facing certain execution.

Yes. Yes.

But how much better for me.

AFTER THE END
A NEW STORY ABOUT C. AUGUSTE DUPIN
(with apologies to E.A. Poe)

By

LISA TUTTLE

I have written before about my quondam friend, the Chevalier C. Auguste Dupin, with whom I long ago resided in an ancient house in a retired and desolate street in Paris, yet never have I described the details of his final case. That it would be of great interest to a very wide readership I was never in doubt, for it involved a series of horrific murders that terrified the public and baffled the police, and without the intervention of Dupin and his superior powers of analytical thought, the killer would never have been found and brought to justice.

The victims were all young women, but there was no discernible connection between them; one was married, one affianced; one a *grisette*, and another the daughter of a lawyer. They were of different classes and lived in different quarters of the city. At first, therefore, the police quite naturally assumed each had been murdered by a different man. There were no suspects, and no one came forward to inform or confess, but when another woman died, the public became convinced one single, bloodthirsty monster was responsible.

Dupin had already recognized the evidence, what he called the killer's *signature*, even while the police resisted the idea.

The problem was how to find the murderer? No matter how he searched for a connection between these disparate women (or their families), Dupin could find nothing. They had lived and died in different *arrondissements*, did not attend the same church or buy their bread from the same baker. The only thing they had in common was their sex and relative youth (the eldest was twenty-four; the youngest, seventeen), and perhaps most importantly, the fact that they did not know their killer. Dupin concluded that the man the popular press had dubbed "The Beast of Paris" was deliberately choosing his victims from a large pool of total strangers, women previously unknown to him, with whom he had no traceable connection.

But who sets out to kill strangers, outside of wartime, for no reason or benefit?

Only a madman. Indeed, the senseless cruelty of the crimes could be the very definition of insanity. Yet, apart from that, the killer did not act like one in the grip of madness. He was cool and calculating. He planned his murders in advance, and possessed sufficient self-control to resist drawing attention to himself. If he was mad, it was only now and then, at times of his own choosing—which surely is not madness at all, but an expression of pure evil. A better name for this monster than "beast" would be "devil," I thought.

By now, some of my readers will have guessed the identity of this devil, and recall the scandal that erupted when the police, acting on the results of Monsieur Dupin's investigations, arrested one Paul Gabriel Reclus. Monsieur Reclus was known as a respectable, wealthy, unmarried gentleman of Paris. Not himself a member of either the government or the press, he had influential friends in both, and as a result, the police found themselves obliged to release him almost immediately, with groveling apologies, for they had no evidence against him. Although convinced by Dupin's argument, constructed from his subtle observations, it amounted to nothing more than a delicate chain of logic. There were no witnesses to any of the murders, and nothing, not a single, solid object or piece of blood-stained clothing, in the possession of Monsieur Reclus to tie him to any one of the crimes. As he showed no signs of guilt or any inclination to confess, the police had nothing with which to convict him, not even an obvious reason for arresting him.

Naturally, they blamed Dupin for leading them astray. The results were quite disastrous for my friend. He did not mind the mockery in the press (although some of the cartoons were particularly savage) and simply ignored those military friends of Reclus who challenged him to a duel (after all, dueling was illegal, however common it might have been among bantam cocks obsessed with their notion of honor), but the charges of slander and libel brought against him in court cost him most of his patrimony to defend. However, there was something far worse than all of that: the secret, subterranean vengeance enacted by Reclus against Dupin, about which my friend dared say nothing. For Monsieur Reclus continued to kill innocent young women. He must have believed himself invincible, untouchable. But now, for his victims, he chose girls who possessed some connection to the one man who had revealed he knew his secret. Because Dupin led a retired and celibate existence, the connections were necessarily remote, of a sort only *he* would be sure to recognize. The first victim worked in the shop where my friend customarily bought his daily bread. The next was the wife of his butcher. Then a bookseller's daughter met her mysterious, violent end.

Dupin realized that unless he could deliver the killer to the police with irrefutable evidence of his crimes—or killed the clever madman himself—more women would die. In addition, he knew that he had little time to act, as he anticipated the killer's scheme was to implicate him in his crimes, planting clews that must eventually lead to the inevitable (although false) conclusion that *Dupin* was the murderer.

The Chevalier's analytical skills were not limited to unraveling mysteries of the past, but extended to predicting what, following a certain course of action, an individual would do next. This, he insisted, was not a matter of intuition, but of observation; it was a purely scientific exercise, and would always be successful so long as the initial observations were sufficient and correct. To me, this seemed to contradict the notion of free will, suggesting human beings were little more than mechanical objects, forced to move in a particular way once their springs had been wound, but his results were such that I could never argue. When he declared that he had worked out precisely when, where, and *who* the killer would next attack, I knew he must be right. The only problem was how to ensure that the police arrived on the scene before the girl was killed, but when Reclus' murderous intentions were still clear enough that his arrest and subsequent conviction would prove inevitable.

To the public, Dupin's skills could seem magical, yet he always insisted they were purely rational. And, in the past, in my previous stories about Monsieur Dupin, I have delighted in explaining the chain of reasoning that led him to feats of understanding which seemed like clairvoyance, mind-reading, or some other of those super-human skills sometimes displayed by people who have been mesmerized.

But I have never written about the case I might once have called "The Devil of Paris," never given all the details of what was to be C. Auguste Dupin's last case. Yes, he solved it, but at a great cost.

Of course, it was not *his* fault the police arrived too late to save the life of Dupin's own cousin. At least they were in time to catch Reclus red-handed, and none of his influential friends were able to save him from the guillotine. In vain did I argue with my old friend that he had performed the great public service of protecting any number of young women from the ravages of "the beast"; sadly he could never allay the guilt he felt about focussing the attention of the murderer on his cousin and the other three blameless young women whose misfortune it was to be connected to men with whom Dupin had commercial dealings. In vain did I argue he could not possibly be held to blame for the actions of that evil creature. His reply was that he should have *known* how Reclus would take his revenge, that he should not have given the police the killer's name without the evidence they needed to arrest him.

His partial failure weighed upon his conscience, and turned him away from the police. They had let him down as much as he had let down the last four victims of Reclus, and henceforth he would take no interest in contemporary crime or current affairs, but would instead dedicate all his mental capacities to questions of historic and philosophical matters. He instructed me never to write about his final case, and although I no longer feel bound by that injunction, neither do I wish to revisit those old days and write of his solving of the case of the beast—or devil—of Paris in the sort of detail I devoted to his earlier exploits. I merely raise the subject as a reminder to my readers, for its bearing on what would transpire later, the subject of this story.

Had I remained in Paris, I sometimes think things might have turned out differently for Dupin—but it was not to be. Even as my old friend was becoming more determinedly entrenched in his studies, retreating from the present day, I received a letter from my father, summoning me home with some urgency to help with the family business. With a feeling of profound melancholy, I bid farewell to the Chevalier, begging him not to forget me, and to write often.

I had, I think, half a dozen letters from him after my return to Baltimore, each one a superb, if not entirely comprehensible, essay on a subject of deepest obscurity, such as the origins of the Kartvelian languages; the meaning of the gigantic stone heads of Easter Island; the manner in which eels reproduce; and a new interpretation of the Mayan calendar. Apart from mentioning certain rare volumes he had been fortunate enough to acquire for his library, he made little reference to the details of his quotidian life, although from the regular changes of address I understood his fortunes were continuing to decline, as he moved to ever-poorer quarters.

That is, until the last letter, in which he mentioned, in a post-script, that he was about to be married and would shortly be departing Paris for his wife's country estate. He mentioned no word of love, nor did he describe the beauty or charm of his intended, although he did inform me that the future Madame Dupin came from a family equal in age and nobility to his own, but far superior in wealth. She had also inherited a library of impressive size. I perceived at once that this was no love match, but a practical arrangement by which Monsieur Dupin might subsidize his bibliophilia.

Unfortunately, he neglected to include his new address, or even his fiancée's name or the location of her library. Surely he intended to inform me once he was settled into his new home, but within days of receiving that last letter, I found myself in a tricky financial situation, and was forced to depart the city abruptly without leaving a forwarding address. Alas, this set an unhappy pattern for the next two years, and as I lived a vagabond existence and moved from Brooklyn to Boston, then from Philadelphia to Poughkeepsie, I could only scour the newspapers for news from France, and quiz any recent visitors for word of him, but to no avail.

Until, at last, one day, in the pages of the *New York Herald*, I glimpsed the name of *C. Auguste Dupin* almost buried in a dense column of black type devoted to a series of shocking deaths—that series of hideous, inhuman killings dubbed by our press "the French Wolf-Man Murders." Although he had no connection with the police or this case (as I discovered after reading the entire article), Dupin's name was invoked by the journalist who fancied he saw some similarities to the murders in the Rue Morgue, and thought the genius who had solved that strange mystery would also be able to explain this one.

At that point, there had been two deaths, within weeks of each other, in the same region of France. One young woman had been bloodily slaughtered in a lonely forest, and the other died in her own bed. Both had had their throats ripped out, apparently by some fierce beast. The girl in the forest had been presumed to have fallen prey to a wolf (very rare in that part of the country, yet presumably not quite extinct) until the second killing, which apart from the setting, seemed almost identical to the first. But how had a wolf come to enter and leave a young lady's bedroom without attracting attention? Sensationalist newspapers and superstitious public alike spoke of that creature which is a man in daylight and a wolf by night: the were-wolf, or *loup garou.*

A week later, the newspaper carried more reports from France. The police were convinced the two deaths were completely unrelated, nor were they murders, despite misleading reports. One woman had been attacked by a wolf, which had been spotted several times in the district. The other had been killed by her own dog, turned unexpectedly savage. Although it had run away, it had been caught and destroyed.

Yet even as this story appeared in our American papers, another woman had died in a quiet country lane in a French village, her throat torn out, and in every other particular her death resembled that of the other two women. Soon enough, that story reached us across the ocean, accompanied by some of the hysteria gripping that region of France, and full of speculation as to the true reason for these deaths.

A surgeon who had examined all three bodies announced his conviction that the culprit was a human being. Not an animal, and certainly not a supernatural shape-shifting creature, but an exceptionally cunning and ruthless man who was driven to kill by some inexplicable compulsion (here he reminded questioners of the Reclus case in Paris a few years earlier)—mad in that way, but utterly rational in his ability to disguise his crimes.

It would have been better for Dr. De La Roche if he had never spoken out, for his announcement did not affect the rising hysteria about the *loup garou,* and three days later, both he and his wife were found dead in their home, their throats savaged in the same manner as seen on the other victims. When I heard that, it occurred to me that even if the police asked for his help, Dupin—now with the safety of his own wife to think about—

would surely refuse. Would he be right to do so? Could anyone else solve this fearful mystery?

My mind therefore was certainly fixed on Dupin, as well as the recent terrible crimes in France, on the evening I attended a session promising "mesmeric revelations" in the home of Mr. D— W— of Elmira, New York.

Displays of mesmerism have been so popular and widespread in recent years that I think I need hardly explain the theory. The gathering at the W— home in Elmira was small and informal, for the parlor could comfortably accommodate no more than a dozen guests. The designated somnambule was the sixteen-year-old daughter of the house, and we had been told in advance that her particular talent, when under the influence of the magnetic passes made by her father, was to become a channel, or medium, through which we might receive the voices of the dead. Particularly likely to speak were those troubled spirits who had recently passed out of the realm of the physical, their deaths so sudden that they had not yet come to terms with their new state.

Even under the rapt gaze of an audience, Miss W— succumbed to the expected strange, sleep-like state quite rapidly. Almost at once she gasped, and exclaimed in French, then, in that same language, began to teasingly scold some gentleman who had, it seemed, taken her by surprise. The one-sided conversation that followed, at first flirtatious, became increasingly bold and salacious as the speaker began to bargain with the male stranger, offering the pleasures of her body in return for payment. I shifted uncomfortably in my seat, but noticing none of my fellow guests responding, realized I must be the only person there who understood the language.

The somnambule—or, I should say, whoever spoke *through*

her—now changed her tone. She seemed nervous, even frightened of the man she had been so intent upon wooing, and there could be no mistaking her terror when she screamed.

At that bloodcurdling sound there was a shocked flurry throughout the stuffy parlor—one lady fainted dead away—and Mr. W— seemed about to try and wake his daughter when I stopped him. Recognizing that we'd heard evidence of a crime, I begged him to question his daughter as to the identity of the spirit.

But Miss W— was only a conduit, and knew nothing of what transpired while she was in this state. Fortunately, the spirit was still nearby. As the only French-speaker, it fell to me to question her, and firstly I inquired her name.

"I am Marie Callot."

That was the name of the third victim of the murderous "wolf-man" of France. I felt a chill, and heard gasps and murmurs from others who also recognized her name from the papers.

How I longed for the aid of Auguste Dupin as I quizzed the victim about her attacker! Perhaps he would have made more of her slender evidence than I could. The girl had not known the man, and had scarcely seen his face in the dark lane where he encountered her. She could only say that she did not think he was a local; he had a Paris accent, and from the fine cloth and fashionable cut of his clothes, she knew he was "quality." No, he did not bite her throat, nor did he metamorphose into a hairy animal. She did not see what sort of knife he held, only felt its rough bite as he slashed her throat and took her life with it.

After I had translated her words for the others, Marie was allowed to depart. I asked Mr. W— if we could summon other victims of this killer so I could question them.

He agreed to try, saying that it was best to summon the

recently departed by name—and thus we called up Dr. De La Roche. I thought a man of science might have the most helpful observations to offer.

When Miss W— began to speak, her tone had dropped by nearly an octave: "Where am I?" growled an unfamiliar voice in French. "Is this Heaven or Hell?"

"Neither," said I, "but a parlor in New York State. We speak to you by means of a medium created through mesmerism."

"Mesmerism! Do you mean that absurd charade still keeps idiots occupied? How long have I been dead?"

"Scarcely more than a week."

"Ah, so I am still in Limbo. And what of Dupin?"

I was quite startled to hear this name issue from the lips of the young medium. "You refer to the Chevalier C. Auguste Dupin?"

"Certainly. When he came to my door—"

Excited, I burst out: "When?"

"Why, on the last morning of my life! I was surprised, yet pleased, thinking that if he had taken an interest, the murders must be solved. And I should hear it first! I invited him inside, to take a bowl of coffee. It was still early, and my wife and I had not yet broken our fast.

"Once we were seated in the morning room, he congratulated me on having solved the mystery. I assured him that I was still very much in the dark.

"'But you know,' said he, 'you *perceived* that the three young women were murdered, killed by a man, not attacked by wolves, dogs, or the frightful *loup garou*.'"

"'Yes,' said I, 'but not the identity of their slayer; that, like his motives, remains mysterious.'

"He denied there was any mystery, and when I asked if he

meant that he could identify the killer, he said, very calmly, that he could name the man, and explain every detail of the three killings.

"Astonished, I asked why he had not told the police. Was it not true they had asked for his help, and he had declined to become involved?

"Yes, he said, that was true. He had decided never to work with the police again after his last experience with them had left him agitated and disturbed. Although he had identified the killer to the police and the man had subsequently been executed for his crimes, Dupin considered he had failed to solve the case.

"I begged him to explain, and he replied that although he had discovered *who* had committed the murders, there remained unanswered the more troubling query: *why*.

"Most crimes can be explained, he told me. A man becomes a killer in a fit of passion—he goes for his knife in a jealous rage, or beats or strangles a woman who repulsed his amorous attentions, or when driven past endurance by a nagging wife. Other killers are more calculating; they kill for revenge, or to remove an obstacle in their path. What reason could there be for a rational man to deliberately choose to murder strangers almost at random?

"I replied that some killers were insane, and it was fruitless to attempt to apply reason to the actions of a madman.

"Dupin replied that it made no sense to describe *this* killer as mad. The man was both clever and rational. He knew that what he did was wrong, but he killed for a purpose, although he understood that his purpose would be considered repulsive by most civilized beings, and if he was caught, he would pay for his crimes with his life. He was quite sane. He made a decision. He had no wish to die, but his desire to kill was so powerful, the reward so great, that he judged the risk of being caught was worth it.

"I stared at the great detective in astonishment, thinking he was joking, but he looked utterly serious. 'Reward?' I repeated. 'Explain to me, sir, what possible *reward* could there be in killing a stranger?'

"Dupin gave me a cold, distant look as he replied: 'Pleasure.'

"'You expect me to believe Reclus killed purely for the pleasure—the, I should say, *imaginary* pleasure of it—and yet you say he was not mad?' I said.

"'He was not mad,' argued Dupin. 'He was a man of superior intellect, and quite peculiarly refined sensibilities, able to feel sensations that would be lost on most. He told me that the pleasure of taking a life was the greatest pleasure he had ever known—it was particularly keen when the victim was a young and beautiful woman, but any death was to be savored.'"

A faint sigh—a melancholy, expiring sigh—issued from the lips of the fair young medium and she wavered a little in her seat.

"I think it is time, we must not overtax her system," said Mr. W—, moving toward his daughter and raising his arms as if anxious to perform the passes that would bring her out of her mesmerized state, but I blocked him.

"Not yet," I said urgently. "Please—just give me a little longer!"

I looked around the stuffy room, hoping one of the other guests would support me, and realized that there would be no help forthcoming from them. The audience had grown bored with our incomprehensible conversation.

"Just a few more questions," I said quickly. "Then I will translate—you see, he is about to reveal the identity of the French were-wolf!"

This caused a satisfactory stir of interest, so I put the question to Dr. De La Roche at once: "But what about the more recent murders? Did you ask Dupin to identify the killer?"

"Of course. He advised patience—all in good time, I think he said—and asked how I could be so certain the killer was a man and not an animal. Was it not true that, as he had read, each of the women's throats revealed the unmistakable tooth-marks?"

"Indeed they did, and I may have chuckled a little as I explained that my closer examination, under a microscope, had convinced me that although the marks had been made by animal teeth, the wounds were not bites. There is a distinction, you see. After examining the pattern of the marks, I felt certain that the wounds had been inflicted by some implement, either artificially made, or the jawbone of some large, carnivorous animal, a wolf or a tiger, wielded by a human hand in such a way as to *mimic* the bite of an animal as it cut the throat.

"'Yet it was not very well done if you were able to recognize its artificiality,' said Monsieur Dupin, frowning.

"I assured him that it had fooled the police and would pass muster with most people, even other doctors, but that I had a great deal of experience with animal bites. Monsieur Dupin looked oddly reassured as he nodded his head. 'You are particularly observant, and very thorough in your examinations,' he said. 'A paragon among men of medicine!'

"As I was modestly denying this, Monsieur Dupin reached inside his coat to reveal what he had hidden there. It was something like the curved blade of a sickle, but lined with rows of sharp teeth, some of them natural animal teeth, others manufactured from glass and steel. At first, I felt only wonder at the sight of it, for I had not yet comprehended why Monsieur Dupin had come to visit me at home, so early in the morning, and I did not realize that the emotion I should have felt was fear, until I saw my own blood spurting out over the white table cloth, and knew it was far too late.

"I tried to ask him *why*, but could barely manage to gurgle as the life seeped out of my body. Yet he understood me well enough, smiling that distant, cold, inhuman smile of his as he replied, 'You may call it madness, but I do not. It *is* the greatest pleasure.'"

If it is true that the mesmerized can channel the voices of the dead, and if I truly spoke to the spirit of a murdered man, still I must ask: can the dead lie? Is his story true, or could it be some nightmare experienced by the soul in Limbo, no more to be believed than the mad visions that fill my own head every night?

There is no doubt in my mind that De La Roche met Dupin, for when I heard the altered voice of the medium describe his "distant, cold, inhuman smile," I could see it myself, with my inward eye, recalling how Dupin, in the grip of his analytical passion, would become frigid and abstract, his expression vacantly staring, his voice rising to a higher tone as if (I sometimes fancied) he was possessed of a bi-part soul, his body inhabited in turn by one of two distinctly different personalities. But never did I for a moment imagine that one of those two selves might be evil incarnate; I always knew Dupin for a prodigy and a wonder, not a monster.

I broke my promise to the rest of the audience and did not satisfy their curiosity by translating the conversation I'd had with the dead French doctor. Instead, I pleaded an attack of the megrims, and staggered out of the house just as soon as young Miss W— was restored to her natural self. The fortunate girl retained no recollection whatsoever of anything that had transpired during her trance, and no one else could enlighten her on the subject of what the Frenchman had said.

I do not want to believe that my old friend has become a killer. But I sense no trickery, and can think of no reason why someone should wish to fool me, or to blacken the name of C. Auguste Dupin.

Perhaps the most terrible thing is that although I do not want to believe it, neither can I wholly disbelieve. Knowing him as I did, I can imagine how his own curiosity and reliance on rationality could have been his undoing. The lack of any *reason* for the series of murders in his last case always preyed upon his mind. However repugnant and absurd, the explanation given by Reclus for his own actions could not be dismissed. The idea of murder as a pleasure might have become a maggot in Dupin's brain, eating away at him until he was finally driven to test the matter for himself.

Once having killed... But here my chain of reasoning breaks down, for I cannot believe that the man I knew, even at his most coldly analytical, could perform such a ghastly experiment. Surely he would not murder a helpless, harmless young woman simply to *test a theory*?

Even if he killed in self-defense, or to save someone else, killing someone who deserved to die... if, in so doing, he had tasted something of the intoxicating pleasure Reclus had promised, might he not have become addicted, driven to kill again?

But no, the idea is too repulsive. It is madness. Only a madman could conceive the notion of murder as "the greatest pleasure." Reclus was mad.

And Dupin?

Dupin, if he has become a killer, must be mad, in the same, seemingly rational way as the man he sent to the guillotine, the man who infected him with his terrible, repulsive idea.

Already, in the day and night that have passed since the mesmeric *séance* of which I have written, fresh reports have reached New York of still more killings in France: two sisters, this time, their throats savagely chewed by an unknown creature.

Yet how can I tell the police what I know? More importantly, how can I convince them? A letter is easily dismissed, and if I made the effort of traveling to France to speak to the people in power there, I should probably find myself locked up. I can imagine how Dupin would respond, with a mocking, pitying smile: "A dead man told you I had killed him? And do you often converse with the dead? This is common in America? My dear friend, I fear you are suffering from a fever of the brain…"

Dupin has the ear of the French police, as I do not, but I have something else. I have the ear of the public, in this country and abroad. My readers will not like this story as much as they liked "The Murders in the Rue Morgue." I admit, I do not like it so much myself. Yet it must be told. I must beg my readers to supply the necessary ending.

THE PURLOINED FACE

By

STEPHEN VOLK

My Dear Lestrade

I doubt you expected a further package from me for Scotland Yard's Black Museum, given that last time you heard from me I was at death's door. But the chill in my bones has passed and my doctor, a brusque devil, with none of the bedside manner of Watson, has told me to get air in my lungs and sun on my face. Whilst in that endeavor this afternoon, I experienced to my alarm something which brought back vividly to life one of the strange cases I investigated with the remarkable C. Auguste Dupin, long cloistered in fusty memory.

The local cinema is not a place I frequent often. I simply wanted somewhere to rest my feet, and can't say I even took note of the film that was playing before I entered the gloom. What unfolded on screen I found both sordid and spectacular, at times a turgid melodrama, but punctuated with moments of the most lurid terror.

It slowly dawned on me as I saw that wretched

underground lake, the abducted girl swept away in a gondola by the Phantom to his lair, that this was an adaptation of a novel I knew all too well. A beautiful soprano in love with a disfigured madman, a tepid variation on Beauty and the Beast: if only the truth, I thought, were as comforting in its roles of monster and victim. And when, in the Bal Masqué scene, the Phantom appeared as the Red Death from Poe's story of that name, the irony tore an involuntary laugh from my throat, somewhat distracting some members of the audience, who hushed me with frowning sibilance.

The gross travesty of what really happened at the Paris Opera first appeared in the pages of Le Gaulois back in the first decade of this century, but now this motion picture, starring the renowned "Man of a Thousand Faces," was spreading that fallacy to the world, projecting it in huge images, with organ accompaniment, for all to see. As I sat there watching the audience squirm and shriek at the monster's unmasking, I thought: If only they knew the truth...

You hold it in your hand, Inspector. Unmask it, if you dare. But I warn you, a decent man will be shaken by what he reads.

Holmes

Many mysteries came to the door of the man in the *Rue de la Femme-sans-Tête*. The district we lived in, the *Île de la Citée*, once thronged with thieves, whores, and murderers, but was now hemmed in by the gray edifice of the *Préfecture de Police*, law courts, and offices of civil servants, a bastion against the unrestrained and malevolent. Safe, but also strangely chill. He and I often yearned to stray into areas of the dissolute, vulgar, and unpredictable. At other times tales of the aberrant and profane beat a path, unbidden, to our door.

To relieve his inveterate boredom—and for the purpose of my further instruction in the science of "ratiocination"—Poe had set up a mirror at the window by which to observe the street below. When the brass bell rang unexpectedly at the *porte-cochère* on that particular April morning, echoing through the apartment, he asked me to report my observations in the short time it took for Le Bon to descend the stairs and return with our visitors.

"A man and a woman," I began, squinting down at our guests. "She seems nervous, delicate, uncertain..."

"'Seems' is not a fact," Poe interjected.

"Very well. I'd say from their relative ages he is her father. She wears a coat from *Le Bon Marché* and a black veil over her face, which indicates she is in mourning. I deduce therefore it is her husband who has died, mysteriously, and it is for that reason they have come. The man is around fifty-five years of age, rotund, and bears an uncanny resemblance to Balzac. Well-fed, and well off, by the cut of his jib. Overcoat worn over his shoulders in the manner of a Hussar. A definite military man. From his sallow skin tone and black hair there is Indian blood in his family tree, or Eurasian, possibly. And—hello?—a dash of red on his cravat. Blood? Good grief, perhaps the perpetrator of the deed is presenting himself to us with all the brazen aplomb of a murderer who thinks he is beyond the powers of detection..."

"Brilliant! That was truly instructive." Poe jumped from his chair and combed his thin, paper-white hair in the mirror. "Instructive in how to arrive at an entirely erroneous conclusion. Remind me not to ask you to fetch me black peppercorns in a field of rabbit droppings." I tried not to affect the disgruntlement of a schoolboy handed back homework that fell ruefully short of the mark. "That is not blood on his cuff, but strawberry conserve. To be exact, the one served with a *kipferl* at the *bijou boulangerie* on the Rue Bertrand Sluizer. Furthermore, he uses mustache wax by Marie Helene Rogeon, is a Corsican, has three brothers, lived in Avignon, the son of a shoe-mender, ran a ballet company, married a woman called Mathilde, and has five children. All girls. None married. Though one is the fiancée of a locomotive driver."

"Heavens above!" My head was spinning. "How on earth…?"

Poe's laugh was high and shrill as he slapped me on the shoulder. "My dear Holmes, forgive an old Southern gentleman his petty amusement! How could I resist teasing you when such an opportunity presented itself? I saw from the reflection that the man is Olivier Guédiguian, manager of the *Opéra de Paris*. The reason I know is very simply I have met him before, at the very *boulangerie* I mentioned: his habitual haunt for *petit dejeuner*. During our conversation he imparted a good deal about his life. At the time he was worried about a malignant superstition having a grip on his stage workers that some kind of, ahem, *specter* was causing damage and maladies of all descriptions. I was able to convince him that it was nothing but a series of accidents and coincidences, each perfectly explicable in its own right, but overall signifying nothing. And certainly nothing *supernatural*—the very word being a contradiction in terms. Metaphysics and philosophy! Why will people waste my time with trivialities!" We heard footsteps on the stair. "And by the way, the dress is from *La Samaritaine*, not *Le Bon Marché*."

I was speechless in the briefest pause before Poe's negro servant opened the double doors and ushered Monsieur Guédiguian and his female companion—*veiled* companion—into our presence. A parrot called Griswold squawked a few bars of the "Marseillaise" before chewing on a ball of nuts. There is no brass name-plate with *Dupin* etched on it down below, but it is curious that those who need his assistance always find him, one way or another.

Guédiguian untied his scarf and rolled it in a ball.

"Monsieur Dupin?"

I have described elsewhere how Edgar Poe lived beyond the date chiseled on his gravestone in Baltimore. Far from being, as is popularly believed, the drunken victim of a "cooping" gang at the elections in October 1849, he encountered that night, by remarkable coincidence, his *doppelgänger*, complete with a one-way ticket to Europe, and sensing escape from the rigors of his former life, swapped clothes with the dying inebriate, abandoning his old identity for an unknown future. He made Paris his secret home, at first in self-imposed exile at the *Hôtel Pimedon*, aided by his friend and translator Charles Baudelaire, assuming—with typical playfulness and black humor—the name of his famous detective of "Rue Morgue" fame: Dupin, and occasionally, under that appellation, helping the French police with their more baffling investigations, as food for a brain no longer with an appetite for mere fiction.

"Monsieur Guédiguian. My pleasure, yet again." As he shook his hand Poe saw our guest eyeing the thin young man standing at the window—myself. "This is my assistant, Monsieur Holmes. He speaks French like an Englishman, but is a master of discretion, as are all his countrymen. You may talk freely."

I met Poe in the guise of "Dupin" when I first came to Paris in my early twenties[1], and once within the penumbra of his intellect, having succumbed to his alluring devotion to his

---

[1] See "The Comfort of the Seine" in *Gaslight Arcanum: Uncanny Tales of Sherlock Holmes*—ed. J.R., Campbell and Charles Prepolec (Edge Publishing, 2011)

science, was unwilling—*unable*—to leave until I had learned all I could from the great man's unparalleled talent for deduction. Little did I know how that learning—or that friendship—would change my life forever.

"Allow me first to introduce Madame Anaïs Jolivet." Guédiguian touched the woman in the veil lightly on the elbow as he led her gently forward. She shuddered with every step as if treading on broken glass, so much so that, had she not possessed a curvaceous and upright frame, I might have taken her for an old crone.

Poe, as was his custom, took her hand to kiss it, and I saw instantly that the hand was not only shivering, but bandaged. She quickly inserted it in her fur muff as Guédiguian guided her to a seat, puffing up a cushion before she settled in it.

Sitting on the arm of her chair, the man seemed exhausted merely from being in her presence, and I feared he would not find the wherewithal to speak. She certainly showed no willingness to do so. It seemed as though all her physical effort went into holding herself in one piece, and a gust of wind might make her tumble down before our eyes. I also realized that the dress I took to be black was in fact navy blue, with tiny embossed *fleurs-de-lis* that sparkled like stars in a summer night. And who, I asked myself, dresses in navy blue whilst in mourning?

"Tea?" enquired Poe as Madame L'Espanaye, the maid, entered with a pot of Darjeeling. "Or something stronger? A glass of Virville? Pernod?" He was a teetotaler since his resurrection, but did not begrudge the pleasures of others, and kept a moderate cellar.

The woman looked up at Guédiguian like a frightened puppy.

"Water," he said. "And a drinking straw. If you please." He took her other hand gently in his own as the maidservant quietly exited, closing the doors after her. "I don't recall precisely how much you know about opera…"

"I know," said Poe, "by a certain deportment and an assessment of the capacity of the lungs that I am in the company of a *prima donna*."

I could not tell if the woman blushed behind her veil, but her chin sank slightly and she let go of the manager's hand in order to avail herself of a handkerchief.

"But, monsieur, that term only puts her within a category of greatness," said Guédiguian. "Madame Jolivet is beyond that. Madame Jolivet is immortal. We are blessed that she walks the streets of this fair city and does not sit in Heaven making the saints weep. When she played Gounod's Juliette she raised the roof of the *Théâtre-Lyrique*. Her Marguerite in *Faust* was outstanding. Those who missed her Pamina in *Die Zauberflöte* or the Countess in *The Marriage of Figaro* missed the supreme roles of the supreme soprano of her generation." I could see my elderly friend sinking in his armchair, his forearms making a bridge and his fingertips touching and separating with patient regularity as he listened. "She is a monument, sir. A monument! To both *coloratura* and dramatic intensity. There is… not another lyric singer… alive… who is… who can rise to the demands of…" The *impresario*'s shoulders sank and he pressed his fingers to the corners of his eyes. "I'm sorry… I'm sorry…"

"Not at all," I offered, sitting at the nearby bureau and opening my notebook.

Poe leapt from his chair the moment Madame L'Espanaye knocked and snatched the tray from her. He knelt in front of the veiled woman's chair and placed it on a foot stool. The glass filled, he inserted the straw and held it out to her. The merest croak of thanks—not even that—emerged from her lips. I would not have credited it as a woman's voice, had you pressed me. And possibly not even human.

She lifted the veil an inch and put the straw in her mouth.

"No," said Guédiguian as he saw Poe reach out his hand, but it was too late to stop him.

"I must."

The veil was raised, in the manner of a groom lifting the veil of his bride on their wedding day to plant a kiss on the lips of his betrothed. Nothing can be more grotesque or appalling an idea in view of what actually greeted our eyes.

I beheld the face of a rotting corpse. No. Half a face. Which, far from diluting the impact, only served to throw it into heightened obscenity by contrast. One eye was lustrous, that of a poor, frightened doe, the other lidless, shriveled, and blistered. The skin on one side flawless and pure, that of a beautiful woman, yet on the other—pitiful thing!—almost non-existent. She was eaten to the bone. I can only describe it, absurdly, as resembling the surface of a burnt sausage. Even that is inadequate. Her right cheek was gone, a flayed cavern in which I could count the teeth in her jaw and see her pink tongue wriggling, her right ear nothing more than a gristly stump. All this absorbed in an instant, and not forgotten in a lifetime.

I heard a death rattle, which was Madame Jolivet breathing with the horrid restriction her injuries compelled. Yet she held Poe's eyes without self-pity. And to his credit, he did not avert his gaze.

"Who did this?"

"We do not know." Guédiguian whimpered and sandwiched his hands between his thighs. "That is why we are here. It happened three weeks ago. Madame has not been well enough to move until today."

"You've spoken to the police?"

"We told them everything."

"Tell *me* everything."

"We had just begun rehearsing *La Traviata*. I had fired the conductor for being a drunk." Guédiguian began to pace back and forth behind her chair, occasionally tweaking it with his fingers as if to steady himself on a rolling sea. "I was calling in favors from old friends to ensure the production didn't run off the rails, but everybody was excited about Madame playing the part of Violetta. I knew it would be a complete triumph."

"How many of the cast had worked with Madame before?"

"That is not vital at this moment." Poe cut me off, his eyes never leaving the *diva*. "Please describe the incident as clearly as you can remember it."

"I must speak for her," said Guédiguian. "The merest exertion of the vocal chords causes her unbearable agony. She will never sing an aria again."

"Madame, not only has your body been cruelly abused," said Poe, "but so too has your soul. In that regard, justice is your only balm and my expertise—my *considerable* expertise—is at your service. Are you happy for Monsieur Guédiguian to continue on your behalf?"

Now self-conscious, the woman lowered the veil before nodding. Her face covered, she became perfection once more. And I could breathe freely.

Poe turned to the manager. "Pray continue."

"One day during rehearsals, at about four in the afternoon, Madame retired to her dressing room for a nap. She gave her boy a swift instruction that she was not to be disturbed. She undressed, put on her dressing gown, and lay on the day bed while upstairs the new conductor, Francesco Mazzini, put the orchestra through their paces. Half-dozing some minutes later—but not too much later, because the music had not changed, it was still 'Sempre Libera'—she remembers hearing the door open, thinking nothing much of it—perhaps it was the boy again, with flowers from an admirer, after all a day did not pass without her receiving some token or other. Suddenly, but not with horror, she felt liquid on her face. It had no obvious odor. Though momentarily startled, she presumed it was water—though why anybody would splash water on her face mystified her. She could only think it was a silly prank. Hardly had that thought begun to materialize when the substance began to burn. And when it did not stop burning, and when she felt the cheek under her fingers turning to mud, she screamed. Screamed till her lungs burst. Horribly, for a few seconds the singers next door took the high notes to be her practicing, then the truth…"

The man's thick hair hung lank. "I'm—sorry…"

"Please, monsieur," Poe urged. "For Madame."

"There is little more to tell." Guédiguian waved a hand spuriously. "The hospital did what they could. They still are doing. But her face is a ruin. Her life is a ruin. They can rebuild neither. If she had a husband… but now…" He swallowed the thought, shaking his head, regretting he had even given it form. "Who would do such a thing? Who?"

"The police conducted interviews?"

"Endlessly. The chorus were becoming hoarse from repeating where they were and with whom. I think the paperwork must be longer than *La Comédie Humaine*."

"Word count is only an illusion of achievement," said Poe. "Over time, and with increasing desperation, the core, the essence, becomes obscured like a diamond lost in a bush of thorns. What is the name of the officer in charge?"

"Bermutier."

"Henri Bermutier. Not the sharpest bayonet in the army, but count yourself lucky you didn't get that lazy pig Malandain."

"It was Bermutier who pointed us in your direction, *Maestro*. He said if any man in Paris could find the solution to the mystery, it was C. Auguste Dupin."

"*Naturellement*." Poe explained that his method demanded he have unfettered access to the scene of the crime, and our new client assured us of his every co-operation, together with that of his numerous employees, whether performers or artisans. "The tea is stewed to the consistency of an Alabama swamp. I shall get us a fresh pot."

"We—we shall decline your kind offer, monsieur..." Guédiguian accurately read the signal of his companion tugging his sleeve. "We have to go. Madame, you see, she is tired... The slightest exertion..."

Speaking for Poe and myself I said we understood completely and any other questions could be answered in the fullness of time.

Neither had removed their coats. Guédiguian offered La Jolivet his arm. Once more Poe took the lady's hand and kissed it, and I sensed she was thankful that he did. Charm sometimes trumped his insensitivity. Otherwise life in his company, frankly, would have been intolerable.

"There is something else I should say, which I fear will shock and displease you." Guédiguian turned back, knotting his scarf. "This incident has rekindled backstage rumors of a *fantôme*. Tongues are wagging that the production is cursed, that the opera house is haunted, that this is merely the beginning of a concerted spree of malevolence from beyond the grave..."

"It always displeases me," sneered Poe, lighting a cigarette from a candle, "when I have it confirmed that the imaginative excesses of the poorly educated know no bounds. But shock? No. I would have been shocked had they not."

"But—beyond the grave? Monsieur Dupin, I confess to you, I was brought up in fear of the Church and in fear of God…"

"Then good luck to you." Poe jangled the bell-pull to summon Le Bon. "But there is no *beyond* in matters of the grave. There is only—the *grave*. The Conqueror Worm and all his wriggling allies in decomposition. If this abominable act tells us anything, it is that the creature we seek is flesh and blood."

"I wish I could be so certain."

Behind Guédiguian, the woman's back was turned, like a silhouette cut from black paper. A long curl of fair hair, colorless as flax, lay on the night-blue of her shoulder. The man placed his hand against her back, and they were gone, like phantoms themselves.

"The quantity used was small, so the assailant must have been close. Very close." Our carriage took us at speed down the Avenue de l'Opéra. To Poe the imposing five-story buildings either side, which had eradicated the medieval city at the mercy of Haussman's modernization, were invisible. "Sulfuric acid, by the lack of odor. Used to pickle silver by jewelers. Readily dissolves human tissue, prolonged exposure causing pulmonary incapacity and tooth erosion. Severely corrosive to most metals, and shows an unquenchable thirst. If a flask of it is allowed to stand uncovered, it'll absorb water from the air until the container overflows, so must be handled with the utmost care. In highly diluted form it is available as a medical laxative. Used in horticulture to eradicate weeds and moss. Also as a drain cleaner…"

"Paris has good need for drain cleaner, I'll give you that. It out-stinks London."

"London has a perfume by comparison." He blinked languorously, acknowledging my presence for the first time in minutes. "Paris was born in filth and blood and other liquids, my dear Holmes. Violence is its beating heart. And freedom will be the death of it."

The Opéra Garnier was not to my taste, but had to be admired. A triumph of engineering, indeed of artistic will, it captured something, if not everything, of its era. Completed only a few years before, the neo-Baroque masterpiece had been commissioned by Napoleon III as part of his grandiloquent and massive reshaping of Paris, designed unashamedly as a flamboyant riposte to the established opera houses of Italy. Over a fifteen-year gestation, its construction had been held up by multifarious incidents and setbacks, from mundane lack of funds to upheavals such as the Franco-Prussian War and the demise of the Empire in favor of a new Republic. As a visual statement, its Imperial glory suddenly spoke only of the former regime in all its dubious splendor, and the politicians, freshly warming their rumps in the seats of office, were inherently ill-disposed toward its existence. The most that was done, in the end, was to change the Opéra's official name on the entablature fronting the loggia from "Academie Imperiale de Musique" to "Academie *Nationale* de Musique." Happily for the craftsmen involved, a difference of only six letters.

Personally I saw the edifice before me as a resplendent example of grandeur and folly in roughly equal measure. With sunlight gilding the figures of Music and Dance on the *façade* and Apollo atop the dome, it was almost impossible to conceive that such an odious crime could have happened under the aegis of such gods and noble virtues.

"Another disfigurement. Almost a prediction, if you believe

such nonsense." As we climbed the steps to the entrance, Poe pointed out Carpeaux's sculpture, which had so shocked the Puritans of Paris in its erotic depiction of *La Dance* that ink was thrown over its marble thighs. "Ink. Acid. I know some critics where the two are synonymous."

If we had doubted the atmosphere of superstitious dread permeating the company, we soon found it illustrated when the doorman almost leapt out of his skin at the sound of our rapping. Poe introduced himself—as "Dupin," naturally—and proceeded to interrogate the individual, a *sapeur-pompier* with a wooden leg, about his actions on the afternoon in question. The fellow was adamant that nobody had entered or left the theater on his watch and he himself never strayed from his post until the doors were locked.

We ascended the Grand Staircase with its balustrade of red and green marble and two bronze female *torchières* in the direction of the foyers.

Poe sniffed like an eager bloodhound as we were surrounded by immense mirrors and parquet, more colored marble, moulded stucco, and sculptures.

"These are the mirrors in which the audience watch the show *before* the show." He looked at the vast room in reflection, and at his own. "This is where they see each other, and themselves. And find themselves on the upper step, or the lower. The inane dance of the socially inclined and the artistically disinterested. I'd wager by law of averages that of the myriad citizens crammed in here on opening night, at least five are murderers."

"A sobering thought."

"On the contrary, a thought to turn one to drink," said Poe. "I should know."

We had lied to the doorman. Our appointment with

Guédiguian was at three. It gave us a full hour to explore unhindered, an opportunity my colleague took to with relish. He had been given extensive floor plans of the Opéra, but nothing, he said, was a substitute for the application of the senses. If there were gods that deserved statuary, Poe declared, it was Sight, Smell, Touch, Taste, and Hearing.

And so we roamed the interweaving corridors, stairwells, alcoves, and landings. Before long it was not hard to imagine a clever infiltrator scampering from floor to floor or room to room unseen. Skulking round the Romano-Byzantine labyrinth, several times I wished for Ariadne's ball of twine, fearful that we had lost our way, while Poe counted his footsteps into hundreds, storing myriad calculations of I-knew-not-what. But then, I seldom did.

A swell of music rose up and I was momentarily reminded of the old adage of a dying man hearing a choir of angels. The gas-lit passageway gave the notes a dull, eerie resonance, making it tricky to know whether the source was near or far. But when Poe opened a door and we stepped into a fourth-level box overlooking the stage, the voices and orchestra took on voluminous proportions.

The tiny figures before us were dwarfed in a five-tier auditorium resplendent in red velvet, plaster cherubs, and gold leaf. The magnificent house curtain with gold braid and pom-poms was raised above the proscenium. And presiding over all—in fact partly obscuring our view—hung the magnificent seven-ton crystal and bronze chandelier which alone, if you are to believe the controversy, cost thirty thousand gold francs.

I am marginally more familiar with *La Traviata* now than I was then, and could not have told you in those days they were rehearsing Act Two, Scene Two—the *soirée* at Flora's house, in which Alfredo, here a beefy man with the build of a prize-fighter, sees his love, the former courtesan Violetta, with Baron Douphol. After winning a small fortune from the Baron, he bitterly rounds up the guests to witness her humiliation—"*Questa donna conoscete?*"—before hurling his winnings at her feet in payment for her "services." Whereupon she faints to the floor.

"She faints in Act One, too," said Poe, paying less attention to the stage than he did to the fixtures and fittings of the box. "Never a good sign."

"More to the point, Guédiguian hasn't wasted any time in finding a new Violetta. I presume that's her understudy."

Poe arched an eyebrow.

As we listened to the guests turn on Alfredo—singing "*Di donne ignobile insultatore, di qua allontanati, ne desti orror!*"— Poe could no longer bear the pain and left the box, muttering that high art was invariably highly dull. The art of the street, the Penny Dreadful and barrel organ, he found more rewarding, he said—and more honest. "I don't know about you, but I have seldom been accompanied by an orchestra in my moments of intimate passion."

"But is there a clue in the play?" I caught up with him in the corridor.

"Why would there be?"

"I don't know. Do you? I've never stepped in an opera house before. I don't even know what *La Traviata* means."

"The Fallen Woman. It is based on *La Dame aux Camélias*, a play in turn based on a novel by Dumas, *fils*—in turn based, some say, on a lady of his own acquaintance. The play was a big success when I first arrived in Paris, especially after it was vilified by the censors."

"For what reason?"

"A high-living prostitute depicted as a victim of society? Especially when she never sees the light? In London, I believe they tried to get an injunction to stop it. But then, it is never entirely a bad thing for a work of art to be pilloried by the Church. In America they say the plot is immoral, though no worse than *Don Giovanni*. Here, it was first performed at the Théâtre Lyrique on the Place de Chatelet with Christine Nilsson in the title role. Too chaste-looking for a harlot, if you ask me."

"You saw it?"

"Yes, which is why I abhor opera with every fiber of my being. Rarely does an art form offend all the senses at once, and the buttocks more than any. Nothing less than the crucifixion of Christ should last more than forty minutes. And God forbid that Judas should sing about it. Though, given time, I'm sure he shall." Keeping up his sprightly pace, he turned a corner. "The truth is, my dear Holmes, I endured this mellifluous obscenity once and did not care for it. In fact, I walked out."

He strode on several yards before replying to my unspoken question, but did not turn to face me.

"You see... the soprano was too old, too obese... almost to the point of being flabby, to play—to *conceivably* play, with any hope of conviction—the part of a young woman dying of consumption." His face creased and twitched with the most intense inner agitation. "That she sang with such—abnormal gusto, with superhuman energy—with such buoyant, lustrous, glowing *health*. And the fact that she was applauded. That people *cheered*..."

He had told me before of Virginia, his cousin and child bride. Her icy pallor, cheeks rubbed with plum juice to fake a ruddy complexion. Her dry lips enlivened briefly with the color of cherries. The coughing of blood onto a pure white handkerchief. He had also, once, intimated that the disease gave spells of excitement, even desire; that there was an aphrodisiac quality to the fading bloom. I think it was this that haunted him most of all. I cannot imagine what he had suffered. To bear helpless witness to a death so inevitable yet so gradual. To see loveliness—one's very reason for living—wither on the vine, and all around feel harangued by the prejudice of others, not knowing whether to blame habits or heredity or himself. Then to be there as the leaf takes to the wind, leaving its heavy load behind…

"From the opening music we are in the presence of death. Eight first and eight second violins portray the frail consumptive. Curtain up on a party scene. We are told the hostess is seeing her doctor. I know that feeling well. I have been in that scene, that room, many times. She wants to enjoy life fully because it is fleeting. Parties will be the drug to kill her pain. I understand that too. They drink a toast because love is life. *Fervido. Fervido…* A fever… A passion…"

The female voice rose again, distant as the angels.

"It is a lie, as all Art lies. There is no aria at the end. There is only the incessant coughs, the swelling of joints, the loss of weight, the cadaverous emaciation, delirium, torment—and, if one is lucky, the uttering of a lover's name."

Straightening his back he walked on, anxious not to meet my eyes, though he would never have admitted it. No more was said on the subject. He had closed a heavy door and I knew I could not open it. Only he could do that, when—and if—he wished.

We found a staircase. Narrow. Badly lit. And descended.

I made to speak, but Poe raised a finger to his lips. We entered the auditorium and the music swelled louder.

We crept nearer to the stage, where Laurent Loubatierre, the tenor playing Alfredo, stood delivering an aria. We settled into a couple of seats off the central aisle, far enough back not to be noticed by the several people with their backs to us who formed a meager audience—costumier, copyist, dramaturge, dance manager, and so on. Or so we thought.

Poe sank in his chair, thin neck disappearing into his collar, long white hair sitting on his shoulders, and eyes heavy-lidded like those of a slumbering owl. I had placed my notebook on my knee, when I was aware that the tenor's notes were falling flat, and looked up to see Loubatierre pinching the bridge of his nose, blinking furiously, then shading his eyes with his hand as he advanced to the footlights.

"I am sorry, Maestro! But this is impossible! I cannot work with such distractions!" He peered out, pointing in our exact direction, straight past the hapless conductor. "Who are these people? You! Yes, you sir! Both of you! Who invited you here? On what authority…?" He became apoplectic. "Somebody fetch Guédiguian! Fetch him *immediately*!" The assorted lackeys threw looks at each other and one, by some mute agreement, ran out to do his bidding. "I cannot continue—I *refuse* to continue—until you reveal yourselves!"

"I shall, gladly." Poe spoke calmly, examining his fingernails. "When the cast of this opera reveal themselves and give a true account of their movements on the day Madame Jolivet was attacked."

"How dare you! This is outrageous!"

"The ravaging of a beautiful woman's face is outrageous, Monsieur Loubatierre. Your indignation merely ludicrous." A couple of ballerinas in the background looked at each other, open-mouthed. And if Loubatierre was already red-faced with anger, he was now virtually foaming at the mouth.

"You told the police you visited Monsieur Rodin the sculptor at his *atelier* on the Left Bank to sit for him, but according to my enquiries Monsieur Rodin has been in Italy and only returned yesterday, for the unveiling of his *L'Âge d'Airain* at the Paris Salon."

"I don't have to account for my whereabouts to you!"

"You might find that you do."

"Who is this man? That is an unspeakable accusation! I have a good mind to thrash him within an inch of his life!"

"I would very much prefer an answer," said Poe with lugubrious contempt. "Need I point out the truism that a man who has recourse to violence usually has something to hide?"

"Beckstein!" Loubatierre, supremely flustered, addressed the most smartly dressed and rotund of the assembled, whom we later came to understand was the opera house's dramaturge. "Throw him out this instant! I insist! I *insist*!"

The singer turned his back sharply, appealing with extravagant gestures to the gods. Other members of the cast hurried on in their tights, bustles, and blouses, trying their best to placate him, though he shrugged off, equally extravagantly, any attempt to do so. Poe, to my amazement, started to applaud and shout "Bravo! Bravo!" which served only to agitate the performer further. The poor man was incandescent to the point of immobility.

"Monsieur!" Guédiguian arrived, puffing. "What is the cause of all this—?"

"Exactly." Poe rose to his feet and shot his cuffs. "Monsieur Loubatierre's behavior is inexcusable."

The tenor rounded on him now, head down and ready to charge off the stage, had he not been held back.

"Monsieur Dupin! Really!" blubbered Guédiguian, whose own cheeks were reddening. "Perhaps you can explain—"

Poe cut in before he could finish, with his habitual air of distraction. "Perhaps *you* can explain, monsieur, why we were able to wander every floor of this building with impunity, not once being asked our identity or purpose of our visit till now. But to wander with impunity is one thing, to escape the building without being seen by the watchmen at every exit, quite another. If we solve that conundrum, we solve the crime. Now, I should like to question the understudy. What is her name?"

Bamboozled, Guédiguian could do nothing better than to answer the question directly. "Marie-Claire Chanaud."

"Excellent. Where is she?"

Guédiguian appealed to his staff for an answer.

"She… she is not here, monsieur," said Beckstein in a thick German accent.

"Not here?" Poe approached the orchestra pit, and I with him. "Then where? Backstage? Bring her out. It is imperative."

"No, monsieur. She has been working very hard. She complained of a dry throat. With nerves, as you know, the throat tightens. And a singer is an athlete. They must take care of their most delicate instrument. We thought it best she went to the dressing room to rest…"

"You left her *alone*? Unprotected?"

I barely had time to register the ferocity in Poe's face as a clatter of footsteps drew my eyes with a whiplash to the wings, where a small boy ran onto the boards, almost tripping over his clogs in his haste. The entrance was so dramatic that for a split second I took it for a part of the rehearsal, until I saw his blanched face and the tiny hand pressed to his chest as he tried to catch breath, ripping the cloth cap from his tousled head as he cried out to Guédiguian:

"Monsieur! *Monsieur!* He's struck again, sir! The Phantom!" His eyes were unblinking and his lip quivering. "He's struck *again*!"

Alarm taking hold in the auditorium, Poe and I wasted not an instant in thundering downstairs and through coffin-narrow corridors in pursuit of the lad, who moments later stood aside in terror of seeing what revolting scene might confront him in the dressing room.

Inside, we saw what he had seen—a large bunch of flowers tied in a red bow propped against the mirror, shriveling on bending, blackening stalks as we stared at them—a sickening picture of decay seen through some kaleidoscope free of the strictures of time, speeding toward dissolution. Beside it, the open pages of a poetry book lay sizzling, Gérard de Nerval's *Les Chimères* turning to acrid vapor in the air. Poe coughed into his handkerchief. I moved forward to enter, but he extended an arm across my body to block the way.

The chair was overturned.

The dressing room—*empty*.

With a terrible, rising certainty that the understudy had been abducted, I ran to the Stage Door, only to find it bolted.

"Here!"

Returning, I saw that Poe had whisked aside the curtain of an alcove to reveal the trembling singer standing there in nothing but her underwear, having narrowly escaped having her face ravaged by the same demon who had attacked Madame Jolivet.

He picked up a cloak and wrapped it round her shoulders.

"Did any of it touch you? Madame? Are you hurt in any way?" She shook her head. "Are you sure? If it fell on your skin... or eyes..." He turned to the loons congregated at the door. "Water! Get water! Now!" She stepped forward, but sagged into his arms.

I grabbed the chair to prop it under her before she fell. "Stand back! She needs air, can't you see? Clear the way. We need to get her out of here."

The two of us lifted her under the armpits and knees and deposited her gently on a wicker basket in the corridor. She was light as a feather.

"Open the Stage Door and let the fumes out. And nobody go in that room. Be careful how you touch anything."

In a few moments water came, and a sponge, and I ran it over her forehead and cheeks. "Did you breathe it in?"

Again the young soprano shook her head, her blue-black curls, which fell considerably below her shoulders, shining. In this semi-swoon, with her almost painted eyebrows and porcelain skin, extreme thinness, and long neck, I suddenly thought her the perfect picture of the phthisic beauty of consumption. Uncomfortably, it made me look over at Poe, who was glaring at her.

"There was no note with the flowers. Who sent them?"

"Dupin!" I protested.

"Allow her to answer, Holmes, please."

"In truth, I do not know," Marie-Claire said. "I simply came to my dressing room and there they were."

"From an admirer," I suggested.

"Precisely," said Poe, crouching at her side, resting the flats of his hands on the silver wolf's head of his walking cane.

253

"The door was bolted!" snapped the stage doorman, Christophe. "You saw it yourself, monsieur. Nobody could have left without me seeing them, I stake my life on it! Nobody living!"

"Tell me what happened," said Poe to the young woman.

"My dresser, Rosa, helped me change out of my costume." Marie-Claire regained her composure admirably, perhaps because her leading man, Loubatierre, now held her hand. "The girls took it away to do some alterations. I ate some fruit and felt a little better, but didn't want to sleep any more so I read my book and combed my hair. It is foolish, but that has always calmed me, ever since *Maman* used to do it when I was little. I think the motion is soothing; it clears the mind. Well, I was gazing at my own reflection, not especially thinking about anything. Perhaps I was wondering who sent the flowers. Many things. Or perhaps nothing. Sometimes nothing at all goes through this head of mine." A smile flickered, accompanying the most nervous of giggles. "Then..."

"You monster," snarled Loubatierre. "Is it really necessary to put Madame through such torture?"

"It is," insisted Poe. "Continue."

"Then I dropped my bookmark and bent to pick it up. I heard a splash, sat up straight again wondering what it was, and I saw this most horrible sight, of the flowers dying, evaporating right before my eyes. Something prevented me from touching them. Thanks be to Jesus, Mary, and Joseph. And in the mirror I saw behind me, perched on my reflection's shoulder, such a face— indescribable! With holes for eyes. Empty sockets, and... and a *beak*, like some storybook witch, not even human at all, more like a bird—a bird with green scales and no eyes. I don't know what it was, but it was the face of some kind of devil, of... of pure darkness..."

Loubatierre kissed her tiny fist.

"I dare not even think what might have happened if I wasn't wearing this." Marie-Claire touched the crucifix on a chain around her neck then kissed it. "It saved me."

Loubatierre, the bear, embraced her.

"In the name of Pity," said Poe, "please do not burst into song." He turned to me. "The flowers were not from an actor. To an actor, flowers before a performance mean bad luck. But they're from someone who knows *this* opera enough to send camellias. So he is someone already in the building. But that is not our culprit. Come with me." He strode to Christophe and addressed him: "Look directly into my eyes and tell me, what color are the buttons on my assistant's waistcoat?"

"Brown."

"And how many are buttoned? Keep looking into my eyes."

"Two."

"There is nothing wrong with your vision. Where were you standing or sitting?" The man shuffled into his position behind the shelf of his booth. "And you did not leave? Nothing distracted you?" The man screwed up his beret in his fists and shook his head. "Then if someone entered you would have seen them."

"Madame saw nobody. I saw nobody. The thing cannot be seen. Doors and walls are nothing to the Phantom. That much is certain."

"Nothing is certain," said Poe.

An hour later we were in the Opéra manager's office. His hand shook as he poured brandies, and to my astonishment expressed concern that the production would be ready for opening night in a few days time.

"Monsieur." I stepped forward to stand beside the chair in which Marie-Claire sat. "You cannot seriously be considering that can happen, even as the remotest possibility, while this criminal is at large and his intent against Madame could hardly be more clear."

"Please, Monsieur Holmes, do not impugn my sensitivity. No man could be more appalled than I, but my position here means I have to think of the Palais Garnier."

"You value the fortunes of the Palais Garnier above a *life*?"

"Of course not. I nevertheless have to bear in mind that if opening night is canceled, people will ask why. The natural consequence of that is the future of the Opéra may be called into question. The government is all too eagerly looking for the appropriate excuse to shut us down. I have to think not only of Madame—with the greatest respect—but every soul working under this roof."

"In any case…" Marie-Claire rose to her feet. "I'm sorry gentlemen, but there is no question of my *not* playing Violetta on opening night. Monsieur Dupin, I appreciate your efforts as a detective, and those of Monsieur Holmes today, but I have waited my entire life for the opportunity to sing this part." Her back ramrod-straight, from a frail, *petite* girl she took on the aspect of an Amazon. "As I see it, if we let the fiend stop us, whoever or whatever he might be, then the fiend has won."

"Admirable," said Poe, resisting a smile as well as the brandy snifter. "Foolish, but admirable."

"But be under no illusion regarding our gratitude, Monsieur Dupin, nor our desperation. Our safety—Madame's safety—is now entirely in your hands." Guédiguian let the import sink in as the golden liquid trailed down his throat, and my own. Marie-Claire had downed hers in one gulp and returned the glass to its tray before we did.

"My father taught me that."

"My father taught me Shakespeare," said Poe. "He was an actor, but a bad one. You should always have enough gum on your beard when you play Lear, or hilarity ensues. Not what the Bard of Avon had in mind. Though entertaining enough to a four-year-old standing in the wings."

Marie-Claire smiled, but I thought of Poe's mother, an actress too, he'd once told me. I didn't know why I hadn't thought before of his obvious connection to the world of theater. It was in his blood: literally so. She too had died of consumption—his "Red Death" to be—coughing up blood on stage as little Eddie watched, mouthing her lines, the audience not even knowing something was wrong as she slumped in agony, thinking the acting peculiarly good that night in Richmond during *Romeo and Juliet*. Inconceivable to think of it other than as a ghastly foretaste of Virginia and the tragedy to come. The first of a catalogue of losses that were to blight Poe's life, and to this mind, the anvil that forged him. The reward being a great writer. But what a price. Too, too much a price, for any man...

C. Auguste Dupin took the fingers of Marie-Claire Chanaud and pressed his lips to them. Her arm was barely bone in her sleeve, the hand itself as fragile as the skeleton of a bird. Her skin white and untarnished, the perfection of a tombstone freshly carved. Her eyes lustrous with the burning of night.

"The curtain will rise," said Guédiguian.

"The curtain *has* risen," corrected my friend the detective with an expression I could not decide was one of fear or of singular anticipation. "Our characters are on stage. Our villain is waiting in the wings. After the interval, we shall begin Act Three. I simply hope we have not paid to watch a tragedy."

* * *

I knew things were amiss whenever he asked me to talk rather than listen, and that night as the gliding Le Bon lit candles and Madame L'Espanaye served us a supper of oven-warm bread and Normandy camembert so ripe it ran from its skin, he demanded to hear my theory.

"Theory?"

"Yes, Holmes. Theory. Of this elusive Phantom. You have been silent. I hope you have been thinking, but possibly I'm in for a disappointment."

"Well…" I had been caught on the hop. Again the schoolmaster and pupil. I lit a pipe of Altadis Caporal, an earthy *tabac gris*. "I think there's a productive line of enquiry in the fact that Guédiguian, the manager, comes from Corsica. From what I have read, certain Corsican families who get money by extortion and intimidation operate within a secret code called *vendetta*—members are obliged to kill not only anyone who besmirches the family honor, but anyone in *their* family, too. Slights and grievances go back decades. There have been four thousand murders—"

"Mostly garrottings and stabbings, with the odd blinding." Poe took the pipe from my mouth, filled his cheeks, and handed it back without a word. "The Corsicans are a predictable bunch. And they like the victim to know precisely why they're doing it. Rarely cultivate a sense of mystery. Quite the opposite. But well done. We can now rule that out. Anything else?" He descended low into his armchair, crossed his legs and put his hands behind his head before expelling the smoke, which rose in an undulating cloud to the ceiling.

"I noticed a proliferation of tattoos amongst the men working behind the scenes. Also the swaying gait common to seamen. According to my researches, many of the stage crew are traditionally hired from ships in port. If a seafarer was seeking revenge against somebody—a captain perhaps, responsible for the loss of a ship... We could look at the records of shipwrecks, the names—"

"And entirely waste our time."

"Forgive me, but why ask for my deductions, if you seek only to dismiss them?"

"I seek only to arrive at the truth. And they are not deductions, Holmes, they are *suppositions*. Flights of fancy. I have told you before that guesswork is the recourse of the buffoon or the police inspector. When we use my methods, we build our house on sound foundations or none at all."

Poe flicked the tails of his coat and sat on the piano stool at his writing desk with his back to me. He lifted a candle-stick to his elbow, unscrewed an ink pot, and started to scratch with his pen, but the real purpose, I knew, was just that—to have his back to me.

I tapped my pipe bowl against the fire surround, but did not take myself off to bed as he perhaps wished. Stubbornly, I stayed. I hoped he might, as a clever man, draw some conclusion from that. But his pride excelled his wisdom that night.

"This Phantom..."

"Phantoms! Demons! Ghosts!" He rubbed the back of his neck without turning. "Do not desert C. Auguste Dupin for the realm of actors and unreason. If that is your desire, Holmes, I tell you now—go home to London. I have no more to teach you."

A lump came to my throat. He was goading me, but I refused to rise to the bait. I would not be his mental punch bag.

"I intend to stay."

Poe did not reply. He remained sitting with hunched

shoulders and the sound of his scribbling nib in the candlelight. I intuited, however—intuition being only a hop and a skip from guesswork, as he might say—that his change in mood was not about me, and not entirely about the nature of the mystery that was testing us so sorely, either.

He crossed the room and yanked the servant cord. When Le Bon came he asked him to deliver a message by hand the following day. "To Colonel Guy Follenvie, postmaster at the Place de Ravaillac. Tell him to meet me on the opening night of *La Traviata* at the Palais Garnier on Friday. The details are enclosed. And remember to tell him to bring Madame Lop-Lop."

"Madame Lop-Lop?" I sniggered, perplexed.

He ignored me. "Are my instructions clear, or are they not?"

Le Bon said they were.

"I have an appointment tomorrow with a saddle maker, name of Hermès," Poe continued, this incongruous piece of information as mystifying to me as the first. "Do not let me sleep after nine. I shall take coffee but no toast. Holmes can do as he pleases."

His tetchiness with the negro confirmed what I had begun to suspect: from what Poe had said in the shadowy corridors of the Opéra Garnier, I knew he had turned over old soil, and that the bones of the most painful recollections imaginable, that of his long lost love, his first and only love, Virginia, had been unearthed. To my dismay, far from being a hero of vast intelligence and indefatigable vigor, the figure in the semi-gloom—Dupin, Poe—now looked like a husk of humanity. Not a god of the dark imagination or giant of literature, but instead a brittle insect crushable under foot.

I stepped closer. "Can I get you—?"

"No."

Reluctantly, I left the room and went to my bed, but did not sleep.

Lying awake, I pondered whether, for all his absolute faith in the appliance of "ratiocination" and his unwavering dedication to that skill in his latter years, the Socrates to my Plato had increasingly built a dam to keep the vast lake of his inner feelings at bay, at no inconsiderable cost, and—after his sudden ill temper tonight—if unchecked or unheeded, one day that dam might burst.

My private concerns over my mentor's wellbeing only contributed to my further ill ease as opening night drew closer. I slept badly, drank excessively, and by the time we arrived at the Opéra Garnier, my nerves were so jangled that the gas-lights of the boulevards swam in my face like Montgolfier balloons. The conflux of so many carriages dispensing their chattering cargo was so overwhelming, I felt palpitations. So unsure of my grip on my senses was I that I swear I saw a man in a peaked cap taking a pig for a walk.

"Lo! 'tis gala night…"

In the cab, Poe lifted a mahogany box onto his knees, unclipped the brass catches, and opened it. Wrapped in red satin lay two flintlocks I recognized immediately as Denix French dueling pistols.

"Our difference of opinion has come to this?" I mused, not entirely seriously.

Poe, stern-faced, handed me one. "I can think of no man I would rather trust when cogent thinking runs aground and the only logical recourse is to a lead ball and gunpowder." This was as much as I could expect as an apology for his recent behavior, and rather more than I was accustomed to. "My home country is big on these things. I hear they often use them in lieu of democratic debate." He blew down one barrel, then squinted along the length of the other. "I'd have picked up a gun for the South in the war, had I been on the right continent."

"No you wouldn't."

He pouted indignantly. "I went to West Point, I'll have you know."

"Don't be ridiculous."

"Kicked out for insubordination."

"Now I'm starting to believe you."

Dressed for the opera in top hats and capes, we joined the milling throng and were carried by the flow of the crowd up the Grand Staircase. It was mildly ironic to think all these theatergoers done up to the nines were coming to see a tale about disease, death, and prostitution, but such is the wonder of art—or of beautiful music, anyway—to make anything palatable.

We met Bermutier in Box "C," as planned, from which we could watch the seats filling below. If the policeman had nerves half as frayed as I did, he concealed it well. He reported that, according to "Dupin's" explicit instructions, there were thirty men in plain clothes placed in strategic positions around the building. Poe repeated his insistence that they be in sight or earshot of each other and Bermutier confirmed that they were, several with *Garde du Corps du Roi* firearms secreted about their persons, and all with batons and whistles. The one thing they lacked, he said, was any rough description of what this malefactor might look like.

"Monsieur Holmes will tell you," said Poe, to my evident surprise.

"Me?"

"Yes, my friend. I guarantee that within the minute you will be telling Bermutier here exactly what our criminal looks like." He looked down upon the audience as he spoke. "What manner of man could hide in a room unnoticed? Hide under the dressing room table, perhaps, invisible? Slip under the Stage Door shelf, unseen by an eagle-eyed doorman? And slip away again, below the eye-line of you or me?"

"Someone of exceptionally, I don't know—small stature..." An idea went off in my mind like a struck match. "Good God! You can't mean—a *dwarf*!"

"Yes. A dwarf. When you remove the impossible... What was your phrase, Holmes? I thought it was rather good..." Poe unfolded a large sheet of paper from his inside pocket and thrust it at Bermutier. "Holmes and I are going to take up position outside the dressing rooms. Your men are covering the back-stage areas and front of house. I've marked this architectural plan with red crosses where I've seen trapdoors or manholes down to the underworld. That's where he will make his escape."

"Underworld?" I was shocked.

"There is a subterranean lake under this building. A labyrinth of canals and vaults almost the equal of that which is above ground. His hiding place, if not his habitation."

"The Phantom was under our feet all the time!" I said.

Bermutier folded the plans and stuffed them in his pocket, tugging the brim of his hat as he headed to the door.

"Take the utmost care, Bermutier," said Poe. "He does not want Violetta to sing tonight. He intends his desecration of beauty to be complete."

The dressing rooms were busy as we took up our positions near the Stage Door. Loubatierre, in his wig as Alfredo, emerged to make his way upstairs, taken aback to see C. Auguste Dupin, detective, walking toward him.

"Merde," said Poe. The traditional "break a leg" of French actors.

"Merde," repeated the *primo tenore* grudgingly, and was gone.

Dressers and wardrobe mistresses with peacock feathers and robes flitted to and fro. A man in a waistcoat continually checked his watch. Christophe was ensconced in his position. I casually asked after the small boy. "We never saw him again. His mother sent a letter saying he was too afraid to come back." Neither of us found that wholly surprising.

"We would do best to split up," Poe said to me. "You stay here, outside the door. I shall position myself in the dressing room with Madame Chanaud." He checked the hammer action of his pistol, turning to go, but I caught his arm.

"You do not believe in demonic forces, and neither do I. But these acts are no less than atrocities. Mindless atrocities. Is it conceivable that pure evil can manifest in a human being?"

"Evil is a convenient label invented by the sanctimonious to describe the unfathomable." He walked to the dressing room door and knocked. "There are only *deeds*, which we may define as good or bad according to our nursery training and the books we read. The deeds of human beings upon each other and the infinitely complex or infinitesimally simple reasons they commit them." He knocked a second time and entered.

I felt strangely alone. As if by magic the corridor was deserted. The chaotic movement of figures all round us had abated: they had all flown to their posts. Actors waiting in the wings for the action to begin—as were we all. Nervous—as were we all. Fearful—as were we all.

Now the man checking his pocket watch was me.

Above, muffled by distance and woodwork, I heard the orchestra practicing in short, unpredictable bursts. Discordant notes seeped through the building and into my bones.

Walking to the Stage Door to test the bolt, I passed the dressing room door, but could hear no voices within. Christophe's chalky pallor matched my own.

I heard a clatter of footsteps from the dark. I caught a rake of a man by the wrist and asked his name. He said, "Rennedon." He stuttered that he had to give Madame her fifteen-minute call. I told him to do it quickly and go.

When he came a second time he looked frightened of me and retreated a step or two. He held up the five fingers of one hand. I jerked my head with approval. He rapped on the door and delivered his message.

"Five minutes on stage, Madame Chanaud!"

Again, I heard no voices from within.

I wondered whether the two were talking in the dressing room or sitting in silence, Edgar Allan Poe and his new dark maiden, the uncanny mirror of his beloved. He could not save his sick wife, and now another young woman played a dying consumptive. Could *she* be saved? And if not, if he failed, if his old enemy, Death, took *her*, as well…

The strings, having tuned up, fell into a chasm of silence.

At that point my concern became acute. Minutes had elapsed since the rake-like man had rattled off. Why did Marie-Claire not emerge? Surely she would be late for her all-important entrance. What was delaying her? It was then that I heard, as if in answer to my unspoken query, the loud *bang!* of the Stage Door.

I spun round. Saw it swing back into place. The chill draft of night hit me. In the same instant, paralyzed, I saw that the bolt had been lifted.

My hand pulled out my flintlock and held it at arm's-length. My mind was racing. Had they not been speaking because *the fiendish assailant was already in the room?* Had I been pacing, stupidly, and checking my watch while—God in Heaven, *was I already too late?*

"Holmes! *Holmes!*"

Poe's cry was one of—what?

I ran to the door, pistol outstretched, and kicked it wide—

The sight that confronted me shocked me to my core. Never, in the many cases I have encountered over the years as a consulting detective in London, in Sussex, or on Dartmoor, was I more stricken by utter horror.

Marie-Claire stood facing me, immobile. I recognized the lilac "courtesan" gown worn by Violetta in Act One, the bell-like shape of the crinoline, the tight-fitting lavender bodice with pagoda sleeves buttoned to the pit of the throat in a white collar, the leghorn hat ribboned in silver-gray tilted off her braided sausage curls. Yet it was not the lack of movement that pinned me to the spot, for she stared at me from a face not merely painted with the stark white of greasepaint, but a face that bubbled and collapsed, the hissing of a deadly steam rising not only from the cheeks and withering locks, but from the breast of the bodice itself, swathing the entire head in a pall of vapor.

No sooner had I absorbed the nightmare image than her hands tore the front of the bodice asunder, popping the buttons and ripping away the collar.

Pulling my cuffs over one hand, I reached out to help—but the swing of her arm knocked mine away.

The features were falling asunder. Nose. Chin. One eye, a hollow, *slid...* Then to my amazement Marie-Claire's gloved hands—no, *gauntleted* hands—tore off her face and flung it aside.

Fizzing, it broke apart against the wall and fell to the floor. A plaster of Paris mask made by any of a dozen workshops along the Seine. The wig of sausage curls came off next, hurled after it, sizzling on the floorboards like a cut of beef on a griddle.

The figure hastily disrobed a leather balaclava to reveal a thin mop of snowy white hair. Even the leather, extending as it did over the shoulders, was blackened and burning in patches where the acid had eaten through the clothing, and Poe wasted no time in divesting himself of it, and the thick brown gloves with it. Last to be thrown aside in a heap were the goggles as he stepped out of the hoops of the crinoline cage.

He ran to a bowl of water and up-ended it over his head, shook the water out of his hair and flattened it back with his hands.

"Did you see it? What did you see?"

"Nothing!"

We were in the corridor. I still brandished my pistol. Christophe the doorman looked like a startled sheep.

"Tell Monsieur Bermutier, the policeman, that the Phantom is in the building," said Poe. "Tell him Monsieur Dupin says the devil has been foiled, but he has escaped underground. It is imperative he send all his men in that direction. *All* his men. You understand?" The man nodded. "Tell him they must descend to the lake. Immediately! Or he will get away. Go. *Go!*"

The man shot off. I started to follow him, but Poe caught my arm.

"No. We go this way."

He swept out of the Stage Door entrance into the dark, not pausing to answer any of the questions rushing through my mind. Not least: if the *prima donna* was not in the dressing room, *where was she*? In the hands of a terrible abductor? And if the monster was secreted, as he had just said, in the Opéra, or *under* it, why on earth were we running *away* from the place as if our lives depended on it?

As we took to the street I kept up with the detective, an incongruous if not ludicrous sight in his flapping skirts and petticoats. Even with trousers and boots underneath, his long white hair and jagged elbows gave him the appearance of a spirited old maid.

Poe dropped to one knee, and I almost fell over him.

He picked up an object from the ground. A theatrical mask with green feather-like marks, eye holes and a large hooked beak.

"*Papa guinea!* Onward!" Poe cried, inexplicably. "Keep up with the pig!"

At first I thought that this was some strange colloquial expression in the French vernacular to which I had not previously been exposed, but no. What we had to keep up with was indeed just that—a pig. A very fat, very pink pig, whose curl of a tail and rear end I now could make out wobbling in and out of the shadows cast by the street lamps ahead.

I was convinced I was going mad. No, that I *had gone* mad. The process was complete and unequivocal. But it was there, in front of me. A pig on a leash, no less, with a man in a peaked cap in tow, keeping up a brisk walking pace with the animal, its ears flapping and its snout rubbing along the pavement like a bloodhound. Poe following—in the billowing dress of a courtesan. And *I* following *him*.

On the boulevards people were laughing and drinking in the harsh, false glare of the cafés as if the garish reds and golds of the theater were bleeding out after us. The signs were phosphorescent—names like La Barbarie, Sans Soleil, or La Bataille—the eerie glow of absinthe and folly, of love affairs not yet begun and long ended. And not a single soul batted an eyelid at three men hastening past, one at least half dressed in ladies garments, with a pig at the end of a rope.

Then I glimpsed him.

The dwarf!

Far ahead, almost out of sight. Scurrying along low to the ground, head down, swathed in a scarlet hood and cape. And soon just that, a *swirl* of red, lost into the crepuscular haze as the Boulevard des Italiens became the Rue St. Marc.

Soon we had left the bright lights of the cafés behind, and lost sight of the hooded bloodstain to whom we were giving chase. Solitary women now lingered in the shadows, hands extending for money, but we hurried past them, interested only in where this path, and this misshapen gnome, clothed in his Red Death cowl, was taking us, and if, in some nether-region of Poe's "ratiocination," this insanity—this unparalleled *absurdity*—made sense.

Whatever trail the beast was following, and clearly the scent was still in its nostrils, took us to the grim environs of the Rue St. Denis of notorious repute, den of vice since medieval times, and the expectation of such did not fall short. Almost every doorway was adorned with a streetwalker showing a leg or sometimes a bare, grubby breast to advertise her wares, with the shamelessness of the desperate and misbegotten. I shuddered at the rough brush-strokes of rouge that were intended to rouse passion, but instead only invoked, to this young observer at least, an overwhelming disgust, tinged with pity. But these specimens—variously termed *comediennes*, *lorettes*, *grisettes*, *les codettes*, or (most dismissively of all) *les horizontals*—did not crave my pity and likely would have bitten my fingers off if I had offered a helping hand.

Our four-legged companion, moving at great speed, spurred only by the occasional "Allez!" or "Vite!" from its master, led us via a murky alleyway to the Rue Blondel.

Its snout dragged us to a doorway with red *faience* tiles on its façade. Snorting, it tugged the man in the peaked cap through into an ill-lit stairwell, where he was unceremoniously grabbed by a bald, nattering Chinaman with rolled up sleeves and the girth of a pannier horse. Poe thrust his arm against the ogre's chest, but one might as well have tried to keep a mastiff at bay with a pipe cleaner. The thug pawed it away effortlessly, and was about to punch him in the nose and quite possibly take the head from his shoulders in the process when, registering that his assailant wore a flouncy pastel-colored dress, he simply burst into laughter. The hearty guffaw was cut short when the barrel of my pistol made a cold circle against his temple.

A wrought-iron staircase led upward.

The pig was first up it. The man second. Poe third. "Don't touch it!" And I came close after, backward, making sure I did not step on the empty bottle of sulfuric acid lying there, still hissing. I kept the oriental giant in my sights the whole way. Even with his animal intellect he knew better than to follow, and I fear I would have put a bullet in him with not a vast amount of provocation.

I pulled aside a red curtain sticky with grime and heard screams ahead. Shrill, girlish screams, and those of men—and of a dwarf, for all I knew.

A cigar-smoking man hastened to pull up his trousers, probably convinced I was a policeman. He stood with his hands in the air and just as quickly his trousers fell.

In another room a fat woman, suddenly shrieking as she saw me, rolled her doughy frame off the bed, revealing a skinny old man secreted in the pillows under her.

My cheeks did not blush so much as burn.

As I followed Poe and pig, each doorway I passed was a window into debauchery. If this was where so-called gentlemen came for their treats, then their play was beyond anything I would have credited, had I not seen it with my own eyes. My education with Poe had been extensive, but this was tantamount to setting foot on another world—not unlike his fantastical account of a trip to the moon.

Pistol in hand, I gaped into unexpectedly grand, if faded, salons with walls adorned with voluptuous nymphs lolling on clouds and men—or gods—endowed with the envy of Priapus. Through another open door I saw a man biting the cloth off sumptuous bosoms while a second woman wore a strapped-on phallus in lurid pink. Then there were the *tableaux vivants*—the Crazed Nun, The Naval Officer's Homecoming, The Naughtiest Boy in School—which added theatricality to ardor, setting copulation and flagellation in a variety of frankly highly unlikely settings for the purpose of pepping up the proceedings. I will not dwell on the proliferation of nakedness or the contortions exhibited, but will remark only that the excitement of the physical organs of both genders was not only evident, but in the main exposed to view with little attempt to recover dignity, or any semblance of embarrassment.

So *this* was the dwarf's abode? One of the *maisons d'abattage* or "slaughterhouses" I had heard about, where a man took a number and waited in line for a woman who had up to sixty *passes* a day? Where adulterers from the mansions of the Champs-Élysées, or off-duty soldiers with a *franc* in their pocket came to roll their clothes into a ball?

A door slammed and the pig squealed. I elbowed past a square-shouldered female sucking an opium pipe.

Ahead of me, the man in the peaked cap was yanking the leash so hard that the pig was standing on two legs, its corkscrew tail vibrating excitedly. He slapped its ears as if admonishing a disobedient infant. In front of him, Poe was holding open a door, the room beyond him thick with darkness.

I snatched a candle from the pipe smoker. Holding it aloft, I joined my friend, who had now lowered to his knees. I shone it over his shoulder. Its glow made a halo of his cloud-white hair, and fell beyond, picking out a shape in the far corner of the room.

A shape I immediately recognized as the dwarf's all-encompassing scarlet cape. A tiny human being was under it, knees tucked up to its chest, trembling, its lungs clearly gasping for air after the exertion of running through the streets, and a kind of throaty sobbing emitting from it in bursts. As my candle entered the room, the hooded head sunk down so that its face was even more completely hidden in shadow.

Poe crept toward the huddled figure on his hands and knees. I caught his shoulder with my free hand. "Be careful. He might be armed." I drew my dueling pistol, but he placed a hand on the barrel and pushed it away.

"Stand back," he whispered. "As far back as possible."

Reluctantly, I obeyed. The candle went with me, and the pistol went back in my coat.

The retreating amber glow threw Poe's shadow longer over the filthy floorboards and onto a grim, stripped bed, its mattress a continent of stains and mildew. The shape, the scarlet bundle, sat sandwiched between it and the peeling wall. The dwarf did not move as Poe moved closer. It merely continued to shudder.

My hand slid into my waistcoat and derived some small comfort from the butt of the Denix.

He moved closer still. I wished I could be sure that this wasn't some damn foolish action of a madman I was watching. The death—the second and *final* death of Edgar Allan Poe, more than worthy of his outlandish fiction: at the hands of a maniac dwarf.

"Don't be frightened." The master of the macabre spoke so softly now I could hardly hear him. "We are not here to harm you..."

He rested back on his heels and reached out one hand. A slender hand, a womanly hand, with the long fingers of a pianist. Or so he was told by a gypsy reading palms in Philadelphia.

My finger dug down for the trigger.

I expected the dwarf to galvanize as the hand grew closer, but it did not. I expected the Phantom to jump forward, to grab, to bite, to resist, to run in sudden desperation to escape—but it did none of these things. Somehow satiated, repentant, inactive, or resigned to its fate, it only breathed. And its breath was a thin kind of mewling.

I imagined the grotesque mockery of human physiognomy that would be revealed under the hood, but what I did not—*could* not—imagine was that, when it was pulled back, the face was that of a little girl no more than eleven years of age.

The gentle mewling continued as she rocked back and forth, the candlelight picking out in silver the pearls of tears coursing down her pretty cheeks as I stepped into the room.

When we left the building at dawn a battalion of street sweepers had begun their daily grind, moving as a mechanical phalanx down the width of the cobbles, brooms sweeping the dirt in front of them in semicircles, pushing all the rubbish into the gutter with the same rhythmic motion of reapers in the field. We saw them on every road on our way home, working like puppets. But all I could think of was the dingy room that lit up as I walked in to it, a faded sampler and a map of the world on the walls, furnished as it was with a rocking-horse, an abacus, a wooden Noah's Ark, and a family of china-headed dolls, in a vile parody of a nursery.

"The pig is a much maligned species." Poe took a curl of sugared orange peel from the tray proffered by Le Bon and dropped it into his open mouth, the sunlight from the window making it a curling sliver of gold. "Just because it lives in its own feces, people presume it is dirty. Nothing could be further from the truth. In fact it is very clean, and highly intelligent. More intelligent than a dog, and it has a more acute sense of smell than a dog, which is why I have undertaken experiments in their relative use to the police. Unfortunately they are not as loyal and obedient as dogs, but once on track are far more reliable than an average black-and-tan Beauceron—though perhaps not as manly at a law enforcer's heel. However, because of their poor eyesight they can detect food with astonishing precision: the reason why for centuries they have been employed to forage for truffles up to three feet underground. The female is used because the smell resembles the male reproductive organs. Dogs, I've found, are, by and large, not sexually excited by fungus."

"Madame Lop-Lop..." I elaborated for the benefit of Guédiguian, who perched his coffee cup on the arm of his chair as I added cream to mine.

"Madame Lop-Lop indeed." Poe sipped his own. "She was used to great effect in uncovering explosives being shipped via Marseilles by a gang of anarchists. They can be trained, you see. In this case, with a reward of food over several weeks, trained to sniff out explosives. Soon afterward she retired, as did Colonel Follenvie, who received a bullet in the leg and took on the old sow as a pet. But her usefulness as a bloodhound was proven. The best snout in Paris. Reason enough to lure her out of retirement for one last case. I devised a concoction of chemicals, tactile enough to stick to the sole of a shoe. Then I knew we could trace our Phantom wherever he, or she, fled…"

Guédiguian shook his black locks with their sheen of macassar oil. Poe's racing intellect and breathless reasoning often left people bewildered bystanders. Today was no exception.

"There were distractions. There always are. The wasteful detritus of any investigation. The tenor Loubatierre being absent and refusing to give an explanation: that confounded me until I had Le Bon follow him, and found he was visiting his ailing father at the mad house in Bicêtre. He simply wished to keep the stigma of insanity in his family a private affair. The other being the dramaturge Beckstein's unrequited love for Madame Chanaud. It was he who sent the mysterious flowers with no card: camellias in symbolic celebration of her role on stage. On our first visit to the theater I noted he wore a pale pink camellia flower in his buttonhole—Lady Hume's Blush, if I'm not mistaken—a secret signal to our *ingénue* that he was in love with her. If she did but care, or even notice…

"Anyway, unimportant! The crucial fact, as Holmes now knows, was Marie-Claire saying that the intruder's face was level with her shoulder. Common sense dictated that only three possibilities existed: the figure was on its knees (unlikely in the extreme); it was a dwarf (which I considered *highly* fanciful); or else it was a child. From her description I had no doubt the infiltrator wore the traditional mask of Papageno the bird-catcher, birdlike itself. Confirmed when we were told the name of the previous production at the Garnier: *The Magic Flute*.

"The problem of the bolt on the Stage Door then presented

itself. Yes, a wire from outside poked through the crack could yank up the bolt to allow entry—any pickpocket in Pigalle could show you that trick in five minutes—but why and how was the bolt *shut immediately afterwards*? At that stage I could not dismiss the notion that Christophe might be an accomplice. Which is why I could not tell you, my dear Holmes, of my plan on opening night. Your most minute gesture or reaction might have betrayed to the doorman the fact that the *prima donna* was not in her dressing room, and as a direct result our elusive Phantom may have been alerted and the chance of capture jeopardized." Poe saw my displeasure. I could not disguise it. "Do not sulk. You thereby give the evidence that my decision was correct. It is not a fault, my good friend, but an observation and an accurate one: you wear your heart on your sleeve, and could no easier lie or deceive than you could remove the beating heart of a starving orphan. Where was I?"

"The bolt," said Guédiguian. "Which was locked."

"Which was locked because Christophe locked it. The man had not seen the *Fantôme* enter or leave—or rather he *did* see it leave, in that he saw the door open and close. Mystified, and thinking he would be blamed for being inattentive when the screams went up, he simply threw the bolt himself and claimed, because he had to, that the door had been closed the whole time. Self-protection being the most powerful of motives.

"My plan then was simplicity itself. The first priority was to remove Madame Chanaud from any possibility of danger. To that end I arranged that she be secreted in your office with two armed guards on opening night. I then went to a saddler to acquire protective clothing, impenetrable to the acid, and a plaster mask, lest the perpetrator see me in the mirror.

"That the criminal was a child I was certain, but a child is not a natural aggressor, it is a natural victim. What was the catalyst for such monstrous acts as these? I needed to know and my fear was that the clod-hopping police force would get in the way. It was imperative to misdirect them, and so I invented the ruse of the underground 'lake'—a fabrication. The most cursory investigation into the building of the Opéra revealed that when Garnier first cleared the ground, water constantly bubbled up from the swamp below. All attempts to pump the site dry failed miserably. Wells were sunk, eight steam pumps were put into operation, to no avail. The only solution was to construct an enormous concrete tank, called the *cuve*, to relieve the pressure of the external groundwater and stop any of it rising up through the foundations. But there is no *lake*, no labyrinth—"

"And no Phantom," I added. "Just an insane and frightened child."

"Do you want cream?" Poe addressed our guest. "Sometimes the bitterness of black is too much for a person to take. I confess to having no such qualm. It's the sweetness that I often cannot take. The universe is black. Blackness is reality. It's a flavor I prefer untarnished."

I had no idea if he thought he was being amusing, but Guédiguian gave a polite smile as if he was.

"Well, the main thing is, thanks to you and Monsieur Holmes, Madame Chanaud sang Violetta on opening night."

"So I believe," said Poe. "That was the precise intention."

"And I have to say she was magnificent." Guédiguian puffed his chest. "You can never be sure with the *claque*, but the whole of Paris is enraptured by her. I've never seen a success like it. She said to tell you her dream had come true after all. And to say when she sang her final aria, Monsieur Dupin, she sang it for you."

Poe tilted his head in the most miniscule acknowledgment, his eyes a little shinier than they were before. He shifted in his chair and examined his cuffs.

"I feel I have endured an earthquake, or a volcano," said Guédiguian, standing. "I felt at times the lava might consume me. But now all is well. The threat has passed. The mystery is solved. And what a mystery! It remains only for me to thank you for saving my business." He extended a hand to Poe, but the writer only stared at it.

"A pity I cannot save your soul, monsieur."

The opera director took a faltering step backward.

"Monsieur Guédiguian, if I were truly covering my tracks, I should enquire as to the motive for the crime. That would be the thought and action of an innocent man. Though I doubt you would know too intimately the actions of an innocent man, would you?"

Guédiguian retreated to his seat, ashen, and sat with his hands between his knees. "I swear. It is not—*not* what you imagine…"

"I am not prepared to imagine, monsieur." Poe stood and buttoned his jacket. "I am only prepared to *know*. And I know I am right in thinking you have bedded both Madame Jolivet and Marie-Claire Chanaud, her former understudy. As well as many singers before them, probably. Perhaps they see it as no less than their duty, and you as no more than your privilege."

"Please…" Guédiguian began sweating profusely and took out a handkerchief to stem the tide.

"'Please'? It is not a question of *please*…" Poe refused to back off. "What I also know is that you regularly frequented the premises of Madame Floch on the Rue Blondel, known as 'Tante Berthe' to her girls. I'm afraid she was very illuminating when I said she might be implicated in some exceedingly violent crimes. Extremely eloquent and forthcoming."

"Don't…" The opera manager cringed, holding his skull in torment. I could only stare as the Master rounded on him, unabated.

"She would not normally divulge the names of her clientele, but for me she made an exception. She said you were amongst that fine coterie of men who have certain proclivities. That is, an insatiable longing for young flesh. To use the untouched and the unknowing for your gratification and—"

Guédiguian shot to his feet. "You can prove none of this! This is preposterous! I am not listening to another word! Who said such—?"

"I heard it from the lips of a child."

Guédiguian stammered. "A child? What child?"

"The child whose bed you took, whose chastity you took, whose childhood you took, for the price of a few francs."

Afraid the opera manager might become aggressive, I got up and stood between them, holding him by the upper arms. He barely made a show to get past me as soon as he saw in my eyes that everything Monsieur Dupin the detective knew, I knew. I think he saw the plain disgust there. As Poe had said earlier, I was fairly inept at masking my emotions. And didn't care if he did see.

"I do not sit in moral judgment. That is between you and your Maker, if you are foolish enough to believe in one." Poe stood at the window, the profile of his supercilious nose against the sunlit panes. "Over weeks and months you visited this child. You knew her in every carnal and intimate fashion. Sometimes you took a toy or doll. She didn't understand she was the merest plaything to you, an object to satisfy your lust. To her, you became special. She looked forward to your visits. I will not say you hurt her, though many others did. On the contrary, perhaps you were the first to show her the illusion of love. Perhaps that was your downfall. You thought nothing of her, but *she* loved *you*. And, in time, came to be sad when you left, and one afternoon followed you.

"That day, having crept into the opera house, invisible, she espied you with Madame Jolivet in all her finery. A beautiful woman adored by the gentleman she thought was hers. She thought, 'Why not me? Would he truly love me if not for her?' The hatred and envy festered in her. She was an orphan. She had not known love, and all her young life had only known those who wanted to use her as a commodity. She saw prettiness and wanted to make it ugly. She wanted those bright, successful women who lit up the stage, and your life, to feel as mutilated and destroyed as she herself was by the countless men who passed through her room. She wanted—"

"Stop!" Guédiguian wrapped his arms around his head. "Stop! In the name of Heaven and all its saints—must you torture me? I am not a criminal!"

"You took what was not yours."

"As a hundred men do in Paris every day!" He scowled. "And worse!"

"I say again: your morality, or lack of it, does not interest me. You can discuss that with a priest, or some other ne'er-do-well. I am, however, interested in your culpability. In respect of your... addiction—and I am far from able to pronounce on anyone's *addiction* to anything—setting in train the events that have generated such pain and anguish."

"Then I *am* culpable. There. I have said it. Could I have known? No! Could I have stopped it, had I known—perhaps! But I did not know! I. Did. Not. Know! How could I? She—"

"Say her name."

"Don't tell me what to—"

"What was her name?"

Guédiguian crumbled. His shoulders heaved and he let out a strangled moan. I helped him to his chair. He slumped in it like a sack.

"Édith."

"Édith Dufranoux," said Poe. "She came with it, according to Madame Floch. But if you ask me, her real name, like her true family, is lost on the winds of time."

Guédiguian wiped a slime of spittle from his lower lip. His eyes could no longer meet ours. I wished I felt an ounce of pity for him.

"You see, monsters come in all shapes and sizes, Holmes," said Poe. "They do not all wear wolf skins. Some wear the utmost fashion in respectability. You do not need to open the covers of a book of horror stories by Poe. You need only look in the mirrors of the Opéra Garnier."

"You are not privy to my mind, Dupin," Guédiguian spat.

"I very nearly am. Do not be sure about that. I am the Man of the Crowd. I walk in many shoes. That is my business. To understand pure logic one must understand its opposite, perversion, when pure instinct is unleashed, unrestrained. The tragedy is, you could not have known the harvest your libidinous appetite would reap." Poe's words took on a melancholy tone as he stared out of the window at a passing world blissfully unaware of the dark, impish secrets we discussed. "You were haunted by the phantom of all kisses: obsessive love."

The opera manager covered his face with his hands.

"What will happen to her? The police..."

"The police know nothing," said Poe. "About you, or about her. As far as Bermutier is concerned, the Phantom of the Opéra

Garnier escaped from their clutches, disappearing forever. A mystery unsolved. I bade him persuade his *gendarmes* not to divulge any details of the crime to the *presse*, but that may be a vain hope that some juice does not seep out of the apple barrel…

"As for the girl, earlier this morning I took her to a woman I know at the Hôtel Dieu, the last bastion of '*La Couche*,' as it is known, the old *Hôpital des Enfants-Trouvés* created as a refuge for the abandoned waifs of the city, amongst other things to prevent them being purposefully maimed and sold as beggars. I have no idea whether she has a chance there of a 'proper' or 'decent' future—whatever that is. She may end up a wastrel or die of cold and hunger on the streets, or drowned in the sewers, or be sold to peddlers and mountebanks for money-making purposes. Or become an opera singer. I can only say that for now she has food and water, the prospect of friends and even adults who do not despise her, and schooling in the ways of Christianity. For a while, at least, she will be safe. Beyond that, her life is her own."

"Can I see her?"

"If you do, I will see to it that everyone in Paris knows what I know."

The opera manager choked and swallowed. "Did she—did she say anything about me?"

Poe glared at the man. "She asked if she would go to the guillotine for her crimes. She said she wouldn't mind if she did. She said she had no fear of dying because she was dead already."

Guédiguian closed his eyes. I cannot remember clearly what he said after that, but he was a man diminished, and the conversation over. In a fatuous gesture to make amends, he proposed, mumbling and almost incoherent, that he would donate some of the opera's profits to the poor, to the workhouse, perhaps expecting us to cry "Bravo!" Poe greeted it with the silent disdain it deserved, and I think thereafter Guédiguian found it difficult to sit much longer in our presence. It took every atom of politeness I could muster to shake his hand, but for all his insistence that he had no morality, Poe did not.

I attempted to give back the gift he had brought us—people often did, as C. Auguste Dupin accepted no fee for his services—but Guédiguian showed me his palms. He did not want it and was now eager to go. When the door closed after him I was left with it in my hands.

"Stradivarius," Poe commented. "You should take it up. There is a power in music 'to soothe a savage breast.'"

He took the rolled-up play bill Guédiguian had brought advertising *La Traviata*—a memento of our adventure, he had said—unfurled it briefly, glimpsing the name of Marie-Claire Chanaud as Violetta, then placed it next to the violin case.

"You knew it was a child all along," I said, gazing into the fire to stop my upset from showing. "Poe, I am constantly amazed at your capacity for casual cruelty. You were prepared for me to… to ridicule myself by talk of a… a maniac *dwarf*?"

"To feel ridiculous is a very small price to pay, my dear Holmes. It was necessary for you to *appear* to deduce that fact convincingly in order to send Bermutier on a hunt for the proverbial wild goose. Before condemning a child to the punitive forces of law and order, I needed to know why it had chosen such vehement and intractable actions."

"Then you see yourself above the law?"

"Not above. Parallel to. Let us debate this another day. Today I find it tiresome. Let us just say I wanted the whole picture to be complete. I am sorry I allowed you to feel foolish—*je suis desolé!*—but it was to that end, I promise. I would never be cruel unless it was for the greater good. Well, almost never." And my anger could almost never sustain itself when I saw that dark twinkle in his eye.

Without calling Le Bon, he fetched our coats from their pegs.

"Will he live with his shame?" I asked, inserting my arms in the one he held up for me.

"Of course he will," said Poe, doing the same in reverse.

"I shall never be able to listen to opera again, after this vile business."

"Crime is vile in all its manifestations. Mysteries abound. We are adrift in an ocean of unknowing. The only respite is to solve them. And until we conquer the great question of non-dimensional creation, the seeking of those solutions will be the essence and eternal vexation of Man. Come, let us go to the Rue du Faubourg Montmartre, to the Restaurant Morot, and talk about the rigors of decapitation. There's a murder in *Le Figaro* today and I'm convinced they have the wrong man. You remember? With its dark fittings and the hat racks above the tables it's like dining in a railway carriage. Vidal will always find a table for me, and he serves the best pig's ears in Paris. You can drink, and I shall watch."

"Amontillado?"

"Please. That is beneath you."

He took my arm. His own was thin. He was a skeleton in a suit by sunlight. It brings a tear to my eye now, but I hardly noticed then a frailty that was increasing with the passing years. Years all too few.

We were, of course, too late. Out of gossip and half-truths the myth was born. If accidents happened at the theater, the stage hands would still ascribe it to their *Fantôme*. He had escaped, but not into the non-existent lake—into stories. Descending with his disfigured face and mask to his watery home. And coming to haunt us from the pages of a book, and the flickering screen.

In the months that followed we had other cases, including that of an extraordinary patient of Dr. Charcot at Salpêtrière, the "Gates of Hell" affair, and the spirit photography of Monsieur Boguet, but none pierced my heart quite as much as the tale of Olivier Guédiguian, whose mask disguised a monster, and little Édith Dufranoux, the true Phantom of the *Opéra de Paris*.

NEW MURDERS IN THE RUE MORGUE

By

CLIVE BARKER

Winter, Lewis decided, was no season for old men. The snow that lay five inches thick on the streets of Paris froze him to the marrow. What had been a joy to him as a child was now a curse. He hated it with all his heart; hated the snowballing children (squeals, howls, tears); hated, too, the young lovers, eager to be caught in a flurry together (squeals, kisses, tears). It was uncomfortable and tiresome, and he wished he was in Fort Lauderdale, where the sun would be shining.

But Catherine's telegram, though not explicit, had been urgent, and the ties of friendship between them had been unbroken for the best part of fifty years. He was here for her, and for her brother Phillipe. However thin his blood felt in this ice land, it was foolish to complain. He'd come at a summons from the past, and he would have come as swiftly, and as willingly, if Paris had been burning.

Besides, it was his mother's city. She'd been born on

the Boulevard Diderot, back in a time when the city was untrammeled by free-thinking architects and social engineers. Now every time Lewis returned to Paris he steeled himself for another desecration. It was happening less of late, he'd noticed. The recession in Europe made governments less eager with their bulldozers. But still, year after year, more fine houses found themselves rubble. Whole streets sometimes, gone to ground.

Even the Rue Morgue.

There was, of course, some doubt as to whether that infamous street had ever existed in the first place, but as his years advanced Lewis had seen less and less purpose in distinguishing between fact and fiction. That great divide was for young men, who still had to deal with life. For the old (Lewis was 73), the distinction was academic. What did it matter what was true and what was false, what real and what invented? In his head all of it, the half-lies and the truths, were one continuum of personal history.

Maybe the Rue Morgue had existed, as it had been described in Edgar Allan Poe's immortal story; maybe it was pure invention. Whichever, the notorious street was no longer to be found on a map of Paris.

Perhaps Lewis was a little disappointed not to have found the Rue Morgue. After all, it was part of his heritage. If the stories he had been told as a young boy were correct, the events described in "The Murders in the Rue Morgue" had been narrated to Poe by Lewis' grandfather. It was his mother's pride that her father had met Poe, while traveling in America. Apparently his grandfather had been a globe-trotter, unhappy unless he visited a new town every week. And in the winter of 1835 he had been in Richmond, Virginia. It was a bitter winter, perhaps not unlike the one Lewis was presently suffering, and one night the grandfather had taken refuge in a bar in Richmond. There, with a blizzard raging outside, he had met a small, dark, melancholy young man called Eddie. He was something of a local celebrity apparently, having written a tale that had won a competition in the *Baltimore Saturday Visitor*. The tale was "MS. Found in a Bottle" and the haunted young man was Edgar Allan Poe.

The two had spent the evening together, drinking, and (this is how the story went, anyway) Poe had gently pumped Lewis' grandfather for stories of the bizarre, of the occult and of the morbid. The worldly-wise traveler was glad to oblige, pouring out believe-it-or-not fragments that the writer later turned into "The Mystery of Marie Rogêt" and "The Murders in the Rue Morgue." In both those stories, peering out from between the atrocities, was the peculiar genius of C. Auguste Dupin.

C. Auguste Dupin. Poe's vision of the perfect detective: calm, rational, and brilliantly perceptive. The narratives in which he appeared rapidly became well-known, and through them Dupin became a fictional celebrity, without anyone in America knowing that Dupin was a real person.

He was the brother of Lewis' grandfather. Lewis' great uncle was C. Auguste Dupin.

And his greatest case—the Murders in the Rue Morgue—they too were based on fact. The slaughters that occurred in the story had actually taken place. Two women had indeed been brutally killed in the Rue Morgue. They were, as Poe had written, Madame L'Espanaye and her daughter Mademoiselle Camille L'Espanaye. Both women of good reputation, who lived quiet and unsensational lives. So much more horrible then to find those lives so brutally cut short. The daughter's body had been thrust up the chimney; the body of the mother was discovered in the yard at the back of the house, her throat cut with such savagery that her head was all but sawn off. No apparent motive could be found for the murders, and the mystery further deepened when all the occupants of the house claimed to have heard the voice of the murderer speaking in a different language. The Frenchman was certain the voice had spoken Spanish, the Englishman had heard German, the Dutchman thought it was French. Dupin, in his investigations, noted that none of the witnesses actually spoke the language they claimed to have heard from the lips of the unseen murderer. He concluded that the language was no language at all, but the wordless voice of a wild beast.

An ape in fact, a monstrous orang-outang from the East Indian Islands. Its tawny hairs had been found in the grip of the slain Madame L'Espanaye. Only its strength and agility made the appalling fate of Mademoiselle L'Espanaye plausible. The beast had belonged to a Maltese sailor, had escaped, and run riot in the bloody apartment on the Rue Morgue.

That was the bones of the story.

Whether true or not the tale held a great romantic appeal for Lewis. He liked to think of his great uncle logically pacing his way through the mystery, undistressed by the hysteria and horror around him. He thought of that calm as essentially European; belonging to a lost age in which the light of reason was still valued, and the worst horror that could be conceived of was a beast with a cut-throat razor.

Now, as the twentieth century ground through its last quarter, there were far greater atrocities to be accounted for, all committed by human beings. The humble orang-outang had been investigated by anthropologists and found to be a solitary herbivore; quiet and philosophical. The true monsters were far less apparent, and far more powerful. Their weapons made razors look pitiful; their crimes were vast. In some ways Lewis was almost glad to be old and close to leaving the century to its own devices. Yes, the snow froze his marrow. Yes, to see a young girl with a face of a goddess uselessly stirred his desires. Yes, he felt like an observer now instead of a participator.

But it had not always been that way.

In 1937, in the very room at number eleven, Quai de Bourbon, where he now sat, there had been experience enough. Paris was still a pleasure-dome in those days, studiously ignoring rumors of war, and preserving, though at times the strain told, an air of sweet naiveté. They had been careless then; in both senses of the word, living endless lives of perfect leisure.

It wasn't so of course. The lives had not been perfect, or endless. But for a time—a summer, a month, a day—it had seemed nothing in the world would change.

In half a decade Paris would burn, and its playful guilt, which was true innocence, would be soiled permanently. They had spent many days (and nights) in the apartment Lewis now occupied, wonderful times; when he thought of them his stomach seemed to ache with the loss.

His thoughts turned to more recent events. To his New York exhibition, in which his series of paintings chronicling the damnation of Europe had been a brilliant critical success. At the age of seventy-three Lewis Fox was a fêted man. Articles were being written in every art periodical. Admirers and buyers had sprung up like mushrooms overnight, eager to purchase his work, to talk with him, to touch his hand. All too late, of course. The agonies of creation were long over, and he'd put down his brushes for the last time five years ago. Now, when he was merely a spectator, his critical triumph seemed like a parody: he viewed the circus from a distance with something approaching distaste.

When the telegram had come from Paris, begging for his

assistance, he had been more than pleased to slip away from the ring of imbeciles mouthing his praise.

Now he waited in the darkening apartment, watching the steady flow of cars across the Pont Louis-Philippe, as tired Parisians began the trek home through the snow. Their horns blared; their engines coughed and growled; their yellow foglamps made a ribbon of light across the bridge.

Still Catherine didn't come.

The snow, which had held off for most of the day, was beginning to fall again, whispering against the window. The traffic flowed across the Seine, the Seine flowed under the traffic. Night fell. At last, he heard footsteps in the hall; exchanged whispers with the housekeeper.

It was Catherine. At last, it was Catherine.

He stood up and stared at the door, imagining it opening before it opened, imagining her in the doorway.

"Lewis, my darling—"

She smiled at him; a pale smile on a paler face. She looked older than he'd expected. How long was it since he'd seen her? Four years or five? Her fragrance was the same as she always wore: and it reassured Lewis with its permanence. He kissed her cold cheeks lightly.

"You look well," he lied.

"No I don't," she said. "If I look well it's an insult to Phillipe. How can I be well when he's in such trouble?"

Her manner was brisk, and forbidding, as always.

She was three years his senior, but she treated him as a teacher would a recalcitrant child. She always had: it was her way of being fond.

Greetings over, she sat down beside the window, staring out over the Seine. Small gray ice-floes floated under the bridge, rocking and revolving in the current. The water looked deadly, as though its bitterness could crush the breath out of you.

"What trouble is Phillipe in?"

"He's accused of—"

A tiny hesitation. A flicker of an eyelid.

"—murder."

Lewis wanted to laugh; the very thought was preposterous. Phillipe was sixty-nine years old, and as mild-mannered as a lamb.

"It's true, Lewis. I couldn't tell you by telegram, you understand. I had to say it myself. Murder. He's accused of murder."

"Who?"

"A girl, of course. One of his fancy women."

"He still gets around, does he?"

"We used to joke he'd die on a woman, remember?"

Lewis half-nodded.

"She was nineteen. Natalie Perec. Quite an educated girl, apparently. And lovely. Long red hair. You remember how Phillipe loved redheads?"

"Nineteen? She was nineteen years old?"

She didn't reply. Lewis sat down, knowing his pacing of the room irritated her. In profile she was still beautiful, and the wash of yellow-blue through the window softened the lines on her face, magically erasing fifty years of living.

"Where is he?"

"They locked him up. They say he's dangerous. They say he could kill again."

Lewis shook his head. There was a pain at his temples, which might go if he could only close his eyes.

"He needs to see you. Very badly."

But maybe sleep was just an escape. Here was something even he couldn't be a spectator to.

Phillipe Laborteaux stared at Lewis across the bare, scored table, his face weary and lost. They had greeted each other only with handshakes; all other physical contact was strictly forbidden.

"I am in despair," he said. "She's dead. My Natalie is dead."

"Tell me what happened."

"I have a little apartment in Montmartre. In the Rue des Martyrs. Just a room really, to entertain friends. Catherine always keeps number 11 so neat, you know, a man can't spread himself out. Natalie used to spend a lot of time with me there: everyone in the house knew her. She was so good natured, so beautiful. She was studying to go into Medical School. Bright. And she loved me."

Phillipe was still handsome. In fact, as the fashion in looks came full circle, his elegance, his almost dashing face, his unhurried charm were the order of the day. A breath of a lost age, perhaps.

"I went out on Sunday morning: to the patisserie. And when I came back..."

The words failed him for a moment.

"Lewis..."

His eyes filled with tears of frustration. This was so difficult for him his mouth refused to make the necessary sounds.

"Don't—" Lewis began.

"I want to tell you, Lewis. I want you to know, I want you to see her as I saw her—so you know what there is... there is... what there is in the world."

The tears ran down his face in two graceful rivulets. He

gripped Lewis' hand in his, so tightly it ached.

"She was covered in blood. In wounds. Skin torn off... hair torn out. Her tongue was on the pillow, Lewis. Imagine that. She'd bitten it off in her terror. It was just lying on the pillow. And her eyes, all swimming in blood, like she'd wept blood. She was the dearest thing in all creation, Lewis. She was beautiful."

"No more."

"I want to die, Lewis."

"No."

"I don't want to live now. There's no point."

"They won't find you guilty."

"I don't care, Lewis. You must look after Catherine now. I read about the exhibition—"

He almost smiled.

"—Wonderful for you. We always said, didn't we? before the war, you'd be the one to be famous, I'd be—"

The smile had gone.

"—notorious. They say terrible things about me now, in the newspapers. An old man going with young girls, you see, that doesn't make me very wholesome. They probably think I lost my temper because I couldn't perform with her. That's what they think, I'm certain." He lost his way, halted, began again. "You must look after Catherine. She's got money, but no friends. She's too cool, you see. Too hurt inside; and that makes people wary of her. You have to stay with her."

"I shall."

"I know. I know. That's why I feel happy, really, to just..."

"No, Phillipe."

"Just die. There's nothing left for us, Lewis. The world's too hard."

Lewis thought of the snow, and the ice-floes, and saw the

sense in dying.

The officer in charge of the investigation was less than helpful, though Lewis introduced himself as a relative of the esteemed Detective Dupin. Lewis' contempt for the shoddily-dressed weasel, sitting in his cluttered hole of an office, made the interview crackle with suppressed anger.

"Your friend," the Inspector said, picking at the raw cuticle of his thumb, "is a murderer, Monsieur Fox. It is as simple as that. The evidence is overwhelming."

"I can't believe that."

"Believe what you like to believe, that's your prerogative. We have all the evidence we need to convict Phillipe Laborteaux of murder in the first degree. It was a cold-blooded killing and he will be punished to the full extent of the law. This is my promise."

"What evidence do you have against him?"

"Monsieur Fox; I am not beholden to you. What evidence we have is our business. Suffice it to say that no other person was seen in the house during the time that the accused claims he was at some fictional patisserie; and as access to the room in which the deceased was found is only possible by the stairs—"

"What about a window?"

"A plain wall: three flights up. Maybe an acrobat: an acrobat might do it."

"And the state of the body?"

The Inspector made a face. Disgust.

"Horrible. Skin and muscle stripped from the bone. All the spine exposed. Blood; much blood."

"Phillipe is seventy."

"So?"

"An old man would not be capable—"

"In other respects," the Inspector interrupted, "he seems to have been quite capable, *oui*? The lover, yes? The passionate lover: he was capable of that."

"And what motive would you claim he had?"

His mouth scalloped, his eyes rolled, and he tapped his chest.

"*Le coeur humain*," he said, as if despairing of reason in affairs of the heart. "*Le coeur humain, quel mystère, n'est-ce pas?*" and exhaling the stench of his ulcer at Lewis, he proffered the open door.

"*Merci*, Monsieur Fox. I understand your confusion, *oui*? But you are wasting your time. A crime is a crime. It is real; not like your paintings."

He saw the surprise on Lewis' face.

"Oh, I am not so uncivilized as not to know your reputation, Monsieur Fox. But I ask you, make your fictions as best you can; that is your genius, *oui*? Mine; to investigate the truth."

Lewis couldn't bear the weasel's cant any longer.

"Truth?" he snapped back at the Inspector. "You wouldn't know the truth if you tripped over it."

The weasel looked as though he'd been slapped with a wet fish.

It was precious little satisfaction; but it made Lewis feel better for at least five minutes.

The house on the Rue des Martyrs was not in good condition, and Lewis could smell the damp as he climbed to the little room on the third floor. Doors opened as he passed, and inquiring whispers ushered him up the stairs, but nobody tried to stop him. The room where the atrocity had happened was locked.

Frustrated, but not knowing how or why it would help Phillipe's case to see the interior of the room, he made his way back down the stairs and into the bitter air.

Catherine was back at the Quai de Bourbon. As soon as Lewis saw her he knew there was something new to hear. Her gray hair was loosed from the bun she favored wearing, and hung unbraided at her shoulders. Her face was a sickly yellow-gray by the lamplight. She shivered, even in the clogged air of the centrally-heated apartment.

"What's wrong?" he asked.

"I went to Phillipe's apartment."

"So did I. It was locked."

"I have the key: Phillipe's spare key. I just wanted to pick up a few clothes for him."

Lewis nodded.

"And?"

"Somebody else was there."

"Police?"

"No."

"Who?"

"I couldn't see. I don't know exactly. He was dressed in a big coat, scarf over his face. Hat. Gloves." She paused. Then, "He had a razor, Lewis."

"A razor?"

"An open razor, like a barber."

Something jangled in the back of Lewis Fox's mind. An open razor; a man dressed so well he couldn't be recognized.

"I was terrified."

"Did he hurt you?"

She shook her head.

"I screamed and he ran away."

"Didn't say anything to you?"

"No."

"Maybe a friend of Phillipe's?"

"I know Phillipe's friends."

"Then of the girl. A brother."

"Perhaps. But—"

"What?"

"There was something odd about him. He smelt of perfume, stank of it, and he walked with such mincing little steps, even though he was huge."

Lewis put his arm around her.

"Whoever it was, you scared them off. You just mustn't go back there. If we have to fetch clothes for Phillipe, I'll gladly go."

"Thank you. I feel a fool: he may have just stumbled in. Come to look at the murder-chamber. People do that, don't they? Out of some morbid fascination…"

"Tomorrow I'll speak to the Weasel."

"Weasel?"

"Inspector Marais. Have him search the place."

"Did you see Phillipe?"

"Yes."

"Is he well?"

Lewis said nothing for a long moment.

"He wants to die, Catherine. He's given up fighting already, before he goes to trial."

"But he didn't do anything."

"We can't prove that."

"You're always boasting about your ancestors. Your blessed Dupin. You prove it…"

"Where do I start?"

"Speak to some of his friends, Lewis. *Please*. Maybe the

woman had enemies."

Jacques Solal stared at Lewis through his round-bellied spectacles, his irises huge and distorted through the glass. He was the worse for too much cognac.

"She hadn't got any enemies," he said, "not her. Oh maybe a few women jealous of her beauty…"

Lewis toyed with the wrapped cubes of sugar that had come with his coffee. Solal was as uninformative as he was drunk; but unlikely as it seemed Catherine had described the runt across the table as Phillipe's closest friend.

"Do you think Phillipe murdered her?"

Solal pursed his lips.

"Who knows?"

"What's your instinct?"

"Ah; he was my friend. If I knew who had killed her I would say so."

It seemed to be the truth. Maybe the little man was simply drowning his sorrows in cognac.

"He was a gentleman," Solal said, his eyes drifting towards the street. Through the steamed glass of the Brasserie window brave Parisians were struggling through the fury of another blizzard, vainly attempting to keep their dignity and their posture in the teeth of a gale.

"A gentleman," he said again.

"And the girl?"

"She was beautiful, and he was in love with her. She had other admirers, of course. A woman like her—"

"Jealous admirers?"

"Who knows?"

Again: who knows? The inquiry hung on the air like a shrug. Who knows? Who knows? Lewis began to understand the Inspector's passion for truth. For the first time in ten years perhaps a goal appeared in his life; an ambition to shoot this indifferent "who knows?" out of the air. To discover what had happened in that room on the Rue des Martyrs. Not an approximation, not a fictionalized account, but the truth, the absolute, unquestionable truth.

"Do you remember if there were any particular men who fancied her?" he asked.

Solal grinned. He only had two teeth in his lower jaw.

"Oh yes. There was one."

"Who?"

"I never knew his name. A big man: I saw him outside the house three or four times. Though to smell him you'd have thought—"

He made an unmistakable face that implied he thought the man was homosexual. The arched eyebrows and the pursed lips made him look doubly ridiculous behind the thick spectacles.

"He smelt?"

"Oh yes."

"Of what?"

"Perfume, Lewis. Perfume."

Somewhere in Paris there was a man who had known the girl Phillipe loved. Jealous rage had overcome him. In a fit of uncontrollable anger he had broken into Phillipe's apartment and slaughtered the girl. It was as clear as that.

Somewhere in Paris.

"Another cognac?"

Solal shook his head.

"Already I'm sick," he said.

Lewis called the waiter across, and as he did so his eye alighted on a cluster of newspaper clippings pinned behind the bar.

Solal followed his gaze.

"Phillipe: he liked the pictures," he said.

Lewis stood up.

"He came here, sometimes, to see them."

The cuttings were old, stained and fading. Some were presumably of purely local interest. Accounts of a fireball seen in a nearby street. Another about a boy of two burned to death in his cot. One concerned an escaped puma; one, an unpublished manuscript by Rimbaud; a third (accompanied by a photograph) detailed casualties in a plane crash at Orleans airport. But there were other cuttings too; some far older than others. Atrocities, bizarre murders, ritual rapes, an advertisement for *Fantômas*, another for Cocteau's *La Belle et La Bête*. And almost buried under this embarrassment of bizarreries, was a sepia photograph so absurd it could have come from the hand of Max Ernst. A half-ring of well-dressed gentlemen, many sporting the thick mustaches popular in the eighteen-nineties, were grouped around the vast, bleeding bulk of an ape, which was suspended by its feet from a lamppost. The faces in the picture bore expressions of mute pride; of absolute authority over the dead beast, which Lewis clearly recognized as a gorilla. Its inverted head had an almost noble tilt in death. Its brow was deep and furrowed, its jaw, though shattered by a fearsome wound, was thinly bearded like that of a patrician, and its eyes, rolled back in its head, seemed full of concern for this merciless world. They reminded Lewis, those rolling eyes, of the Weasel in his hole, tapping his chest.

"*Le coeur humain.*"

Pitiful.

"What is that?" he asked the acne-ridden barman, pointing at the picture of the dead gorilla.

A shrug was the reply: indifferent to the fate of men and apes.

"Who knows?" said Solal at his back. "Who knows?"

It was not the ape of Poe's story, that was certain. That tale had been told in 1835, and the photograph was far more recent. Besides, the ape in the picture was a gorilla: clearly a gorilla.

Had history repeated itself? Had another ape, a different species but an ape nevertheless, been loosed on the streets of Paris at the turn of the century?

And if so, if the story of the ape could repeat itself once... why not twice?

As Lewis walked through the freezing night back to the apartment at the Quai de Bourbon, the imagined repetition of events became more attractive; and now further symmetry presented itself to him. Was it possible that he, the great nephew of C. Auguste Dupin, might become involved in another pursuit, not entirely dissimilar from the first?

The key to Phillipe's room at the Rue des Martyrs was icy in Lewis' hand, and though it was now well past midnight he couldn't help but turn off at the bridge and make his way up the Boulevard de Sebastopol, west on to Boulevard Bonne-Nouvelle, then north again towards the Place Pigalle. It was a long, exhausting trudge, but he felt in need of the cold air, to keep his head clear of emotionalism. It took him an hour and a half to reach the Rue des Martyrs.

It was Saturday night, and there was still a lot of noise in a number of the rooms. Lewis made his way up the two flights as quietly as he could, his presence masked by the din. The key turned easily, and the door swung open.

Street lights illuminated the room. The bed, which dominated the space, was bare. Presumably sheets and blankets had been taken away for forensic tests. The eruption of blood onto the mattress was a mulberry color in the gloom. Otherwise, there was no sign of the violence the room had witnessed.

Lewis reached for the light switch, and snapped it on. Nothing happened. He stepped deeply into the room and stared up at the light fixture. The bulb was shattered.

He half thought of retreating, of leaving the room to darkness, and returning in the morning when there were fewer shadows. But as he stood under the broken bulb his eyes began to pierce the gloom a little better, and he began to make out the shape of a large teak chest of drawers along the far wall. Surely it was a matter of a few minutes work to find a change of clothes for Phillipe. Otherwise he would have to return the next day; another long journey through the snow. Better to do it now, and save his bones.

The room was large, and had been left in chaos by the police. Lewis stumbled and cursed as he crossed to the chest of drawers, tripping over a fallen lamp, and a shattered vase. Downstairs the howls and shrieks of a well-advanced party drowned any noise he made. Was it an orgy or a fight? The noise could have been either.

He struggled with the top drawer of the teak chest, and eventually wrenched it open, ferreting in the depths for the bare essentials of Phillipe's comfort: a clean undershirt, a pair of socks, initialed handkerchiefs, beautifully pressed.

He sneezed. The chilly weather had thickened the catarrh on his chest and the mucus in his sinuses. A handkerchief was to hand, and he blew his nose, clearing his blocked nostrils. For the first time the smell of the room came to him.

One odor predominated, above the damp, and the stale vegetables. Perfume, the lingering scent of perfume.

He turned into the darkened room, hearing his bones creak, and his eyes fell on the shadow behind the bed. A huge shadow, a bulk that swelled as it rose into view.

It was, he saw at once, the razor-wielding stranger. He was here: in waiting.

Curiously, Lewis wasn't frightened.

"What are you doing?" he demanded, in a loud, strong voice.

As he emerged from his hiding place the face of the stranger came into the watery light from the street; a broad, flat-featured, flayed face. His eyes were deep-set, but without malice; and he was smiling, smiling generously, at Lewis.

"Who are you?" Lewis asked again.

The man shook his head; shook his body, in fact, his gloved hands gesturing around his mouth. Was he dumb? The shaking of the head was more violent now, as though he was about to have a fit.

"Are you all right?"

Suddenly, the shaking stopped, and to his surprise Lewis saw tears, large, syrupy tears well up in the stranger's eyes and roll down his rough cheeks and into the bush of his beard.

As if ashamed of his display of feelings, the man turned away from the light, making a thick noise of sobbing in his throat, and exited. Lewis followed, more curious about this stranger than nervous of his intentions.

"Wait!"

The man was already half-way down the first flight of stairs, nimble despite his build.

"Please wait, I want to talk to you." Lewis began down the stairs after him, but the pursuit was lost before it was started.

Lewis' joints were stiff with age and the cold, and it was late. No time to be running after a much younger man, along a pavement made lethal with ice and snow. He chased the stranger as far as the door and then watched him run off down the street; his gait was mincing as Catherine had said. Almost a waddle, ridiculous in a man so big.

The smell of his perfume was already snatched away by the north-east wind. Breathless, Lewis climbed the stairs again, past the din of the party, to claim a set of clothes for Phillipe.

The next day Paris woke to a blizzard of unprecedented ferocity. The calls to Mass went unrequited, the hot Sunday croissants went unbought, the newspapers lay unread on the vendor's stalls. Few people had either the nerve or the motive to step outside into the howling gale. They sat by their fires, hugging their knees, and dreamt of spring.

Catherine wanted to go to the prison to visit Phillipe, but Lewis insisted that he go alone. It was not simply the cold weather that made him cautious on her behalf; he had difficult words to say to Phillipe, delicate questions to ask him. After the previous night's encounter in his room, he had no doubt that Phillipe had a rival, probably a murderous rival. The only way to save Phillipe's life, it seemed, was to trace the man. And if that meant delving into Phillipe's sexual arrangements, then so be it. But it wasn't a conversation he, or Phillipe, would have wanted to conduct in Catherine's presence.

The fresh clothes Lewis had brought were searched, then given to Phillipe, who took them with a nod of thanks.

"I went to the house last night to fetch these for you."

"Oh."

"There was somebody in the room already."

Phillipe's jaw muscle began to churn, as he ground his teeth together. He was avoiding Lewis' eyes.

"A big man, with a beard. Do you know him, or of him?"

"*No.*"

"Phillipe—"

"No!"

"The same man attacked Catherine," Lewis said.

"What?" Phillipe had begun to tremble.

"With a razor."

"Attacked her?" Phillipe said. "Are you sure?"

"Or was going to."

"No! He would never have touched her. Never!"

"Who is it Phillipe? Do you know?"

"Tell her not to go there again; please, Lewis—" His eyes implored. "Please, for God's sake tell her never to go there again. Will you do that? Or you. Not you either."

"Who is it?"

"*Tell her.*"

"I will. But you must tell me who this man is, Phillipe."

He shook his head, grinding his teeth together audibly now.

"You wouldn't understand, Lewis. I couldn't expect you to understand."

"Tell me; I want to help."

"Just let me die."

"*Who is he?*"

"Just let me die... I want to forget, why do you try to make me remember? I want to—"

He looked up again: his eyes were bloodshot, and red-rimmed from nights of tears. But now it seemed there were no more tears left in him; just an arid place where there had been an honest fear of death, a love of love, and an appetite for life. What met Lewis' eyes was a universal indifference: to continuation, to self-preservation, to feeling.

"She was a whore," he suddenly exclaimed. His hands were fists. Lewis had never seen Phillipe make a fist in his life. Now his nails bit into the soft flesh of his palm until blood began to flow.

"Whore," he said again, his voice too loud in the little cell.

"Keep your row down," snapped the guard.

"A whore!" This time Phillipe hissed the accusation through teeth exposed like those of an angry baboon.

Lewis could make no sense of the transformation.

"You began all this—" Phillipe said, looking straight at Lewis, meeting his eyes fully for the first time. It was a bitter accusation, though Lewis didn't understand its significance.

"Me?"

"With your stories. With your damn Dupin."

"Dupin?"

"It was all a lie: all stupid lies. Women, murder—"

"You mean the Rue Morgue story?"

"You were so proud of that, weren't you? All those silly lies. None of it was true."

"Yes it was."

"No. It never was, Lewis: it was a story, that's all. Dupin, the Rue Morgue, the murders…"

His voice trailed away, as though the next words were unsayable.

"…the ape."

Those were the words: the apparently unspeakable was spoken as though each syllable had been cut from his throat.

"…the ape."

"What about the ape?"

"There are beasts, Lewis. Some of them are pitiful; circus animals. They have no brains; they are born victims. Then there are others."

"What others?"

"Natalie was a whore!" he screamed again, his eyes big as saucers. He took hold of Lewis' lapels, and began to shake him. Everybody else in the little room turned to look at the two old men as they wrestled over the table. Convicts and their sweethearts grinned as Phillipe was dragged off his friend, his words descending into incoherence and obscenity as he thrashed in the warder's grip.

"Whore! Whore! Whore!" was all he could say as they hauled him back to his cell.

Catherine met Lewis at the door of her apartment. She was shaking and tearful. Beyond her, the room was wrecked.

She sobbed against his chest as he comforted her, but she was inconsolable. It was many years since he'd comforted a woman, and he'd lost the knack of it. He was embarrassed instead of soothing, and she knew it. She broke away from his embrace, happier untouched.

"He was here," she said.

He didn't need to ask who. The stranger, the tearful, razor-wielding stranger.

"What did he want?"

"He kept saying 'Phillipe' to me. Almost saying it; grunting it more than saying it: and when I didn't answer he just destroyed the furniture, the vases. He wasn't even looking for anything: he just wanted to make a mess."

It made her furious: the uselessness of the attack.

The apartment was in ruins. Lewis wandered through the fragments of porcelain and shredded fabric, shaking his head. In his mind a confusion of tearful faces: Catherine, Phillipe, the stranger. Everyone in his narrow world, it seemed, was hurt and broken. Everyone was suffering; and yet the source, the heart of the suffering, was nowhere to be found.

Only Phillipe had pointed an accusing finger: at Lewis himself.

"You began all this." Weren't those his words? "You began all this."

But how?

Lewis stood at the window. Three of the small panes had been cracked by flying debris, and a wind was insinuating itself into the apartment, with frost in its teeth. He looked across at the ice-thickened waters of the Seine; then a movement caught his eye. His stomach turned.

The full face of the stranger was turned up to the window, his expression wild. The clothes he had always worn so impeccably were in disarray, and the look on his face was of utter, utter despair, so pitiful as to be almost tragic. Or rather, a performance of tragedy: an actor's pain. Even as Lewis stared down at him the stranger raised his arms to the window in a gesture that seemed to beg either forgiveness or understanding, or both.

Lewis backed away from the appeal. It was too much; all too much. The next moment the stranger was walking across the courtyard away from the apartment. The mincing walk had deteriorated into a rolling lope. Lewis uttered a long, low moan of recognition as the ill-dressed bulk disappeared from view.

"Lewis?"

It wasn't a man's walk, that roll, that swagger. It was the gait of an upright beast who'd been taught to walk, and now, without its master, was losing the trick of it.

It was an ape.

Oh God, oh God, it was an ape.

"I have to see Phillipe Laborteaux."

"I'm sorry, Monsieur; but prison visitors—"

"This is a matter of life and death, officer."

"Easily said, Monsieur."

Lewis risked a lie.

"His sister is dying. I beg you to have some compassion."

"Oh... well..."

A little doubt. Lewis levered a little further.

"A few minutes only; to settle arrangements."

"Can't it wait until tomorrow?"

"She'll be dead by morning."

Lewis hated talking about Catherine in such a way, even for the purpose of this deception, but it was necessary; he had to see Phillipe. If his theory was correct, history might repeat itself before the night was out.

Phillipe had been woken from a sedated sleep. His eyes were circled with darkness.

"What do you want?"

Lewis didn't even attempt to proceed any further with his lie; Phillipe was drugged as it was, and probably confused. Best to confront him with the truth, and see what came of it.

"You kept an ape, didn't you?"

A look of terror crossed Phillipe's face, slowed by the drugs in his blood, but plain enough.

"Didn't you?"

"Lewis..." Phillipe looked so very old.

"Answer me, Phillipe, I beg you: before it's too late. Did you keep an ape?"

"It was an experiment, that's all it was. An experiment."

"Why?"

"Your stories. Your damn stories: I wanted to see if it was true that they were wild. I wanted to make a man of it."

"Make a man of it."

"And that whore…"

"Natalie."

"She seduced it."

Lewis felt sick. This was a convolution he hadn't anticipated.

"Seduced it?"

"Whore," Phillipe said, with infinite regret.

"Where is this ape of yours?"

"You'll kill it."

"It broke into the apartment, while Catherine was there. Destroyed everything, Phillipe. It's dangerous now that it has no master. Don't you understand?"

"Catherine?"

"No, she's all right."

"It's trained: it wouldn't harm her. It's watched her, in hiding. Come and gone. Quiet as a mouse."

"And the girl?"

"It was jealous."

"So it murdered her?"

"Perhaps. I don't know. I don't want to think about it."

"Why haven't you told them; had the thing destroyed?"

"I don't know if it's true. It's probably all a fiction, one of your damn fictions, just another story."

A sour, wily smile crossed his exhausted face.

"You must know what I mean, Lewis. It could be a story,

311

couldn't it? Like your tales of Dupin. Except that maybe I made it true for a while; did you ever think of that? Maybe I made it true."

Lewis stood up. It was a tired debate: reality and illusion. Either a thing was, or was not. Life was not a dream.

"Where is the ape?" he demanded. Phillipe pointed to his temple.

"Here; where you can never find him," he said, and spat in Lewis' face. The spittle hit his lip, like a kiss.

"You don't know what you did. You'll never know."

Lewis wiped his lip as the warders escorted the prisoner out of the room and back to his happy drugged oblivion. All he could think of now, left alone in the cold interview room, was that Phillipe had it easy. He'd taken refuge in pretended guilt, and locked himself away where memory, and revenge, and the truth, the wild, marauding truth, could never touch him again. He hated Phillipe at that moment, with all his heart. Hated him for the dilettante and the coward he'd always known him to be. It wasn't a more gentle world Phillipe had created around him; it was a hiding place, as much a lie as that summer of 1937 had been. No life could be lived the way he'd lived it without a reckoning coming sooner or later; and here it was.

That night, in the safety of his cell, Phillipe woke. It was warm, but he was cold. In the utter dark he chewed at his wrists until a pulse of blood bubbled into his mouth. He lay back on his bed, and quietly splashed and fountained away to death, out of sight and out of mind.

* * *

The suicide was reported in a small article on the second page of *Le Monde*. The big news of the following day however was the sensational murder of a redheaded prostitute in a little house off the Rue de Rochechquant. Monique Zevaco had been found at three o'clock in the morning by her flatmate, her body in a state so horrible as to "defy description."

Despite the alleged impossibility of the task, the media set about describing the indescribable with a morbid will. Every last scratch, tear and gouging on Monique's partially nude body—tattooed, drooled *Le Monde*, with a map of France—was chronicled in detail. As indeed was the appearance of her well-dressed, over-perfumed murderer, who had apparently watched her at her toilet through a small back window, then broken in and attacked Mademoiselle Zevaco in her bathroom. The murderer had then fled down the stairs, bumping into the flatmate who would minutes after discover Mademoiselle Zevaco's mutilated corpse. Only one commentator made any connection between the murder at the Rue des Martyrs and the slaughter of Mme Zevaco; and he failed to pick up on the curious coincidence that the accused Phillipe Laborteaux had that same night taken his own life.

The funeral took place in a storm, the cortege edging its pitiful way through the abandoned streets towards Montparnasse with the lashing snow entirely blotting out the road ahead. Lewis sat with Catherine and Jacques Solal as they laid Phillipe to rest. Every one of his circle had deserted him, unwilling to attend the funeral of a suicide and of a suspected murderer. His wit, his good looks, his infinite capacity to charm went for nothing at the end.

He was not, as it turned out, entirely unmourned by strangers. As they stood at the graveside, the cold cutting into them, Solal sidled up to Lewis and nudged him.

"What?"

"Over there. Under the tree." Solal nodded beyond the praying priest.

The stranger was standing at a distance, almost hidden by the marble mausoleums. A heavy black scarf was wrapped across his face, and a wide-brimmed hat pulled down over his brow, but his bulk was unmistakable. Catherine had seen him too. She was shaking as she stood, wrapped round by Lewis' embrace, not just with cold, but with fear. It was as though the creature was some morbid angel, come to hover a while, and enjoy the grief. It was grotesque, and eerie, that this thing should come to see Phillipe consigned to the frozen earth. What did it feel? Anguish? Guilt?

Yes, did it feel guilt?

It knew it had been seen, and it turned its back, shambling away. Without a word to Lewis, Jacques Solal slipped away from the grave in pursuit. In a short while both the stranger and his pursuer were erased by the snow.

Back at the Quai de Bourbon Catherine and Lewis said nothing of the incident. A kind of barrier had appeared between them, forbidding contact on any level but the most trivial. There was no purpose in analysis, and none in regrets. Phillipe was dead. The past, their past together, was dead. This final chapter in their joint lives soured utterly everything that preceded it, so that no shared memory could be enjoyed without the pleasure being spoilt. Phillipe had died horribly, devouring his own flesh and blood, perhaps driven mad by a knowledge he possessed of his own guilt and depravity. No innocence, no history of joy could remain unstained by that fact. Silently they mourned the loss, not only of Phillipe, but of their own past. Lewis understood now Phillipe's reluctance to live when there was such loss in the world.

Solal rang. Breathless after his chase, but elated, he spoke in whispers to Lewis, clearly enjoying the excitement.

"I'm at the Gare du Nord, and I've found out where our friend lives. I've found him Lewis!"

"Excellent. I'll come straight away. I'll meet you on the steps of the Gare du Nord. I'll take a cab: ten minutes."

"It's in the basement of number sixteen, Rue des Fleurs. I'll see you there—"

"Don't go in, Jacques. Wait for me. Don't—"

The telephone clicked and Solal was gone. Lewis reached for his coat.

"Who was that?"

She asked, but she didn't want to know. Lewis shrugged on his overcoat and said: "Nobody at all. Don't worry. I won't be long."

"Take your scarf," she said, not glancing over her shoulder.

"Yes. Thank you."

"You'll catch a chill."

He left her gazing over the night-clad Seine, watching the ice-floes dance together on the black water.

When he arrived at the house on the Rue des Fleurs, Solal was not to be seen, but fresh footprints in the powdery snow led to the front door of number sixteen and then, foiled, went around the back of the house. Lewis followed them. As he stepped into the yard behind the house, through a rotted gate that had been crudely forced by Solal, he realized he had come without a weapon. Best to go back, perhaps, find a crowbar, a knife; something. Even as he was debating with himself, the back door opened, and the stranger appeared, dressed in his now familiar overcoat. Lewis flattened himself against the wall of the yard, where the shadows were deepest, certain that he would be seen. But the beast was about other business. He stood in the doorway with his face fully exposed, and for the first time, in the reflected moonlight off the snow, Lewis could see the creature's physiognomy plainly. Its face was freshly shaved; and the scent of cologne was strong, even in the open air. Its skin was pink as a peach, though nicked in one or two places by a careless blade. Lewis thought of the open-razor it had apparently threatened Catherine with. Was that what its business had been in Phillipe's room, the purloining of a good razor? It was pulling its leather gloves on over its wide, shaved hands, making small coughing noises in its throat that sounded almost like grunts of satisfaction. Lewis had the impression that it was preparing itself for the outside world; and the sight was touching as much as intimidating. All this thing wanted was to be human. It was aspiring, in its way, to the model Phillipe had given it, had nurtured in it. Now, deprived of its mentor, confused and unhappy, it was attempting to face the world as it had been taught to do. There was no way back for it. Its days of innocence had gone: it could never be an unambitious beast again. Trapped in its new persona, it had no choice but to continue in the life its master had awoken its taste for. Without glancing in Lewis' direction, it gently closed the door behind it and crossed the yard, its walk transforming in those few steps from a simian roll to the mincing waddle that it used to simulate humanity.

Then it was gone.

Lewis waited a moment in the shadows, breathing shallowly. Every bone in his body ached with cold now, and his feet were numb. The beast showed no sign of returning; so he ventured out of his hiding place and tried the door. It was not locked. As he stepped inside a stench struck him: the sickly sweet smell of rotten fruit mingled with the cloying cologne: the zoo and the boudoir.

He edged down a flight of slimy stone steps, and along a short, tiled corridor towards a door. It too was unlocked; and the bare bulb inside illuminated a bizarre scene.

On the floor, a large, somewhat thread-bare Persian carpet; sparse furnishings; a bed, roughly covered with blankets and stained hessian; a wardrobe, bulging with oversize clothes; discarded fruit in abundance, some trodden into the floor; a bucket, filled with straw and stinking of droppings. On the wall, a large crucifix. On the mantelpiece a photograph of Catherine, Lewis, and Phillipe together in a sunlit past, smiling. At the sink, the creature's shaving kit. Soap, brush, razor. Fresh suds. On the dresser a pile of money, left in careless abundance beside a pile of hypodermics and a collection of small bottles. It was warm in the beast's garret; perhaps the furnace for the house roared in an adjacent cellar. Solal was not there.

Suddenly, a noise.

Lewis turned to the door, expecting the ape to be filling it, teeth bared, eyes demonic. But he had lost all orientation; the noise was not from the door but from the wardrobe. Behind the pile of clothes there was a movement.

"Solal?"

Jacques Solal half fell out of the wardrobe, and sprawled across the Persian carpet. His face was disfigured by one foul wound, so that it was all but impossible to find any part of his features that was still Jacques.

The creature had taken hold of his lip and pulled his muscle off his bone, as though removing a balaclava. His exposed teeth chattered away in nervous response to oncoming death; his limbs jangled and shook. But Jacques was already gone. These shudders and jerks were not signs of thought or personality, just the din of passing. Lewis knelt at Solal's side; his stomach was strong. During the war, being a conscientious objector, he had volunteered to serve in the Military Hospital, and there were few transformations of the human body he had not seen in one combination or another. Tenderly, he cradled the body, not noticing the blood. He hadn't loved this man, scarcely cared for him at all, but now all he wanted was to take him away, out of the ape's cage, and find him a human grave. He'd take the photograph too. That was too much, giving the beast a photograph of the three friends together. It made him hate Phillipe more than ever.

He hauled the body off the carpet. It required a gargantuan effort, and the sultry heat in the room, after the chill of the outside world, made him dizzy. He could feel a jittering nervousness in his limbs. His body was close to betraying him, he knew it; close to failing, to losing its coherence and collapsing.

Not here. In God's name, not here.

Maybe he should go now, and find a phone. That would be wise. Call the police, yes... call Catherine, yes... even find somebody in the house to help him. But that would mean leaving Jacques in the lair, for the beast to assault again, and he had become strangely protective of the corpse; he was unwilling to leave it alone. In an anguish of confused feelings, unable to leave Jacques yet unable to move him far, he stood in the middle of the room and did nothing at all. That was best; yes. Nothing at all. Too tired, too weak. Nothing at all was best.

The reverie went on interminably; the old man fixed beyond movement at the crux of his feelings, unable to go forward into the future, or back into the soiled past. Unable to remember.

Unable to forget.

Waiting, in a dreamy half-life, for the end of the world.

It came home noisily like a drunken man, and the sound of its opening the outer door stirred Lewis into a slow response. With some difficulty he hauled Jacques into the wardrobe, and hid there himself, with the faceless head in his lap.

There was a voice in the room, a woman's voice. Maybe it wasn't the beast, after all. But no: through the crack of the wardrobe door Lewis could see the beast, and a red-haired young woman with him. She was talking incessantly, the perpetual trivia of a spaced-out mind.

"You've got more; oh you sweetie, oh you dear man, that's wonderful. Look at all this stuff."

She had pills in her hands and was swallowing them like sweets, gleeful as a child at Christmas.

"Where did you get all this? OK, if you don't want to tell me, it's fine by me."

Was this Phillipe's doing too, or had the ape stolen the stuff for his own purposes? Did he regularly seduce redheaded prostitutes with drugs?

The girl's grating babble was calming now, as the pills took effect, sedating her, transporting her to a private world. Lewis watched, entranced, as she began to undress.

"It's so... hot... in here."

The ape watched, his back to Lewis. What expression did that shaved face wear? Was there lust in its eyes, or doubt?

The girl's breasts were beautiful, though her body was rather too thin. The young skin was white, the nipples flower-pink. She raised her arms over her head and as she stretched the perfect globes rose and flattened slightly. The ape reached a wide hand to her body and tenderly plucked at one of her nipples, rolling it between dark-meat fingers. The girl sighed.

"Shall I... take everything off?"

The monkey grunted.

"You don't say much, do you?"

She shimmied out of her red skirt. Now she was naked but for a pair of knickers. She lay on the bed stretching again, luxuriating in her body and the welcome heat of the room, not even bothering to look at her admirer.

Wedged underneath Solal's body, Lewis began to feel dizzy again. His lower limbs were now completely numb, and he had no feeling in his right arm, which was pressed against the back of the wardrobe, yet he didn't dare move. The ape was capable of anything, he knew that. If he was discovered what might it not choose to do, to him and to the girl?

Every part of his body was now either nerveless, or wracked with pain. In his lap Solal's seeping body seemed to become heavier with every moment. His spine was screaming, and the back of his neck pained him as though pierced with hot knitting-needles. The agony was becoming unbearable; he began to think he would die in this pathetic hiding place, while the ape made love.

The girl sighed, and Lewis looked again at the bed. The ape had its hand between her legs, and she squirmed beneath its ministrations.

"Yes, oh yes," she said again and again, as her lover stripped her completely.

It was too much. The dizziness throbbed through Lewis' cortex. Was this death? The lights in the head, and the whine in the ears?

He closed his eyes, blotting out the sight of the lovers, but unable to shut out the noise. It seemed to go on forever, invading his head. Sighs, laughter, little shrieks.

At last, darkness.

Lewis woke on an invisible rack; his body had been wrenched out of shape by the limitations of his hiding-place. He looked up. The door of the wardrobe was open, and the ape was staring down at him, its mouth attempting a grin. It was naked; and its body was almost entirely shaved. In the cleft of its immense chest a small gold crucifix glinted. Lewis recognized the jewelry immediately. He had bought it for Phillipe in the Champs-Élysées just before the war. Now it nestled in a tuft of reddish-orange hair. The beast proffered a hand to Lewis, and he automatically took it. The coarse-palmed grip hauled him from under Solal's body. He couldn't stand straight. His legs were rubbery, his ankles wouldn't support him. The beast took hold of him, and steadied him. His head spinning, Lewis looked down into the wardrobe, where Solal was lying, tucked up like a baby in its womb, face to the wall.

The beast closed the door on the corpse, and helped Lewis to the sink, where he was sick.

"Phillipe?" He dimly realized that the woman was still here: in the bed: just woken after a night of love.

"Phillipe: who's this?" She was scrabbling for pills on the table beside the bed. The beast sauntered across and snatched them from her hands.

"Ah... Phillipe... please. Do you want me to go with this one as well? I will if you want. Just give me back the pills."

She gestured towards Lewis.

"I don't usually go with old men."

The ape growled at her. The expression on her face changed,

as though for the first time she had an inkling of what this John was. But the thought was too difficult for her drugged mind, and she let it go.

"Please, Phillipe..." she whimpered.

Lewis was looking at the ape. It had taken the photograph from the mantelpiece. Its dark nail was on Lewis' picture. It was smiling. It recognized him, even though forty-odd years had drained so much life from him.

"Lewis," it said, finding the word quite easy to say.

The old man had nothing in his stomach to vomit, and no harm left to feel. This was the end of the century, he should be ready for anything. Even to be greeted as a friend of a friend by the shaved beast that loomed in front of him. It would not harm him, he knew that. Probably Phillipe had told the ape about their lives together; made the creature love Catherine and himself as much as it had adored Phillipe.

"Lewis," it said again, and gestured to the woman (now sitting open-legged on the bed), offering her for his pleasure.

Lewis shook his head.

In and out, in and out, part fiction, part fact.

It had come to this; offered a human woman by this naked ape. It was the last, God help him, the very last chapter in the fiction his great uncle had begun. From love to murder back to love. Again. The love of an ape for a man. He had caused it, with his dreams of fictional heroes, steeped in absolute reason. He had coaxed Phillipe into making real the stories of a lost youth. He was to blame. Not this poor strutting ape, lost between the jungle and the Stock Exchange; not Phillipe, wanting to be young forever; certainly not cold Catherine, who after tonight would be completely alone. It was him. His the crime, his the guilt, his the punishment.

His legs had regained a little feeling, and he began to stagger to the door.

"Aren't you staying?" said the red-haired woman.

"This thing..." he couldn't bring himself to name the animal.

"You mean Phillipe?"

"He isn't called Phillipe," Lewis said. "He's not even human."

"Please yourself," she said, and shrugged.

To his back, the ape spoke, saying his name. But this time, instead of it coming out as a sort of grunt-word, its simian palate caught Phillipe's inflexion with unnerving accuracy, better than the most skillful of parrots. It was Phillipe's voice, perfectly.

"Lewis," it said.

Not pleading. Not demanding. Simply naming, for the pleasure of naming, an equal.

The passers-by who saw the old man clamber on to the parapet of the Pont du Carrousel stared, but made no attempt to stop him jumping. He teetered a moment as he stood up straight, then pitched over into the threshing, churning ice-water.

One or two people wandered to the other side of the bridge to see if the current had caught him: it had. He rose to the surface, his face blue-white and blank as a baby's, then some intricate eddy snatched at his feet and pulled him under. The thick water closed over his head and churned on.

"Who was that?" somebody asked.

"Who knows?"

It was a clear-heaven day; the last of the winter's snow had fallen, and the thaw would begin by noon. Birds, exulting in the sudden sun, swooped over the Sacré Coeur. Paris began to undress for spring, its virgin white too spoiled to be worn for long.

In mid-morning, a young woman with red hair, her arm linked in that of a large ugly man, took a leisurely stroll to the steps of the Sacré Coeur. The sun blessed them. Bells rang.

It was a new day.

THE CONTRIBUTORS

EDGAR ALLAN POE (1809–49) is possibly one of the best known genre writers of all time. He saw himself as primarily a poet—his most famous poem probably remains "The Raven"—but it is with his tales of mystery and imagination that he has become synonymous. Stories such as "The Masque of the Red Death," "The Pit and the Pendulum," "The Fall of the House of Usher," "The Black Cat," and of course "The Tell-Tale Heart" have cemented his place in horror history. But some critics have also labeled him the originator of the detective story (due to "The Murders in the Rue Morgue"), while others see him as an early forerunner in the science fiction genre. Greatly admired and imitated, his work has been adapted for film and television many times, most notably by Universal Studios in the 1930s, Roger Corman in the 1960s, and by the Italian Master of Suspense Dario Argento and *Night of the Living Dead* director George A. Romero in the 1990s.

MIKE CAREY was born in Liverpool, but moved to London in the 1980s after completing an English degree at Oxford. He taught English and Media for several years before resigning to become a freelance writer in 2000. Initially he worked mainly within the medium of comic books, coming to prominence with the *Lucifer* ongoing series at DC Vertigo. Since then, he has written *Hellblazer* for DC, *X-Men* and *Fantastic Four* for Marvel, *Vampirella* for Harris and *Red Sonja* for Dynamite Entertainment. He also wrote the Marvel Comics adaptation of Orson Scott Card's *Ender's Shadow*, and has recently launched a creator-owned book at Vertigo, *The Unwritten*, which (in collected format) has made the *New York Times* graphic novel bestseller list several times.

More recently, Mike has moved into prose fiction with the *Felix Castor* novels, supernatural crime thrillers recounting the exploits of a freelance exorcist, and (under the pseudonym of Adam Blake) with mainstream thrillers such as *The Dead Sea Deception*. Along with his wife Linda and their daughter Louise he has co-written the fantasy novel *The Steel Seraglio*, soon to be published in the UK as *City of Silk and Steel*. His movie screenplay, *Dominion*, is in development with US producer Intrepid Pictures and UK's Slingshot Studios.

SIMON CLARK's latest novel, *Inspector Abberline & the Gods of Rome*, blends crime and the occult into a horror-thriller set in nineteenth-century England. His other books include *Blood Crazy*, *This Rage of Echoes*, *Death's Dominion*, *Vengeance Child* and the award-winning *The Night of the Triffids*, which continues the story of Wyndham's classic *The Day of the Triffids*.

WESTON OCHSE is the author of nine novels, most recently *SEAL Team 666*. His first novel, *Scarecrow Gods*, won the Bram Stoker Award for First Novel. He's also had published more than a hundred short stories, many of which appeared in anthologies, magazines, peered journals, and comic books. His short fiction has been nominated for the Pushcart Prize and been Bram Stoker Award finalists. FYI, his last name is pronounced "oaks." According to Harlan Ellison, "Weston Ochse sounds like a stately trailer park or a nursing home where good people go to die." The trailer park lives in the Arizona desert within rock throwing distance of Mexico. For fun Weston races tarantula wasps and watches the black helicopters dance along the horizon.

YVONNE NAVARRO lives in southern Arizona, where by day she works on historic Fort Huachuca. She is the author of twenty-two published novels and well over a hundred short stories, and has written about everything from vampires to psychologically disturbed husbands to the end of the world. Her work has won the HWA's Bram Stoker Award, plus a number of other writing awards. Visit her at www.yvonnenavarro.com or www.facebook.com/yvonne.navarro.001 to keep up with slices of a crazy life that includes her husband, author Weston Ochse, three Great Danes (Goblin, Ghost, and Ghoulie), a people-loving parakeet named BirdZilla, painting, and lots of ice cream, Smarties, and white zinfandel. Her most recent novels are *Highborn* and *Concrete Savior*, the first two books in the Dark Redemption Series. Only once in a great while does she fight it out, er, co-write with her husband.

JONATHAN MABERRY is a *New York Times* best-selling author, multiple Bram Stoker Award winner, and freelancer for Marvel Comics. His novels include *Assassin's Code, Flesh & Bone, Ghost Road Blues, Dust & Decay, Patient Zero, The Wolfman,* and many others. Non-fiction books include *Ultimate*

Jujutsu, *The Cryptopedia*, *Zombie CSU*, *Wanted Undead or Alive*, and others. Jonathan's award-winning teen novel *Rot & Ruin* is now in development for film. He's the editor/co-author of *V-Wars*, a vampire-themed anthology, and was a featured expert on The History Channel special *Zombies: A Living History*. Since 1978 he's sold more than 1200 magazine feature articles, 3000 columns, two plays, greeting cards, song lyrics, and poetry. His comics include *Captain America: Hail Hydra*, *DoomWar*, *Marvel Zombies Return*, and *Marvel Universe Vs The Avengers*. He teaches the Experimental Writing for Teens class, is the founder of the Writers Coffeehouse, and co-founder of The Liars Club. Jonathan lives in Bucks County, Pennsylvania with his wife, Sara, and their dog, Rosie. www.jonathanmaberry.com

JOE R. LANSDALE is the author of over thirty novels and two hundred short pieces, articles, and stories. He has been awarded The Edgar, The Grinzani Cavour Prize for Literature, nine Bram Stokers, is a Grandmaster of Horror, and a Lifetime Achievement Award recipient from The Horror Writers Association. His work has been made into films, and he is Writer in Residence at Stephen F. Austin University. He is the Grandmaster and Founder of Shen Chuan Martial Arts and has been inducted into both the International and United States Martial Arts Hall of Fame.

ELIZABETH MASSIE is a Bram Stoker Award- and Scribe Award-winning author of horror novels, short horror fiction, media tie-ins, mainstream fiction, historical novels, and non-fiction. More recent works include *Desper Hollow* (horror novel), *Naked, On the Edge* (collection of horror short fiction), and *Homegrown* (mainstream novel). She is the creator of the Skeeryvilletown slew of cartoon zombies, monsters, and other bizarre misfits. In her "spare" time she manages Hand to Hand Vision, a Facebook-based fundraising project she founded to help others during these tough economic times. Massie lives in the Shenandoah Valley of Virginia and shares life and abode with the talented illustrator/artist Cortney Skinner.

LISA TUTTLE began writing while still at school, sold her first stories at university, and won the John W. Campbell Award for Best New Science Fiction Writer of the year in 1974. Her first novel, *Windhaven*, was a collaboration with George R. R. Martin published in 1981; her most recent is the contemporary fantasy *The Silver Bough*; and she has written at least a hundred short stories—science fiction, fantasy, and horror—as well as essays, reviews, non-fiction, and books for children. Born and raised in Texas, she now makes her home in a remote, rural part of Scotland.

STEPHEN VOLK is best known as the creator of the notorious BBC-TV "Halloween hoax" *Ghostwatch* and the award-winning British TV drama series *Afterlife*. He co-wrote the recent big screen ghost story *The Awakening* starring Rebecca Hall and Dominic West, while his other credits include Ken Russell's *Gothic* and William Friedkin's *The Guardian*, as well as standalone scripts for Channel Four's *Shockers* and the short film *The Deadness of Dad,* which won him a BAFTA. His short stories have been finalists for British Fantasy, Stoker, and Shirley Jackson Awards, and have appeared in several Best-of anthologies. His first collection, Dark Corners, was published in 2006, followed by the acclaimed novella *Vardøger,* while 2013 sees the publication of *Whitstable*, his new novella featuring Peter Cushing. Visit his site at www.stephenvolk.net

CLIVE BARKER was born in Liverpool, England, where he began his creative career writing, directing, and acting for the stage. Since then, he has gone on to pen such bestsellers as *The Books of Blood*, *Weaveworld*, *Imajica*, *The Great and Secret Show*, *The Thief of Always*, *Everville*, *Sacrament*, *Galilee*, *Coldheart Canyon*, *Mr. B Gone*, and the highly acclaimed fantasy series *Abarat*. As a screenwriter, director, and film producer, he is credited with the *Hellraiser* and *Candyman* pictures, as well as *Nightbreed*, *Lord of Illusions*, *Gods and Monsters*, *The Midnight Meat Train*, *Clive Barker's Book of Blood* and *Dread*. Mr. Barker lives in Los Angeles, California.

THE EDITORS

PAUL KANE is an award-winning writer and editor based in Derbyshire, UK. His short story collections are *Alone (In the Dark)*, *Touching the Flame*, *FunnyBones*, *Peripheral Visions*, *Shadow Writer*, and *The Adventures of Dalton Quayle*, with his latest out from the award-winning PS Publishing: *The Butterfly Man and Other Stories*. His novellas include *Signs of Life*, *The Lazarus Condition*, *RED*, and *Pain Cages*. He is the author of the novels *Of Darkness and Light*, *The Gemini Factor*, and the bestselling *Arrowhead* trilogy (*Arrowhead*, *Broken Arrow*, and *Arrowland*), a post-apocalyptic reworking of the Robin Hood mythology. His latest novels are *Lunar* (which is set to be turned into a feature film), and the short Y.A. novel *The Rainbow Man* (as P.B. Kane). He has also written for comics, most notably for the *Dead Roots* zombie anthology alongside writers such as James Moran (*Torchwood*, *Cockneys vs. Zombies*) and Jason Arnopp (*Doctor Who*, *Friday The 13th*). Paul is co-editor of the anthology *Hellbound Hearts*—stories based around the Clive Barker mythology that spawned *Hellraiser*—*The Mammoth Book of Body Horror*, featuring the likes of Stephen King and James Herbert, and *A Carnivàle of Horror: Dark Tales from the Fairground* (PS).

His non-fiction books are *The Hellraiser Films and Their Legacy* and *Voices in the Dark*, and his genre journalism has appeared in such magazines as *SFX*, *Dreamwatch*, and *DeathRay*. He has been a Guest at Alt.Fiction five times, was a Guest at the first SFX Weekender, at Thought Bubble in 2011, plus The Derbyshire Literary Festival, Edge-Lit, and Off the Shelf in 2012, as well as being a panelist at FantasyCon and the World Fantasy Convention. His work has been optioned for film and television, and his zombie story "Dead Time" was turned into an episode of the Lionsgate/NBC TV series *Fear Itself*, adapted by Steve Niles (*30 Days of Night*) and directed by Darren Lynn Bousman (*SAW II–IV*). He also scripted *The Opportunity*, which premiered at the Cannes Film Festival, *Wind Chimes* (directed by Brad "*7th Dimension*" Watson), and *The Weeping Woman*—filmed by award-winning director Mark Steensland and starring Tony-nominated actor Stephen Geoffreys (*Fright Night*). You can find out more at his website www.shadow-writer.co.uk which has featured Guest Writers such as Neil Gaiman, Charlaine Harris, Dean Koontz, John Connolly, and Guillermo del Toro.

CHARLES PREPOLEC is a freelance writer, editor, and reviewer. His articles, interviews, artwork, and reviews have appeared in *Scarlet Street*, *Sherlock*, *All-Hallows*, and *Canadian Holmes*, as well as the *Doctor Who* fanzines *Peladon Press* and *Into the Vortex*. He has been acknowledged for various research contributions to *Starring Sherlock Holmes* (Rev. Ed. Titan Books 2007), *Sherlock Holmes On Screen* (Reynolds and Hearn 2002), *Christopher Lee: The Authorised Screen History* (Reynolds and Hearn 2001), *In All Sincerity... Peter Cushing* (Xlibris 2004), *Heroes & Monsters: The Unofficial Companion To The League Of Extraordinary Gentlemen* (Monkeybrain Books 2003), and spent two years editing news for actor Christopher Lee's official website www.christopherleeweb.com

Alongside his frequent collaborator Jeff Campbell, he has edited five Sherlock Holmes anthologies—*Curious Incidents Vols. 1 & 2* (Mad For a Mystery Publications 2002 & 2003), *Gaslight Grimoire: Fantastic Tales of Sherlock Holmes* (EDGE SF&F 2008), *Gaslight Grotesque: Nightmare Tales of Sherlock Holmes* (EDGE SF&F 2009), and *Gaslight Arcanum: Uncanny Tales of Sherlock Holmes* (EDGE SF&F 2011). Currently in the works is a revival anthology of new stories featuring Arthur Conan Doyle's "other" character—*Professor Challenger: New Worlds, Lost Places* (EDGE SF&F 2014).

An active Sherlockian for more than twenty-five years with Calgary's *The Singular Society of the Baker Street Dozen*, he was designated a Master Bootmaker in 2006 by *The Bootmakers of Toronto*—Canada's national Sherlock Holmes Society. He maintains an online presence via www.sherlocknews.com, as well as www.bakerstreetdozen.com, and currently resides in his hometown of Calgary, AB, Canada with his wife Kristen and their cat Karma.

ENCOUNTERS OF SHERLOCK HOLMES

EDITED BY GEORGE MANN

BRAND-NEW TALES OF THE GREAT DETECTIVE

The spirit of Sherlock Holmes lives on in this collection of fourteen brand-new adventures. Marvel as the master of deduction aids a dying Sir Richard Francis Burton; matches wits with gentleman thief, A.J. Raffles; crosses paths with H.G. Wells in the most curious circumstances; unravels a macabre mystery on the Necropolis Express; unpicks a murder in a locked railway carriage; explains the origins of his famous Persian slipper and more!

FEATURING ORIGINAL STORIES FROM
Mark Hodder • Mags L Halliday • Cavan Scott
Nick Kyme • Paul Magrs • George Mann • Stuart Douglas
Eric Brown • Richard Dinnick • Kelly Hale • Steve Lockley
• Mark Wright • David Barnett • James Lovegrove

WWW.TITANBOOKS.COM

THE HARRY HOUDINI MYSTERIES

DANIEL STASHOWER

THE DIME MUSEUM MURDERS
THE FLOATING LADY MURDER
THE HOUDINI SPECTER

In turn-of-the-century New York, the Great Houdini's confidence in his own abilities is matched only by the indifference of the paying public. Now the young performer has the opportunity to make a name for himself by attempting the most amazing feats of his fledgling career—solving what seem to be impenetrable crimes. With the reluctant help of his brother Dash, Houdini must unravel murders, debunk frauds and escape from danger that is no illusion...

"Magician Daniel Stashower pairs [Sherlock Holmes] with Harry Houdini (who was a friend of Conan Doyle)... This is charming... it might have amused Conan Doyle."
New York Times

"In his first mystery, Stashower paired Harry Houdini and Sherlock Holmes to marvelous effect." *Chicago Tribune*

WWW.TITANBOOKS.COM

THE FURTHER ADVENTURES OF SHERLOCK HOLMES...

A LIBRARY OF ORIGINAL TALES OF THE GREAT DETECTIVE

WWW.TITANBOOKS.COM